sionate scenes, their efforts to build a meaningful partnership outside the bedroom make this a mature addition to any Regency shelf. An impressive debut."

—*Kirkus Reviews*

"Debut author MacGregor brings England's Regency era to life in this sparkling launch for the Cavensham Heiresses romance series. This charming tale features a refreshing array of happy families, solid relationships . . . The book's promise of a delicious story is well realized, building anticipation for future installments."

—*Publishers Weekly*

"Newcomer MacGregor delivers a well-paced, powerfully plotted debut where love and revenge vie for center stage. Here is a romance that reminds readers that love is complicated, healing and captivating. MacGregor's characters are carefully drawn, their emotions realistic and their passions palpable. Watch for MacGregor to make her mark on the genre." —*RT Book Reviews*

"Readers, rejoice! We have a new writer to celebrate. Janna MacGregor writes with intelligence and heart. *The Bad Luck Bride* is a full-bodied romance about what it truly means to love, to forgive, and to heal. Plus, it introduces us to characters we will enjoy as they grow and develop. Smart, smart romance."

—*New York Times* bestselling author Cathy Maxwell

"Delightful! Janna MacGregor bewitched me with her captivating characters and a romance that sizzles off the page. I'm already a huge fan!"

—*New York Times* bestselling author Eloisa James

"*The Bad Luck Bride* is a stroke of good luck for readers—the intricate plot, arresting characters, and rich emotional resonance will leave you swooning."
  —*New York Times* bestselling author Sabrina Jeffries

"Janna MacGregor's *The Bad Luck Bride* is a seductive tale filled with suspense and unforgettable characters. A must-buy for historical romance readers."
  —*USA Today* bestselling author Alexandra Hawkins

"A diamond-bright debut, with a passionate heroine and worthy hero to root for."
  —Maggie Robinson, author of
  The Unsuitable Secretary

The
GOOD, THE
BAD, AND
THE DUKE

JANNA
MACGREGOR

St. Martin's Paperbacks

This is a work of fiction. All of the characters, organizations, and events portrayed in this novel are either products of the author's imagination or are used fictitiously.

THE GOOD, THE BAD, AND THE DUKE

Copyright © 2018 by JLWR, LLC.

All rights reserved.

For information address St. Martin's Press, 175 Fifth Avenue, New York, NY 10010.

ISBN: 978-1-250-29597-2

Our books may be purchased in bulk for promotional, educational, or business use. Please contact your local bookseller or the Macmillan Corporate and Premium Sales Department at 1-800-221-7945, ext. 5442, or by e-mail at MacmillanSpecialMarkets@macmillan.com.

Printed in the United States of America

St. Martin's Paperbacks edition / December 2018

St. Martin's Paperbacks are published by St. Martin's Press, 175 Fifth Avenue, New York, NY 10010.

10 9 8 7 6 5 4 3 2 1

To Anthony—Two sentences weren't enough, but you lucky dog, you went home with the heart-shaped rock.

Acknowledgments

From the first words I wrote in *The Bad Luck Bride*, Paul hounded me for his own story. How could one so dissolute and selfish become a hero? There's only one answer—by being a very charming but persistent fellow. He always demanded to be in every story even if it was only a mention. *The Good, the Bad, and the Duke* would never have been written without my fabulous agent, Pam Ahearn. As soon as she read the first scene that Paul ever appeared in, she told me that I had to write his story. Needless to say, Paul charmed Pam, also.

My marvelous editor, Alexandra Sehulster, is pure genius. She helped me craft these characters into a special couple, and their story was a joy to write. Saying thank you isn't enough. It was my honor to work with you on this book.

Marissa Sangiacomo, Meghan Harrington, Mara Delgado-Sanchez, and the rest of the team at St. Martin's Press, I'm so lucky to have you all behind me. The art department at St. Martin's Press and Jon Paul Ferrara have my special gratitude, also. The cover for Paul and Daphne's book is not only gorgeous, but it's pure romance.

Holly Ingraham, I can't say thank you enough. You are simply brilliant. More important, thank you for believing in me and my stories. Corinne DeMaagd, you are the best teacher any writer could have. Your skills at editing are only surpassed by your warmth and friendship. Kim Rozzell, thank you. Everything you touch sparkles with class and wit. You make it seem so easy. Simply put, you're a force to be reckoned with.

Without you, my dear readers, none of this would have happened. From the very first, you encouraged me to write Paul and Daphne's story. From the bottom of my heart, thank you for believing that Paul was worthy of his own tale. I truly have fallen in love with this couple, and I hope you do, too.

Finally, I couldn't do any of this without the love and support of my own darling rogue. Thank you, Greg, the author of my romantic life.

Prologue

S oon, she'd face her nemesis in hand-to-hand combat.

Or a more apt description was "hand-to-paw combat."

She was Lady Daphne Hallworth, a proud name synonymous with bravery.

She always said that mantra when she needed courage, and today she would not lose. An innocent's life was at stake, and Daphne would defend it until the bitter end.

A trickle of sweat cascaded down the side of her face. Her mother had instructed her repeatedly that women do not sweat. Only horses sweat, while men perspire and women glisten. Whatever it was, Daphne bent her head to wipe the offending nuisance away. With a stealth-like maneuver that reminded her of her enemy, the dribble evaded her swipe and attacked her eye. The stinging salt forced her to blink several times to relieve the pain.

Swoosh. Out of nowhere, a forced gust of air assailed her.

The angry magpie darted close, and Daphne ducked her head. As best she could, Daphne ignored the screaming and furious bird. Instead, she focused on her opponent—one that possessed an intelligence and cunning that knew no limits—her older brother's cat, Athena.

Taking advantage of the magpie's frantic calls and repeated swoops around Daphne's head, her adversary approached from the far-left flank.

All things considered, Daphne loved Athena. The orange-striped cat cuddled with her late at night when she couldn't sleep.

But this was war.

Daphne would make it up to the cat this evening. She'd sneak some pheasant from tonight's dinner and wrap it in one of her linen squares, if there were any left over from their skirmish.

Thankfully, the mother bird returned to her nest in the mighty oak tree. Now Daphne could prepare for the next battle. Slowly, so as not to draw attention, she took a piece of linen and dunked it in the bucket of water. She was down to her last five pieces. Earlier, she'd taken one of her mother's best table coverings and ripped it into squares the size of a man's handkerchief.

Such was the cost of war. Finery and fripperies were worth the sacrifice for the greater good. When doused in water, the fabric transformed into a projectile, a weapon that her adversary loathed and feared.

Of course, when her mother, the Marchioness of Pembrooke, discovered her best linen tablecloth destroyed, Daphne would face a blistering lecture and some harsh punishment. Most probably, her mother would forbid she have any tarts for the next week. They were her only weakness in life, and her mother would consider the destruction of the antique linen worthy of such a chastisement.

If only her mother would forbid her from eating kippers.

She hated kippers. When served for breakfast, the little herrings always appeared to be staring straight at you.

With a sigh, Daphne wadded the linen into a wet ball. Forgoing tarts would be worth the sacrifice if she succeeded in guarding the precious life behind her to safety.

"One step closer, Athena, and you'll be wearing this as a mobcap for your face." Daphne aimed the sopping missile.

"What are you about, imp? Why are you fighting with your brother's cat?"

Of all the rotten luck.

Paul.

She didn't need her brother's charmingly arrogant but affable friend interfering now—not when another battle loomed before her.

Lord Paul Barstowe, the second son of the Duke of Southart, studied the nest, then surveyed the lawn in front of him. Scraps of material littered the ground, making it look like it had snowed linen. "Are you in some sort of epic battle?"

"Yes." Daphne drew her shoulders back and defiantly tipped her chin. She pointed at a nest of twigs and grass she'd constructed on the ground with a makeshift wall of briar branches surrounding a tiny bird. His black and white wings constantly fluttered as he tried to escape the little sanctuary she'd carefully crafted around him. "Athena wants him for dinner."

Paul surveyed her from top to bottom. Her black hair had escaped the confines of her bow and mud covered her half boots. "Instead of a well-groomed sister of a marquess, you look like a mess of dirt, grime, and sweat."

"Dirt, grim, and glisten," she said in an authoritative manner. "Only horses sweat. Mother says girls glisten and boys perspire."

"What do pigs do?" A tiny smile broke across his lips.

"Are you calling me a pig?" She narrowed her eyes in challenge.

He quickly subdued his humor. If provoked, she might be more dangerous than the angry magpie hurling squawks their way. "No. If recollection serves, pigs don't sweat, glisten, or perspire," he said. "That's why they wallow in the mud."

"Astounding," she answered incredulously.

"Never mind. Once your governess finds the depth of your dishevel you'll be punished, I'd wager."

Once a pristine white, the color of her simple dress resembled the dirty coal-infused fogs that smothered London on cool autumn days. The sash around her waist had somehow come untied, and the ends had turned black where she'd dragged it along the ground as she defended her territory and the baby bird.

"It's my governess's fault I look like this." Daphne waved her hand down the front of her dress. "She won't let me wear Alex's hand-me-down breeches and shirts. Who would want to wear a dress when gathering briar branches?"

"Indeed. Who would?" Sympathetically, he grinned. There was no sense in making the point, but he highly doubted if a single bath would clean the filth she'd managed to attract today.

"My governess will make me put myself to rights before I'm allowed any dinner." She shrugged her shoulders. "It makes little difference. I came prepared to spend the night. I have plenty of provisions and a warm blanket."

His gaze darted from hers to the cat that crouched in preparation to strike. The tip of Athena's tail flickered in warning of an impending pounce, one that would lead to victory with the spoils of war, namely the baby magpie, in her mouth.

"Get down." Daphne grabbed his arm as she ducked.

The mother bird squawked as she flew past without any consideration for their position. This time she'd reserved her screeching fury for Athena and swooped low over the cat's back. Athena darted in a zigzag pattern toward the kitchen.

Paul inhaled sharply as his gaze raked over Daphne's bloodied arms. Scratched and bruised, she had suffered a severe thrashing from something, most likely an angry cat. Normally, Athena didn't live up to her namesake, the goddess of war. Alex's cat much preferred prowling around the kitchen for any scraps that might have dropped and expressing her thanks with a quick rub against the cook's legs and a purr. But having wet linen repeatedly hurled at its head would give any cat cause for attack. "Did Athena do that to you?"

She shook her head. "I tripped and landed on the bramble branches."

With a slight tug, he straightened out her arms to study her injuries. His hands dwarfed her smaller ones, reminding him she wasn't just a hellion on a mission but a little girl. Some of her dress stains were the result of dirt, but far more of the brown blotches were dried blood. Her impressive conviction to save the little bird perplexed him. Didn't most little girls prefer needlework, painting, and playing with dolls?

He pulled her gently toward the house. "Those scratches must hurt. Let's get you inside and cleaned up."

"I'm not leaving him." She jerked her hands away and pointed at the bird on the ground.

Paul drew a deep breath and glanced at the fountain in the courtyard. The gurgling water soothed and encouraged him to practice sufferance as he exhaled. Sometimes he lost his patience with Lady Alice Hallworth, Alex's youngest sister, who had a tendency to whine, but never Daphne. Her confidence and moral compass defied her young age. Only her bottom lip sticking out betrayed her stubbornness, a trait that she had in abundance. "That magpie came close to attacking you. This isn't worth you getting hurt. You can't change Athena. She's born to hunt. You need to let nature take its course."

Daphne blew a stray wisp of hair out of her eyes. "I'm not changing nature or Athena's behavior. I'm just modifying it a tad." She turned her unyielding gaze to him. "I'm not scared of the magpie."

Had he ever been that stalwart in his principles or that innocent?

Perhaps when his mother was alive and he'd had her undivided attention. Once she was gone, no one paid much heed to him or his needs. His father's interests had focused solely on his older brother, Robert, the ducal heir. Paul's priorities then had changed to shocking his sire with his wayward actions—gambling and drinking to excess. He learned early that if he lived up to his reputation as a firebrand his father paid some mind to him.

"Come, Daphne. I'll escort you inside. You need a bath, and your nursemaid should attend to your wounds."

"Not until I know he's safe." She crouched next to the little bird on the ground.

He hopped and fluttered his wings, almost managing to become airborne. His brothers and sisters squeaked and tweeted in encouragement. Their little chorus of protests grew more frantic the longer their mother was gone from the nest.

"I have an idea," Daphne offered. "Would you help me? I asked Alex earlier, but he had estate work to attend to. Alice is looking through the latest fashion plates Mother received from London."

He didn't miss the slight crinkle of the little hoyden's nose at the word "fashion."

"What do you have in mind? I don't have much time." Paul brushed his hands together. "Lucky for you, I haven't lost my sense of adventure. I'm always game for anything completely inappropriate."

Daphne rolled her eyes, then stood. "This is life and death we're discussing. Not some stupid prank of schoolboys."

She was deliberately piquing him. "Schoolboys? Seriously?"

"Of course. Pardon me," she mocked. "Ever since you and Alex returned home from university, you both have preened and paraded like peacocks. Eton must offer a requisite class on offensive male behavior."

He knew better than to quarrel with a tart-tongued spitfire, but she needed correction. He took a challenging step closer. "Haven't you been taught that a man's honor and character are something to be cherished and guarded?"

She shook her head. "No. I've been warned they're very fragile and to take heed when around one."

The little rapscallion never ceased to surprise him with her quips. He threw back his head and laughed. For the life of him, he couldn't resist and tapped her on the nose. "Well done, minx."

With a dip of her head, she swept her hands out to the sides and delivered a courtly bow. A heated flush, one undoubtedly caused by his praise, crawled up her neck to her cheeks.

Though filthy, Daphne was really quite adorable the way she straightened her shoulders to try to quash her embarrassment. Pembrooke was quite fortunate that he had such an entertaining little sister. With a slight grin, he turned his attention to the nest in the tree. With little trouble, he could scale the oak's branches, deposit the bird, and be down before anyone, namely that obnoxious mother magpie, returned. "Here's what we'll do. I'll climb the tree and put the little fellow back in his nest. Then we can both leave this battlefield and prepare for the evening."

"You'll do that?" she asked.

The adulation in her gray eyes made his throat cinch

tight. No one ever looked at him like that. He scrambled madly to come up with something to say that would shock or at least disabuse her of the notion that he deserved her admiration. He'd made it his life's mission to be outrageous.

"Paul?" Daphne pulled on his sleeve. Once she had his full attention, she continued, "I tried to climb the tree, but couldn't reach the second branch to pull myself up." Suddenly, she smiled. "My opinion of you has changed. It proves you are worthy of my friendship."

At least someone, even if she was an imp, appreciated his company. Perhaps she could have a conversation with his father. She could certainly go toe-to-toe with the old man.

"Would you sit by me at dinner tonight?" She bounced on her feet like a bobber on a pond. *"Pleasssse."*

"I can't. Your brother and I are dining in the village this evening."

Her face fell as if he'd stolen her favorite pastry from her plate. Immediately, he regretted sharing that tidbit.

"To see your favorite barmaids and make fools of yourselves as you play hazard until the dawn?" Her mouth dipped into a frown. "Boys have all the fun. It's so unfair."

"To make up for the all unfairness in life, how about I promise to take you riding tomorrow?" Paul shrugged out of his coat. "We'll ask Pembrooke and Alice to join us."

"Really?" Excitement blazed in her eyes, turning them from gray to silver. "That would be lovely."

In seconds, he had managed to hoist himself onto the first branch. "Give him to me, will you?"

Daphne carefully scooped up the baby bird, then gently placed him in Paul's outstretched hand. The small claws of the bird's feet and downy-soft feathers tickled his palm. He carefully placed the bird in one of his waistcoat's front pockets.

Without much fanfare, he pulled himself up to the second branch, then spread his body halfway across the limb. He reached into his pocket and found the soft quiver of feathers. Gently, he pulled the bird free, then placed him back in the nest with his brothers and sisters. A chorus of chirps and tweets greeted him on behalf of his benevolent actions.

Without warning, the mother magpie descended in a rage and seemed to surround him in every direction with a flurry of feathers. Attacking and screeching in hysterics, she beat her wings around his head and pecked at his face. He covered himself with one arm and tried to shoo her away. She managed to find a place where his cheek was exposed, then pecked him without mercy.

"Bloody hell." The pain of an ice pick plunging into his face would have hurt less. He scrambled backward from the nest, mindful of the branch below, then plummeted to the ground with a thud and landed on his back.

A trail of hot blood ran down his cheek where the bird had brutalized him. He rolled to his feet. The magpie kept swooping at them, so he grabbed Daphne's hand and pulled her away from the tree to escape any further attacks.

"I hope that doesn't leave a scar." She handed him a piece of her mother's table covering. "What people say about you isn't true."

He stopped, completely speechless, and stared for a moment, then took the square of material and wiped the blood from his face. He grimaced, then schooled his features so his characteristic aloofness returned, replacing his earlier ease and warmth. He shouldn't have let a snip of a girl past his defenses.

The rays of the setting sun tangled in Daphne's black tresses, painting them mahogany. The bits of twigs and leaves twined in her hair completely ruined the effect. His gaze slid past her to the orange horizon. His behavior was becoming infamous if a nine-year-old girl had heard rumors about him. He shrugged into his riding jacket and picked up the hat and gloves he'd discarded. Uncomfortable with her steely gaze, he adjusted the cuffs of his shirtsleeves. Appearing not to have a care in the world, he strolled toward the front of the house.

He shouldn't be bothered with gossip and nonsense. Yet an irritating vexation niggled and nagged his thoughts until it awoke his curiosity. Suddenly, he stopped and pivoted on one booted heel. "What exactly do *they* say about me?"

"That you're selfish and arrogant. In short, that you're only concerned with your own needs." She softened her next words. "But you're not."

"You should pay attention to their warnings." He slapped his gloves against the palm of his hand, then lifted a brow in challenge. His chest tightened at the biting truthfulness of her words.

"If I was insensitive, I apologize." She presented an empathetic smile, but the slight tightening around her unusual silver eyes betrayed her uneasiness.

God, he hated any type of sympathy. He was his own man and didn't want or need any coddling.

"I'm just trying to help," she said. "Let me give you some advice. Don't ever gamble. The swans in our pond have more acting skills than you." She tied the dirty sash of her dress. "You need to school your facial expressions. As your friend, it's my duty to help. Cook made some special raspberry tarts just for me. I'll share with you." Taking his hand in hers, she tugged him toward the kitchen entrance. "Besides, what I say is not my opinion, but a simple truth. Your countenance is easy to read."

"How so?"

"Your eyes betray you," she said.

"Now I'm receiving the most unusual deportment

lessons from a nine-year-old hoyden." He smiled down, hoping he hid his unease. "Let me give *you* some advice." From his coat pocket he retrieved the unusual rock he'd found earlier during his ride and gave it to her. "Every time you feel the need to save someone, remember this piece of limestone. You'd do well to harden that organ in the middle of your chest and only think of yourself."

Daphne studied the stone in the palm of her hand. "It's shaped like a heart."

She peered up at him and smiled. Her teeth were straight and even except for the hole where her recently lost left canine tooth used to reside. Without a hint of guile or contrived innocence, her lopsided grin hurt far greater than the stab from the bird. He didn't deserve any type of admiration.

"Thank you. It's a beautiful stone. Now I'm ready for a tart. Shall we?" she announced.

When she tried to slip her hand in his once more, he stepped out of her reach. "You eat my share. I must go, Daph." He turned and quickened his pace, hoping she wouldn't follow.

Who knew that Lady Daphne Hallworth, a little girl no less, could be the one who made his dissatisfaction with himself almost unbearable?

Chapter One

Autumn
Sixteen years later
The London residence of the Duke of Langham

Paul relaxed in the leather chair that sat directly in front of the Duke of Langham's mahogany desk. In so many ways, the piece resembled the duke—massive, dark, but with an inherent warmth that made a person want to settle in for a long afternoon of pleasure mixed with work.

That was the allure of Langham. As one of the most respected—not to mention powerful—members in the House of Lords, his acceptance of Paul by being the first to stand at the end of Paul's introductory address to the noble institution had made Paul's welcome by its members easier. Everyone had followed the duke's example and stood. As the sound of clapping and cheers echoed through the chambers, Paul finally had allowed himself to relax.

His peers accepted him.

However, the duke's nephew-in-law, Paul's oldest but estranged friend, Alexander, the Marquis of Pembrooke, had been one of the last to stand when Paul received a standing ovation for his speech.

The marquess's act of disdain that day still stung but wasn't much of a surprise. Their former friendship had been destroyed by Paul's selfish acts. But Pembrooke's brief note offering condolences on the death of Paul's brother three months ago meant the world to him. Paul kept it on his desk as a reminder of all the things he'd lost in his life, but it also represented hope. If Pembrooke thought enough to pen a note, then perhaps Paul could redeem himself in his former friend's eyes.

"I'm not the only one who has noticed the amount of work you're doing to familiarize yourself with the upcoming parliamentary session next year," Langham offered. "It shows your commitment. Lord Kenton may offer you a position on one of his committees. If you want it, I'll see that it happens."

"I'd appreciate your help. I can never repay you for your kindness." Paul glanced at his little finger where the large ruby in his signet ring flashed like fire. Every Duke of Southart had worn it since William III had bestowed the stone as a thank-you for the first duke's valiant service. For Paul, the ring was not a symbol of his father, but a symbol of Paul's family. It should have been Robbie's, but Paul wore it in Robbie's place. For that reason alone, it meant something to him. "I couldn't have made such strides without your thoughts and guidance."

The duke waved his hand through the air as if it were nothing. The fact that he'd allowed Paul entrance into Langham Hall after Paul had jilted the duke's niece years ago on the night of their engagement ball spoke of the duke's forgiving nature.

He swallowed, hoping to relieve his unease at such painful memories. He'd been desperate that night. Gambling recklessly trying to win back all the money he'd lost. Pembrooke had come to rescue him, but in return for buying Paul's debts, Pembrooke demanded that Paul release Lady Claire Cavensham, Langham's niece, from the betrothal. Based upon Paul's behavior at the gambling hells, Pembrooke thought he wasn't good enough for the duke's niece.

Which in hindsight was true—much to Paul's own disgrace. He did as asked, not thinking of the ramifications, by breaking with her at their engagement ball, and Pembrooke had quickly married Claire within the week to save her from the *ton*'s vicious rumors. Now Lady Claire was the Marchioness of Pembrooke.

"Langham"—he cleared his throat hoping that brief moment would summon forth the right words—"I truly am sorry for my previous behavior when I was engaged to your niece."

The duke slowly leaned forward and focused his hawklike gaze on Paul. Moments slipped by, causing their earlier ease with each other to grow tense. Finally, the duke finished his examination and leaned back in his chair. "There's no need to revisit the past. What you need to concentrate on is your current and future actions. They'll define your worth as the new Duke of Southart."

Paul nodded. "That's one of the things I want to discuss. I'm starting a new charity, a hospital that specializes in the treatment of rheumatic fever, to honor my late brother, Robbie. It'll be a place for patients who have no other alternatives for care, and hopefully, it'll provide research opportunities for the top medical professionals in that area of study."

A smile tugged at the duke's mouth, and his blue eyes flashed with delight. "That's a noble cause, and one you should be passionate about."

"I am," Paul answered truthfully. He'd been thinking of starting this endeavor for years, ever since Robbie had first become ill.

"How can I help?" the duke asked.

"I've instructed my solicitors to find a suitable property. And I hoped you'd come to a benefit soiree I plan to host in several months—" Before he could continue, Pembrooke and Nicholas, the Earl of Somerton, entered the room. While Pembrooke had married the duke's niece, Somerton had married the duke's daughter, Lady Emma Cavensham, now the Countess of Somerton.

"Come in, gentlemen," the duke called out in greeting. "Southart and I were discussing his plans for a new hospital in honor of his late brother. Grand idea, don't you think?"

Paul stood and nodded in greeting.

Somerton answered Paul's nod with a brief one of his own, but Pembrooke visibly stiffened his shoulders and stared at him as if he were an intruder.

"It's an admirable goal," Pembrooke finally said. "However, completing such a project takes dedication, hard work, and gravitas. Traits you always seemed to lack. Unless you've acquired them in recent years." One arrogant eyebrow arched slowly. Silence descended at the curt denouncement.

Somerton shook his head. "Pembrooke, enough."

"Things haven't changed, I see." The duke exhaled and gently drummed the fingers of one hand on the desktop. "Perhaps you'd both like to join us, and we could discuss this in more detail."

Arm in arm with smiles on their faces, Somerton's wife, Emma, and Lady Daphne entered. Both women were attractive, but Paul's gaze fixated on Daphne. She'd turned into a real diamond of the first water. She was breathtaking.

As soon as Daphne saw Paul, her eyes widened. "Paul . . . I mean, Your Grace. How wonderful to see you."

The excitement in her voice rang through the room. All he could do was grin. "Lady Somerton," he answered. "Lady Daphne, the pleasure is all mine."

Emma nodded in return, but Daphne's smile grew bigger. The brilliance in her unusual gray eyes reminded him of simpler times when they were all younger—and all true friends. They'd certainly been more at ease with one another's company.

She broke away from her friend, then approached Paul. Her happy greeting caused the tightness in his chest to ease.

He took her gloved hand in his. Though her hand was covered, he could detect the inherent softness of her skin. Unable to resist, he gently squeezed, signaling his pleasure at her welcome. "Congratulations. I understand your mother married Somerton's father. I wish both of them happiness."

"Thank you. I'll give Mother and Renton your regards." Still holding his hand, she executed a perfect curtsy. "We're all so happy for their union. An added benefit is that Alex and I have a new stepbrother, Somerton."

"And he has a new stepbrother and stepsister. I'm envious," Paul said. "But very happy for all of you."

"My condolences to you on the recent passing of your brother and father." She squeezed his hand in return.

"Thank you." He was desperate for the comfort she offered and made the mistake of holding her hand a little too long.

"Daphne," commanded Pembrooke.

She dropped his hand as if burned, then turned to her brother. "Alex, I didn't see you." She hesitated for a moment.

But it was long enough for Paul to see the division that lay between him and Pembrooke extended to Daphne as well. Without another word, she went to stand beside her brother. The awkwardness in the room grew until it became unbearable for Paul. He quickly took his leave from the duke and Lord and Lady Somerton, then forced himself to face Pembrooke.

Daphne's brother had his head bent to hers in a private conversation.

"Why not welcome him?" she murmured. "The duke has."

"He may be the Duke of Southart now, but he hasn't changed. He promises nothing but disappointment. Remember what he did to Claire." Alex bit out the words. "Stay away from him."

Daphne glanced his way while her brother engaged in a conversation with Langham.

A flush of heat threatened to overtake Paul.

She bit her lip, then dropped her gaze.

They both were aware Paul had heard every word.

Three months later—exactly three days before Christmastide
The London residence of the Duke of Southart

Paul resisted the urge to straighten the cuffs of his shirt, a habit he acquired years ago when confronting his father in this very room. He stared into the glass of brandy. This particular vintage had been his father's favorite until he and his older brother, Robert, had replaced three bottles with rust-colored water. His father hadn't punished Robbie, but Paul couldn't sit down for a week without a pillow underneath.

"Would you?"

"Would I what?" Paul glanced from the glass into the bottomless green eyes of Devan Farris. He was in London for Christmastide ready to receive his new assignment in the church. What made Devan unique was his steadfastness. He was the only man who hadn't given up on Paul, and he was Paul's last true friend in the world. It made little difference that Devan happened to be the most unusual vicar who had ever resided in Easton, a tiny village located five miles north of Paul's duchy.

It was still difficult to refer to Southart as such. Six months ago, his father—with probable infinite pleasure—had shocked everyone with his death just two days after Robbie's passing from rheumatic fever, a lasting souvenir from his severe bout of scarlet fever. Robbie's death had been expected, as his health had declined rapidly over the last three years, but their father's sudden passing surprised everyone. The doctor had concluded the duke's heart had suddenly stopped. Paul had a better diagnosis; his father had died of a broken heart. The contrary act had made Paul the new Duke of Southart, even though he still considered himself the second son, the spare heir—just like his father had.

Perhaps he always would. His gaze skimmed his azure merino wool dress coat with diamond buttons and black silk pantaloons. He dressed like a duke, but beneath the wrappings of his position in society and wealth, he was still the same man—one who had lived a life full of mistakes and regrets. However, he'd change all that with the creation of his hospital.

"Would you swive the new Duchess of Renton? Though she's old enough to be our mother, she's still grand looking." Devan rose from the settee and poured another glass of brandy. "How many times do I have to go through the entire *Debrett's* listing of married women in the *ton*? You used to be marvelous fun at this game. Now a day-old dumpling has more appeal. By the way, this swallows like a whore's—"

"For the love of God, Farris. You're a man of the church." Paul shook his head and chuckled. His old friend could always make him smile with his outrageous comments and game of "Would You Swive?"

"Need I remind you that I'm considered one of the most devout of my profession?" Devan's arrogance transformed into an expression of a dutiful clergyman ready to hear confessions. "Oh, I can give my flock a pious look. I can recite a couple of pieces of verse as I bow my head and close my eyes. As I whisper a trite prayer, they all think I'm the holiest thing that ever came into this world." He threw back his head and laughed. "I love my work."

The joy in Farris's face was contagious, and Paul grinned in return. For the moment, this was exactly what he'd needed to steal away his grief from losing his family—meaningless fun with a friend.

"Of course, if they only knew that I can swill whisky along with the best of men. Besides, I'm proud of the fact that I've raised my fair amount of hell and have never been caught," Devan boasted.

"I taught you everything you know," Paul quipped.

"No, I taught you . . . except the women part. How in the devil you could seduce the Countess of Velton is beyond me." Devan squinted and shuddered.

His reaction reminded Paul of sour lemons.

"In defense of the old dame, it was out of respect." Paul had only bedded her once, but it was a fond memory. Twenty years older and with the patience of Job, she'd taught him all sorts of sensual delights. At the age of seventeen, he had known nothing about women. Lady Velton had sought his attention at a house party, then had kindly taught him every seduction technique she'd acquired in her thirty-plus years upon the earth. With all that bountiful knowledge, he could take a woman on a sensual journey in bed that she'd never forget. In return, he found his own satisfaction knowing that when he took a woman to bed she was treated like a queen. He lifted his glass in Lady Velton's honor for a weekend that had proved well worth his time, and he hoped that she considered him worth her time.

"You're a simpleton when it comes to women," Devan countered.

"Careful, my friend." Paul leaned back and regarded him with a half-lidded gaze. "I'm not a simpleton, but I am a simple man, one with simple tastes and simple goals."

Devan grunted in response.

"I adore beautiful women, vintage champagne, fine clothes, and the worst gambling hells I can find." Paul set the brandy aside and rose from the richly appointed mahogany desk. The Moroccan leather chair moaned, protesting like a cast-aside lover. He circled the massive piece of wood and made his way to the side table, where he poured a glass of champagne. He lifted the glass in the air, but Devan shook his head.

"I'm fine with this," the vicar answered. "By the way, how goes the search for a property for the new hospital?"

"My solicitors found a perfect location. I trust their judgment and directed them to place a suitable bid on the property."

"Sight unseen?" Devon raised a brow.

"Yes, I didn't want to lose it," Paul said. "Apparently, someone else is interested in it."

Both raised their glasses to each other.

"To the hospital," Paul toasted.

"To the hospital." Devan nodded. "And friends old and new."

Paul exhaled loudly. "Why did you choose a profession in the church? With your new assignment forthcoming, you'll likely settle in a small town with nothing to offer but a constant view of cows chewing their cuds."

Devan tilted his head as he considered Paul's question. "Well, as the fourth son of an earl, I didn't have many options in life. I could have gone into the military, but how bourgeois. There's only so much entertainment to be had in the daily cleaning of weapons." He leaned forward. "What other choice did I have? Let me tell you a secret few know. As a man of the church, I'm revered. I always have a tea or dinner invitation readily offered from the various families of my parish." He shrugged his shoulders. "I can flirt with the prettiest women in town, and no one bats an eye."

"Give it up. Come live at Southart. The duchy's rectory is a lovely place, and you could settle into a life that I guarantee will be fulfilling. You'll have my wretched soul to watch over. That should keep you busy until the end of your days."

When Devan examined him with a razor-sharp gaze, prickles of unease raised the hair on the back of Paul's neck. An image of Devan pulling away the layers of sins and misdeeds while trying to find something redeeming inside increased Paul's discomfort. Such a task as finding anything worthwhile in his rotten soul would take the vicar years or, most likely, eons.

"That came out of the clear blue. Feeling nostalgic this time of year, my friend?" Devan tilted his head.

"Hardly. I received another note and vowel from my father addressed to 'The Great Disappointment, my baseborn son.' The solicitor sent it over this morning."

"Christ," Devan said. "Your father's cruelty knows no bounds. What's the amount of the vowel?"

"I owe the Reynolds fifteen pounds. This makes the third one in three weeks. He's haunting me from the grave." He laughed, but the sound held no humor. "The vowels are all such little amounts. Why did he save them? I could have paid these amounts years ago."

Devan shrugged his shoulders, but his gaze never left Paul's.

"I'll tell you why. He's humiliating me." Paul allowed his carefully constructed image of a bored and pampered aristocrat to melt away. He commanded a deep breath to dampen the bite of pain that appeared at the most inopportune times. On most occasions, he managed to tame the misery residing close to his every thought and deed. This moment was a watershed. His grief over his father's sudden death was a constant mystery. He and his brother had been close for siblings, but his father had treated him as if he were something the cat had dragged into the house in the blackest part of night. When Robbie had discovered Paul's beating by their father's hand over the brandy prank, Robbie had entered their father's study and not emerged for an hour.

Their father had never touched him again.

Nevertheless, his father found other ways to punish Paul. The constant look of disgust on the duke's face whenever forced to address his younger son's misdeeds always reminded Paul of someone holding his nose so as not to suffer contamination from the stench. His father continued to find more ways to torment Paul beyond the grave. The old duke's personal solicitor had written that he possessed a personal letter addressed to Paul from his father. Once he returned from holiday, he'd deliver it himself and answer any questions Paul might have.

He'd always wondered if it wasn't some divine plan that his father had died within days of Robbie's passing. It ensured his father was never disappointed in him again—ever.

Perhaps the heavens thought the old duke needed a permanent hiatus from Paul's mischief, or it took pity on Paul and swept the curmudgeon into its welcoming arms.

Most likely, it showed that maybe his father had no interest living in a world where Paul was his only son.

When Paul's mother had been alive, she'd spent every available moment with Robbie and him, which was very unusual for a duchess. Once Robbie had reached the appropriate age, the duke had insisted his heir leave the nursery. Paul would have been lost if it hadn't been for his mother's tender attention. However, all that changed less than two months later when she'd succumbed to an illness and died within days.

Paul would have been inconsolable, since their father never much acknowledged his grief over his duchess's death. But Paul's brother had defied their father and spent the next month in the nursery and schoolroom proving his stalwart love for his little brother.

Even still, Paul missed the stoic, regimented old duke. The daily challenge of getting a rise out of the old man and watching his visage turn fifty hues of scarlet had been Paul's favorite pastime.

"I need your friendship." The burn inside the middle of his chest threatened to take his voice away. "I kept my sanity through mourning because of you," he said in a low tone.

Devan placed his crystal glass of brandy on the side table and approached. He rested his hand on Paul's shoulder and squeezed. "You had plenty of friends. The problem with you, *Your Grace,* is that you've *bloody* rejected the ones closest to you."

Paul choked on his champagne. The vile curse coming from his friend's mouth didn't shock him, but the truth of Devan's words stole his breath. Indeed, he'd destroyed nearly every relationship he'd ever had except his brother's and Devan's friendships. Though Devan was a vicar, he still counted as a true friend, but maybe because of his profession he possessed more tolerance than most.

"Don't mince any words in consideration of my tender feelings." Paul cleared his throat. "I've told you those friendships are gone forever."

"No." Devan smirked, then huffed a dismissal. "You're making it too easy on yourself. You'll never be happy unless you try to repair those friendships you've ruined."

"It's hopeless." Paul took another sip of champagne.

"Hardly," Devon cajoled. "When you approached the

Duke of Langham, he was very willing to support you and your hospital charity."

"He wanted something in return. My support for his upcoming bills in the House of Lords."

Devan rolled his eyes. "That's the way the members of Parliament work together. Plus, Pembrooke attended your speech in the House of Lords before the winter break. Last week, Somerton sat with Pembrooke at White's while you read the evening post at the next table. Five years ago, such a thing wouldn't happen."

"Pure coincidence. Neither spared a glance my way." Paul shook his head. "How do you know such things?"

"The *Earrrrl of Larrrrkton* made mention." The roll of the *r*'s in the title emphasized Devan's contempt for his oldest brother. "Even a man of the cloth has to go home every once in a while and make amends for his transgressions. Larkton wanted my head for refusing to marry the lovely Miss Barbara Overfield."

Paul whistled softly. "I admire your brother's good taste. She's one of England's wealthiest heiresses and of marriageable age. Now that the Cavensham heiresses have been gobbled up, there aren't many left."

"Call me old-fashioned, but I believe there should be some attraction between a couple. She constantly chatters. Between the two of us, neither of us would ever let the other get a word in edgewise." Devan returned to collect his brandy and sat in front of the blazing fireplace at a small ebony table with an intricately carved chess set. "Besides, you're wrong. If you consider familial relations by marriage, there's a new Cavensham heiress. Remember Lady Daphne Hallworth?"

"Only in the loosest of terms." *What a liar.* Yes, he still remembered her as a young girl, one he spent many an hour teaching to play chess and whist. He rubbed the scar on his cheek courtesy of the magpie. She thought him noble that day, and it was one of his fondest memories. He couldn't recall anyone ever thinking of him that way since. Then, when he'd seen her at the Duke of Langham's home, her happiness at meeting him had made Paul feel mighty—almost as if he could become chivalrous—until she bore witness to his shame.

"Details, old man," Devan said. "She's Lady Pembrooke's sister-in-law and the stepsister-in-law to Lady Somerton, both former Cavenshams. The lovely Lady Daphne recently came into a fortune left to her by her late aunt on her mother's side. Close to forty-five or fifty thousand pounds if *The Midnight Cryer* has it right."

"I'd heard rumors." Paul tipped the glass and finished the rest of the champagne.

"She's a beauty with a handsome fortune plus a dowry to match." Making himself at home, Devan arranged the chess pieces to his liking. "I've met her several times at *ton* events, but once the new Season rolls around, if I'm still in London, I plan to become better acquainted."

Paul's gut twisted into a knot. An intense flame of dislike coursed through him at his friend's brazen declaration. They both knew that Devan craved financial freedom from his brother, but the pious bastard wasn't worthy of touching one obsidian-colored hair on her head.

Who was he to judge?

He let out a silent sigh. He'd pursued marriage with Lady Claire Cavensham and Lady Emma Cavensham, all in an effort to win his father's approval. His father wanted one of his sons to marry into the Cavensham family as a way to align the Southart and Langham dukedoms. With Robbie's sickness, that left Paul with the duty. But he'd failed miserably by insulting one, Lady Claire, the previous Duke of Langham's daughter, then summarily being dismissed by the other, Lady Emma, the current Duke of Langham's daughter. His floundering efforts with the

Cavensham heiresses had kept the London gossips twirling in unabashed glee for months. Not to mention, it'd kept the pockets of Martin Richmond, the publisher of *The Midnight Cryer,* flush with cash.

"I see the gleam in your eye." Coaxing Paul to join him, Devan waved his hand in front of the board. "Before you get any ideas in that ducal brain of yours, clean your house. Pembrooke and Somerton may not feel comfortable with you, but you can change that. Set things right with them before you try to steal the lovely Lady Daphne from me."

The muscles in Paul's jaw tightened until his teeth gnashed together. "You see intrigue in the least likely of places."

"In all the years we've played 'Would You Swive?' you've placed the Duchess of Langham, the Marchioness of Pembrooke, the new Duchess of Renton, the Countess of Somerton, the Marchioness of McCalpin, and all her lovely sisters in the 'gladly' column. You've even included the queen, my own mother, and my sister in the 'out of respect' column at the risk of my wrath." Devan narrowed his eyes. "All those times, you've never made mention of Lady Daphne. Oversight? I think not."

"I thought we only played with married women." When the full force of his friend's examination fell on him, Paul adjusted his stance to withstand the all-seeing gaze. "Lady Daphne's a young girl."

"What rock have you been hiding under? There are whispers she's permanently on the shelf since she's twenty-five. Rumor has it that she believes no man is good enough to marry. She always keeps herself separated from the crowd and finds the highest perch to peer at the throng whenever she attends an event. She almost appears as if she was looking for someone." He shook his head slightly. "I'll try my hand at bringing her down from her nest. In my opinion, she's not too young or too old. Like Goldilocks's

memorable words of wisdom, she's just right, and the
perfect marriageable age, *Your Grace,*" Devan mockingly
offered, then resumed setting up the chessboard.

"What makes you think I'd be interested in her?" Paul
flicked an imaginary piece of lint from one of his sleeves,
then straightened his cuffs. He bit the inside of his cheek
at the nervous tic.

"Your response makes me wonder about your real interest in the lady," Devan said.

Paul flipped the tails from his expertly tailored dress
coat as he sat down. "Pembrooke would slaughter me if I
even looked in her direction."

"White or black?" The joyful clicking of the marble
pieces stilled as Devan finished arranging the board.

"Black. In my house, black moves first. It goes with my
personality."

"As you wish, *Your Grace,*" Devan taunted.

The room quieted except for the cheerful pop from the
crackling flames in the fireplace. After they had made several moves each, the vicar directed all his attention at
Paul. "Have you thought about how you're going to keep
your promises to your brother?"

On his deathbed, Paul's brother had made him promise
he'd reform his wicked ways and be the duke both Robbie
and their father expected. Paul ran his hand over his face in
a poor attempt to wipe the grief and memories aside.
Robbie had been his champion, the only one who believed
there was any good in Paul.

Now it was doubtful that anyone did.

Even *he* doubted his own worthiness.

Devan stared out the window into the black night.

"Looking for divine inspiration?" Paul asked.

"No, God doesn't mingle in matters such as yours. You
have to be your own savior. The hospital and your work to
build political alliances in the House of Lords are an

excellent start. But you never know what the future holds. Perhaps there's a great woman for you, one who will lead you on a merry chase?" Eventually, Devan returned his attention to Paul. "My friend, a woman who believes in you would provide all the more reason to get your house in order."

Paul tapped his finger twice against the top of the black queen. "You may have a point with your observation regarding Miss Barbara Overfield."

Devan's eyes widened. "You weren't to infer I meant her."

"I'm not referring to Miss Overfield. Didn't you say that neither of you would allow the other a word in edgewise?" Paul exhaled a breath feigning exasperation. "I meant you don't know when to stop talking."

As he watched Devan flounder for a witty response, Paul considered all the reasons why he had to attain order in his house before he'd consider marriage. First, he had to finish his father's silly game of running around London and paying gambling debts. Second, he had more than enough to keep him occupied, namely his estates and his work in the House of Lords. Third, and most important, he didn't want any distractions as he tried to mend the broken relationships he left in his wake before he took his title.

Daphne Hallworth was the last person in the world he'd consider as a suitable bride.

Her family hated him.

Chapter Two

The next day
The Marquess of Pembrooke's London residence

N*ooooooo, Truesdale!"* The volume of Lady Margaret's wail bordered on a bloodcurdling scream. A banshee would seek shelter from the noise that erupted from Lady Margaret's mouth.

Daphne stopped mid-stride.

The piercing sound echoed repeatedly, almost growing in volume as it ricocheted through the Pembrooke home's entry.

The cacophony created by numerous servants who were tasked with organizing the luggage immediately halted.

Ignoring everyone but her twin brother, she pushed him in the chest. "*Don't,*" she yelled. I don't want *your smelly pug* next to *Minerva.*"

The servants froze in the atrium as if suspended in time. Various chests, bags, and other items that would accompany Daphne and her family to their ancestral home, Pemhill, for the Christmas holidays rested on their shoulders or in their arms. No one dared moved for fear another shrill shriek was forthcoming. Even the stoic and regimented butler, Simms, who'd served the

Pembrooke family for years, grimaced at the earsplitting sound that had emanated from Margaret.

The household had become an unruly madhouse when everyone—Daphne, her family, and the servants—had gathered in the entry this morning. Trunks, toys, and valises lay scattered and piled in the center of the black and white marble atrium floor. Claire and Alex's twins, Lord Truesdale and Lady Margaret, had placed their pets next to each other in the center of the room. Truesdale's pug, Percival, and Lady Margaret's cat, Minerva, detested each other. Throughout the morning, each had growled or hissed in the other's direction from their respective cages, adding to the mayhem.

The stillness in the room vanished when Lord Truesdale answered Margaret's push in the chest with one of his own. "*Maggie, Percival* was here first. *Minerva* doesn't belong here."

"Don't call me *Maggie*. I hate that name." Another howl of frustration erupted from Margaret, who did what only a four-and-a-half-year-old could do in such a situation.

She dropped to the floor in a heap and sobbed.

Daphne rushed to pick up her niece while dodging a footman who held her trunk on his shoulder.

"My lady, pardon me. I didn't see you. Where shall I put your things?" the liveried footman asked. Apparently, he thought it safe to approach the little girl.

Margaret threw her arms around Daphne's neck and started to bawl. She gently patted her niece's back. "Shh, it's all right," Daphne soothed. She turned her attention to the footman. "Just put them under the stairs for now."

He nodded as if nothing were amiss, then headed in the opposite direction.

"Greene, over here. I need your help," another footman

called out. With the crisis averted, the servants continued their work.

Daphne ignored the shouts and thumps of trunks being set on the floor. "Sweetheart, it'll be fine. They won't ride together in the same carriage on the way to Pemhill."

Margaret wiped her nose across Daphne's blue velvet traveling gown. "But Minerva's unhappy, Aunt Daph."

"I'll take her." Alex appeared from nowhere and picked up Margaret from Daphne's arms. "Last night both of them were so excited for today. I doubt between them they got a wink of sleep."

"Remember how we used to be before Christmas? They'll sleep the entire way to Pemhill." Daphne released Margaret to Alex, then discovered her sister-in-law, Claire, beside her with a sleeping Truesdale in her arms.

"He surrendered first," Claire said.

"Darling, let me take him," Alex offered. "He's too heavy."

"You can't hold both," Claire answered as she bent her head and pressed her lips on top of her son's forehead. While still holding Truesdale, she bent and pressed another kiss to Margaret's cheek. The little girl closed her eyes, then tucked her head next to her father's neck, crushing his cravat.

Just then, the door flew open, bringing a brisk winter breeze into the entry along with Daphne and Alex's mother, the new Duchess of Renton. Her husband, the Duke of Renton, stood by her side.

"Good morning, darlings. Have we missed anything?" the duchess called out. When she saw a sleeping Margaret and Truesdale in their parents' arms, she smiled. "My little lambs are exhausted, aren't they?"

Alex kissed his mother's cheek while holding Margaret. "Welcome to the madhouse, Mother. Renton, see what you married into?"

"A loving family." The duke chuckled. "We're here to pick up Charlotte's last belongings. If you don't mind, I invited Emma and Somerton to join us for the holidays."

"Excellent. We'll all be together as a family should be during the holidays. Come with me," Alex said. He wove his way through a sea of luggage and servants still cradling his daughter in his arms, while the duke walked beside him.

"I'm going to lay Truesdale on one of the sofas in the sitting room until we're ready to leave." Claire glanced at Daphne. "Oh, Daph, I hate to tell you this, but your traveling gown is stained from this morning's skirmish. I'm so sorry."

"It's not a problem." Daphne dismissed her sister-in-law's regret with a wave of her hand, then looked at her gown. Margaret had wiped the remnants of her tears and her nose across the bodice. "I've plenty of time to change my gown. The carriages won't depart at least for another hour or so."

The words became lost in the pandemonium as her mother and Claire had already left to settle Truesdale in the rose sitting room away from the hubbub.

With a sigh, Daphne dodged another footman who balanced a small trunk on his shoulder, then made her way to her room.

A short time later she emerged from her chambers. After Daphne had changed, she'd taken a few minutes and written in her journal about Margaret and Truesdale's latest skirmish. She checked her reflection in a hallway mirror and pinched her cheeks. She straightened the black lace trim around her neck and wrists, then smoothed her hands down the soft white velvet dress with coordinating red velvet spencer. With her straight black hair pulled back in a simple chignon trimmed with a red velvet ribbon, she was ready for the journey. She hoped her travel with her brother and sister-in-law to Pemhill would be easy.

It certainly would be different.

Since her mother had married the Duke of Renton, she lived with him now. For the first time ever, Daphne's mother, the former Dowager Marchioness of Pembrooke, would not travel with the family to the ancestral seat. Instead, she and her new husband would leave for his ancestral home, Renton House, and spend a few private days together before joining the rest of the family on Christmas Day.

Without hesitation, Daphne had decided to live with Claire, Alex, and their three children. She'd spent her entire life at the Pembrooke family estates and planned to remain doing the same until her circumstances changed. Her family hoped the changed circumstance was marriage.

Daphne had a different idea. She'd been working for months with architects, builders, carpenters, and even Dr. Camden, the trusted family physician who had delivered Alex and Claire's children, on the ideal property for her new charity. She'd instructed her solicitor to place a bid two weeks ago on the location, Winterford House. It would be perfect for the unwed mothers' home she planned to establish.

Daphne wrinkled her nose as she made her way downstairs. The holidays would be especially joyous and celebratory this year. She relished the upcoming New Year and the new beginnings it would offer to her personally.

Without taking a breath, she swept her gaze about the entryway of the family's London townhouse. Something was definitely amiss. The atrium was completely devoid of servants, luggage, or any of the other hustle and bustle of a busy household preparing to travel for the holidays.

Daphne shook her head to clear the nightmare from her thoughts.

They couldn't have.

Her family was gone. Daphne closed her eyes and

clenched her hands into fists. They'd forgotten her. Once again, she'd been overlooked. Ever since she'd had her introduction to society, she'd tried to be the ideal daughter and sister. She never raised a ruckus.

Always aware of her position in society, Daphne presented the persona of a perfect lady—always the good girl, always the quintessential Hallworth. She was even careful whom she danced with at society events.

If any hint of fun could be construed as scandalous, Daphne refrained from participating, even when she desperately wanted to be in the thick of things. She'd claimed this high standard even though it chafed to subdue her own wants and desires. Determined to be flawless in her actions and deeds, she'd behaved properly for years, ever since her sister, Alice, had died. It was her way to help her mother and brother with their grief. They never had to worry about her behavior.

Being left at home was her reward for being everything genteel and circumspect.

She was invisible.

She straightened her shoulders. It was beyond foolish to jump to conclusions. Once her family realized she was at home, they'd return posthaste. Such a thought failed to wrestle the worm of worry that burrowed deep. They'd left to celebrate the holidays without her.

The under-butler Tait McBride entered the atrium, then stopped. He blinked his whisky-copper eyes slowly like an owl taking in its surroundings. "My lady, why aren't you on your way to Renton House with your mother, Her Grace?"

"Why would I go to Renton House with my mother?" Daphne asked.

Tait clasped his hands behind his back. "The marquess informed Mr. Simms, who informed me, that you were traveling with the duke and duchess."

Her mother and new stepfather would not want her bumping along like a fifth wheel on a carriage in their early days of wedded bliss. "I told my mother I was traveling with the marquess and the marchioness."

With that thought, the truth slammed into Daphne, and she fought to maintain calm. If Alex thought she was with her mother and her mother thought she was with Alex, they wouldn't discover she was missing until Christmas Day.

She was truly home alone.

Bloody hell. She would not cry.

"What are your plans?" Inwardly, she winced at her tone. It was almost accusatory, and she scrambled for something else to say to Tait. "What I meant is, I'm in somewhat of a quandary."

That slight glimmer of compassion in his eyes made Daphne cringe inside. This was one of the few times she appreciated her obscurity. She'd developed a talent for hiding her emotions ever since her sister had died. Over the years, she'd had opportunities to hone her craft without others witnessing her failures and disappointments.

Daphne despised having to ask him to wait with her, and for an instant she had an overwhelming need to push him out the door. Only then could she lick her wounds in private. But she needed him—at least until she found her way to Pemhill.

"I plan to spend Christmastide with my mother, but I promised Mr. Simms I'd see everyone off before I headed over to her residence." Tait glanced at the greatcoat and modest beaver hat resting on a kitchen chair. "He'd have my head if I left you here alone."

"Is anyone else coming to your mother's home for the holiday?" she asked. "I don't want to ruin your plans or inconvenience your family."

"No. It's just me and my mother." Tait's eyebrows drew together.

She hesitated, but she had little recourse. "I hate to impose, but would you and your mother stay with me? I hope it'll just be for a while, until I . . . decide what the best course of action is."

He nodded once. "There's no one in the stables. If I could find a courier, shall I hire him to take a message?"

"No." The confidence in her voice never wavered, but in that moment she understood her niece's need to throw herself on the floor for a good cry. "It's doubtful anyone realizes that I'm not with either my mother or my brother and his family." She swallowed in an effort to tame her disappointment. "The truth is I might have to spend Christmas here in London."

"Say no more, my lady. My mother is the type of woman that would welcome helping you. She'd relish the opportunity to work again. Besides, she's an excellent cook." An affectionate smile tugged at Tait's lips. "As a matter of fact, she's waiting for me at the butcher shop with her Christmas goose. It's our tradition that I escort both her and the goose home. Would it be acceptable if I meet and tell her our plans have changed? She'll worry otherwise. You're welcome to join me, if you like."

"Go to your mother. But I think it wise that I stay here just in case Lord Pembrooke discovers I've been left in London." There was little chance of that occurring, but if by some miracle someone realized she was home alone with no family, she wanted to be here. "Take your time. I'm sorry that I'm inconveniencing you both. Please bring your mother here, if she doesn't mind waiting. Of course, the goose is welcome, too."

Tait chuckled as he put on his hat and coat. "I will escort them both here. Thank you, Lady Daphne." With a tip of his hat, he was out the door.

With a sigh, she secured and locked the door, then returned to the entry. She pulled her trunks to the center of the room and started to pace. If Alex arrived, she wanted to have her lecture memorized with a delivery that would blister his ears. Her well-crafted image of the perfect sister be damned. This was way beyond the pale for her to forgive. Imagine if she'd forgotten him—at the holidays, no less. She swallowed most of her indignation and closed her eyes.

That wasn't fair to Alex. He was a wonderfully kind and loving brother. He'd never deliberately hurt her, and she loved him dearly. She felt the same for her mother. The truth was they both thought she traveled with the other. Her heart plummeted, and she blinked rapidly to prevent the scalding tears that threatened. She had to face her new reality. As an adult, she wasn't the first priority for either of them, and it was perfectly understandable. They were married, with new and different responsibilities.

Numb with the knowledge that she was truly alone, Daphne sat on her trunk. This had to be what it was like to live as a spinster. Just like a clump of dust under the bed, no one really saw you, no one really wanted you, but everyone knew you existed.

Her chest tightened, but she refused to allow her disappointment to run roughshod over her emotions. She would ignore the pain. She was a master at it after all the years of practice.

A deafening silence greeted her. She'd never been alone in the house before. With all the fires dampened and the curtains drawn, the house had turned bitterly chilly. The lack of light reminded her of her own dimness. Suddenly, the wind whipped against the windows while intermittent gusts moaned menacingly as they skated down the brick chimney in the adjacent salon. She clasped the collar of her red spencer tighter at the eerie sounds.

She rubbed her temples and narrowed her eyes.

If neither her family nor any of the servants traveling

with the family had realized she was alone, her best course of action might be to hire a carriage and an escort to Pemhill. She quickly rejected that plan. If someone came for her, their carriages might pass by each other on the road. She forced herself to inhale deeply, settling her heartbeat into a familiar rhythm. Perhaps she could stay with Emma, her best friend.

"No!" She pressed her hand to her forehead. She had the worst luck in the world. Emma had mentioned that she and Somerton were leaving for Cambridge earlier in the week. This morning, the Duke of Renton had announced he'd invited Emma and Somerton to join the rest of the family at Pemhill once they were finished in Cambridge.

There was no one left in town. There was only one conclusion she could draw. She'd spend the holiday alone in London.

She straightened her shoulders, vowing she'd have her own jolly Christmas. If anything, she'd use this time wisely to examine her life and solidify her plans for her own residence. No longer would she depend upon her family. Without delay, she'd call on the family solicitor, Mr. Fincham, and direct him to find her a place she could call her own. With her inheritance from Aunt Beatrice, she had more than enough to lease or purchase a small townhouse in the city, establish her own household, and open her charity. No one, not even Alex, could tell her otherwise. She'd live her life the way she saw fit. Never again would she accept the hateful, dull nomenclature of "good girl." Whatever she wanted she would go after.

In the past, she'd listened to her brother's arguments that she not create a home for unwed mothers. Alex thought that it would ruin her socially if she created and worked in such an institution. It made little difference if she was ruined or not. She'd forgo any plans for marriage, as this charity would have her heart and devotion completely.

Just as Alex and their mother had other priorities, so did Daphne. She'd thought about establishing such a charity for years, ever since she had worked at Claire's charities and at Emma's bank for women. It would be her contribution to help women forge a better life. No one should have to suffer a lifetime because of a mistake or because someone took advantage of her.

Selfishly, if Daphne could help one unmarried woman escape the heartache of an unexpected pregnancy like her sister, Alice, had experienced, then whatever sacrifices Daphne had to make would be minuscule in comparison to the relief it would offer her.

Suddenly, the wind wailed, shaking the entry windows. The atrium seemed to close around her, suffocating in its silence. Her heartbeat accelerated trying to outrun the invading quiet. She would not feel sorry for herself. Nor would she be scared in her own home. She needed a diversion, some exercise to take her mind off things.

Her first order of business with her new independence was to make her way to Mr. Fincham's office. If a carriage came for her, let the family wait until she was ready to leave. With a deep breath designed to fill her with courage, she wrote Tait a quick note of where she'd gone. She threw her heavy wool cloak over her gown and spencer, then retrieved her reticule that contained a few coins and her most precious possession—her journal.

Chapter Three

If rain had a fragrance, then snow was a sensual feast. The scent of spruce and a whiff of clean linen tinted the air. The surroundings seemed to sparkle in decoration for the season.

When Daphne's thoughts were clouded much like the gray sky overhead, she liked to walk. With determination fueling her every step, Daphne made quick work of the distance from Mr. Fincham's office to her favorite small park in Mayfair. Unfortunately, the solicitor had closed his office for several hours, and instead of waiting, Daphne had chosen to walk back to Pembrooke House through the park.

Even the eerily deserted streets didn't give her pause as she continued on her way. Except for the occasional street vender crossing through Mayfair, she didn't pass another soul. In her present mood, it suited her perfectly.

With a swipe of her handkerchief, she cleaned her favorite granite bench, then sat, facing a small frosted fountain. The thin layer of ice gave the appearance that the fountain had been gilded in silver.

She'd survived other tragedies and disappointments in her life, and she'd survive this utterly humiliating day.

It would not defeat her.

Daphne tilted her face at the sky. Several snowflakes gently floated through the air and danced upon her face. She'd enjoy this outing even if she was alone. Afterward, she'd go home and fix herself tea, then perhaps try her hand at baking tarts. She'd show her family and herself she could make it quite nicely on her own.

She placed her ermine muff beside her, then pulled out a sharpened pencil and her journal from her reticule. Normally, she wrote with a quill and ink and kept the journal under lock and key in a secret trunk in her room. When she traveled, she'd place the precious volume in her reticule to keep it close. Writing in the small red leather journal outside in the open air brought a new type of freedom. The book held every secret thought, desire, and idea that she wanted to remember. Some were wicked and wanton and others biting and cruel. The majority of her writings were so personal she found it hard to read them. The ones after her sister's death were especially painful. At the memories of her sister's passing, everything stilled within Daphne as the claiming grief threatened to climb from its abyss and take control.

Her entire family had been lost in their mourning over Alice. Her brother and mother had dealt with Alice's death individually. Several times, she'd approached them but been gently rebuffed when she mentioned how much she hurt. She couldn't blame them. Their agony was as acute as her own was. The only difference? They couldn't bring themselves to discuss it.

When her father had died, Daphne, Alex, her young sister, Alice, and their mother had all grieved together. His passing wasn't a forbidden secret like Alice's death.

But then her father hadn't taken his own life either.

Daphne pushed her sadness and disappointment aside. She took a deep breath of the cold air, then shivered before she set the pencil to the fine parchment. It was time she created other memories.

"My lady?" Deep and smooth like a rare and perfectly aged wine, his voice embraced her from behind. She glanced over her shoulder, and his ice-blue gaze held hers as he pulled the glove from his hand slowly, one finger at a time, like an erotic overture to a kiss. "Are you alone?"

All she could manage was a nod.

With his bare hand, he cupped her cheek and brought her close enough that his frosted breath kissed her lips. The warmth from his fingers flooded her body in a silken heat. Her earlier chill fled as if exorcised.

"Come home with me," he begged with a wicked grin that promised every sort of sensual pleasure. His lips trailed across the sensitive skin below her ear. He playfully nipped the tender lobe. "I want to hear you scream my name as you climax. Then I'll enter you slowly"—the deep cadence dropped to a whisper—"ever so slowly."

His gaze held hers captive, and she moaned.

"I want to hear my name on your lips. Say it," he commanded. "Say my name."

His thumb traced the outline of her lips. She took it into the warm cavern of her mouth and sucked. He groaned a heady sound. Her tongue pressed against the sensitive tip. He drew a deep breath, but his eyes flashed a dark blue reminiscent of lightning over a crystal-clear lake.

She'd turned the tables on him.
"Say it." His demand transformed into a
prayer. "Please, my lady?"

"Please, m'lady?" The soft voice of an angel caused Daphne to look up from her writing in a daze.

She slammed her journal shut and pushed it inside her reticule while forcing her prurient thoughts into a semblance of submission. Before her stood a street urchin no more than eight or nine. Though his clothing was several sizes too big, the thick wool guaranteed he was warm. A fine wool scarf wrapped around his neck provided the finishing touch to the haphazard ensemble.

"Might ye have a coin to spare, m'lady?" He pulled the scarf away from his throat and scratched. "Blasted thing is i'chy." He tilted his head and grimaced. "It would mean the world to me if I could buy me poor ill mather a Christmastide present. Bu' our landlawd demanded the rent last night." He pulled out the pockets of his jacket to prove he had no coin. He blinked slowly, and several fine snowflakes caught in the ridiculously long length of his dark brown lashes. "Anythin' you could spare would be a gift."

A Christmas angel in the form of this small boy had come to remind her there were more important things to remember of the season besides her predicament. The lad's concern wasn't for himself, but his dear mother. He set a perfect example for how she should concentrate her efforts on others and not herself.

She bestowed her best smile and thanked her lucky stars she hadn't been caught writing such salacious things. Her heart still raced from the wicked sensual images she'd summoned of her dream lover.

"Let me see what I can find." She pulled a guinea from her reticle and then pulled it shut. "Here you are."

The boy held out his hand, and Daphne placed the coin

on his palm. "Perhaps you'll have enough to get yourself a little something, too."

"Yor like manna from the bloomin 'eavens." He pocketed the coin, then executed an exaggerated bow. "In celebration o' the most 'oliest o' seasons, m'lady."

Daphne stood in the slippery snow and answered with a slight curtsy, the movement requiring she extend her hand with her reticule for balance.

With a swift swipe of his hand, he ripped the reticule from her grasp, causing her to jerk forward. She lost her footing and fell into a heap of black wool cloak.

Her sweet angel had transformed into a little pirate before her eyes.

His brilliant brown eyes widened in shock. "Forgive me, m'lady." The little wretch tipped his hat, then ran.

Stunned for a moment, Daphne couldn't move. Then as her anger rose, she clenched her bare hands into fists. If she truly thought herself independent, then she needed to be her own savior. She'd pursue the boy on her own. He'd left the park, but there was enough snow that she could follow his footsteps.

Daphne struggled to untangle her legs from her cloak. As off-balanced as a newborn filly, she hoisted herself off the ground. She took a deep breath for courage, then started after the little urchin.

Through the park and down the street, she briskly walked the trail he'd left. When she got to the corner of the street and turned, she spied him. He was tearing through her reticule. No doubt counting the spoils of his thievery.

He looked up, and they made eye contact. For a moment, they just stared at each other.

"I just want my reticule and journal." She kept her voice calm. "I'll give you the money. You can go home then."

Without answering, he ran down the street.

"Stop, you little miscreant!" She really didn't give a

farthing whether she ever got the reticule or her money back. All she wanted was her journal. If she lost it, it'd be akin to having her every memory stolen and her heart ripped out of her chest. It had her entire life in it. It contained every despicable thought and feeling she'd ever experienced. It held her hopes and dreams. It possessed her most wicked desires.

Above all, it bore witness to her grief over losing her sister, and if any of that were read, lives would be ruined.

After three blocks, the boy reached the quiet streets on the outskirts of Mayfair. He chanced a glance back.

"Stop, please!" She slipped on the snow that had started to accumulate on the ground. The soles of her new half boots offered no traction on the slick walkway. "You can have everything except the book."

The distance between them had increased. Throwing caution to the wind, she accelerated into a full run. No matter how unladylike her appearance, she couldn't lose him. Her lungs started to protest the exercise and the cold.

Suddenly, he darted down a short alley. Without questioning the wisdom of her pursuit, she followed. He rounded another corner and proceeded straight ahead. Once he crossed St. James's Square, he headed toward the theatre district.

Her throat burned from inhaling the cold air. Her right side screamed with a splitting pain. She dismissed her discomfort. Only after she retrieved her journal could she afford the luxury of taking stock of her aches and injuries.

They rushed passed the Theatre Royal Haymarket. Several carriages lumbered down the snowy streets. The little thief darted between them, then headed in the direction of Seven Dials. If he made it into that unsavory area of town, he would be gone forever. She was not foolish enough to attempt to visit that part of London without proper escort.

Unexpectedly, he scampered into one of the gambling hells across the street that littered the area. Daphne slowed to a hurried walk so as not to draw attention to herself in the populated neighborhood. Elegantly dressed men and coaches with their attendants littered the street.

Once she reached the building, she would knock at the gambling establishment's door and ask the majordomo to find the little devil for her. As soon as he was delivered to her, she'd retrieve her journal, then turn him over to the nearest authorities. She'd brush her hands of him.

Holiday cheer, indeed.

With a quick glance in both directions, she started across the street, then suddenly stopped.

In front of the Reynolds Gambling Establishment, larger than life, was the Duke of Southart.

Proof that any luck she possessed had evaporated. Under no circumstances would she cross the street with him there. If he spoke to her, she'd have no choice but to be rude. He'd undoubtedly want to know why she was at the Reynolds. To engage in a conversation with him would invite unwanted speculation that either the family accepted him or, worse, she was interested in him. Though Alex and Paul were at times civil to each other, their friendship had never recovered the affection they had held for each other. Like most feuding families, hers had supported their own. If Alex didn't want Southart's friendship, then the family respected those wishes.

She exhaled, and the vapor of her breath rushed forward as if wanting to join with the crowd gathered around him. She studied his form. Tall with blond hair and with a charming demeanor to match, the duke cut a striking figure. Men surrounded him as if begging for his attention. There was no denying he was handsome. Some said he was the handsomest man in all of England.

Unfortunately, she agreed. He was beautiful. He'd always

been kind and attentive to her, particularly when she was a little girl. But she was no longer a little girl. She could admire him from afar, but that was all she could do.

She chuckled under her breath. That must be why she fantasized about Southart in a completely inappropriate manner. He was an ideal lover on the pages of her journal. He was gorgeous and tender in her daydreams, but he wasn't real.

Thus, making him the *perfect* man—one she didn't have to answer to like a husband who would object to her opening a home for unwed mothers. More important, one she didn't have to pretend *perfection* around like she did with her family. It was exhausting keeping things on an even keel since Alice's death.

As she watched him, he turned his gaze to hers. She pulled the hood of her cloak tighter around her face. He took off his gloves, tugging at one finger at a time, the movements slow and deliberate as if he were teasing her. Good lord, the man could make the simple act of taking off his leather gloves a seduction.

Daphne had little choice but to find another entrance. She had to retrieve her journal as quickly as possible.

Perhaps Southart was leaving.

Inside her chest, her traitorous heart beat a little faster in hopes he'd just arrived.

Chapter Four

Paul stood in front of the Reynolds, an establishment known for high-stakes gambling. Only a few coaches and hackneys decorated the street. Two boys acting as attendants guarded the horses owned by the nobs, rakes, and other dissolute society hounds who were the regulars at the Reynolds. Such mongrels saved their affections for lady luck rather than concern themselves with the comfort and care of their employees or the poor creatures that conveyed them from one low-life haunt to another.

He was—or had been—just like them. With a deep breath, he allowed the bitter cold to cleanse his lungs. It was a shame the air couldn't clean his conscience. He'd spent so many nights and days at the Reynolds. A pure waste of precious time that he'd never reclaim. Time he should have spent with Robbie, easing his pain and keeping him company in his last years.

He'd wasted money also but had recovered the massive amount of gambling losses. Fate had been kind to him, but he couldn't see it at the time.

When Pembrooke had bought Paul's vowels, then forced him to renege on his engagement to Claire, Paul's old friend's actions had been solely for revenge—an act that had first infuriated Paul. Pembrooke had thought his youngest sister, Lady Alice Hallworth, and Paul had formed a liaison that resulted in the poor girl's pregnancy and subsequent suicide. Like an avalanche, Alex wouldn't stop in his plan to ruin Paul. After Alex had married Claire, the truth eventually unfolded as it always did. Paul hadn't laid a hand on Alice, and in time Alex had discovered the truth of Paul's innocence. In the end, a very much-in-love-with-his-wife Pembrooke had returned Paul's vowels.

In hindsight, Pembrooke's deeds were a blessing. Alex's bold acts had curtailed Paul's incessant gambling, a forced habit to gain his father's attention. It had cost dearly in other ways besides his lost time with Robbie.

Paul had lost Pembrooke's friendship. Though they pretended to be civil with each other, it was readily apparent in Pembrooke's attitude that he'd not welcome Paul's company. Like a broken plate glued together, it may appear whole, but if one looked close enough, the crack was still there ready to split open again.

Against a sudden blast of frigid air, he squared his shoulders, his formal black greatcoat billowing around him. Tonight, he'd pay the gambling debt his father had left him, then put the Reynolds and that chapter of his life to rest. He'd keep his promise to Robbie and accept his role as duke with all its responsibility and its accompanying respectability.

There were advantages to being a duke. He was treated like a national treasure or a rare bird. They looked at and sometimes admired him, but for the most part, people kept their distance. Perhaps they feared getting pecked.

But the unanswered question remained: When a duke claimed the title, why didn't anyone make mention that it was so damned lonely? The simple feat of finding trustworthy confidants—let alone friends—was practically impossible.

"Southart, surprised to see you back at the Reynolds," greeted Edgar Farnsworth, the Earl of Howton. Tall and in his mid-thirties, Howton was in charge of the Committee of Privileges. How fitting, since his position was as stuffy as his title. The man's cheeks flamed. "I'm here to pay a debt for my youngest brother."

Paul nodded at the clearly embarrassed man. "I'm paying a debt also. One just brought to my attention."

"I see." Howton tugged at the brim of his hat. "Well, Merry Christmas. Excellent speech you gave this week."

Paul nodded his thanks.

An old acquaintance, Richard Pearce, the Marguess of Warwyk, joined them. "Southart, you're here playing again?"

"No, I have to see someone," Paul answered.

Warwyk nodded. "I needed a little entertainment myself, since my wife and I stayed in town over the holidays. We've a dinner engagement with her family this evening. One of those uncomfortable affairs where everyone looks down their noses at everyone else." He shook his head and muttered, "Families. Must be going."

Without another word, both men left. The mention of family sent a pang through Paul's chest. This would be his first Christmas without Robbie—without any family. Most would say he was blessed with riches, estates, and a noble lineage. Yet he considered himself rather poor in all the things that mattered in life, love and friendship. He quickly dismissed his melancholy, which could only be attributed to the season.

Before he climbed the steps to the entrance, the massive ebony doors opened. In a smart evening uniform of the maroon and gold Reynolds colors, the establishment's majordomo greeted him. Boisterous yelps of joy at fate's kind hand along with the accompanying moans of despair when luck—the true definition of a fickle beast—inevitably departed the tables, then rushed into the night.

"Evening, Your Grace." The man beamed a smile, one he undoubtedly reserved only for the most elite upper crust with deep pockets. "Welcome to the Reynolds. We're delighted you decided to join us this evening."

Paul nodded in return and proceeded into the establishment. There was no use in correcting the man's presumption that he was here for entertainment purposes. The garish lights that surrounded the perimeter of the large entry were designed to lead a man into the gambling club's main rooms where tables of hazard, vingte-et-un, faro, and dice were strategically placed for ease of play. A raised stage marked the center of the room. In the middle of the stage, two giant desks faced each other. One was for the croupiers who ensured no one cheated. The other was reserved for the exclusive use of the Reynolds brothers. The desk's height provided for an unrestricted view of the gambling floor, so Thomas Reynolds and his brother, Forest Reynolds, could reign over all activities.

Surveying the room from afar, Paul immediately found himself steeped in the thick scent of the patrons' desperation and debauchery. Brightly painted serving wenches passed through the crowded floors with endless trays of spirits. Designed to get a man foxed, the house increased its odds the patron would gamble heavier if he was inebriated.

It was a well-orchestrated but macabre play, one where fortunes were lost every night. Never mind that lives were ruined. Like a powerful break in a billiards game, men on a losing streak careened from table to table, desperate to find some luck.

Thomas Reynolds caught his gaze. He said something

to his brother, then with an ease only the most confident of men possessed, he approached Paul. Once he was within earshot, he dipped a bow. "Your Grace, we're honored to have you this evening."

"Good evening, Mr. Reynolds. I'm here to pay an old note I discovered in my account books," Paul drawled in the most bored, aristocratic voice he could summon. Anxious to leave the soul-rotting establishment, he wasted little time with pleasantries. "Would you lend some assistance . . ."

His words trailed to nothing when his gaze fixed on a corner where the partially concealed majordomo stood embroiled in a heated discussion with a woman who had her back turned to Paul. Dressed in a white gown better suited for an Almack's affair, she gesticulated quickly as she spoke. If the majordomo moved an inch closer, she would hit him with her hands as she made her point.

The man towered over her as he shook his head. Instead of intimidating her, it seemed to have the opposite result and incited another round of arguments from the young woman. Whoever she was, she would shortly be leaving the Reynolds. They only allowed men in its hallowed halls. If she was looking for a place to gamble, she'd have better luck at the Beauchamp House, where women and men were free to play together.

The majordomo had started to sputter in outrage at her latest comment. Paul's gaze strayed to her velvet dress, which emphasized her straight backside and hugged her plump, perfectly shaped bottom, which begged for a man's touch. Whoever she was, she was simply magnificent in her demeanor. Paul couldn't tear his eyes away from the lovely vision with ebony hair tucked in an elegant chignon.

Completely ignoring the majordomo, she glanced at the side exit leading to the kitchen. The instant he caught her profile, Paul's stomach dropped in a free fall. The curve of her exquisite cheek and the tilt of her lovely head held him spellbound. With the faintest of fragrances wafting his way, the allure of her scent captivated him.

He *knew* that woman.

What in the devil's name was Lady Daphne Hallworth doing in the Reynolds?

If she had to spend the night in the gaming hell, Daphne would find a way to enter into the Reynolds kitchen before the sun rose the next day. It was beyond the pale that she had to argue with an overgrown baboon disguised as a man in formal livery two sizes too small.

"Women aren't allowed here," warned the majordomo. He had the audacity to take her by the arm and pull her toward the back of the building.

She dug in her heels and twisted away from his formidable bulk. "Please. I just need to see the kitchen. If he's here, I won't take but a minute."

"He isn't here, miss. Garland works here as a runner in the evenings. Most of that time he dawdles in the kitchen with the cook Elsie. He's always hiding in her shadow begging for food. Tonight, he and Elsie have the night off." The majordomo snorted. "Now listen here, I'm not above throwing you out myself if you won't leave on your own accord."

"Now just a minute, sir," Daphne interrupted. "I happen to be—"

"Lady Moonbeam," a voice behind her announced. "My escort for the evening."

The deep sound wrapped around her in a polished smoothness that reminded Daphne of a calm bay at night off the Adriatic Sea. It was smooth as glass, but she knew that beneath the surface there lurked unfathomable danger. The Duke of Southart could blow everything out of the water for her with one word or command.

Why had she even wanted him to be here?

She turned and faced him. He moved in front of her and blocked the view of the gaming room. His cool gaze locked on hers, and the slight smile made him even more handsome than she remembered. Lit from within, his eyes blazed with a hint of temptation or mayhap seduction.

Most likely, it was just surprise.

Daphne exhaled and pushed her consternation aside for another day. She had to find the kitchen. The cook would know the whereabouts of the boy.

"Come, Moonbeam," Paul whispered. He'd leaned close enough that she could smell his fresh, clean sandalwood scent. He extended his arm in a command for her to take it, then directed his attention to the major baboon. "Why don't you alert my footman that Lady Moonbeam and I are ready to retire for the evening."

"Yes, Your Grace." The majordomo nodded and snapped his fingers at one of the attendants who worked the floor of the gambling hell. As if a piece of rubbish, he held Daphne's cloak between two fingers. She reached for it, but Paul easily intercepted it and casually laid the black wool garment over his arm.

Before she could say a word, the summoned attendant was halfway out the door.

She and Paul faced each other like two ships ready to commence fire on the open seas. "You had no right to interfere." She ignored Paul's offered arm, and there was enough hiss in her voice to alert him that she wasn't happy. "And quit calling me that ridiculous name."

Paul grinned, and it transformed him from an arrogant aristocrat accustomed to getting his way into a man who took her breath away. Without taking his eyes from hers, he addressed the majordomo. "My good man, you've seen what type of mood she's in. Might there be a place where Lady Moonbeam and I might have an intimate conversation for a few minutes before the carriage is brought to the door?"

"Of course, Your Grace. If you and *Lady Moonbeam* will follow me."

Chapter Five

Paul waited until the majordomo shut the door to the private room before he addressed Daphne. "Imagine my surprise and pleasure to find you standing in the middle of the Reynolds. Unfortunately, for both of us, women aren't allowed, and there's no exception for the sister of the Marquess of Pembrooke." With a purposeful insouciance, he strolled to the side table against the wall where an open bottle of chilled champagne waited for him. He'd say one thing for the Reynolds brothers—they took care of their guests whether expected or not. "May I pour you a glass?"

"No, thank you." Daphne straightened her shoulders.

Her prickly mood and appearance reminded him of an inquisition, and he was the examiner.

Interesting, since he hadn't asked her a single question— yet. He poured a glass and, without taking his eyes from hers, took a sip. An excellent vintage, but too sweet for his tastes. He much preferred the brut variety, so he replaced the glass. "Moonbeam, I thought with our history, you'd share without me having to ask." He feigned a sigh and placed his hand over the middle of his chest.

"Please stop calling me Moonbeam." She tipped her head and regarded him like an unwanted interruption. "To answer your question, I'm looking for someone."

"Aha." Though he said it in a lighthearted manner, his stomach twisted at her confession.

The thought that Daphne Hallworth would risk her reputation for some reprobate who frequented a place such as the Reynolds made him want to curse the vilest oaths he could conjure. There wasn't a single man in the place he'd allow to attend her.

Shocked at the intensity of his feelings, he drew a deep breath. The only reason for such a strong reaction had to be his protective instincts. He was simply concerned for her welfare, much like a brother. Granted, he'd seen her at Langham's house and at a handful of social events, but they barely spoke. Yet she'd always left an indelible impression on him. The reason didn't escape him. She was striking.

He shook his head to clear such inane thoughts. He would never *ever* in his entire life as a reprobate consider Daphne Hallworth a sister. "Who is it?" He asked the words with a nuance designed to learn her secrets.

"No one you would know." She turned toward the door. "I'll leave you to your evening, *Your Grace*."

"Stop, please. Someone might recognize you." In a stealth move, he followed her. By the time she'd twisted the knob, he rested his palm against the door, thwarting her escape. "Moonbeam, you can't go out there without a proper escort. Where you go I go."

She turned around and flattened her back against the door in a show of defiance. "Please, I would hate to ruin your plans or festivities."

The urge to whip out a witty quip fell silent when he caught Daphne's gaze. She looked like a devil's angel with her dark hair, ethereal silver eyes, and those strawberry-colored lips. Any sin she offered, he'd have no hesitation rising to the challenge.

He leaned in close. Her chest rose and fell with a rhythm that drummed like a well-crafted metronome, and his heartbeat joined into the melee with abandon. Daphne's warmth and her delightful scent of lavender and woman transformed into a witchery he couldn't resist. He drew nearer until his breath mingled with hers.

"You're not ruining anything." He lowered his voice. "In fact, my night became much more interesting since a beautiful moonbeam appeared." Her allure called to him, and powerless to resist, he brushed his fingers against her cheek. The silkiness of her skin could soothe the most savage and jaded of beasts.

Her black lashes drifted down when she leaned just a fraction closer. His chest swelled in response. She was affected as much as he was.

"Shall we sit until your carriage is ready?" Her breathless sigh was a welcome distraction and indicated her wariness was fading.

"After you." Taking several steps back, he swept his arm toward a matching pair of club chairs that faced the fire. Her quick acquiescence meant it would take little effort on his part to find out whom she intended to meet.

A gentle smile adorned her face and locked him in place. She charmed him in returning one to her. When she held her smile a little too long, he instantly recognized his mistake. With her hand behind her, she opened the door and flew down the hall without a look back.

"*Bloody hell,*" he muttered. If she returned to the game floor, her reputation would be in tatters if some lowlife libertine recognized her. There was only one thing he could do—he gave chase.

He, the Duke of Southart, had to catch a moonbeam.

* * *

Daphne rushed down the hall and hoped she was headed toward the Reynolds kitchen. Ever mindful, she kept her head averted in case she met an employee. As she passed an exquisite red-lacquered cabriole side table, she picked up a discarded serving tray. If people thought she was some serving wench sans painted face, she stood greater odds of making it to the kitchen before she faced an unwanted escort out of the establishment.

"What's your hurry, l-lub?" A very inebriated oaf swayed before her with a hiccup. "Luv, I mean."

Belying a quickness for such a drunkard, he placed his hands around her arms and drew her near. The stench of alcohol and cheroot combined into a miasma that made her stomach protest. Before she could fight him off, another man pulled her free. She found her backside nestled against a hard, broad chest and her bottom pressed against a set of iron legs. Instinctively, she fought to free herself from the man's embrace.

"Easy, Moonbeam. I've been looking for you," Paul's voice teased her from behind. Without warning, his lips pressed against her cheek, then traveled close to her ear. "Turn around and hold me close. Pretend we're lovers," he whispered.

Paul wouldn't have to ask twice. With a tremulous breath, she turned, then folded her arms around his neck and pushed up on her tiptoes. She was surely going to hell after this. If anyone in her family, particularly Alex, could see her now, they'd likely explode into a thousand pieces of disbelief and anger. But she had little choice if she wanted to keep her identity a secret. She pressed her lips to his earlobe. "Thank you," she murmured.

She drew a breath, forcing herself closer to him. The scents of sandalwood, lemongrass, and pure male melded in a heady mixture that turned intoxicating. There was little doubt. Paul, the devil himself, could lead any woman, including her, on a merry dance to utter ruin.

She'd do well to remember that simple fact.

But that was the least of her worries. Her only goal was retrieving her journal.

"S-Southart, I saw her first," the drunkard slurred. "She looks like a bloody virgin angel in that garb. Since when did the Reynolds require the help to wear costumes?"

"Bennington, it's a treat for the holiday season. Now run along, as true love can't be denied. Moonbeam and I have a special tryst we've planned all evening."

"Bloody unfair. Makes no difference if they're whores or ladies. They always melt for you. Even when you were nothing but the spare." Bennington tried to stare at Paul, but he kept stumbling and catching himself.

"Watch your tongue," Paul growled, and Bennington fell backward. "She's a lady."

"Of course she is, Southart. You always did have a fanciful imagination." Bennington guffawed at his own quip. When he tried to slap one knee, he missed, resulting in him falling into a heap in the middle of the hallway.

"Have a good nap, old fellow." Without missing a step, Paul threw her discarded cloak around her shoulders and pulled her hood into place.

She'd completely forgotten about her wrap. If she kept this pace of losing articles of clothing, she'd not have anything to wear by the end of the week. It was of little consequence. The only thing she needed to survive the holiday was retrieving her lost journal. "I can't leave until I visit the kitchen."

"Why? I never took you as the domestic sort." He quickly surveyed the hall. "There's no one roaming about. We should leave."

"I lost something," she said.

"What?"

"Something small," she answered with a scowl.

"A spoon? A teacup?" he joked. "An embroidered apron? Perhaps your favorite tarts?"

His humor made the depth of his blue eyes twinkle. He'd remembered her weakness for tarts. She couldn't resist his charm and laughed. "It's none of your concern, but I thank you for your help. I can find my way from here."

"A secret recipe, hmm?"

"Good evening, Your Grace."

"Wait. Let me come with you." The sincerity of his tone and the candor in his expression gave her pause. "This place is besieged with secret passageways, hidden corridors, and paths that lead nowhere. What if someone grabs you again? You're not safe here alone. I can help you find the kitchen and give you an escort outside."

"You know all this?" She arched a brow. "How could I forget? You frequent this place."

"A wound straight to the heart." He feigned a stumble backward. "That's in my past, Moonbeam."

"Why help me?"

"I thought tonight I might like to try something different. Perhaps, I'll be the one in shining armor instead of my usual black." The silky sensuality in his voice promised her a taste of the forbidden.

"As in knight?" she asked, ever mindful that he held a power reminiscent of a potent elixir over most women.

"Yes. But if you prefer black, then black it shall be." The raspiness in his voice reminded her of a cat's tongue when it licked you—signaling you were chosen as a token of affection.

Daphne leaned close ready to answer, "Black," then stopped. She couldn't succumb to his seduction. Not tonight. Not ever. But it would save precious time if he'd take her to the kitchen, since she only had a vague understanding of where it was.

As if he knew she struggled with her decision, he added, "I can get you to the kitchen where there is a secret exit. You can find your recipe or whatnot, then I'll see you safely away."

"Thank you," she murmured, still not certain if this was the best plan, but time was not on her side. The quicker she recovered her journal, the quicker she could put this nightmare behind her.

He glanced down the hall where they came from. "No one is coming. Follow me. Tell me what you're looking for."

"My bag."

"Seriously? In the Reynolds?" he said with a raised brow. Without waiting for her answer, he strolled down a short hallway that looked like a dead-end and pushed aside a bookshelf. Magically, it rolled easily, as if on wheels.

"I've never seen the like." The bookshelf contained real books but moved with the ease of a sliding door. "I'd have never found that opening."

"Proving I'm a knight in shining armor," he replied. He swept his hand in front of him as if inviting her to tea with the queen.

She stepped inside to another world. The sounds of pans and pots banging along with the bustle of people preparing meals surrounded them. "This is amazing."

He nodded, then surveyed the room. "We shouldn't tarry. It appears no one is paying attention to us, but I guarantee the Reynolds brothers have already been alerted that we're in their kitchen. Whatever you're looking for, find it, and we'll leave."

Without responding, she walked through the kitchen searching for the boy. There were no hiding places that she could see, but that meant little if the kitchen entrance was any indication of the possible niches a boy could hide in. Paul stayed by her side without drawing much attention. Several of the footmen had nodded their way, but the rest of the staff ignored them.

"Any luck?" Southart asked.

Suddenly, the door of the kitchen rolled open, and the majordomo swept his gaze across the room until he found them. He shook his head as if dismayed, then started toward them.

Paul lifted a hand in greeting and held his other arm for her to take. "No need for your services, my good man. We bid you adieu."

For a moment she hesitated, as she didn't want to leave until she found the boy and her journal.

"Come, Moonbeam," he coaxed.

With a deep sigh and an even deeper reluctance, she capitulated.

Southart pulled aside a small curtain, exposing a door. When he opened it, they were outside the Reynolds in a small side alley. He started to escort her to the front of the building. "You may never find your bag. Is there something valuable in it?"

Her breath caught at his words. "Please. I must go back."

"Lady Moonbeam, not tonight. I'll visit tomorrow and look for it."

"Why would you do that?" she asked incredulously.

"To prove I'm a knight in shining armor. Now, do you have a way home? My carriage is out front. I could take you." Without warning, he stopped and pulled her close. Abruptly, he propelled them toward the closed shop of a cobbler on the other side of the alley and didn't stop until the dark awning covering the shop door concealed them.

"What are you doing?" Her voice betrayed the small pang of disquiet that had unfurled in her thoughts. This was the man who had besmirched her lovely sister-in-law. He was practically an enemy.

But an enemy who had helped her this evening. Immediately, she thought of a stroke of lightning, something brief and brilliant—a coup de foudre. His efforts were simply a splash of brilliance in the dark night, nothing more.

"We can't leave that way." He searched her face and something akin to panic made his ice-blue eyes shine like a finely cut aquamarine stone. "We'll have to walk completely round the building."

He took a step back and peered down the alley toward the back of the building. A garbled moan drew her attention toward the front of the establishment. Under the cold haze of a street lamp, several dozen or so feet from the Reynolds side entrance, a man leaned against the wall. Bobbing her head in a frantic and awkward dance, a woman was on her knees directly in front of him.

"That's it. Deeper, take me deeper," he crooned. He put his gloved hand on top of her head and pushed her lower.

The woman adjusted her stance, leaving a clear view of what she was doing. The man's erect member jutted like a sword toward the woman's mouth. Daphne knew she should turn away, since ladies shouldn't bear witness to such a shocking escapade. Yet she couldn't. Her curiosity was stronger than her sense of decorum. The woman appeared to be kissing his erection, then trying to eat it.

Though her upbringing didn't provide for such an education, she'd overheard several conversations between the under-maids who loved to gossip. When she first heard men sought pleasure like that, she'd thought it disgusting. Now she wasn't certain what she thought. Her own breath deepened trying to dampen her racing heartbeat.

The man in the alley released a loud groan that lasted an eternity while the woman held still. With a pop of her lips, she released his organ and proceeded to wipe her mouth.

Gently, Paul pulled her back into darkness the overhang offered, then rubbed a hand over his face. "Daphne, your brother would kill me if he had any inkling what you were watching."

The old Daphne would be sputtering a protest at the ribald crudeness of the couple. But after today's events, she could do anything she wanted, even watch the exchange between the woman and the man. She bit her lip in a poor effort to thwart the laughter that threatened at the vulgar banter and interaction between the two. Paul moved close enough that his greatcoat brushed against her cloak. The sensation caused the fine hairs along her arms to stand straight up at attention, and she shivered.

"You're cold," Paul declared.

She took a deep breath of the frigid air. "No. Just curious at the levity of the conversation."

"You hellion." He brought her into his arms. If she wasn't mistaken, his lips pressed against the top of her head. "You are incorrigible. And I adore—"

"Southart? Is that you?" A different man from the one who'd been pleasured by the whore crept closer.

Paul's eyes widened. "I'd recognized that snake's hiss anywhere. It's Martin Richmond from *The Midnight Cryer*."

"The gossip rag?" Her throat tightened in a panic.

There were ways of having one's reputation ruined that were self-inflicted and couldn't be avoided—like running a home for unwed mothers. However, to have it revealed she was outside the Reynolds with the Duke of Southart while prostitutes serviced their clients was another matter. The future of her home would be in jeopardy—even before she purchased it. With her reputation in tatters, no one would seek her help. Nor would anyone associate with her if they thought she was watching or, God forbid, if they thought she was involved in such salacious activities.

"Don't hide your little dove from me," Richmond drawled, coming closer. "Not after all the nights we've shared together at the Reynolds."

"What shall we do?" Panic laced her words.

"You could walk away, and I'll try to engage him. Stay close by, though." His brow creased after he said the words. "That's a bad plan. Another man might stop you."

"You could kiss me." The words just escaped, but she didn't have time to disavow them. Quickly, she jerked at the wool hood of her cloak until her face was hidden.

"I beg your pardon?" Paul slowly drew away, and the shock in his eyes was almost laughable if they weren't in such dire straits. "What did you say?"

"Kiss me," she pleaded.

"You want me to defile you in order to protect you from ruin?" He dipped his head slightly, then shook it. The gesture either meant he would deny her or, she hoped, he was trying to make sense of what she was asking. "That's your plan?"

She drew back and studied his face. His eyes were half-lidded. The lines of his mouth had softened, and his lips had parted.

"Southart, did you hear me?" The man's voice grew more insistent.

For five bold heartbeats, she refused to look away from his gaze. On the sixth beat, she made the mistake of glancing at his lips once again. Full, wide, and perfectly formed, they mesmerized her, and she lost her count. Time stood suspended, refusing to move like an early morning fog holding tightly to a moor.

Oh God, she didn't have time for such silly musings. Without wasting another half second, she wrapped her arms around his neck and brought his lips to hers.

Any other rational woman would have run away rather than kiss the Duke of Southart, a known libertine and a man her family hated.

But when his mouth touched hers, she thanked the heavens.

It was a stroke of good fortune that tonight she'd lost every common sense she'd ever possessed.

Chapter Six

The moment Paul's lips brushed hers, he found himself sinking. Sinking into a chasm that he hadn't expected. She molded her body next to his, and the effect intoxicated him. When he pulled her closer, she moaned the sweetest sigh of pleasure, then pressed her mouth against his harder, demanding more from him.

There was no doubt he needed more from her.

How could such a small, gentle woman be so fierce, so resolute, so tempting? In his arms, she melted and nurtured within him things that he hadn't even understood were missing. Things like the feel of absolute rightness that this woman's touch brought forth. Things like the yearning to be a better man.

This wasn't supposed to be a seductive kiss, but one designed to keep Martin Richmond from discovering Daphne's identity.

Like a warning shot, the thought that this was Pembrooke's little sister cleared his senses. He was only pretending to enjoy the kiss. He was only protecting her. He needed to keep repeating that supposed truth so as not to get lost in her. His recalcitrant heart kept missing beats the more her sweet mouth pressed against his. Somehow, she reached a place deep inside his chest and squeezed until she had him worshiping her mouth like a heathen ready to convert to any religion she offered. He'd gladly become a proselyte in the house of Daphne Hallworth as long as she'd continue to kiss him.

Through the thick layers of wool that separated them, their bodies melded together, and he could feel her feminine softness unfurl around him. He imagined her breasts pushed against his chest with her nipples hardening from the pleasure. Would the areolae around those incredible nipples match the deep pink of her cheeks, or would they be a dark crimson like her lips? His cock swelled, then twitched in eagerness for an answer.

For holy hell's sake, she was a well-bred lady, the sister of a highly respected marquess, and he was kissing her in the back alley of a gambling hell.

He was insane to be thinking about her breasts.

He was insane to be kissing her.

Thankfully, reality was highly overrated. If this was insanity, he welcomed it.

His tongue teased the crease of her lips and elicited another slight moan, an aphrodisiac too strong to resist. She opened for him, and he swept his tongue against hers. Mating with hers. The sweet taste of her mouth caused an aching want that grew until he couldn't contain it. He groaned, "Moonbeam."

She didn't let him think or react but continued her relentless response. She encouraged him to take more. He obliged as only a scoundrel would. His tongue danced with hers in an endless waltz. He explored every secret space and learned what she liked. She wasn't tentative, but the responsive tangles of her tongue indicated she'd been kissed before—probably by some officious stumbling gentleman or a bumptious peer who lacked the finesse to make her desire spiral. He gentled his mouth and drew out this brief glimpse of heaven until he had naught to do but surrender to the teasing passion that swirled around them like an electrical storm. Her slight moan seduced him, and he wanted to hear it over and over. If the world collapsed around them, he dared think he'd not notice.

"Southart, let her come up for air," a voice clamored beside them.

Richmond's deep tenor brought Paul out of his frenzy, and he reluctantly pulled away. When he took one look at her innocence and the muddled desire on her face, he was useless to care who called his name. Her swollen lips made every decadent desire within him explode like Friday fireworks over Vauxhall. Forced to catch his breath, Paul rested his forehead against hers.

"Southart, you knave."

Paul turned partway to address the interloper and shoo him away, then remembered it was Martin Richmond, the publisher of *The Midnight Cryer*. With a single swipe of his quill, he could ruin Daphne. Paul didn't give a fig about himself. He was crawling out of the gutter on his own. Any hit he'd take wouldn't cost him much . . . but Daphne was as pure as the December snow flirting with the cold London night.

He smiled in a half grin that he only hoped wasn't too much of a sneer and nodded at Richmond before turning his attention back to Daphne. He brought his lips to her ear. "Moonbeam, I'll do my best to convince him to leave. Perhaps it'd be best if you stay quiet?" he whispered, then nibbled the tender skin of her earlobe. Without a second thought, he stole another kiss from the bounty of her beautiful lips.

She tilted her head slightly and nodded. She seemed to

shudder against him, and he tightened his arms around her. A primeval urge rose within him to protect her with everything he possessed. The flush of her cheeks and the sway of her body meant he needed to get both of them out of there, and quickly. Much more of their incendiary passion and they'd both burn to the ground.

"Richmond, can't you see that I'm busy?" Paul turned his head and found the man no more than two feet behind him. Paul held Daphne close.

She dropped her hands from his shoulders, then pulled the hood of her cloak around her head, ensuring her face was covered. Then she burrowed close as if seeking sanctuary in his arms. Paul's anger rose that she felt fear over Richmond's presence.

"Oh, you've found a lusty beauty this evening, Your Grace," drawled Richmond. "Perhaps you might introduce me to your ladybird?"

Richmond tried to peek, but Daphne scooted in the opposite direction. Paul's arms tightened his hold of her, and he bent slightly over her lithe body. No matter what happened, Daphne would remain his secret.

"You know me better than that. I don't share. She's my special luck charm this evening." The blood in Paul's veins pounded. He wouldn't credit Richmond's presence for such a strong physical reaction. It had to be the remnants of his passion still flaming.

"I didn't realize that you were back to gambling at the Reynolds, *Your Grace*." Richmond enunciated the words with a hint of scorn. "That's news I'm certain *The Midnight Cryer*'s readers would take quite an interest in."

Daphne stiffened in his arms at the mention of Richmond's paper, the biggest gossip rag in all of London. With his gloved hand, Paul tucked her head against him closer. Her breathing had calmed, but she stood stock-still like a rabbit desperate not to become the fox's prey.

"Then you sorely must be lacking any real news." Paul glanced back at Richmond. "Publish what you want. Now if you'll excuse us, the lady and I are late for our next appointment."

"Pardon my interruption. If you change your mind and want to share, or if your *Moon-glow* tires of you, send her my way." Richmond laughed, but the sound held scant humor. After a long pause, he executed a quick turn and entered the Reynolds.

"Do you think he recognized me?" Daphne whispered. The quiver in her voice was unmistakable.

"No." Grudgingly, he released her from his arms. "But we should leave quickly. He may come sniffing here again. This is one of his favorite places to get stories."

He looked down and straightened her hood. The slight adjustment only revealed her swollen red lips. The thought pleased him that only he knew the real reason for their delectable color. "Come. Let me take you home."

She stood frozen like a captured ice princess staring at him. As if awakening and breaking out of her cage, she shook her head. "No, I must return to the kitchen."

"Not tonight, sweetheart." He fought the urge to kiss her again. "It's too dangerous with Richmond prowling the establishment. I'll come tomorrow and look for your reticule."

Reluctantly, she nodded. "Let's go."

No matter what the cost, she'd find her little thief. Even if she had to loiter all day in a hired carriage outside the gambling establishment, she'd wait until he arrived, then grab him before he could enter the Reynolds. The idea that the majordomo actually had threatened to throw her out was inconceivable. She only wanted to stop in the kitchen to see if he was there. Even though she didn't discover the little boy's full name, she knew they called him Garland.

With such a name, he should be easy to find. She released the breath she'd been holding. She prayed Garland still had her journal. If he'd been there tonight, she could have put this nightmare behind her.

Truthfully, that was the only thing she'd change about the evening.

Daphne kept her head down to block the wind. She'd just shared the kiss of her dreams with Paul. No matter what happened in the days to come, she'd tuck this evening in a special place of her heart and never share it with anyone. His lips fit perfect against hers, and when he deepened their kiss she could imagine taking him to bed.

If she had her journal, she'd record every moment and every sensation she'd experienced. Their passion was more powerful than she could ever have contemplated. Their kisses could change the earth's orbit.

Oh God, what was she thinking? This was the Duke of Southart. Such kisses were probably a daily, if not hourly, occurrence for him.

She sighed and pushed such thoughts aside. She had to concentrate on her journal. With Southart by her side, she walked around the building to his waiting carriage. All she wanted to do was find a large fire and cuddle with four blankets. There was little else she could do except return to the Reynolds the next day and find Garland or at least the cook he favored.

Could the night become any more fraught with unwelcome interruptions or the risk of discovery? Daphne bit her lip and winced. Her lips were tender, and if she didn't take heed they'd likely be chapped and cracked by the morrow. She twisted her cloak in one hand, desperate for warmth. Her gloves offered little comfort. She could hardly move her poor fingers, frozen harder than the Thames at a frost fair.

They rounded the corner, and the wind assaulted her

with such a force that it stole her breath and pushed against her so hard, she had to stop. Paul gently grasped her arm in support. It was as if the wind were conspiring to keep her by the duke's side.

One of Paul's liveried footmen appeared from nowhere, the perfect cue for Daphne to take her leave. "I—I wish you a Happy Christmas, Your Grace."

"You're mistaken if you think I'm leaving you to your own devices. Why don't you have your man take your carriage home. I'll escort you personally to your brother."

When he leaned close, the intense blaze in his blue eyes captivated her. Too entranced by his nearness, she fought for the perfect words to dissuade him from his mission. She increased the distance between them. Finally, the fog lifted from her mind. "There's no need. I'll hire a hackney."

Paul's eyes widened. "A hackney? Ladies do not hire hackneys. Besides, who knows if you'll be able to find one? I'll take you home."

She nodded once. There was little else she could do. She had no money.

Paul's gaze locked on hers. "What are you about, Moonbeam?"

She swallowed and prayed her courage hadn't deserted her. *The mercurial beast.* "With the weather, it seemed unfair to have one of our carriages prepared for the short excursion."

His stare could have melted the snow from Mount Kilimanjaro. She didn't say another word. Slowly, a smile that would have charmed a snake out of the Garden of Eden creased his lips and made his eyes blaze in brilliance. "Shall we, Moonbeam?"

"Quit calling me that silly nickname."

He laughed, and the sound rumbled deep within his chest. Like a welcome ray of sunshine, the sound warmed her insides and reminded her of the cavalier boy from long ago. Such a simpler time, one she remembered fondly.

Without another word, Paul escorted her across the street to his waiting carriage. The attending footman opened the door, and Paul took her hand to lend assistance. Once she settled into the forward-facing seat, he followed and closed the door.

Her heart pounded at the idea Paul could soon discover her true circumstances of being alone, without any family. What she needed was a diversion. She pulled aside the silk curtain covering the window. "I think this is highly improper for me to be alone with you without a chaperone—"

"Improper? For you or for me?" The humor in his voice apparent. "You just kissed me senseless out in the cold and you're worried about a chaperone?"

She curled back into the luxurious velvet cushion.

"Let me answer for you. I find you inside a gaming hell, arguing with the establishment's majordomo, and honing your acting skills by impersonating a serving wench. I think it's safe to say that neither of us is really worried about a proper escort."

His deep baritone battered her resolve to fight him. She turned slightly and snuck another glance out the carriage window.

He followed the direction of her gaze. "There's no escaping me, Moonbeam."

"Why do you insist on calling me that?" She really didn't give a whit for the ridiculous moniker, but it served the purpose of steering their conversation to another topic. Besides, her actions were her own, and she didn't have to answer to anyone—even Paul.

The carriage gently lurched into movement, and the silence weighed heavy like a thick wool blanket between them. Instead of a peaceful quiet, the air crackled with tension. Like a specter created out of her own doubts and fears, Paul emerged from the darkness of the other side of the carriage and edged closer to her. With his long legs framing hers, she felt surrounded.

"Daphne?" The deep vibration of his words reminded her of a lion's gravelly purr. "I've always been game for intrigue. You've roused my interest. What were you doing in the Reynolds besides looking for your reticule? You can tell me."

She'd heard one of the great beast's rumbles once when Alex took her to a visiting circus. The adult lion had stared at her, and his dark eyes had glittered with a savage need to devour her, much like the man across the seat glaring at her.

She straightened in her seat and vowed not to turn into a simpering idiot in front of him. Nor would she turn away. "It's none of your concern."

"I think you made mention that it was *none of my concern* inside the Reynolds. But that's no fun. I'll tell you a secret." As he took off his evening gloves, he allowed his gaze to sweep from the top of her head to her toes. "I called you Moonbeam for two purposes. First, the word popped into my mind when I heard your conversation with the majordomo. Second, the lights in the Reynolds cast a blue-black glow to your hair, highlighting the silver-gray of your eyes. Simply put, you reminded me of a moonbeam."

Coming from another man, she might have believed it a compliment, a lovely one at that. But such words oozed from him. He was a consummate flirt and a practiced trifler with woman.

For a fleeting moment, she allowed herself the luxury of imagining he meant what he said. Such a thought helped chase the chill that encased her in its cold claws, but her fingers were still frozen like icicles. She clasped her hands and brought them to her mouth so she could blow warm air over them.

"Where are your gloves?" he asked.

"In my lap." She held them up as proof. "They offer little warmth. I normally wear a muff."

He reached over and clasped her hands between his. Gently, he rubbed back and forth. The warmth and strength in his large hands and long fingers started to break apart the stinging pain in her fingers.

"Where is your muff?" The lion's purr had returned.

"I lost it."

One eyebrow shot up in disbelief.

"In the park close to home," she vaguely offered.

The carriage slowed to a stop in front of her brother's home, saving her from offering more details. The merry glow from the chandelier reflected off the windows above the entry door. It gave the appearance of an occupied household busy with holiday celebrations.

She stole one more glance inside the carriage. The light from the street lamp streamed into the blackness and fell across his face. Unguarded, he appeared almost like the boy he used to be. In the center of his right cheek, a faint scar, the souvenir from the magpie, marred his skin. Such a defect didn't diminish his beauty, only enhanced it as a sign of chivalry. He was the most devilishly handsome man in all of England.

Before the footman opened the carriage door and she lost her courage, Daphne leaned forward and placed her lips against that scar. The warmth of his skin and hint of evening bristles tickled her skin. No matter what life had in store for their individual futures, that fateful afternoon sixteen years ago had irrefutably intertwined their pasts together. He might not even remember the day, but she did.

It was the day he'd given her a heart-shaped rock. More important, he'd sacrificed his safety for her and that little bird. He'd put her and her beliefs before his own wants and needs. How times had changed. How they had changed individually over the years. He was a duke, a powerful one at that. She wondered if he was as selfish as rumors claimed. Tonight, he didn't appear selfish in the least. He'd helped her.

There was little to be gained with such thoughts.

Now she was a spinster ready to take control of her own destiny, one that meant she'd give up her position in society and the promise of her own family and all that life entailed. Such a sacrifice was worth it if it helped save one woman from Alice's fate.

The end of the night might very well be the last time she and Paul were ever alone together. As the patron of a home for unwed mothers, she shouldn't dally with men, particularly Paul with his reputation. Yet tonight was different. Though she didn't recover her journal, she did receive the precious gift of his kiss and the honor of all his attention devoted to only her, even if it was only for an hour. She'd remember everything about this night.

"Thank you for this evening," she said against his warm skin. Slowly, she drew away, knowing she'd soon breach a distance that would break the magic between them. Inevitably, she turned toward the carriage door. More than anything, she wanted to tell him tonight meant the world to her. Tell him what his kiss meant to her.

"Daphne?" He reached for her and gently turned her face to his. "Are you upset?"

"No, not really." She released a sigh. "I've much on my mind."

With a creased brow, he nodded. "May I escort you in?"

She drew away from his touch. "There's no need. Tait is waiting for me."

"Indulge me. I'd like to." Before she could decline, he hopped down from the carriage and held out his hand. "Please?"

Reluctantly, she took his fingers in his hers. In response, he squeezed hers gently almost in encouragement.

His eyes searched hers, and she prayed she'd safely hidden her longing and the accompanying sadness.

"Are you crying?" The tenderness in his voice was almost seductive. Who would believe that the Duke of Southart could actually be concerned for her feelings? "Is it because I kissed you? I apologize."

He regarded her as if trying to discover all her secrets. In response, she stared back determined not to divulge anything. Yet his regard weakened her resolve.

This couldn't be the man who'd insulted her sister-in-law or made an offer for her best friend out of the blue. He was the one person her brother found completely unacceptable.

But here—before her now—he acted like the perfect gentleman.

"That's not it," she said. She blinked while wrestling her wayward sorrow back into the carefully crafted vault she'd created in her heart. For good measure, she grinned as best she could. "If memory serves me, I'm the one that kissed you."

"Immaterial details," he said with a wave of his other hand. "I shouldn't have done it, but at the time, I thought I was keeping you safe. . . ." He let his words drift to nothing.

"Please, let me take the credit. I'll be the rakehell this evening," she said dismissively. Without letting go of his hand, she started to walk toward the door.

He took a deep breath and exhaled. "Truth be told, I allowed myself to get carried away. I enjoyed kissing you."

"Good, because I enjoyed kissing you." She glanced at his face. His befuddlement had an endearing quality to it. To set him at ease, she continued, "Now let's not mention it again."

"Of course. A lady's desires are always my top priority. But let's make one thing clear." He lifted a brow in challenge. "I'm the rakehell. You can be the big, bad scoundrel."

"You can't give up your title of a bounder for one evening?" she teased.

"Of course you may borrow the term 'bounder.' But never 'rakehell.' That's mine," he said without an ounce of guilt. "I've earned every letter of the word. But to appease you, I'll allow you to borrow the title of rake for the amount of time that you kissed me."

"You make me dizzy with your explanations." Daphne laughed.

"I always aim to please," he offered.

Always the consummate under-butler, Tait waited for them inside the front door. "Lady Daphne, welcome home. I was a tad worried."

"I was detained." Daphne handed her cloak to Tait and glanced at Paul trying to decide whether to ask him to stay or not. If she did ask him, she'd have to explain her circumstances, a story perhaps best left untold.

With a sheepish smile, Tait bowed. "May I take your coat, Your Grace?"

"Is Lord Pembrooke here?" Paul directed his question to Tait as Paul slipped off his black greatcoat and handed it and his tall beaver hat to the under-butler.

The dark undertones in his deep voice reminded Daphne of a deep mulled wine, one she could savor and never tire of even if he was reading aloud his duchy's financial reports. Yet this was no time to moon over the man when he was asking for her brother. Before she could answer, Tait stepped in and performed the duty for her.

"Your Grace, Lord and Lady Pembrooke are not available. I'm sorry to add that I'm not certain when they'll be receiving next. Would you care to leave a card?" Tait's delivery was every bit as polished as their butler Simms.

Paul raised a dubious brow, making Daphne's decision easy. After everything they'd shared tonight, she'd tell him the truth of her circumstances. She had little to lose at this point. He might be able to help her, considering he was intimately familiar with the Reynolds.

"Tait, would you mind seeing about some refreshments? His Grace and I will be in the study."

Chapter Seven

❧

Daphne sat motionless like a porcelain doll. Alex's desk had captured her full attention. For some insane jealous reason, Paul wanted to bash it into pieces.

"Where *exactly* are your brother and his wife?" He ignored the gingerbread and tea on the side table. Instead, he sat beside her on the sofa.

"They're not here," she said.

"That's evident, sweetheart. If Pembrooke were here, there wouldn't be any way he'd allow me to be alone with you like this. Hell's fury is like a slap from a kitten's paw when compared to your brother's wrath."

She refused to look at him and continued her study of the desk.

He moved closer to her and rested one arm behind her on the sofa's frame. "When will they return?"

She scooted toward him, and he wanted to cry out in triumph. Daphne Hallworth was comfortable enough with him to lean against him. Gently, he nuzzled the side of her head with his nose. Loosely twisted in an elegant chignon, the midnight-black hair threatened to fall in waves. The hairpins had lost their moorings from the sea of black curls. It was wicked, but he nudged the pins again.

He never claimed to be a saint.

When a couple of pins slipped free, the rest followed, surrendering the fight. All that glorious hair fell in ripples around her shoulders. Her lavender scent rose to greet him.

She turned and blinked slowly. "I can't say."

Unable to resist such beauty, he twisted a handful of hair around his fist, then released it. Like a soft silk river, streams of black ran through his fingers.

Her enchanting eyes widened, and her breathing grew rapid. He wanted to kiss her senseless, but he wrestled his self-control back into some order. He had other concerns, though none as pleasing as her sweet, sensual kisses.

"Sweetheart"—he continued to nestle his nose against her head in hopes of lowering her guard—"you're lying."

He must be losing his touch with enticing women, as she bristled and her back straightened.

"I'm not lying," she protested and gave him her undivided attention.

Well, maybe he hadn't entirely lost his ability in the charm department. Her interest in the desk had waned.

"Of course you're not," he agreed. "I'd call it . . . an economical use of words or, perhaps, a concise confabulation, a vague vernacular, or a penurious parlance. Each has a nice poetical ring to it." He trailed his forefinger down her nose.

She pushed his finger away. "You're calling me dishonest."

"I would *never* say something that vile." He shook his head. "Well, maybe I would, but certainly not about you. Let's say you're lacking terminological exactitude when you answer my questions. That has a nice refined quality to it, wouldn't you agree?"

Her skin was returning to its normal creaminess after

being out in the cold, but her cheek color was high. He had little doubt that she'd be glorious to make love to. The thought of all the things he could teach her about pleasure made him exhale in longing. He scooped up another handful of black silk. He was getting bloody hard just from playing with her hair. He could only imagine the frenzy he'd experience if he had her in his bed for a week. A month and they'd have London in flames.

He pushed the pleasurable thoughts aside, as he needed to determine why exactly Daphne found the Reynolds so fascinating that she had to visit it alone.

"Moonbeam, there's not a single footman in attendance, not a single maid swooning at my feet, and the ubiquitous Simms is nowhere to be found. Now, if the staff is having a Christmas party downstairs, I say let's join the festivities."

She gracefully stood, and the defeated slump of her shoulders wrenched an emotion free from the middle of his chest. But it had to be his imagination. He didn't care about anything but himself. With a huff of breath, he dismissed the odd feeling.

She walked across the large expanse of the study and stared through the French doors that led into a small courtyard surrounding a magnificent fountain. Daphne's father had commissioned the piece years ago. It brought forth fond memories of warm spring days. He and Alex had played for hours in the fountain as boys. Where had Daphne been? They should have included her. But she'd always been with Alice, reading, painting, embroidering, and doing all the other things girls did with one another.

As he studied her silhouette framed by the door, he experienced an epiphany. Alice had been closer than just a sister—she had been Daphne's best friend. Just as he mourned Robbie's passing and the loss of Pembrooke's friendship, she'd lost Alice.

Without second-guessing his decision, he made quick work of reaching her side. He took her hand and led her back to the fire. She sat without his encouragement, and he joined her on the large navy brocade settee that faced the fire. He laced his fingers with hers. She turned her attention from the fire to him and exhaled—the sound poignant.

Something changed between them in those minutes. Like the stars in perfect alignment, his understanding grew that they both struggled in their losses, and they shared that bond together. Only she was pure and he was nothing but wicked. God, he shouldn't soil her beauty or pureness with all the sins he'd committed.

"I'm humiliated to speak of it, but you deserve an answer," she said. The defiant tilt of her chin brought forth memories of her as a hoyden, one who no matter the sacrifice would do what she thought was right—no matter the consequences. She was a woman who would do as she pleased.

He found her beguiling and exceedingly desirable.

But oddly, there was a slight change in her demeanor. She could have been staring at a gallery portrait of a stuffy ancestor, one in the long line of her family, and wondering whether to leave it or store in the attic. The lack of emotion took him aback. It had to be his imagination, but her normal vivaciousness and the ever-present sparkle in her silver eyes had dimmed—just a smidgen.

"Just so there's no misunderstanding later, I'm not leaving London or this house," she challenged.

"And you're telling me this why?" Such an illogical reaction, but he placed their interlaced hands on his thigh. The need to touch her, feel her warmth, was overpowering.

She stared at their hands for a moment. "This morning, my family left to celebrate the holidays without me. Both my mother and brother thought I traveled with the other. Even the servants didn't realize I was left alone." Her voice so soft, he strained to hear the words. "My under-butler Tait realized what had happened, as he was the only one left in the house. Earlier, I'd sent my lady's maid home so she could spend Christmas with her family." Daphne regarded him as if trying to determine if she could trust him.

"That's very kind of you. I can't imagine many ladies who would give their maids the holidays off." He squeezed her hand. "She's lucky to have you."

"I'm lucky to have her." She grinned slightly. "Tait's plans were to spend Christmas with his mother in London. I considered hiring a carriage to take me to Pemhill, but thought I'd wait to see if Alex came back for me. However, I've decided to remain in London. I asked Tait if he would stay with me. His mother is here, too."

His respect for the young under-butler increased dramatically. Loyal, the man had the good sense to stay for his mistress's safety.

Whatever she studied in the fire must have given her the courage to continue. "I made him promise not to send a note to Alex."

He couldn't help but stare at her as a suffocating silence descended. "Why don't you want Alex to know? You can be at Pemhill by tomorrow's nightfall. I'll send a carriage with one of my maids as a chaperone."

"Stop. You promised not to interfere."

The firmness in her voice was tinted with something else, perhaps hesitation. Whatever it was, it tore a piece of his heart away. "Daph, I didn't promise. Pembrooke and Claire are probably worried sick for your safety."

"They won't be worried until days later." The soft light from the candles enhanced the beauty of her hair. "You see, until my mother and the Duke of Renton travel to Pemhill on Christmas Day, no one will know that I'm here.

I thought about going to Emma and Somerton, but I forgot they're traveling to Cambridge."

"She's still your best friend?" he asked.

She nodded with her head bent. "She and Somerton will join my mother and his father at Pemhill."

"Don't you want to be with your family?" He didn't hide the incredulity from his voice. If he had the opportunity to spend the holidays with a loving family or with Robbie just one more time, it would take the devil himself to stop him.

"Of course, but now I have to stay in London," she replied testily.

There was only one reason to stay in town. "Let me guess. It has something to do with the Reynolds."

She nodded once, and a soulful sigh escaped, one that reminded him she was vulnerable and alone in a big house with only Tait and his mother in attendance. All he wanted to do was gather her in his arms until whatever it was that plagued her never bothered her again.

He wouldn't let her escape from explaining what was keeping her in London. "Tell me."

"I was looking for someone, a boy who frequents the establishment."

"There are no boys there." He didn't keep the growl out of his voice. "Only reprobates, scoundrels, rakes—"

"You were there," she challenged.

"Proves my point entirely," he countered.

"Stop saying such derogatory comments," she hissed. "You drive me mad with your cavalier attitude and the way you belittle yourself. You're so much more than that."

For once, he didn't have a "cavalier" response. No, she'd rendered him speechless. She couldn't actually think of him any other way than as a scoundrel, could she?

"Let me continue, please." She lifted her chin.

Good God, "magnificent" was the only word to describe her when her pique was high.

"The majordomo explained the boy I'm looking for is a street urchin about ten or so. He spends his time in the kitchen." She stood silent for a moment, then squared her shoulders. "I must find him."

"Why?" he asked.

She stared at the floor and didn't answer.

"Does this have something to do with the Duchess of Langham and Claire's charities for orphans?" He strolled to the Robert Adam side table that held Alex's liquor selection. "Do you mind?"

She shook her head. "I should have offered you one earlier."

Once she started this story, she'd undoubtedly need a calming drink.

There was little doubt he would. Searching the selection, he found the bottle of his father's favorite brandy. The sight caused a smile to tug at his lips. In retaliation for his father hitting him, Paul had stolen one from the Southart estate and given it to Alex. After all the years, Alex still possessed it. Choosing another bottle, he poured a fingerful of brandy for both of them, then walked to her side. "I poured one for you."

Without taking the drink, Daphne recounted her story. As the last words melted into silence, she stood before the fire with her back facing him.

"A reticule is hardly worth ruining your reputation, Moonbeam." He used her nickname to put her at ease.

Finally, she turned to face him, and he almost dropped both glasses at the sight. The ashes in the fireplace possessed more color than her face.

"You don't understand," she whispered.

The uncertainty in her voice cut him in two. He set the

glasses on the nearest table, then pulled her to him. Her arms tightened around his torso as if only he could keep her upright.

"Help me understand," he said.

With her forehead resting against his chest, Daphne released a woeful sigh. "I don't care about the reticule either. But it contains my journal." She lifted her gaze to his. "I've written things that would destroy my family and others. Personal things about my siblings and personal things about me. If it lands in the wrong hands, then my family is ruined, not to mention me."

She suddenly pulled away, and the immediate sense of loss overpowered him. "I'll find the boy and retrieve your journal."

Pure panic radiated from her as her chest heaved wildly like a chimney bellows. "You can't. Tait will accompany me. I'll go back tomorrow and wait in the carriage for Garland to appear."

"Let me point out the obvious," he drawled. "Tait is the least competent person to retrieve your book. He couldn't fight off a fly if it decided to attack. Besides, I'm familiar enough with the Reynolds staff and its patrons that I can quickly find this journal of yours while keeping you safe."

Adorably, she bit her lip as she considered his logic. "What an excellent idea. With you beside me, we'll be in and out in a trice. No one need know what's inside my journal."

"You can't come with me. It would be inviting a scandal. If you're discovered there, you're ruined. Completely. We were lucky that you weren't recognized tonight." There was no way except for a month filled with thirty Sundays that Paul would ever consider taking her. On her own, she was fresh meat for the carnivores who prowled through the night masquerading as gentlemen.

Hadn't he just described himself? No, he'd kissed her

to save her reputation. But if he was truthful with himself, he wanted to spend this time with her. She was a delightful woman full of love and seemed to enjoy his company also.

"If you won't take me, then Tait will." She crossed her arms in front of her chest.

The pose had the unintended effect of lifting her breasts, like an offering on a platter. Like a starving man, he groaned and ran his hand over his face, hoping to tame the wild and edgy response of his body.

She smiled for the first time since she arrived at home, causing her face to glow.

Something shifted within him. A crack opened up, allowing a want to crawl out from the depths of his soiled soul and emerge, shaking every manacle free. He didn't recognize it at first, but it was something uncontrollable. It resembled a yearning, a hunger that could consume him, and only she could satisfy it. If desire would destroy him, then he'd relish every minute of it. A lightness released within him that he hadn't felt in ages, maybe never. Like a heavy-linked chain had loosened and he experienced freedom for the first time.

She and her haunting eyes and bewitching mouth had caused it.

No. It wasn't lust.

It was more powerful. In that moment, he forced himself to breath deep. Ordinary scents of the library—leather, brandy, fire, books, paper, and ink—combined. Yet his nostrils flared, desperate to consume an exotic scent that wafted gently toward him.

Her innocence combined with the fragrance of lavender wrapped around him and squeezed. He almost laughed aloud at the absurdity that this woman might dare threaten his sense of self. Suddenly, everything surrounding him grew eerily silent. Even the crackling of the fire quieted.

She took a step toward him.

That's when he caught it, the real power that could destroy him. The faint whiff of her essence, a woman desiring him, and her accompanying look—fleeting as it was—a pure, unfettered look of adoration.

He'd been desired before, but never with that look.

She thought him noble.

He stumbled back a step.

He closed his eyes and took another deep breath, desperate to recapture the scent. God, to have someone see goodness within him was a heady desire. Like a cold, sobering rain shower, reality intruded. All the hateful things he'd done to her family marched into his forethoughts— her brother, his longtime friend, he'd tried to ruin. He'd disparaged her sister-in-law, and the shame of it still singed his soul. He'd let her sister suffer.

But from nowhere, his true self, the selfish beast he'd nurtured for years, pummeled his last remaining brief hope. He was nothing but a rogue. No matter how hard he tried, he couldn't change. He only lived for himself.

Everything inside him roiled in revolt and pain. He had to escape now, or he'd find himself emasculated by his own wants. He'd not soil her goodness with his own rot.

He closed his eyes and groaned. "There's only one solution. I'll take you, and together we'll find your journal." For liquid courage, he downed one fingerful of brandy then reached for the other. "Do you mind?"

"No, be my guest. I'm not thirsty."

God almighty, he was. "Parched" didn't even describe his thirst. What in the devil had he gotten himself into?

"I want something in return." Wasn't that always his creed? Think of himself first. "I want to mend my relationship with your brother. You can help me."

"How?" She laughed. "You made quite the mess of it all by yourself."

"That's true, but a fine upstanding sister such as your-self would have a lot of influence."

"What are you about?" she scoffed. "He forgot me. How much influence is that?"

"I'd never forget you," he said sincerely.

She rolled her eyes.

"I never have."

"Please. Spare me the trite words," she said dismissively.

All his bad acts had come home to roost. He really wanted to give her a compliment, and she threw it in his face. "I'm serious. I promised my brother that I'd repair my broken friendship with Pembrooke."

"Why would you make that promise?" she asked.

"I think Robbie was worried I wouldn't have anyone except for my friend, Devan Farris." He shrugged his shoulders. "Maybe Robbie wanted me to cleanse my soul."

"I can understand a brother wanting to protect his sibling. The only thing I can promise is I'll try," she said hesitantly. "But you must help me with the Reynolds."

This was not the way to mend his broken relationships with the Hallworth family, particularly Pembrooke. But when had Paul ever done the right thing? Certainly not when he wanted something. He was living proof that you couldn't change a tiger's stripes to spots.

Tonight, the only thing he wanted was her.

But he couldn't have her.

"Agreed. Now I must be on my way. I hope you have a lovely evening." Without another word, he walked briskly toward the door.

"Paul, stop. We need to discuss the arrangements in greater detail." The sound of relief and hope in her voice was pure and sweet like music.

He heard her cry out for him to stop again, but he kept walking, his boot heels clicking against the black and white marble tiles like a drum sergeant ordering him forward. He made quick work of retrieving his own coat and hat. Her steps followed his.

Paul forced himself to lock gazes with her. Before she could utter a word of protest, he nodded once. "Good night, my lady." He didn't look back as he rushed out the door.

Otherwise, he might change his mind and do the only proper thing—refuse to take her to the gambling hell.

Only when his carriage was safely away did he let his desire have free rein. He wanted what her look had promised—a life with a woman who could love him.

Yet he knew the truth. He could never earn her love or risk his heart. For he wouldn't be able to bear the utter revulsion in her liquid silver eyes when she discovered how dissolute and disreputable he truly was.

Chapter Eight

~~~~~

Devan took a drink of whisky, then shook his head. "That'll clear the cobwebs. Today proved Dante didn't know what he was talking about." He exhaled a sound very much like exhaustion. "There are no circles of hell—it's a straight path, and I took it today in the company of my brother. But it can wait until later. Now you have my undivided attention."

The devilment in his friend's voice irritated Paul, but after he'd been so bemused last night, it helped to tell the incredible tale to his friend. Once he'd retired for the evening, he hadn't fallen asleep until hours later, as visions of Daphne Hallworth stole his every thought.

"I found Lady Daphne at the bloody gaming hell." Paul eased his body into his favorite chair in the library, a massive armchair covered in leather with scrollwork details and carved spiral uprights that his great-grandfather had commissioned. Paul had personally brought it down from the attic as a tribute to his father. The ornate piece was out of place in the room decorated in the neoclassical design his father favored. If his father were here, he'd roar his disapproval and rail at Paul's lack of taste. For some odd reason, the simple act of placing the chair in a position of prominence pleased Paul to no end. "We went out the hidden kitchen door. You know the one?"

Devan nodded, then took another sip.

"One of the Reynolds whores was servicing a man on her knees."

Devan emphatically shook his head. "I believe the proper term is 'Cyprians weaving their magic.' The establishment doesn't employ your everyday light-skirts. Those women are beautiful."

"I agree," Paul said. "However, I never fancied how they were treated."

"The Reynolds takes advantage of those women."

Paul nodded. "There's more. Lady Daphne saw everything."

His friend's eyes grew wide, then he let out a bark of laughter. "I wish I could have seen the two of you together. The consummate Lothario and the wide-eyed virgin bearing witness to a cock being serviced."

"A 'Lothario' implies that I deceive women. Is your opinion that low of me?" Paul asked.

Devan shook his head. "Never. You don't deceive anyone. You're too busy seducing. A more innocent description for you is 'a rake.' Will that satisfy your honor?"

The teasing in his voice grated Paul's somewhat frayed nerves.

"They should have been taking bets inside the Reynolds as to who had the wider eyes, you watching the delectable Lady Daphne watching such a scene or her at the shock of what she saw," Devan offered.

"Oh no, my friend, it's worse." Paul set down his full glass of champagne, then started to pace. "Martin Richmond saw me outside and had the audacity to approach. I had my back to him. She told me to kiss her, and frankly, I froze. All of a sudden, she kissed me. I went along with it. If Richmond thought I was out there with a whore, it was worth the chance he'd leave us be."

"That's smart thinking on her part." Devan studied his glass, concentrating as if it were a crystal ball with all the answers. "So, how does the fair Lady Daphne kiss?"

"Sometimes you're so juvenile. Or are you just foxed? Why I entertain your nonsense is beyond me."

"Because you know I have your best interests at heart." Devan's demeanor changed from humorous to grave. "Must I beg? Give me a prurient bone. It's been at least six months since I've even had a scent of a woman, let alone a kiss."

"Enough of the jokes." Paul's humor at Devan's shenanigans faded. There was serious business afoot. "He wants to meet her."

"Lady Daphne?"

"Moonbeam. That's what I called her tonight, so others wouldn't recognize who she was." But the real reason was because when he'd first seen the soft light kissing her cheeks she looked as ethereal as any celestial body in the sky. If he shared that with Devan, Paul would never hear the end of it.

"Moonbeam?" Devan claimed the closest chair and howled in laughter. "Good God, this gets better and better, Your Grace."

"As a man of the church, you're not supposed to blaspheme." The arrogant arse was begging Paul to plant a facer.

Once Devan fought his laughter under control, he smoothed a hand down his waistcoat and wiped his eyes. "There's a special dispensation during the holidays."

Devan's perfect delivery of a pious expression caused Paul to roll his eyes.

"Everyone's heart overflows with love for our fellow man and the holy spirit." Then his friend pursed his lips like a cat's arse, and his eyes flashed with laughter once again. "But 'Moonbeam'? Your Grace, where's the suave seducer we've all come to love and respect?"

Without giving a tinker's damn, Devan laughed again.

Paul stopped his pacing and returned to his champagne. The bubbles rushed to meet him. At least the beverage held some respect for him. He ran a hand over his face to clear his maudlin mood. Now he was attributing human emotions to a glass of wine. He downed the glass without coming up for air. "You're supposed to be my friend, my spiritual counselor."

Devan walked to him and grabbed one of Paul's shoulders. "I am your friend. But you need to see the humor in this situation. She twisted you into a homemade noodle."

Paul opened his mouth to argue, but Devan put up his hand to stop him. "Why was Moonbeam there?"

Paul briefly debated how much of the story to tell, then decided he'd share everything. He had the utmost faith in Devan's discretion. "A boy, who works as a runner for the Reynolds, stole her private diary, a journal where she's recorded her private thoughts. I promised I'd help her find it."

"What you're doing for her is a kind thing," Devan said. "She's rightfully concerned that someone will find this journal and use it to harm her or her family. If *The Midnight Cryer* gets wind of this diary, she'll face ruin."

Paul nodded in agreement. "She's bloody terrified. I know I promised her, but I shouldn't take her. Besides, it's in my character to break such a promise."

Devan shook his head. "You'd be miserable if you did."

"But I should try to talk her out of going. She can't risk going to the Reynolds." Paul began to pace, hoping it'd clear his thoughts. "I'll get the damned thing for her and return it. She doesn't need to be involved."

Devan lost all signs of his earlier mirth. "Did the

thought ever occur to you that she doesn't want you to see what's inside?"

"What are you getting at?"

"Every single one of us has a dark side that battles relentlessly for supremacy. Perhaps she writes to cleanse herself, like her own personal communion." Devan tilted his head slightly in a signal that usually preceded a lecture. "You above all others should understand that desire. You're constantly seeking an easy way to purify your soul."

Paul put up his hand for Devan to stop. "Not tonight, please. I'm in no mood for a sermon."

Ignoring him, Devan continued, "If Lady Daphne writes about her demons and desires, then all the more power to her. It makes no difference to any of us. So, if she writes about plotting murders by poison or perverted tales that would make the devil cringe, I say, it's her business and no one else's."

"I don't care what she's written." Paul stopped his pacing, then turned his full attention to Devan. "I'm the last person to think ill of anyone else."

"I never said that you did care. But this is something very personal to her. From what you've described, she's going to go with or without you. If you're with her, then you can assist if she needs help. Her brother will be undoubtedly grateful."

Gratitude wouldn't be Pembrooke's reaction. Pure unadulterated fury would most likely be the marquess's response once he learned of Paul's attention to Daphne while she was alone in the city. "I told her I'd help her if she'd help me mend my friendship with Pembrooke."

Devan shrugged. "Quid pro quo. I see the wisdom in that. You're both invested in the outcome."

There was more to it than that, but he wouldn't share it with Devan. When he'd held her in his arms, he'd experienced a connection, a closeness that had been missing since Robbie's death. Perhaps it was worth the risk. Their closeness was something that he'd never experienced before. His friendship with Devan represented a bond, a familiar one at that, but nothing like the friendship he experienced with Daphne tonight.

"Friendship"—such a curious word. The thought that he and Daphne were friends punched him in the gut like two schoolboys showing affection toward each other. The truth was that he needed her much more than she needed him. If there was one thing he lacked in his filthy rich and obscenely blessed ducal life, it was friends and family.

Such a revelation proved there was only one thing to do.

It would be his honor, as a friend, to accompany her to the Reynolds. If she needed help, she'd not have to rely on a stranger. She could rely on him. At least he could assist her until her brother returned, and why shouldn't he do it? Though a debauched rake, he could act appropriately when needed.

He and Daphne were friends after all.

When Daphne dressed, her thoughts were consumed with Paul and their sensuous kisses. He was not the type of man she should trust, but last night he'd been a charming ally and, frankly, a valiant accomplice who wanted to help— never mind the fact that he was an expert at kissing.

Whether the night was memorable because of the passion they'd created together or because she'd been alone with him at a gambling hell made little difference. Either way, he was like a forbidden fruit, and she'd just taken a bite out of the poisoned apple and survived.

It wasn't too far-fetched to say that she wanted more.

For once in her life she had chosen something for herself—a night with someone unacceptable in almost every conceivable way. He was a man her family didn't approve of, and he was wicked in so many ways. But for her, the simple reason that Paul was helping her recover her journal in return for her assistance in repairing his friendship with her brother made her even less leery. Why would he spend his evening with her unless he truly felt something for her? She wasn't naïve enough to believe he'd changed completely. Based upon Alex and his friend Somerton's comments, they thought he'd never change his dissolute ways.

Yet last night he'd only had eyes for her and she'd relished that power. She'd chosen not to be invisible with him, but to show her true wants and wishes.

Her courage was increasing in strength. This morning, she'd received a note from Mr. Orham, the owner of Winterford House, stating that per her request, the Pembrooke family physician, Dr. Camden, had scheduled a visit this morning. Mr. Orham went on to ask for the pleasure of her company afterward to discuss her bid on the property.

Her plans were coming along nicely. It was another step in her start to build a life for herself, one that would allow her to protect unwed women from the heartbreak of an unwanted pregnancy. Daphne had seen enough heartache to know she couldn't save everyone who needed her, but if she could save just one life, all her sacrifices would be worth it.

Within the hour, Tait had hired a hackney and had escorted her to Winterford. She pushed her musings aside and concentrated on the lovely grounds in front of her. The fountain was shut down for the winter, but the expertly kept gardens were clearly visible even through their winter sleep. The property would offer the women an oasis within the city.

"Lady Daphne, do you need me to view anything else?" Dr. Wade Camden asked. The handsome and serious-minded doctor stood beside her. His tawny hair and the capes of his greatcoat waved gently in the chilly breeze.

He was a gifted physician who had delivered Alex and Claire's children. He'd also delivered Emma and Somerton's daughter. It said a great deal that they trusted him to bring their children into the world. Daphne had relied on the good doctor's opinion when she'd met with the architects for the remodel of the home. His first recommendations had been to incorporate birthing and examination rooms for the residents.

"No." Daphne smiled. "You've generously given your time to me. I appreciate your advice for future expansion. If this effort proves successful, then women would flock from all over London."

Dr. Camden rocked backed on his heels and surveyed the grounds. "It'll be more than successful, I'm afraid." His brow ceased into neat lines. "You'll have not only women from London, but also women from the surrounding areas seeking your assistance. They'll need this refuge. There will be no other place like it."

All she could do was nod at his truthful pronouncement.

"A midwife approached me yesterday." His visage creased into a scowl. "Her name is Grace Arthur. An obnoxious woman, but she's highly talented and sought after in town. She might have a patient who'll need your services."

"Really?" Daphne raised her hand to her heart.

"I don't know the specifics yet, but she's a lady. Her family wants her to disappear out of the country until the baby's born, but she's refusing. The father is on a secret assignment for the Home Office and doesn't know of the pregnancy." He exhaled, the sound poignant. "Her family is threatening to cut her off and disown her if she continues with her plans. She's convinced the baby's father will marry her once he returns."

It was Daphne's most ardent wish to provide a haven

from the ridicule and the condemnation that would fall on these women once their families discovered their pregnancies. Though Alice hadn't suffered such a travesty, she'd suffered in her own way without seeking any help.

"That gives me all the more reason to open the home sooner rather than later." She reached into her pocket and pulled out a calling card. "Will you see that she gets this? As soon as I can complete the purchase, we'll open up the home for her if she needs it."

He took the card and placed it in his waistcoat pocket. "I'll do that, my lady."

"Thank you again, Dr. Camden."

"It's my pleasure, my lady. I'm a firm believer in the home's necessity. Please let me know if you need anything else," he offered. "Mr. Orham is waiting to speak with you."

They said good-bye to each other, and Daphne headed back inside to speak to the building's owner. It was fortuitous that he'd asked to speak with her, as she'd inquire when her solicitor could call and they could sign the purchase agreement. She quickly found Mr. Orham, a man in his late seventies, in the front sitting room.

"Thank you, Lady Daphne, for coming today. I don't know how to say this." Mr. Oldham examined the floor. Finally, he lifted his gaze to hers and pursued his lips. "I'm sorry, my lady. My son found another bidder this morning, and reluctantly, I agreed to entertain the bid. Imagine my surprise when I received it this morning sight unseen." He slowly shook his head. "It's greater than your bid. Actually, it's more than the asking amount."

"Pardon me?" she asked incredulously.

"I'm as shocked as you are. Because you've worked tirelessly on determining the suitability of the land and building for your home, I wanted to let you know immediately so you could discuss this with your solicitor and your brother. Perhaps they could advise you."

"Neither the marquess nor my solicitor has anything to do with my decision, Mr. Orham," she stated firmly. She bit the inside of her cheek to keep from delivering a blistering lecture at the inference that she didn't have the wherewithal to make a decision by herself.

She exhaled, but it did little to reduce her aggravation at the news. She'd budgeted carefully for the purchase and the renovations of the building and the attached lands. The home would not be an attractive charitable foundation. No outside monies would come into its coffers. It wasn't like Claire's charities for retired soldiers or war widows and their children.

Her home would cater to the women whom society viewed as wanton and loose in their morals. Thus, Daphne wouldn't have much luck with charity balls or fund-raising auctions. Members of the *ton* were the only ones who had the money for such contributions. They'd most likely throw their money out a carriage window rather than send in a donation to keep her home for unwed mothers running. It would take most of her inheritance to keep it operational for years to come. She didn't see how she could offer any more. Even if she asked Alex for help, he would likely refuse. He was dead set against the idea from the beginning.

With what she'd learned from Dr. Camden this morning, she needed to open the home as soon as possible. A woman was in desperate straits, and Daphne would not lose it to another bidder.

"Someone else is interested in the building?" The idea was simply incredible, as the building had sat vacant for over a year. Daphne clenched a fist in her skirts but kept the reaction to herself. She'd spent the last several months against Alex's wishes with architects, craftsmen, and Dr. Camden evaluating the building for its suitability as a home. "I thought you told me I was the only one?"

Mr. Orham gently shook his head. "I'm sorry, my lady."

"As am I." She asked calmly, which was remarkable, as she wanted to scream, "I was under the impression we had an understanding?"

"The property purchase requires a written contract, and your solicitor hasn't sent one to me." Little beads of sweat covered his brow. "I want to be fair, my lady, since you were the first to show any interest. But—"

Daphne winged an eyebrow waiting for the "but."

"I'll sell you the property if your bid matches the current one on my desk," he said meekly.

"And what is that bid?" she asked. If he said double the amount, she'd have to consider it. The location was perfect for her needs. The lands and the building were beautiful. The home on the inside was charming and comfortable. The only renovations required were the rooms Dr. Camden suggested plus several living areas enlarged. For heaven sakes, she'd already selected the name—Aubrey's Place. It was Alice's middle name. It wouldn't embarrass her family, but it would be true to Alice's memory.

"The bid is thirty thousand pounds," he answered.

"What?" she gasped. "That's three times the asking amount."

The man had the good grace to flinch. "I'm sorry, my lady. That amount will ensure that my wife and I are comfortable in our old age, plus provide a nice inheritance for our children."

After last night with Paul and his lovely company, she thought things might be changing in her favor. She bit her lip in consternation. This had nothing to do with luck, and she'd not give up without a fight. "I don't know if I can spend that amount," she answered.

"I understand, my lady. However, I wanted to give you the opportunity to raise the bid."

"May I ask who is bidding against me?" Granted, it was a stately home, but it lay on the outskirts of London. If she found out their identity, perhaps she could convince them to withdraw their bid for purely philanthropic reasons.

"Of course, Lady Daphne," he answered. "I'm sure you'll understand after I tell you. He's very powerful and not to mention rich. He's—"

Just then, the door swung open. The Duke of Southart, looking too magnificent for his own good *or hers,* stood in the doorway.

"Mr. Orham, have you signed the papers? I'm ready to proceed. This will make the perfect location to build my hospital." His gaze shifted to hers, and the hint of shock radiated from his blue eyes. "Moon—I mean, Lady Daphne, what a pleasure to see you here this morning."

Without acknowledging Paul, she directed her attention to Mr. Orham. "After all the effort I've expended on your property, I beg of you, give me two weeks to reevaluate the bid." Without waiting for an answer, she left without another word.

It was a shame that her anger didn't stay in her stead. Perhaps she would learn exactly what the Duke of Southart was up to.

She'd been a fool to even entertain the concept she could trust him.

As she took Tait's hand to climb into the hackney, Paul's baritone voice rang through the cold winter air. "Lady Daphne, wait."

She proceeded to settle in the forward-facing seat. Tait's gaze ricocheted between her and Southart. "My lady?"

"Ignore him." Not that anyone could. Wherever he went, he caused a stir. She released a breath, blowing a frosty steam in front of her. Her time would be better spent going over the projected finances for Aubrey's Place, and determining a way to find Garland and her journal without the duke. "Tell the driver I'm ready to leave."

Tait nodded, then turned to address the driver.

From nowhere, Paul leaned into the carriage. His frame filled the doorway, blocking most of the light. The scent of snow and sandalwood wafted toward her, and her traitorous lungs breathed it in like heaven-sent ambrosia.

"Daphne, we need to talk," he said as he climbed into the carriage.

"I didn't invite you inside." She directed her gaze to the vehicle across the way with the Duke of Southart crest emblazoned across the black enamel. "Your carriage is over there."

"And you're in here." He lifted a brow and smiled. "Please. After last night, I think we owe it to each other, don't you?"

"What do I owe you?" She wanted to snap at him, but miraculously, she kept her anger in check.

"You owe me nothing, but I owe you an explanation. Mr. Orham explained that you were interested in the building and land, too. If I'd known, I wouldn't have bid on it."

The earnest look on his face was almost her undoing. But she steeled herself against it and turned to gaze out the window. She couldn't trust him. "Please. You bid three times the asking price. You knew exactly what you were doing."

"I've directed my solicitors to find a location for a hospital I want to build. They sent word this property was available, and they thought it would be a perfect location." From the corner of her eye, she caught him reaching over in her direction. Within seconds, his hand covered hers. "Would you look at me?"

Reluctantly, she did as asked, fully expecting to find a man who knew how to charm his way out of everything.

Instead, she discovered he looked worried, and that simple fact confused her. "I've spent an inordinate amount of time finding the right building, location, architects, and builders. I can't begin to tell you how angry I am that you swoop in with your 'dukeness' and ruin my plans."

"Dukeness?" The worry on his face slowly transformed into confusion. The sight would have been comical if she weren't so angry.

She took a breath and tried to gather her thoughts. "I should have known better than to trust *you*."

"Why are you looking at the property?" He squeezed her hand.

In response, part of herself that had shared so much with him last night encouraged her to confide in him, but she fought the urge. "Business opportunity," she answered. When he didn't respond, she sighed. "I'm thinking of starting a charity, and this property would have been perfect."

"What kind of charity?" he coaxed.

"Why do you want to know? Will it change your mind about bidding?" The challenge in her voice surprised him. He leaned back but didn't release her hand.

"I'm interested in you and what you want to do." The deep thrum of his voice could soothe a raging river. "And to answer your second question, I'm not certain I can withdraw my bid."

"You can do whatever you want." She lifted one brow in challenge. "You're the Duke of Southart. To answer your question, I'm starting a home for unwed mothers." She expected him to withdraw even farther in horror, but he leaned close and studied her. There was no condemnation in his eyes, nor were there any arguments forthcoming about how inappropriate such an endeavor was.

He released her hand and leaned back against the squabs of the hackney. The fine wool of his black greatcoat and fur of his elegant beaver hat were in startling contrast to the worn leather of the seats.

"That's a noble endeavor, Lady Moonbeam."

"Please, don't call me that." She glanced at her gloves. "It would be best for both of us if I not see you anymore."

"What about the Reynolds?"

"It's not your concern." Last night, she'd had Tait hire a runner to try to find the boy in Seven Dials. So far, he hadn't found him. No one knew of a Garland or an Elsie. Daphne's only chance was to show up at the gambling hell this evening before the cook reported to work. "I'll ask Tait to escort me to the Reynolds. Thank you for all your help."

She'd said it. The words necessary to cut all ties between them. Instead of feeling justified in her response, emptiness stole through her. He'd been so kind and attentive to her. She couldn't remember when a man had actually expressed an interest in her and her wants.

"It wouldn't be best for me, Daphne."

The deep hum of his words reminded her of the brandy he'd drunk last night. The warm, rich sound caressed her, and she shivered in response. She shook her head in a desperate attempt to clear her thoughts. "I can't."

"You can." He drew close again, only this time he didn't touch her. A mere inch separated their lips. She made the mistake of looking into his eyes where the brilliant blue seemed to burst with an emotion she couldn't identify. "We're friends. You can do anything you want with me."

She bit back the need to laugh at his statement.

"Daphne, let me come with you tonight. If it's not too late, I'll find another property. Please, let's be friends."

A sudden heat bludgeoned her cheeks at his plea. Her thoughts tangled, but she refused to look away in embarrassment—she'd not hide anymore. "I'm changing the terms of our bargain from last night. I want Winterford and your assistance in finding my journal. In return, I'll help with Pembrooke."

"I accept your bargain. Shall we seal it with a kiss?" His breath smelled of peppermint and coffee, a heady scent that wrapped itself around her.

She nodded once, proving she was weak when it came to his kisses.

Gently, he brushed his lips against hers.

When he pulled away, she wanted to groan in disappointment. His touch reminded her of a soft spring breeze, and she wanted to be enveloped in it.

"There's nothing I want more than to kiss you until we're both senseless." He picked up his hat and placed his hand on the handle of the carriage. "But first, I'm going to see if I can rescind my bid. I'll not disappoint a friend." He captured her gaze. "Whatever it takes, Daph, I won't disappoint *you*. You're my friend. However, tonight, you're my Moonbeam. Until tonight, my lady."

In an instant, he was out the door. Her lips still tingled from his touch.

Oh God, what had she just agreed to?

Chapter Nine

After this morning's revelations, Daphne had almost sent a note telling Paul not to bother coming over. She didn't need or want his help—particularly after discovering she was in competition with him for her ideal location for Aubrey's Place. Yet he was so persuasive, and she'd come under his spell. He almost seemed eager to help her on both the building and the journal.

Daphne tugged the bodice of her silver satin gown up an inch higher. The black lace overlay and jet-black beading made the gown shimmer like black diamonds in the candlelight. She straightened her shoulders and tugged the bodice again for good measure. The dress really didn't need adjustment, but as nervous as she was, it gave her something to do. Paul would be there within the half hour to take her to the Reynolds tonight. She had to find a way to wrestle her wayward emotions into some order so she appeared to be a woman in control of her world.

A task easier said than done. Her heart still fluttered every time she thought of last night's kiss. Though she liked to think she was creative, Daphne never in her wildest dreams or fantasies could have imagined that kissing

Paul would be such an incendiary event. One kiss contained enough explosive heat that she found herself blasted from her dull, ordinary life to one that could only be described as extraordinary.

With a sigh, she considered the rococo style of Louis XV chairs upholstered in a variety of hues consisting of currant reds, peony pinks, and plush ivory. Thankfully, all were strategically placed in the salon, so she could pace the length of the room without any obstacles. The brocade furniture coverings with their floral and striped patterns showered every square inch with a merry brightness. It was her favorite room in the house, and her darling sister-in-law, Claire, had sought her advice when it needed redecorating. But even with such luxurious surroundings, she couldn't find any comfort or keep her thoughts contained.

Truthfully, she'd never felt such lightheartedness since Alice had died—such buoyancy the result of the delightful Duke of Southart. He'd been an attentive gentleman, and something had shifted between them last night. When she'd adamantly opposed his help and explained that only she and Tait could retrieve the journal, Paul's protectiveness had mildly surprised her. Could he really feel anything for her? Did his possessiveness mean something else?

"Blast it!" she exclaimed to no one. Such fantasies and desires were best left for others. He was a rake of the first order, and she was . . . what? An invisible young woman who skated closer and closer to spinsterhood.

She squared her shoulders at such a thought. Even at the age of twenty-five she was still young, and now had an attractive inheritance attached to her name. She could do anything she wanted without having to answer to anyone. Her life was her own and no one, not her mother, not society, not even her brother, could dictate her actions anymore. As her own person, she would not allow her future or the promise of a happy life be circumvented by others or their expectations. Hence, she'd go forward with her plans for the women's home.

The Duke of Southart had made her realize that about herself last night. His playfulness and concern for her well-being proved that her company could bring joy to others and to herself. Heaven knew, she'd never been as happy as when he kissed her last night. He demonstrated she could feel real desire and, as importantly, desired. She stopped her frantic steps and allowed the heady sensation to take control of her mind and body. She'd never felt such yearning with a real man—only her fantasy characters.

The plush pastel Axminster carpets muffled the sounds of her steps. If only they could quiet her erratic thoughts. Tonight, she needed her wits about her if she wanted to retrieve her journal with as little fanfare as possible. That was what she should be concentrating on instead of the handsome and charming Duke of Southart.

"My lady, His Grace, the Duke of Southart, is here," Tait announced. He stood aside as Paul entered the room.

Paul's height made him tower over the under-butler. His broad shoulders appeared almost sculpted in a black wool evening coat and light gray waistcoat with sterling buttons. His expertly tied cravat was set off by a ruby pin. The deep red stone caught the glow of the fire and sparkled all the way across the room. It was almost sinful how the black pantaloons set off his muscular legs.

Southart's gaze locked with hers, and she couldn't look away even if she wanted. Somehow all the years of comportment training that had been instilled by her governess, Mrs. Burnside, rushed to the forefront in a mishmash of rules and protocol. Her old persona would have waited for him to approach her as good manners dictated.

But not now—not tonight.

Life was too short to waste on good manners when the

Duke of Southart stood so close. She shed every ounce of restraint she possessed and ran to him. He held out his hands, and she unabashedly clasped them in welcome.

Inside, every nerve vibrated in awareness until a riot of heat overtook her. God, she was staring at him like he was the most exquisite tart in Gunther's Tea Shop.

"Lady Daphne, how lovely you look this evening." His eyes crinkled with undeniable mirth at her struggle.

She bit her lip to keep from laughing in triumph.

"Cat got your tongue, my dear?" he whispered. With his back to Tait, he took her hand in his and bowed over it. Instead of kissing the air, he turned her hand until her wrist was exposed. His warm lips caressed the tender skin, and she visibly inhaled at his touch. He lifted his head slightly, and his familiar lopsided grin appeared. "Are we still friends?"

"You rogue," she whispered delightfully. "Yes, we're still friends."

She playfully tried to snatch her hand away, but he held it firm. Once more he pressed his soft lips against her wrist. But this time, his hot tongue licked the pounding pulse in her wrist. Inflamed by his touch, her center seemed to melt into a liquid rush of heat, and a small moan escaped, causing her to turn away in embarrassment.

"Don't." His whisper was so low that, for a moment, she questioned if she'd heard him correctly. He straightened but didn't release her hand.

Without looking at the under-butler, she dismissed him. "Thank you, Tait."

Once the click of Tait's heels grew fainter, Paul focused on her lips, then his crystal clear blue eyes captured hers. "Don't turn from me. Tonight, when we walk into the Reynolds, you'll be disguised as my lover. We'll be completely enchanted with one another."

She should be shocked, but the magical cadence of his

words was an elixir, one that bewitched her. As part of
her reformation, she would take everything he offered
and more. She stole a peek at his face, and his earlier grin
had disappeared to be replaced by an intense stare that
caused her heartbeat to pound.

"Oh." It was the only response she could muster.

Without releasing her hand, he took a step back and
studied her gown. His gaze swept from the bottom of her
feet to the top of her head before returning to the décol-
letage of her dress. "You look beautiful, but may I?" His
visage held a questioning look.

"May you what?" she asked. Heavens, it was hard to appear nonchalant. Not when he examined her so closely.

"Adjust your sleeves," he said.

She nodded in answer.

Slowly, he reached up and pushed the cap sleeves of her
gown down her arms a good three inches. Her shoulders
were immediately bare. But that fact didn't faze her. What
brought an immediate heat to her cheeks were her breasts,
which threatened to burst from her stays in revolt.

She chanced a glance at her chest. The heat across her
face turned into an inferno when she saw the darkened outline of the areolae of her breasts peek out from under her
stays. Without thinking she placed her palm over her heart,
hoping she'd stop her nipples from popping out to parade in
the open. Her gaze flew to his. His eyes seemed to smolder
as he took in every detail of her chest.

She drew a deep breath to calm her embarrassment.

He stepped closer, but his hand never left her shoulder.
He bent his head as if to whisper some great secret in her
ear. His warm breath smelled of peppermint, and it teased
her sensitive lobe. After what felt like a year, he brushed
his lips against her skin. His touch wasn't a kiss, but more
like a taste. He inhaled deeply like a predator that contem-
plates how nervous its prey is before the kill.

She laughed quietly at her own response. This was Paul—of course, she'd expect such behavior.

He leaned away and fixed his gaze upon hers. "Sweetheart, last night you looked like a virgin completely out of your realm. Remember I had to make up that ridiculous story that you were an actress the Reynolds brothers had hired as a serving wench for holiday entertainment?"

Her chest rose and fell as she fought for breath. The movement drew his attention to where her palm still lay flattened against her chest. In defiance, she tilted her chin and pulled her dress up. "It worked, didn't it?"

"Love, he was foxed and, might I add, would've believed anything I told him." He chuckled and leaned close again to divulge another secret. "We'll not repeat that performance. It's too dangerous. Someone might recognize you. If you insist upon going in there, then you'll go as my unparalleled paramour."

Her eyes widened. Like a slow embrace, the sensual words spoken in his sinfully deep voice enveloped her.

She stepped closer and smelled him just as he'd done to her. The fragrant sandalwood and his unique masculine scent marked her. She held his scent as long as she could before she released her breath. He lifted his hand and gently traced a path across her shoulder and down her arm. His fingers danced across her skin, pulling the fabric down inch by inch.

"All right?" he asked.

"Yes, do what you want," she murmured. At that moment, she didn't care what he did as long as he kept touching her.

"Moonbeam, never tell a man that. You should tell him exactly what you want." The hunger in his eyes belied the soothing tone of his voice. "A beautiful woman like you deserves everything and anything. Someone worthy who'll appreciate all your intelligence and wonder—all that makes you unique. Only you can say what you want."

The words floated around her like a warm, gentle stream.

"It's the man's job to cater to your every whim and desire. Wouldn't you agree?"

Speechless, she could only manage a nod. Was he seducing her? This had to be what Eve felt when she was in the garden. However, the man before her was no snake.

"Now tell me." His finger took a lazy path upward across her bare shoulder to her neck. With the back of his forefinger, he gently caressed her in a rhythm that made her insides jelly. "What do *you* want?"

Through the tangled web of sensuality he'd woven around her, she replied, "Everything."

"You're a wicked, wicked woman, Lady Daphne Hallworth." He slowly drew away. With a rumbling, rich laugh that permeated every inch of her body, Paul held out his arm for her to take. "I think you and I are going to become the best of friends this evening. On the way to the Reynolds, perhaps you could define 'everything' for me."

At that moment, he could have escorted her to a cow pasture and she'd have been delighted. That was his true allure. Lucky for her, he was her escort this evening. Within no time, she'd have possession of her journal. With his talent and charm, he would have everyone eating out of his hands within fifteen minutes.

For her, it had only taken five.

Chapter Ten

If the lovely woman sitting across from Paul had expected his seductive manner to continue in the carriage, then she was sorely disappointed. Only when they stopped in front of the Reynolds would Paul give Daphne his undivided attention and explicit advice for behavior inside the gambling hell.

He ran his hand over his face. Why had he acted in such a horrible fashion at her home? Instead of instilling an air of confidence and making her comfortable, he'd behaved like a devilish scoundrel ready to pounce on her innocence.

Without turning his head, he stole a glance at her face. The most perfect hue of pink tinted her complexion. Her face glowed in the moonlight. The voluminous material of her black cloak covered the womanly curves hidden beneath the folds, but he knew the depths of her beauty.

Paul shifted slightly to relieve the tightness of his pantaloons. His erection hadn't ceased since he'd seen a glimpse of her breasts and those extraordinary dusty pink nipples, which, if he was honest, were more perfect than he'd ever dared dream. In fact, his cock was currently throwing a temper tantrum that it had been teased without any promise of a release in the near future. All he could think about was how her luscious breasts would taste and feel in his mouth. He loved their shape, like round, firm apples ready to be bitten, then licked so not a single sweet taste would be missed.

A slight groan involuntarily escaped as Paul adjusted his stance and leaned slightly forward to hide the devastating effect she was having on him.

Of all the moronic acts he could have accomplished at her home, the idea he'd actually considered seducing her topped the list. For God's sake, she was Pembrooke's sister, a virgin, and deserved someone who would treat her like the precious gift she was. He stole another peek and found her staring in return. Though her expression didn't give her away, he could practically hear the questions swirling in her head about his standoffish behavior.

If he wanted to win back Pembrooke's friendship, seducing his sister was not only bad form but also a sure way to get himself killed. Yet his own mind wouldn't quit the relentless cry that he close the distance between them and kiss her until neither of them knew what day it was.

"Paul?" She leaned forward. The subtle movement caused her cloak to gap open in the front. The creamy whiteness of her chest taunted him in the near darkness of the carriage. There was no denying it—he now suffered incredible discomfort from a raging erection that refused to behave. He hadn't felt this way since he was sixteen and still a randy virgin.

Thankfully, he didn't have to answer, as the carriage slowed to a stop. Though he expected the streets to be void of sound, jovial laughter and the noise of shifting hooves of horses greeted them from outside the coach's warm cocoon. Inside, with Daphne sitting across from him, he still had her all to himself, even if he couldn't touch. Once they left the carriage, any interloper who dared threaten to converse, much less look at her, would face his wrath.

Pity the miscreant who wanted her attention.

He closed his eyes and exhaled. He was worse off than he thought. He was contemplating bodily harm to some faceless person who hadn't even done anything.

"Paul," she said a little bit more loudly. "Are you all right?"

No, he wasn't all right. He'd lost his mind several London street blocks ago. "Yes, I'm fine."

"You seem out of sorts. You have ever since we left Pembrooke House." The soft words held enough of a lilt that they carried across the coach. It had to be his imagination, but they seemed to kiss his cheek.

He could only reach one conclusion—he was a bloody fool.

"I apologize for my earlier behavior." He'd said the words hoping they'd relieve his guilt and restore his confidence as a proper duke. Instead, he felt as if he were a sniveling child, one who apologized without any real remorse.

He wasn't really sorry for teasing and playing with her at Pembrooke House. Her entire face had been alight with sheer delight, then it slowly softened to an exquisite emotion that could only be described as desire when he drew her dress down her arms.

He was surely going to hell for seducing an innocent.

Biting one lip, she tried to hide her smile. It made her even more beautiful. "You seem to apologize frequently around me. Am I a bad influence?"

The silver-pewter of her eyes flashed with laughter and a little something that made the distance between them spark with sexual tension. Whatever this was between them electrified him. Every particle of his body throbbed with an acute need to gather her in his arms and kiss her until she begged for more. He tightened both hands around the edge of the seat to keep from reaching for her. The more he squeezed, the more the leather squealed in protest.

What was it about her that made her so irresistible? He'd been with other beautiful women who were definitely more accomplished as seductresses. But her innate grace and sense of self captivated him. Naturally, a rake such as himself would be drawn to someone as pure as her. Wasn't that what rakes did? Despoil perfect flowers. He ran his hand over his face again hoping to clear every lascivious thought. He'd not allow his own dirty hands to touch her, not after what he'd done tonight.

This evening he would be her protector. He'd be her friend. They'd find her journal, then she'd help ease the distance between Pembrooke and him. His job would be finished. He'd have no other reason to be in her company alone. After he returned her home this evening, he'd check on her tomorrow, wish her a happy Christmas, and then wait for her brother to return to town that evening. He'd call on Pembrooke the next day and explain what had happened. Pembrooke would thank him and extend an invitation for a drink, where they'd mend their disagreements. Perhaps they'd even drink coffee and read the papers at White's again. Paul would even invite Alex and Claire to dine with him. He'd invite Somerton and Emma also. Once Somerton saw that Alex had given up his grievances, Somerton would follow suit.

If only it'd be that simple. He'd managed to alienate his friend Nicholas St. Mauer, the Earl of Somerton, when they were young at university. Paul had played deep at hazard one night without the funds, and Somerton had signed for his debt. When Paul had written his father for the money, the duke ignored him.

He'd alienated his friend over a damn gambling debt.

Another loss. He gritted his teeth. He hoped Daphne's adventure in London would be the catalyst to mend the wounds he'd inflicted that destroyed their friendships all those years ago. By helping her, he would make the three of them friends again. That's all he had to remember.

He couldn't think of the gentle swell of her perfect breasts ever again.

She tilted her head and regarded him. "Paul, what are we doing? We've been sitting here for several minutes." She raised her hand to rap her knuckles against the coach roof signaling she was ready to depart.

"Before we exit, I have something for you." He cleared his throat in a poor attempt to purge his thoughts. She lowered her hand when he handed her a half mask that would conceal her eyes and nose. One half was painted black and the other white. Clear crystals and silver foil neatly lined the edges and the openings for the eyes. The mask was elaborate, but the ties that would secure it around her head were simple black ribbons. With her dark hair, it would be difficult to see the ribbons, thus giving the illusion she was a Venetian temptress looking for a lover during Carnival.

"It's beautiful," she whispered. Her fingers tenderly skated over every inch of the mask. "What is it?"

He let out an unsteady breath. She caressed the mask like a lover. "It's a Columbina mask. My mother brought it home from Venice the last time she visited. I want you to wear it tonight. It'll disguise you. No one will dare approach you with me by your side."

"Thank you. That's clever thinking," she offered. "Will you help me put it on?"

Holding the mask to her face, she turned away from him until she was barely seated on the bench cushion. He reached to tie the ribbon, and their fingers entangled. The urge to pull her against him while he inhaled her sweet scent almost overpowered him. Suddenly, her fingers tightened against his, and he hissed.

"You'll need to take off your gloves to tie the ribbons, I'm afraid."

She *should* be afraid, as he was very afraid. Afraid he'd kiss her in this very carriage and never stop until they were both lost in each other's arms.

"Of course." Passion threatened to explode inside him. His own words sounded guttural.

He made quick work of removing his gloves. As he raised his hands to tie the ribbons, his fingers shook. He took a deep breath and commanded himself to relax. In seconds, the mask was secure.

When she twisted around to face him, he felt as if he'd been punched in the gut. Once again, she refuted his claim that he could manage anything.

Describing her as an ethereal creature was like describing the moon as a circle in the sky. Her loveliness was heavenly. Her skin seemed to shimmer in the faint glow of the carriage lantern. The mask did indeed disguise her, but he knew the hidden depths of her beauty. Her expressive eyes and the familiar tilt of her lips spoke a language that only he could understand.

With a shake of his head, Paul tried to dismiss such fanciful thoughts. "Are you ready?"

"In a moment." She scooted close to him. "About this morning, I meant what I said about fighting to win the bid for the estate. But I want you to know that I'll do everything in my power to help you with my brother. It's reassuring that you're here with me." The smile on her lips was radiant.

"Of course," he said. "There's no place I'd rather be than with you here tonight, my dear friend."

If possible, her smile became brighter. It reminded him of sunshine peeking around a cloud. "Whatever happened today won't impact how we deal with each other tonight."

With a deep breath, he tapped the window with his knuckles. Immediately, the door opened, and he jumped out. As soon as Daphne placed her slim hand in his, Paul came to a realization that gave him some, but not nearly enough, relief from his complete befuddlement.

All of his discomfort with Daphne could be attributed to his agreement to be friends.

What a ludicrous bargain.

How could they be friends if all he could think about was seducing her?

Chapter Eleven

❧

Instead of feeling ridiculous in the mask, Daphne felt like a siren. The delicate crystals embedded in the papier-mâché were a delightful touch. For this one night she could act like her heart desired without anyone ever knowing her identity or her true self.

Elegantly tall, with an innate grace, Paul escorted her to the entrance of the Reynolds Gambling Establishment, where the doors magically opened, eager to do the bidding of the Duke of Southart.

Daphne understood the exact feeling.

"Good evening, Your Grace." The majordomo smiled, then puffed out his chest for a proper bow. His smile brightened even more when his gaze settled on Daphne. "Lady Moonbeam, what a delight and surprise to see you again."

Daphne bowed her head slightly in acknowledgment but didn't utter a word. Though it was Christmas Eve, every table had patrons playing, and the boisterous noise of the gambling operation was almost deafening.

Like meerkats popping from the ground in every direction, men lifted their heads from their cards or dice to stare. Slowly, the sound in the room died. Initially the patrons' attention focused on Paul, but soon all eyes were riveted to her. She cast a quick glance down to ensure that her breasts hadn't made an unannounced visit. Thankfully, everything was in order. As the men still stared, she allowed herself a quick perusal of the room.

That was the beauty of the mask. She could see them, but they had no idea who she was. She saw several of her friends' brothers in attendance. At another table, there were several peers who had no business playing cards of any sorts, as their estates were nearly bankrupt.

Before she could continue her study, Paul pulled her close, and she shifted her gaze to his.

"You little vixen. I believe you're enjoying this." With his thumb and forefinger, he gently clasped her chin and tilted her face. "I may have to challenge every man here for your affections."

She couldn't help but laugh at his statement. "I never took you for the jealous type."

"Generally, I'm not. However, with you here, I am a little put out." The laughter in his voice made her smile. "I'm usually the one they're gawking at." He tightened his arm around her waist, bringing her closer to his warmth. He lowered his mouth to her ear. "They're jealous of me."

"Your Grace, what is your preference this evening?" the majordomo asked.

"Perhaps a private room. We won't be long." Paul pressed his lips to the pulse point on her neck below her ear. The blatant move marked his claim that she was his to the throng. Though the crowd also keenly watched Paul, he gave no hint of disquiet. "My lady and I are looking for the boy named Garland."

"The little bugger was here earlier begging for scraps. He's partial to Elsie, one of the cooks. If anyone knows where he is, she will." The majordomo rocked back on his heels. "He didn't steal anything, did he? He's been known to have sticky fingers, and if the boy has taken something of yours, Mr. Reynolds will take restitution out of the little bugger's hide."

Daphne sucked in an angry blast of air. Granted, she'd been livid at Garland for stealing her journal, but she'd never strike him as punishment. Such a barbaric thought immediately caused her ire to rise.

"Which Mr. Reynolds?" she asked, disguising the anger in her voice. Once she discovered the correct brother's identity, she'd give him a lecture that would make the devil himself blush.

Paul took her hand in his and intertwined their fingers. With their hands still clasped, he brought hers to his mouth for a kiss. "We just want to talk to the lad about a mutual acquaintance."

"We don't allow women here, but since she's with you, Your Grace, and it's Lady Moonbeam, I'm sure an exception can be made since you won't be long," the majordomo said. "If you'll follow me, Your Grace."

With quick steps that belied a man the majordomo's size, the man escorted them to the same room they were in last night. After he saw to their comfort, he left.

"Your misstatement was excellent thinking. That was brilliant to say we were looking for someone that Garland might know." Daphne settled into the leather chair closest to the door. When Garland entered, she would not let him escape. Besides, it gave an excellent view of Paul's lean but muscular form.

He arched one perfect eyebrow. "Are you accusing me of lying?"

She shook her head. "I believe the term is 'economical use of words.'" She tapped her chin with one index finger. "Or is it 'terminological inexactitude'?"

Before she could finish, a brisk knock sounded on the

door. Without blinking, Paul kept his gaze locked on hers. "Enter."

A young woman about Daphne's age crossed the doorway and curtsied. Her clothing appeared neat and clean, but the apron tied around her neck was colored with a fine dusting of flour. "Your Grace?"

"Yes," Paul answered. "And you are?"

"Elsie Qulin," she offered. "I'm one of the cooks here. I understand you wish to speak to Garland. Normally, he's always underfoot, but tonight he's gone home. He wants to be available for Christmas deliveries tomorrow. The butcher that supplies the Reynolds likes to use him when things are busy."

"And where exactly is home?" Daphne asked.

Elsie's gaze bobbed between Paul and Daphne. "Beggin' your pardon, my lady. I didn't see you there. Garland won't tell me. But I expect it's in Seven Dials." She bowed her head. "The boy's had a rough time of it. I don't think he has any family."

Daphne's eyes widened. No telling what kind of dismal lodging the lad might find from the fiercely cold weather.

"Can you find him for us?" Paul poured a glass of champagne and handed it to Daphne. "Take a sip, Moonbeam. You're as white as a sheet."

Elsie narrowed her eyes suspiciously. "I must ask, what would you be wanting with Garland?"

"He has something that belongs to me." Daphne didn't wait for Paul to answer. "All I want is for him to return it. There won't be any punishment, I promise."

"What is it you think he's taken?" Elsie asked.

"A book of sorts," Paul answered. He sat on the arm of Daphne's chair and slung his arm across the back. "Moonbeam and I want it back. Anything she wants, I try to get for her." Like an attentive lover, he gently played with her hair. "Can you find him and make him return it to us?"

"For all that's holy, he stole from a duke," she muttered before she nodded her head. "Aye. You have nothing to worry about, Lady Moonbeam. I'll get your book back for ye." The cook looked to the floor and shuffled her feet. "Is there anything personal in it?"

"Well, yes—" Daphne struggled with how much to divulge to the woman.

The most salacious smile appeared on Paul's lips. When Daphne started to blush, he straightened his cuffs. "My darling Moonbeam keeps a thorough record of her titillating social calendar. She's afraid she'll miss an important event and offend the powers that be in the demimonde. There's nothing else important in the book."

If only that were true.

Elsie returned Paul's smile as if enchanted. "Thank the merciful heavens it's nothing more than a calendar, Your Grace. You see, I've taught Garland how to read and write. Took to it like a fish swimming in water." She heaved a huge sigh. "He's developed quite a business of selling tidbits and pieces of gossip to Mr. Richmond. I'd hate for him to cause you any distress."

"It causes me distress that Moonbeam is out of sorts. Would five guineas make it worth your while to ensure that the book is returned promptly without anyone knowing the contents?" Paul asked. He stood and poured Daphne another glass of champagne and handed her the glass, then settled back on the arm of the chair, completely relaxed.

She wasn't even aware she'd finished the first glass. When the cook had mentioned Richmond, everything within her had revolted in horror. Mr. Richmond of *The Midnight Cryer* could ruin her with a single swipe of his pen.

"Indeed, it would, Your Grace. That's very generous. With that amount, perhaps I can get the boy off the streets,"

Elsie said. "Can you come the day after tomorrow? I most probably won't see the scamp until the day after Christmas."

By then, Alex would be back in town. Her brother would never allow her to leave the house for the Reynolds once the family returned. She bit her lip and willed herself to summon every ounce of confidence she possessed. She was her own woman now and could do what she wanted when she wanted. Besides her plans for Aubrey's Place, and leasing a house, she needed to secure her own carriage, which would require groomsmen and a driver. Her future household would require even more servants. Such was the cost of independence, and she'd spend whatever was required to have her freedom.

"That will work, Elsie." As soon as Daphne said the words, her faith in her own abilities doubled. She would control her own life from now on.

Paul cleared his throat. "If Moonbeam is detained, I assume you'll give the book to me."

"Of course, Your Grace." Elsie nodded. "I must be getting back to the kitchen."

The cook turned to leave.

"Miss Qulin," Daphne said. "Since you're helping me with my lost book, if you and Garland need anything . . . any help, I would be honored to offer assistance. I'll be staffing my household within the next week or so."

"Is His Grace setting you up as his mistress?" Elsie asked without a hint of embarrassment. "Lady Moonbeam, I don't carry tales, and frankly, I don't care who you are. But I need to be certain of steady employment. You understand."

Daphne gasped at the crudeness of Elsie's question, and her cheeks immediately flushed. "No. I'm setting up my own household. As long as you work hard and are honest, you and Garland would have a place with me."

"Thank you for your Christmas spirit, Lady Moonbeam. I might just take you up on your offer." Elsie smiled and her eyes shone with an undeniable love for the boy. "I want to keep Garland off the streets, and a household away from here might be the answer to my prayers. It'd keep him away from the gambling hells and Seven Dials."

In response, Daphne reached for her hand and squeezed. She marveled at the strength in the cook's hand. No matter how strong on the outside, they were all weak when it came to people they cared about. Her simple offer gave Elsie something to look forward to, and Elsie's gratitude provided Daphne with something much more—the knowledge that she could unleash a power within herself that the universe would envy. She could make a difference in someone's life. What she couldn't do for Alice, she could do to help others who found life's journey too difficult to bear on their own.

Paul made quick work of the distance between them. "Excellent, Elsie. I'll meet you the day after tomorrow." He pulled a coin from his pocket. "A token of our good faith."

"Thank you, Your Grace. I report to work midafternoon. I'll have the boy and the book for you." Without a by-your-leave, Elsie turned and quietly shut the door.

Two days were an eternity to wait before she had her journal back in her possession. Never again would she allow it to leave her sight. "I need to search for him. If I'm not successful, then I'll come with you to meet Elsie."

"Once Pembrooke arrives in town"—Paul set his glass down—"he won't allow you within a mile of this place. I'll have two of my groomsmen set up a watch outside the butcher's shop. Once they have him, one will come and find me. I'll get your journal."

"I can't let you or your staff attend me on Christmas." She shook her head vehemently. "I'll ask Tait."

"Moonbeam, once Garland sees you, he'll run. He won't suspect my groomsmen. They won't wear their Southart livery."

"That might work." Though it wasn't her intent to obfuscate or confuse the matter, she would be present at the Reynolds the day after tomorrow if Paul and his groomsmen weren't successful. With a plan in place to find Garland, she allowed herself to relax.

Now there were more pressing opportunities before her, and she planned to enjoy them.

Like spending time alone with Paul. Tonight made her believe the possibilities were endless. For now, all her worries had popped like the bubbles in her champagne glass. It was time to celebrate, and she planned to do just that.

"Are you ready, Your Grace?" The purr in her own voice made her feel like a Cyprian who was ready to take control of the night. Never in her life had she ever felt this desirable. No doubt the cause was her mysterious mask and the magical man beside her.

"After you, Moonbeam." The smile on his face was pure wickedness. "I would hate for you to find another man to escort you home."

"I only go home with one specific man when I leave the Reynolds," she offered.

"Let's keep it that way, shall we?" The sensual promise in his voice matched hers. He opened the door with a flourish that the Prince Regent's head footman would no doubt envy. Once she was in the hallway, he offered her his arm, and they walked together toward the main entrance.

At the end of the hall, a man leaned against the doorjamb to the main gambling room. With his back to them, he appeared to be surveying the room, looking for someone. One of the Reynolds brothers stood with him. When Reynolds made a move their way, Paul whisked open a door and gently led her inside. He immediately followed and locked the door behind them. Surrounded in darkness except for one lone candle that burned on the window ledge, Daphne felt his warm breath tickle the back of her neck. He pulled her close, her back pressed against his hard chest.

"Martin Richmond and Thomas Reynolds. I think it best if we avoid them for a few minutes," he whispered. He released her from his embrace.

She grumbled at the loss of his heat—at the loss of him.

Without acknowledging her dissatisfaction, Paul turned his attention to the door and bent his head, then pressed his ear to the panel. The low ebb of two men conversing came closer. With the stealth and sleekness that reminded her of a large predator cat, Paul closed the scant distance between them and leaned close. "We'll stay here until they leave."

She nodded, then strained to hear the conversation. The thick door muffled the words. The men had stopped directly in front and didn't appear to be leaving. She chanced a glance around the room that could only be described as tiny. It appeared to be a storage pantry of some sort. Silver platters, bowls, eating utensils, crystal wineglasses, and compotes were displayed like neat little soldiers ready for service when the call came for their elegance to grace the gambling hell's famous private dining rooms.

Unhurriedly, a slight grin tugged the corners of Paul's mouth. Good lord, but the man was handsome on so many different levels. Physically, he was a masterpiece of toned muscles, no doubt attributed to his love of riding. When he'd held her in his arms, she melted every time, and the attractiveness of his face could keep her enthralled for decades. Simply put, he was the type of man who would age beautifully and still have women fawning over him when he was eighty.

The clouds cleared and the light from a brilliant moon glided through the window. The reflecting snow enhanced the moon's glow. The light kissed his face and illuminated the liveliness of his eyes. If she wasn't mistaken, there was real affection reflected in their depths.

Daphne ignored the qualms and doubts that had started to sprout like weeds after a warm summer rain. Tonight, she was a caterpillar emerging from her cocoon. The man of her desires was before her, and she was Lady Moonbeam, a woman who knew her destiny, a woman who would pursue whatever this was between them.

Tenderly, she reached for his cheek where the radiance of the night's glow embraced him. The sharp angles that defined the contours of his face caused a wonderful shimmer to course through her body and left her slightly breathless. He leaned toward her and closed his eyes at her touch. She brushed her lips against his, then withdrew for just a moment.

In the moonlight, she could see his face clearly. His features were impassive, but his eyes told another story. Along with the remains of his earlier warmth and fondness, desire blazed.

Without hesitation, she touched his lips with hers again. In response, he cupped her cheeks, and a slight moan escaped him. He returned her kiss with one that grew bolder and sweeter in its intensity. She needed more of him, so it was only natural that she open her lips. Without hesitation, he accepted her invitation. As his tongue mated with hers, she reached inside his evening coat and unbuttoned his waistcoat. In response, he deepened their kiss. Emboldened, she slid her hands up his chest. The soft linen of his shirt didn't stop the radiant heat of his body from surrounding her. Desperate for more, she melted against him.

She ran her palms slowly inch by inch across the cloth

that covered his hot skin. The contours of his upper body were more magnificent than she could have ever imagined, and the sinewy cords of muscles fascinated her. As she traced each solid rib and the breadth of his chest, Daphne felt like a cartographer, an explorer discovering each sensual swell and rise beneath her fingers.

When she rubbed her palms over his small, firm nipples, he moaned again. He suckled her bottom lip before playfully taking a nip. With little warning, he took possession of her mouth again, and in a matching move, one of his hands crept to the lowered bodice of her gown.

As his tongue stroked hers, he gently tugged the edge of her bodice downward, forcing the stays to lower as well. Her groan was swallowed by his continuing kiss. She ached for him to touch her breasts—so tender from desire.

"Touch me," she whispered, practically begging.

When the cool air hit her nipples, they tightened into hard pebbles. Desperate to find relief, she arched into his hand where his clever fingers found one breast. He cupped it in his hand, and she whimpered, the pleasure so acute.

"Is this what you meant by 'everything,' Moonbeam?" he whispered as he tugged her gown and stays lower. In the back of her desire-muddled mind, Daphne remembered where they were and who was outside, so she resisted the urge to cry out for more. With his hand, he explored the sensitive skin until he reached her nipple.

Powerless to hold it in, she gasped.

"I feel it, too, Daphne," he whispered before he lowered his head and gently sucked her nipple into his mouth. The agony of the pleasure was almost too much. Somehow, she swallowed the need to cry out, but let out a low whimper. In answer, he continued to attend to her swollen nipple by sucking until she thought she couldn't bear the exquisite torture anymore. As if he realized her breaking point, he gentled his kiss, then teased it with his tongue. He repeated the pattern as he pulled her waist tighter against him. The hard, swollen length of his erection pressed against her.

Unable to resist, she moved against him. It wasn't enough. Her senses were whipped into a frenzy of longing—of wanting to touch him. Every part of her seemed charged waiting for an explosion. Wanting relief, she pushed harder.

But she had no idea what relief. Every kiss, every touch, every taste made her want more and more.

"Moonbeam"—his lips trailed up her neck leaving heat and desire behind—"what do you want?"

"I told you. Everything." She leaned her head back as far as it would go to give him more access to the sensitive skin.

"Do you trust me?" His lips teased as they tasted.

She drew away, and the intensity of his gaze made her feel as if she were on fire. "For tonight," she answered.

He chuckled. "I'm happy one of us does, because I'm not certain I trust myself. Not with you here in this moment."

They stared at each other until they reached a silent accord. She reached behind and untied her mask. She didn't need it with him. She'd shed her invisibility and show him everything about herself. Drawing close, she took his hand in hers. With infinite care, she raised her skirt with their entwined fingers.

Once the skirt was past her knees, he brought her close as he pushed his leg between hers, spreading them apart. Without breaking contact, Daphne pushed against his thigh. She relaxed slightly, then repeated the motion again. There was a promise of something deeper, some sort of resolution. Driven and almost frantic, she continued to push. Tingles of pleasure burst free, then ricocheted through her body.

But that only made her want him more, and only he

could provide her with the key that would unlock this obsession.

Paul lifted one of her legs to his hip. Instinctively, she wrapped it tightly around his backside. The position allowed her to grind herself harder to pursue her pleasure, and she moaned in gratitude.

"Slowly, sweetheart," he whispered in her ear. "It's not a race. Enjoy the journey." His tongue traced the curl of her outer ear.

By now, she was panting and hot. Forget the ricocheting. Wild need careened through her. Paul pulled her closer as she ground herself against him. Pleasure twined itself through every limb. She slowed her movements and allowed herself to experience every nuance of the exquisite sensation.

Paul took possession of her mouth, and she was sure he'd discover her every secret. If he continued pleasuring her this way, she'd gladly give him every single one. When she gasped for air, he kissed his way up to her ear again.

"If we were in my carriage or at my home, you could use something else besides my knee to find your release." As they moved together, he cupped her bottom tight. He nestled his nose right beside her ear. "You could use my finger, my mouth, then perhaps you'd let me use my tongue."

With a vision of him kissing that place on her body, she pushed her center harder against him, then surrendered to the waves of pleasure that pounded through her, congregating and combining into a vortex. Her whole body felt weightless and suspended a thousand feet in the air, then dropped. But instead of breaking, she dissolved into sensations that exploded through every inch of her as she whispered his name.

Unable to hold herself up, she collapsed against him, struggling to catch her breath. Her heartbeat still raced but slowly started to return to its natural rhythm. Paul held her close, placing light kisses on her cheeks, the tip of her nose, and, finally, her tender mouth.

"That was an amazing sight, Moonbeam." The smooth richness of his voice caressed her as he gently rubbed the back of her neck. "You shattering into a million pieces while I held you in my arms. I don't think I'll ever forget this night."

Daphne might have fantasized about making love to him, but truthfully, she knew very little of the act. Though she was a little bashful, she summoned the courage to glance at his face. "Is it always like that? I thought people screamed and howled in passion?"

"It's always delightful if you're treated well and with respect." His expression was almost tender. There certainly wasn't any judgment in his eyes. "To answer your last question, I never scream and howl." He lifted one brow as if determining the suitability of a table wine. "I've never seen the need. Besides, it's gauche."

If anyone saw him now, they'd perceive him as the most arrogant duke in all of England. But through his haughty veneer she recognized he was protecting himself.

Perhaps he thought she'd demand an offer of marriage because of the intimacy they'd just shared. He needn't fear. With Paul's history with her brother, it was highly doubtful both men would ever grow comfortable or come to an agreement if she married Paul. Alex was too protective of her. However, she'd do everything in her power to help the men find their way back to some sort of friendship.

Was she actually thinking of marrying him? She gently shook her head. Her mask must possess some special power that made people forget reality.

"It's late. We should leave." She carefully placed some distance between them and swept her gaze downward.

There was enough light from the moon that she could clearly see his pantaloons.

Bloody hell. Mortified, she clamped her eyes shut.

Where she'd rubbed herself against his leg, a huge wet spot the size of a hothouse rose in full bloom appeared. Heat spread like wildfire from her chest to her face. Quickly, she adjusted her stays and gown to hide her breasts. She bent her head and placed her hand on her forehead as she struggled to come up with an apology.

Excuse me, but your pantaloons are ruined because I acted like a harlot in your arms.

If only she *were* a moonbeam. When a cloud covered the moon, she could disappear like a puff of air.

There were no other options at this point. She'd just apologize and be done with it.

She caught his gaze, and the effect caused her to battle another round of heated cheeks. "I ruined your garment," she whispered. "I'll have Tait order you a new pair."

He bent his head in the direction she pointed, and the despicable oaf had the audacity to laugh. And it just wasn't a chuckle. It turned into an uncontrollable fit of mirth. To make matters worse, it was the truly wicked type—silent bouts of laughter. Unable to take any more humiliation, she donned her mask and made her way for the door.

In two seconds, she was whisked around and found herself in his arms again. He buried his face against her neck, where his irritating laughter slowly dissolved. "I'm sorry." Making a last stand, a renegade snort of laughter escaped. He pulled away, biting his lip to keep from dissolving into laughter again. "Sweetheart, if you could have seen how flushed your face was."

Another assault of heat bludgeoned every inch of her. Under no circumstances would she tolerate his mocking. She'd not allow anyone to treat her this way—not now. Not after she'd found the courage to look deep inside and discovered that she—Daphne Hallworth—deserved to find happiness.

Without warning, she pushed him away and glared. He stumbled backward but elegantly caught his balance. He stood frozen before her. An immediate somberness descended between them. He drew a deep breath and regarded her with a seriousness she'd never seen from him.

She'd not back down. Even if she lost his regard, she'd not withdraw within herself again. Livid at his behavior and her response, she allowed her thoughts to spill into the room. "You're not a gentleman. My inexperience isn't for your amusement."

"You know my reputation." Though he whispered, the curtness in his voice was unmistakable. "I'm not a *gentleman* and never claimed to be."

"That's an excuse." She practically spit the words.

Neither of them would break eye contact.

After a moment, he bent his head and rubbed the back of his neck. "You're right. I apologize. I'm at a loss here as to how to act or what to say, so bear with me. I want to learn. I want to be a gentleman."

The earnestness in the words caused her heart to trip in her chest.

He cleared his throat and looked out the window. She waited for his inevitable glib retort that would change the subject.

After a long silence, he surprised her when he captured her gaze. "As a child, I developed this nasty habit, one which served me well until now. It'd helped defuse my fear of retribution and made my embarrassment manageable when my father would summon me to deliver a punishment, normally a blistering, then a lecture. I'd laugh silently just to infuriate him all over again."

"Your father hit you?" She tried to keep her voice calm, but nothing infuriated her more than an adult hitting a defenseless child. "That's horrible."

"He stopped after Robbie intervened once." He cleared his throat. "But if I laughed, my father would become so livid that he'd forget why he wanted to punish me in the first place. He'd throw me out of the room just to get me out of his sight." He shrugged his shoulders. "It'd saved countless confrontations. It was a stupid reaction, and I'm sorry."

The pain in his eyes tore a hole in her wall of defense.

"I thought perhaps—" He exhaled. "I thought you might have become disgusted with what we'd done or disgusted with me."

She shook her head. "I found it remarkable. I'm sorry, too."

"You have nothing to apologize for. I responded poorly, proving I'm a lout, but, hopefully, a trainable one." His voice deepened. "May I hold you?" The words so low she didn't know if she'd heard them correctly. He moved closer. "Please."

She nodded.

Gently, as if she were fragile treasure, he took her in his arms. "What we shared was extraordinary. When I sensed your arousal, it made me burn." He held her closer and his engorged length pressed against her stomach. "I still burn for you, Moonbeam. You're like an affliction, and I'm not certain I want to be cured."

The tenderness in his words extinguished her earlier indignation. She blinked slowly, struggling to understand what had just happened. He brushed his lips against hers, the touch slow and infinitely gentle. Immediately, she felt cherished—wanted.

Slowly, his endearing roguish smile appeared. "Regarding my clothing, don't worry. These will be saved and on permanent display for my enjoyment. They'll always remind me of our night together."

"That's ridiculous," she protested and pulled away.

As only a duke was wont to do, he ignored her outburst and held out his arm for her to take. "It's time to go. No one is out in the hallway. Let's gather your cloak and my coat, then be on our way. After you, my darling Lady Moonbeam."

Chapter Twelve

Dancing with only one heeled shoe would have been less awkward than the ride back to Pembrooke House. Neither Daphne nor Paul said a word. Both were obviously lost in thought. She ought to tell him there was no harm done this evening. Yet she found it difficult to start the conversation that she expected nothing from him except his friendship. Even if she wanted more, it was a waste of time to dwell on circumstances that couldn't be changed.

She straightened her shoulders when the Southart carriage pulled to a stop in front of her house. Apart from them and the few patrons that haunted the gambling hells, London appeared completely deserted. No one would know Paul had escorted her home without a chaperone except for the ever-present Tait, who currently sat in the driving box.

Daphne swallowed her trepidation and pushed forward. She wanted to discuss the logistics of their next meeting at the Reynolds. By then, her family would have returned to town. By her calculations, her mother would arrive at Alex and Claire's estate, Pemhill, by noon tomorrow, Christmas Day. Within that hour, Alex would ride ahead of the rest of the family to find his missing sister. If Daphne had possessed a little more forethought, she should have sent a note to arrive at noon with instructions not to spoil his holiday, as she was perfectly happy and quite content on her own. Of course, Alex didn't need to be privy to the fact that Paul had kept her in excellent company.

Staring down at the carriage floor and clearly pensive, Paul rested his elbows on his strong legs with a grimace marking his handsome face. The stillness of the night was broken by the jangling of the horses' bridles as the beasts shook their heads—the sound reminiscent of Christmas bells.

She never wanted the nights to end when she was with Paul. He was fast turning into a favorite habit, one that would eventually lead to heartache when they parted company for good. It couldn't be helped. She needed him, and she needed all her wits about her if she wanted to convince Paul to take her to the Reynolds the day after tomorrow if they didn't find the journal before then. Whatever happened, she had to find Garland and retrieve her diary.

"Paul?" Her gentle query had the intended effect. When he lifted his head, it forced him to leave his thoughts. "Would you care to come in? I believe it best if we discuss our return to the Reynolds."

He nodded once. "It's best if we have this discussion inside. You're not going to approve of what I'm going to share."

With those cryptic words, he tapped a knuckle on the door. Almost instantaneously, a handsome liveried footman opened the door.

Well, there was one thing she could always count on. The Duke of Southart was never predictable—in either his actions or behavior.

Paul's acceptance to spend additional time with Daphne was a bad idea—of the worst kind.

Why in the devil did he agree to come inside? Pure torture, her swollen red lips resembled the color of early summer strawberries.

Strawberries were his absolute weakness. Within the halls of Southart House, his ducal estate, he was notorious for eating every single one in sight. He took a deep breath to tame the raging passion that still coursed through his veins. His cock throbbed from the constant need to find a release from his desire. When was the last time he'd suffered this type of misery? He had no memory of aching this way, not since he was an adolescent.

Indeed, this had been a terrible mistake.

Across the salon, Daphne walked toward him, holding two glasses of brandy. Without saying a word, he memorized every graceful step. She resembled a dancer whose every nuanced move enchanted those lucky enough to witness such perfection.

How pathetic was he? He was turning into a romantic fool.

She'd chosen the rotgut brandy that his father had worshiped. *Devil take him.* However, Paul was the Duke of Southart now, and whatever he damned well wanted to drink he would. The blurry image of his father's fury disappeared like dying embers in a fireplace. It was Christmas Eve, and Paul relished the idea of spending it in the lovely company of a beautiful lady—his Moonbeam.

Daphne handed him a glass, then settled beside him. The movement caused her memorable lavender scent to waft gently over him. He inhaled deeply, and immediately, the memory of holding her in his arms as she reached her climax pounded through him with the force of an explosion that could rearrange the universe.

Completely unaware of her effect on his sanity, she studied the brandy as she swirled the liquid around the glass. "The day after tomorrow, if your groomsmen don't find Garland, I'll meet you outside the Reynolds. Then we'll go in together and find the boy."

Without taking a sip of the foul brew, Paul placed his glass on the table beside him. He turned and rested his arm on the back of the sofa. Unable to resist her soft hair, he gently played with a few silken strands that had come loose when she'd taken off her mask.

"The risks are too great, Daphne." Tenderly, he stroked her hair.

Daphne settled in the crook of his arm and closed her eyes, enjoying his tender attention. "The risks are too great if I *don't* accompany you," she whispered.

"What might those be, sweetheart?" He wanted her lulled into a sense of comfort and security with him. Whatever she feared, he wanted her to tell him so he could eliminate the threat.

Like waking from a dream, she opened her eyes and turned to face him. When her knees touched his, she didn't pull away.

The rhythmic clench of her hands in the delicate fabric of her skirts betrayed her turmoil. "My journal contains my private thoughts. You see"—her voice dropped to a low hum, one that required he bend his head closer to hear what she was saying—"there are letters that I wouldn't want anyone to see. Particularly my mother and brother."

"What kind of letters?" He traced his finger along the curve of her chin, and she lifted her gaze to his. "Tell me," he coaxed.

Her lovely gray eyes glistened with tears, and it practically ripped his heart out of his chest. He kept his eyes locked with hers and her delicate chin in his hands. She blinked slowly and swallowed, an effort designed to keep her tears at bay.

"I've written scathing letters to my sister in that journal. There's no denying it's morbid, but I was livid with

Alice after she died." She looked away from his gaze. "If Alex or my mother see what I've written, it would tear open every wound that Alice's death ever inflicted."

"Why were you so angry with her?" He took Daphne's hand in his and squeezed.

She shook her head once. "Please don't ask, as I won't answer."

"Fair enough." He had to tread lightly, since there was unspeakable grief and pain in her sister's passing. He had no idea if she was aware that Alice had taken her own life. Paul knew only because Pembrooke, who had been beyond all reason when his sister had died, had spoken of it that miserable day years ago. "Let me share something."

She nodded.

"I have a small ebony box sitting on my desk. It's innocuous but serves a very specific purpose. Sometimes when my grief won't leave me be, I imagine putting it in that box on my desk. I can ride or work without the overwhelming weight. When I'm ready to return to it, it's safe and waiting for me."

She drew a deep breath, then regarded him. It wasn't skepticism in her eyes but hopefulness. "I've never thought of that before. If I'm enjoying myself at a party or with friends, I feel guilty for not grieving."

"I've experienced the same. It sounds silly, but if you try that sometime, it might help," he said. "Whenever you speak of Alice, I can't help but compare it to my loss of Robbie."

"In some ways," she said hesitantly and squeezed his hand in return.

"Different in others, too." Oddly, the idea of sharing his grief and the truth of his family's regard for him with Daphne was something he wanted and hoped would be cathartic for her. "When Robbie passed, I thought I'd lost everything. I can honestly say he was the only person in

the world who loved me for who I was, even if he wanted
me to become a better person. Only someone who loves
you takes such an interest. I see you as having the same
type of love for Alice as Robbie had for me."

She rubbed her thumb over his, the repetitive movement
soothing. "Didn't your father love you?"

His chest tightened at the question. To keep from exposing too much, he wanted to look away, but he forced
himself to hold her gaze. How many times had he asked
himself the same question only to arrive at the same conclusion? "I don't think so, Daph."

Her expression clouded. "Oh, Paul"—rancor laced her
voice, and her eyes had darkened to a shade that reminded
him of a torrential thunderstorm—"what a despicable
man." She shook her head slowly. "My father was distant.
He never had much to do with Alice or me, but I never
once doubted he loved me. Every child deserves that security growing up."

The emotion on her face reminded him of something
he'd only seen once—Robbie's fury when he'd discovered
Paul had been beaten by his father over the brandy escapade. She was angry for him. Such a look could only be
described as "heady," and it caused the steady beat of his
heart to trip. Just like she had been the champion for that
magpie years ago, she'd have been his champion against
his father. "May I share something with you?"

She nodded.

He hadn't felt this close to another human being since
Robbie passed. The idea that he would share so much of
himself was uncharted territory. But he'd not shy away
from this chance to become closer to her.

"That day you saw me at Langham Hall with the duke,
I was discussing a new project. I envision starting a hospital to care for people stricken by rheumatic fever. I plan
to recruit the most brilliant minds in the field, from every

continent in the world. If they are working for the comfort of the patients and making strides in eradicating the disease, then I want to employ them."

"That's wonderful." Her breathtaking eyes flashed with an enthusiasm that was simply intoxicating. "With you and your duchy behind the effort, it'll be a smashing success."

Easily, she could keep him mesmerized for days. Months or years would be a closer match, but he wasn't even certain that would be long enough.

"At some point, I'll expand the hospital into other buildings, each designed to treat an illness that seems insurmountable. With today's medicine and the brilliantly trained minds coming out of the top universities, there will be cures for the dreaded diseases that plague us." Unable to contain his excitement, he stood. "I'm hosting a charity soiree. The invitations were sent out over a month ago. I've invited your whole family, but no one has responded."

His first inclination was to offer a charming grin, but he thought better of it. Instead, he gave her his honesty. "I hope you'll come."

"I'd like to come." The tenderness in her expression took his breath away.

He leaned closer to watch her brilliant eyes turn silver. "The event will provide a way to introduce the endeavor to my peers. With their support and, hopefully, contributions, I'll be able to start work on renovating the building I bid on."

"You mean the building I want?" One lovely brow arched so delicately that he had a sudden urge to kiss it.

"Now, Moonbeam, I won't lose you or your friendship over a building," he answered.

She shrugged one shoulder in feigned indifference. "Go on. I want to hear the rest of it."

"That area of London is perfect, as the vacant land is plentiful and perfect for expansion."

She stood facing him directly, then took his hands in hers. The gentle touch stole any remnants of his reservation at sharing so much of himself this evening. "It's a marvelous thing to honor your brother like this."

"Robbie was taken from us too early. There are hundreds of other families facing the same hurdles, and I want to make their path easier. As the heir to the previous Duke of Southart, Robbie had the finest medical care available. But it still wasn't enough. Imagine what a working-class family must face with this disease." He walked to the fireplace and stared into the blaze of red and blue flames. "I also want to do it for selfish purposes. I've never done anything just for philanthropic reasons," he drawled.

Again, he used an arrogant and vain tone to hide his true feelings.

"What is your selfish reason?" The dulcet tones in her voice called to him and he could only do one thing—tell her the truth.

He turned to her and dropped his shoulders, immediately lowering his guard. "This event will help me a great deal, both personally and with the added benefit of repairing my soiled reputation. If my fellow members of the House of Lords see that I take my responsibilities seriously, perhaps they'll consider supporting and sponsoring some of my causes in Parliament."

"All of that is understandable, but why do I sense you're hesitating?" Her eyes locked with his.

Every inch of him felt exposed. He couldn't look away even if he wanted to. Her allure was a magnet, and he couldn't fight the power of her gaze.

When he didn't speak, a shadow of unease, or perhaps it was doubt, crossed her face.

He spoke quickly, hoping it would restore her faith in him. "I'm hoping that my efforts will prove I'm trying to make amends to your brother and Somerton. They hold a very low opinion of me. No doubt, they still believe I'm a debauched libertine who frequents unsavory gambling clubs and other scandalous endeavors."

She bit her lips. That was exactly her regard of him, too. She'd even insulted him about his presence at the Reynolds the night he found her there.

"I don't gamble anymore." He lowered his voice, hoping she heard the truth in his words. "Nor do I engage in illicit relationships with women. That's behind me."

"Then why were you at the Reynolds that day?" she asked.

He exhaled. She deserved an explanation. "My father found an interesting way of entertaining himself beyond the grave. He has his solicitor deliver old debts that I accrued but missed paying when I was gambling like a rakehell. I receive one every week or so. Yesterday, I was trying to pay one from the Reynolds that he'd left me." He stepped closer to her. "That is when I saw you arguing with the majordomo."

She clasped her hands together and nodded. He'd never seen her so tentative or unsure. But his Moonbeam was stalwart in the face of a challenge.

My Moonbeam. Where did such an idea come from?

"I ran after Garland and planned to follow him into the Reynolds, but when I saw you there, I hesitated. I didn't want to have to explain myself. I went around the building and found my way inside."

"Lucky for me, I found you. I wouldn't have changed anything about that night except finding the journal. But, Daphne, please listen. I'm serious about reforming my reputation and proving I'm worthy of your brother's friendship once again." Her sharp gaze split him in two, and he'd do anything to make himself whole and deserving of her regard. "I want to prove myself to you."

She continued to stare at him. He stiffened, ready for whatever judgment she might pass on him.

"You're not saying anything," he said.

"No. I didn't realize how much Alex's friendship meant to you." She hesitated briefly. "Or mine."

"It does. But after the way I behaved toward you tonight, I'm sure you have your doubts about my ability to change." He clasped his hands behind his back, then stole a glance at the fireplace. "I shouldn't have touched you. As a newly reformed rake and hopefully trainable duke in the fine art of being a true gentleman, I apologize for my earlier behavior. I'd like to ask for your forgiveness."

"Paul, stop. If anyone should apologize, it should be me for taking advantage of you. I was the one who instigated our slip of proper decorum." Her cheeks heated to a marvelous shade of red.

For once in his life, he'd act like a gentleman. "Perhaps we should consider marriage?"

"Please don't." She held up her hand as if to prevent the words from reaching her. She swallowed, and the movement emphasized her long neck, one of her most elegant physical qualities. "For both of our peace of minds, let's not jeopardize our friendship with words that we both might regret. If you don't ask for my hand, then nothing changes."

"You shouldn't think you've compromised my honor when it was entirely the other way around. Truthfully, I'd do it all over again." The words, thick and unsteady, betrayed his unease with the whole conversation. To add injury to insult, his heart clashed with his brain over the wisdom of her suggestion. For that singular moment, the idea of marrying her caused a lightness he hadn't felt in years. But he pushed it aside. There was no way she could want him. She couldn't marry him and risk alienating her family. "You're correct as usual, Moonbeam. Thank you for saving us." He kept his tone light in hopes of restoring their earlier intimacy. "Perhaps it would be best if we spoke of this tomorrow."

"Speaking of tomorrow, would you care to break your fast with me?" she asked.

The husky timbre of her voice made him want to gather her in his arms. Perhaps he should and convince her to marry him. Instead, he clasped his hands behind his back and regarded her. "What about Pembrooke?"

She waved her hand in the air, dismissing any worry about Alex. "The earliest he'll return is late in the evening. Besides, if I want to invite a friend to join me for a meal, why would he care?"

"It's obvious why he would care. If you were my sister, you'd better believe I'd damn well care."

"What? If I invite a gentleman over? It's a good thing you're not my brother then." She smiled, and it completely disarmed him. "Or a gentleman."

Good lord, she was flirting with him.

And he loved every word she uttered.

He couldn't recall the last time he'd been so caught up in conversation with a woman. He closed the distance between them and matched her captivating smile with one of his own. Unable to resist, he smoothed a mutinous strand of hair behind the delicate skin of her ear.

"You make my own wickedness pale in comparison to you, Moonbeam," he murmured. Suddenly, he remembered Devan. "I invited my friend, Mr. Devan Farris, to spend the day with me. May I bring him along?"

"The more the merrier, as they say," she quipped.

He lifted one brow in question. "Are you sure?"

"Of course." She wrinkled her nose as if he were talking nonsense. "It's Christmas tomorrow. We're friends celebrating the day together."

"Marvelous idea, my beautiful Moonbeam. My very

own holiday present." He took her cheeks in his hands and pressed the softest kiss against her lips, one that he hoped spoke of friendship and true regard.

Her eyes fluttered closed, and she leaned against him.

With infinite regret, Paul pulled away, but not before kissing her perfect nose. "Speaking of tomorrow, it's growing late. I still have a few errands left this evening. Until tomorrow, Lady Moonbeam." He took her hand and pressed his lips against it.

"You are such a rogue." Her breathless response caused him to smile.

"A friendly rogue, my lovely Daphne." His voice turned low and seductive. "Shall I bring the mistletoe?"

Chapter Thirteen

After Paul took his leave, Daphne navigated or, a more apt description, floated her way to the kitchen where both Tait and his mother, Mrs. McBride, were surrounded by a forest of cut evergreens, holly branches, ivy vines, and the most essential greenery of them all, mistletoe. The clear scent of pine and cedar hung heavy in the air.

She informed them of her plans for the morrow. Mrs. McBride's eyes widened at the news, but she brought her own enthusiasm to the festivities as she made suggestions for entertaining Daphne's guests. Singlehandedly, Tait took on the task of decorating the entry hall, small dining room, and salon in preparation for tomorrow's breakfast.

As Daphne made her way to her bedroom, her contentment grew. Tomorrow would be perfect, and a memory that would always bring her joy. Mrs. McBride joined her shortly and helped her undress. A bath had been prepared, and the steaming water was an invitation she couldn't resist. Daphne washed her hair, then dallied as long as she could in the water until it grew cold. Mrs. McBride insisted upon brushing Daphne's hair by the fire until the long length was dry.

"My lady . . . I don't know how to ask this," Mrs. Mc-Bride said.

"What is it?" Daphne looked in the mirror and caught the older woman's gaze.

The lovely gray of her hair shimmered, a perfect contrast to her brown eyes that matched Tait's. Though somewhat plump, she moved with the efficient ease of a woman who was accustomed to making decisions and managing busy households. She was handsome, and her eyes contained the most delightful twinkle that indicated a kind spirit who enjoyed her holidays.

"Well, I've never been shy." She took another sweep of the brush through Daphne's hair. "But I must ask why are you entertaining the duke and his friend tomorrow? Aren't you worried about your reputation?"

If only Mrs. McBride knew how worried she was. She turned in her chair so that she and Tait's mother could look at each other face-to-face. The woman standing before her could be a strong ally. Daphne made the only possible decision. She would trust Mrs. McBride.

"I had my journal in my reticule when a boy stole it." Daphne tightened her lips as she gathered the strength to share more. "I've written *personal things* in that journal, Mrs. McBride." She forced herself to hold the woman's gaze as she confessed more. "Things that were from my heart. Things that could hurt the ones I love."

Mrs. McBride grasped Daphne's hand in hers, the warmth comforting.

"I need the duke. He's helping me find the boy and, hopefully, my journal. He's sent some of his staff to wait at the butcher shop where the boy is supposed to work tomorrow. He instructed his footmen to bring the boy to him as soon as they found him. I wanted to be close to His Grace during the day." Heat flooded her face. "And . . . I didn't want to be alone tomorrow."

"My lady, say no more." She smiled and gently patted Daphne's shoulder. "I kept a journal when I was your age and have ever since," she whispered. "I know the things that are contained within such a book. Every time you pick up a quill to pen a note or jot a thought, you entrust a small piece of your heart, the ones that belong to you and only you, in between the covers for safekeeping. It's how you find yourself when you're lost."

"I'd never considered it that way, but yes." Instead of being stunned at Mrs. McBride's revelation, Daphne experienced a rush of confidence, a certainty that she was pursuing the right path in life.

Mrs. McBride gently took Daphne's hand in hers again. "You need to find those pieces of your heart."

"Thank you," Daphne whispered. "You're like my kindred spirit."

"Kindred spirits stick together. We're the only ones who can value the importance of our own thoughts." With an efficient precision she must have acquired from her years of running Mr. Bertram's household, she walked to the door. "I'll have a feast prepared that will rival the Prince Regent's table tomorrow, my lady. The duke will never want to leave your side."

After Mrs. McBride took her leave, Daphne sat at her dressing table and stared at the mirror. It wasn't her own reflection that held her attention. It was Paul.

Every thought, every word, and, thankfully, every touch she'd experienced in his company she memorized. As she replayed the events of the day, Daphne could only surmise one truth. Her friendship with Paul, though not tangible, had turned into something very real and concrete. When he'd shared the horrible treatment he received from his father, she'd kept her temper by the most merger of threads. If the old duke were alive, she'd have given him a piece of her mind.

The old man didn't deserve such a wonderful son. No wonder Paul was so self-deprecating. The more she saw of him, the more she realized what a remarkable man he was. Building a hospital in remembrance of his brother was a wonderful undertaking. His plans for the endeavor would truly benefit the community. Most of London would much prefer such an endeavor over her own home for unwed mothers.

She pushed such a negative thought aside. Her dream would help and comfort others whom society wanted relegated to the hidden shadows. The best course would be to help Paul find another location. After Christmas, she'd put her efforts toward finding another place, one not too far away from Aubrey's Place.

If she were honest with herself, she wanted more of him. The idea of marriage was a distant dream, but she wanted love. It was too early in their friendship to determine if she could fall in love with him. Most people believed reformed rakes made the best husbands, but she had her doubts. Could they really shelve their previous dissolute and debauched lives and devote themselves to one woman? Such an event would be as rare as the Thames frozen solid. Possible, but not probable.

Once, she'd considered Paul such a rake. To be fair, she'd really thought of him more charitably—he was a loveable libertine. Although she didn't believe the rumors about Paul that were rife in the *ton,* he tried to make her think his behavior was lewd. Yet his attitude and treatment of her were a direct contradiction to such a reputation.

Daphne pulled aside the curtains that surrounded her high four-poster bed. Massive and ornate, it'd been in the family since King William and Queen Mary held the throne. After blowing out the candle on the bedside table, she climbed the three steps and tucked herself in bed. She embraced a pillow and gazed through the window. Stars glittered in the sky like living, breathing organisms.

She allowed her thoughts to return to Paul and the way he'd held her when she found her release. If she had her journal, she'd correct all her tame, flat descriptions of such an event. Discovering pleasure with him could only be described as heaven, the most moving and wonderful experience she'd ever had with another person.

As she drifted to sleep, she only thought of one thing she wanted for Christmas.

She wanted him in her bed.

"You bought her a present?" Devan scowled as he examined the box in Paul's hands. "When did you find the time? I thought you were with her until late last evening."

Tied in a festive red ribbon, the wooden box contained Daphne's old ermine muff he'd found last night after directing his driver to swing by the park near her house.

Covered in snow, the muff was ruined. There was no other way to describe it. The snow had matted the fur, and the leather had cracked from the cold. The only thing he could do was stop by the furrier on the way home, wake the poor man up from his slumber, and purchase a new one for her. He'd paid twice the asking price as a way to make up for the inconvenience of getting the man out of bed. Though similar to her old muff, the new one was made of an ermine fur slightly darker with a large moonstone pin in the center. It reminded him of her eyes, and he couldn't resist purchasing it for her. It gave him another reason to call her Moonbeam.

"I thought it a nice gesture since she's invited us into her home to celebrate."

Devan leaned back against the leather squab and stared. "Do you seriously believe me so gullible that I'll accept that explanation? Be honest about your feelings. You're trying to win her over." He stuck his nose in the air and sniffed much like a hunting dog that caught the scent of a fox. "I think you're wooing her."

When he tried to deny such a statement, the words stuck in his throat. He swallowed, and instinctively he tightened his hands around the box. "Where do you come up with these ideas? You should be thinking of why you're missing the Christmas church service this morning."

"I attended early morning services, hoping to find out my next assignment." Devan shook his head. "No luck. Besides, isn't it obvious? I'm playing chaperone."

"There's no need for a chaperone." At least not today. Yesterday was another story. He'd tossed and turned all night as he'd recalled how lovely and sensual she'd felt in his arms. Never before had he seen such uninhibited passion in a woman.

Regardless of how much he wanted her, he shouldn't have touched her. She was a well-bred lady, and he'd pleasured her like she was his. He glanced through the window as Daphne's home came into view. He'd spent half of his childhood with Pembrooke at that residence. Strange that he now considered the familiar house as Daphne's when he'd always considered it Pembrooke's home.

It'd been several years since his falling-out with Pembrooke. In all that time, Paul had seen Daphne at various social functions but always kept his distance in fear she'd not have anything to do with him. That was another waste of the years. She'd have welcomed him as a friend.

Both he and Devan alighted from the carriage and strolled to the front door. Before he could grab the brass knocker, Tait swung open the door.

"Happy Christmas, Your Grace." The under-butler's joyful enthusiasm was infectious.

"Happy Christmas to you." Paul turned to Devan. "Mr. Farris, this is Tait, Lord Pembrooke's under-butler."

Daphne appeared next to Tait in the doorway. "Your Grace, I'm so honored that you could come. Mr. Farris, it's a pleasure to see you. Please come in." She stood aside, and Tait opened the door completely.

The entry had been completely transformed into another world. An enormous silver vase filled with evergreens and red roses sat in the middle of the vestibule table. The staircase to the family private rooms had boughs of evergreens twined around the banisters. The smells of delicious baked goods and mulled spices surrounded them. Though the decorations in the house were lovely, it was the vision before Paul that held his attention and admiration.

Daphne stood before him in a deep, dark red velvet gown that was breathtaking. It set off her black hair and gray eyes perfectly.

"Happy Christmas." Paul kept his voice purposely intimate, as the greeting was only for her. He pulled her away from Tait and Devan's discourse on the perfect method of collecting mistletoe. "You are absolutely"—he stepped back and looked his fill—"enchanting."

"Thank you." Her dulcet voice reminded him of a first kiss between lovers. A lovely flush of pink colored her chest as it made its way to her cheeks.

"It's my pleasure." He presented the box. "This is for you."

Daphne glanced at Tait and Devan. Their conversation had turned into an argument over which trees harbored the best mistletoe.

Without a word, she grabbed his hand and led him into the salon. When she dropped his hand, he felt almost light-headed without her touch. She rushed to a table beside the fireplace and picked up a package. "This is for you."

When their fingers touched, the urge to take Daphne in his arms almost overpowered him. Before he took the present, he caressed her wrist. Her strong pulse sped as he traveled his finger across the soft skin.

"Thank you." Without letting go, he led her to the sofa. It was inconceivable that excitement bubbled inside of him like an eight-year-old finally allowed to dine at the table with the adults. "Let's open them together."

He untied the twine that held the paper around the package. Based upon the shape, he imagined it was a book. Perhaps a book of poetry he could read to Daphne while his head rested in her lap. He had the perfect spot for them—Willow House, the property he'd inherited from his mother. A stately willow stood guard over a clear blue pond. Serene and tranquil, it was one of his favorite places in the world. He wanted to take her there.

He shook his head to clear such fantasies. His wild musings were directly attributed to the restless night he'd experienced.

"You found my muff!" The sparkle in her eyes reminded him of a diamond. She held up the piece of fur that looked like a drowned rat.

"Look deeper inside the box," he instructed.

She bent over the box. "Oh my . . ." As her voice trailed to nothing, she lifted the new fur muff from the box. Her breath caught at her first sight of the pin. "It's beautiful."

"Not as much as you."

Her eyes flew to his. The joy on her face was simply stunning. "Thank you. It's exquisite. What is that stone? It's so unusual."

He couldn't look away, nor did he want to. "It's a moonstone."

Her eyes widened.

"I couldn't think of a more appropriate gift after our adventures."

"I'll cherish it forever." She leaned over and pressed her

lips to his cheek. Completely oblivious to the effect she had on him, she sat on the edge of the sofa. "Open yours."

He peeled the paper back slowly. Mildly surprised, he thumbed through the blank pages of a book. Bold and masculine, the black leather journal had an embossed magpie in gold leaf centered on the front. "It's lovely. Thank you."

"I was afraid it might be too dull. But after yesterday, I couldn't wait to give it to you. You can jot down plans for the hospital. Make notes of your meetings with architects, physicians, staff, and, of course, a new location." She shrugged her shoulders. "Those sorts of things."

His heart pounded against his chest as if trying to reach her. She believed in him and his plans. He leaned and pressed his lips against her cheek in a like manner as she'd just done to him. Only this time after the kiss, he trailed his lips to the sensitive lobe of her ear. "I adore it. You were thoughtful to think of it. It's perfect, just like you."

"You're such a scoundrel."

He gently bit the lobe of her ear. "Ah, you're starting to recognize my strengths."

She playfully batted at his arm, then stood. "Shall we see where Mr. Farris is? Otherwise, it'll prove I'm a terrible hostess, since I've left him alone too long."

Reluctantly, he agreed and stood. As they neared the door, he caught sight of a bundle of mistletoe hanging above the door. He stilled and waited for her to precede him. When she entered the doorway, he called out, "Wait."

In the doorframe, Daphne stopped and faced him with a quizzical look on her face. "Is something wrong?"

Paul shook his head. "Wait for me right there."

She gifted him with a dazzling smile that made him want to kiss her even more. When he reached her, Paul pointed at the mistletoe, then took her in his arms. Deliberately slow, he lowered his mouth to hers. When skin touched skin, everything within his body slowed except his heart, which pounded harder, encouraging him to make this kiss as special as she was. Daphne moaned slightly and tilted her head to have better access. On a whimper, she opened her mouth, inviting him to deepen the kiss. The soft velvet beneath his fingers emboldened him to caress her as he held her.

"Ahem, *Your Grace*," Devan drawled as he pulled out his timepiece. "A little unseemly to be monopolizing the hostess's attentions at this time of the morning."

Daphne's desire-filled eyes darted up to his, and she stepped away. Her passion melted faster than an iceberg in the Mediterranean Sea.

"Your timing lacks any sophistication," Paul growled.

"I would never dare interfere with your holiday celebrations, *Your Grace*," he mocked. "But I'm hungry, and Mrs. McBride is waiting to serve us in the dining room."

"In a moment." Paul debated whether to pull Daphne back into his arms for another kiss. "He's such a spoilsport."

Daphne looked up and caught his gaze. "Perhaps we should go eat. Mrs. McBride's worked all morning on our feast."

He touched his nose to hers. Her small gasp of surprise and gentle laugh were payment enough for the pleasure they both had to forgo because of the interruption. "Whatever my Moonbeam wants."

She lightheartedly swatted at his chest. Before he could offer his arm, Devan extended his. His friend had sidled up to them without Paul even noticing. Such was the effect of Daphne's luscious kisses. Every one of his senses seem to be on holiday.

Daphne politely took Devan's arm as she started a conversation about the history of the house. She exhibited her prowess as a marvelous hostess as she shared various tidbits about relatives of long ago and whispered about ghosts that haunted the halls. Within moments, she had him laughing over some quip.

A vision of Daphne tilting that gorgeous head of hers as she charmed his guests through Southart Hall popped into his thoughts like an unsinkable cork on a calm lake. She was politically astute; she'd developed friendships with the most benevolent and magnanimous members of the *ton* through her charity efforts; and, more important, he enjoyed her company immensely.

The thought of her warming his bed brought forth a welcomed heat. Perhaps he should seriously consider an offer of marriage. After all, he was the Duke of Southart and needed an heir.

Such musings weren't surprising. She was perfection. She didn't allow him to escape his true feelings. She listened to him. When they were together, everything slipped away—the outside world, all sounds, thoughts, time—everything except the two of them.

Devan twisted slightly and caught Paul's gaze. "*Your Grace,* thank you for allowing me to escort our delightful hostess to the dining room. She's already granted me a boon of a mistletoe kiss after breakfast."

Paul's stomach twisted into a hundred knots.

Devan had the audacity to smile as if delivering an uplifting sermon, then winked. "Rest assured, I won't be so boorish as to do it in front of everyone."

Paul grunted in response.

Repairing his friendships with Pembrooke was not only a good idea but also one that needed to be made as quickly as possible.

He didn't want to lose her to another.

Daphne swept her gaze down the table. Mrs. McBride had outdone herself on the preparations. Fruitcakes, Christmas puddings, eggs, rashers of crisp bacon, sausage, sliced oranges, and a variety of dried fruit and nuts decorated the table.

Daphne had planned the meal and offered to help, but Mrs. McBride had assured her that she could manage everything. Yet Daphne had insisted and enjoyed the tasks immensely. They'd even made her favorite apple tarts with cinnamon. It was something she'd never done before and now looked forward to doing in her own home.

This proved that she could be happy. She'd tried Paul's suggestion and locked her grief over missing Alice in a special mahogany box. It currently sat on the north windowsill of her apartments upstairs. For this morning, she'd allow her guilt and grief to rest as she celebrated with her friends.

Mrs. McBride currently stood at the buffet refilling a plate with freshly baked tarts. The scent of apples sweetened the fragrance of the evergreens that decorated the table.

"Lady Daphne, would you care for another cup of tea?" Sitting to the left of her, the vicar held the pot in the air.

"No thank you. Perhaps His Grace would care for more?" she offered.

"I'm finished as well." Paul sat to her right with a relaxed stance, but he still reminded her of a lion. With his long fingers, he played with the handle of his cup. "That's the third time you've asked if she wanted more tea. She's declined the previous two times. Perhaps you should take the hint she doesn't want any more."

"I've always been an optimist, Your Grace." Mr. Farris waggled his chestnut-colored eyebrows. "Third time charmed."

Before she could answer, Tait entered the room with Claire's cousin by his side. The under-butler's eyes had widened to the size of saucers. "My lady, Lord William Cavensham," he announced.

Though she tried to keep her face nonplussed, her heart shuttered when she caught William's gaze. Lord William Cavensham, the Duke of Langham's youngest son and Claire's cousin, stood with one brow raised. Earlier Daphne had asked Tait to turn away any visitors, since she didn't want anyone to know she was entertaining two gentlemen by herself. She forced herself to remain calm. This was William—he was practically family. However, he was close to Claire, more like a brother than a cousin. Which meant he'd tell Claire or Alex that she'd entertained Paul and Mr. Farris on Christmas Day.

With a sigh, she tried to relax. Her next conversation with Alex had just became more complicated with William's appearance. It couldn't be avoided. She'd already planned to tell her brother that Paul had called upon her out of concern. But now she'd have to explain her reasons for inviting him to dine with her. If Alex became angry, then so be it. She wanted Paul's company.

"Thank you, Tait." She stood and made her way to William.

He took her hand and bowed over it. "Merry Christmas, Daphne. I didn't know you were home . . . or entertaining." He held up a portfolio. "I have some documents that Pembrooke needs."

"Would you care to join us?" Terrified he'd ask a few pointed questions of her guests, she prayed he had other plans. "No doubt you have other engagements that you must be off to."

"I don't. I'm waiting for my brother, McCalpin, to return to town tomorrow. . . ." His words trailed to nothing as he glanced around the room.

When his eyes filled with a sudden fierce sparkling, it left little doubt there were fireworks in her future.

"Southart, Happy Christmas," William drawled in a voice that reminded her of hardened honey. "Farris? My

God, how long has it been? Not since university when you were locked outside the dormitory without any clothing. Why aren't you standing at some pulpit this morning bestowing words that we're all doomed to hell and soon will be smelling brimstone?"

Instead of being insulted, Devan beamed. With a wipe of his mouth, he threw down his serviette, then crossed the room and shook William's hand. "Happy Christmas, my friend. I'm actually changing parishes next month. I wanted to enjoy London before I'm exiled to Northumberland or some remote desolated village in the outskirts of nowhere. Sit down and join us."

With his face frozen in a mask of indifference, Paul looked on but didn't join the exchange.

William locked his gaze with hers. "If I'm not interrupting?"

"Of course, please join us." She extended her hand to the chair next to Devan.

William chose the chair at the end of the small rectangular table. From that angle, he had a clear view of everyone. Mrs. McBride set a plate service in front of him, but William waved her off. "Just tea for me."

Clearly uneasy he'd admitted William into the house, Tait loitered by the buffet, ready to be of service.

Paul didn't say a word. Instead of his prior relaxed pose, his posture had stiffened like a hound ready to attack. His normal radiant warmth was gone. In its place was nothing but ice.

William completely ignored the chill in the room and took a sip of the tea that Mrs. McBride had served him. With a sigh, he leaned back in his chair and surveyed the three of them.

After taking a long gander, Will turned his focus solely on her. "Tell me, Daphne, how is it that you're spending

Christmas at home alone without Pembrooke and Claire? Are they still at Pemhill?"

Desperate to find the right words, she straightened in her chair and looked down at her plate. "Well, yes—"

"I believe that Pembrooke and Lady Pembrooke are returning today." Paul leaned back in his chair in challenge.

"Paul, I can speak for myself." She spoke quietly.

"'Paul' is it?" William queried with an arched eyebrow. The tension in the room was palpable.

"Yes, it is," Daphne answered. She glanced from Paul to William. Both men were staring at each other like two bulls ready to fight.

"I see. Of course, that makes perfect sense." William smiled without any real humor. "You know what else I see?"

Paul tilted his head. "Please enlighten us."

"My pleasure," William said. "I see five people." He pointed to Tait and his mother. "Two witnesses." He directed his index finger at Devan. "A vicar." Then he pointed first at Paul, then at her. "A groom and a bride. Is this the wedding breakfast?"

Daphne stood. "What?"

"Is this the wedding breakfast?" With an annoyingly earnest face, William enunciated the words carefully.

"You are out of your bloody mind." Paul stood beside her.

"Then you married Tait?" William laughed at his own joke.

"Don't talk nonsense, William. It doesn't become you." Daphne let the rebuke sail across the table. She'd not let her perfect morning descend into the absurd.

"Wait, Daph. Hear me out. You couldn't have married Farris, as no one else in the room could have performed the ceremony," William countered.

"She didn't marry me," Paul growled.

"I didn't marry him."

She and Paul protested at the same time. Their voices combined into a litany that held a hint of guilt.

"If you haven't married and aren't about to, I can only assume all is innocent here." Holding Paul's gaze, William issued the words as a challenge.

With a stare that could have burned the entire house to the ground, Paul spit out the words, "You assumed correctly."

"Excellent." William stood. "I'll not keep you from your revelries." He reached into his leather portfolio and extracted some papers. "I picked up two special editions of today's *Midnight Cryer.* One for you and Emma. I pay attention. I know how you and she enjoy the scandals. I haven't read it, so tell me if you find anything of interest." When he reached the door, he handed the portfolio to Tait. William turned to Daphne and pointed to the mistletoe over his head. "Shall we share a Christmas kiss like we always do?"

Flames of heat were the only things kissing her cheeks at that moment. Without looking at Paul, she made her way to William. She tilted her cheek for a peck.

"I'll not see him hurt you like he did Claire. He will not dally with you, then throw you aside. We'll make him think you're mine," William murmured under his breath. Then without warning, he took her in his arms and swept her into a kiss.

Startled, she pushed him away. She'd expected a brotherly kiss, but this was anything but. Though Lord William Cavensham was a handsome man, Daphne felt nothing for the kiss—certainly not like Paul's incendiary kisses. "I don't need protection from him."

William released her. With a devilish grin, his gaze flew to Paul's and settled. "You look like a lid on a pot on the verge of exploding from the heat." He turned to her. "I'm sorry, Daph, but you're family. Trust me."

Without warning, William tried to kiss her again.

"Don't." She deftly turned in such a manner that he kissed her cheek. "He will not hurt me."

"Get. Your. Hands. Off. *Her*." Paul's words were eerily quiet, but there was no denying the menace in his voice. "She doesn't want you to kiss her."

"Do you think she wants to kiss you?" William's voice was uncharacteristically innocent. Everyone in the room was aware that the tone was purely to infuriate Paul.

"William, stop. He's a guest in my home," Daphne whispered.

William's attention turned to her. "You better hope your brother doesn't discover what you've done. It'll become the most popular bet at White's tomorrow, I'll wager."

"What are you talking about?" Devan asked.

William held her gaze as he answered the question. "Whether Pembrooke locks Daphne up or kills Southart first."

"Lady Daphne, I'll see Lord William to the door." Paul stood and walked toward them as if nothing were amiss. But the clenched muscles of his jaw revealed the extent of his dismay.

William nodded his farewell to Devan and then to her. The smirk on his face foretold that he was looking forward to his conversation with Paul. She rushed to follow them both to ensure no blood was drawn.

"Lady Daphne, leave them be." The graveness in Devan's smoky whisper caused her to jerk his gaze to him. "You should see this." He raised his head from the edition of *The Midnight Cryer*.

She made her way to his side while a deep foreboding sprouted like a noxious weed in her stomach. All thoughts to follow Paul were forgotten. Without a word, she took the paper from Devan's hands.

Her worst nightmare lay before her in black and white.

Chapter Fourteen

THE MIDNIGHT CRYER'S SPECIAL
CHRISTMAS EDITION

Gentle readers, we have a gift for you.

For the pleasure of your Christmas celebration, we'd like to share with you a page out of the diary of a young woman who supposedly lives in Mayfair. We just purchased the entry late last night proving Christmas miracles do occur! We don't know her identity just yet, but let's just say . . . we won't leave any stone unturned until we unmask her. We strive for excellence in our pursuit of the truth. Never fear! Once we have her name, we'll let you know her identity immediately.

Suddenly, Daphne regretted eating that last tart, as her stomach rolled itself into knots. Struggling for composure, she swallowed her nausea and made her eyes focus on the next paragraph.

* * *

Without warning, he swept me from the garden path into the shade of several trees. With a sweep of his arm, he pushed aside the branches of a stately willow heavy with an abundance of leaves. I took his hand and pulled him close. My finger traced the beautiful outline of his cheeks until I found the scar, the only imperfection on his right cheek, the only flaw on his beautiful face. With ice-blue eyes, he studied me. He caught my hand and brought it to his lips. His touch caused the sweetest hunger, a longing that only he could assuage.

"I'll forever find myself beholden to that magpie." *He touched his lips to the pulse on my wrist.*

How long had we been parted!

I slid my hand around his neck and pulled him close. My lips mated with his as I unbuttoned his coat. I would not allow this opportunity to fall through my fingers. He was my lover. We'd been parted for days, and I hungered for his forbidden touch—for his body. With deft hands, he unbuttoned my gown.

Gentle reader, did this titillating entry capture your interest? We hope so, as we're actively negotiating the purchase of the rest of this scandalous diary from a longtime informant, an intrepid young boy who came about this journal honestly. He has a nose for business and promises that the book is filled with similar entries. There's mention of even more dishonorable family secrets.

Today's question begs an answer. Would she seduce him? Would a lady really have allowed such liberties from a "forbidden" man?

Alas, whoever she is, the fact remains—she's

already ruined! We'll reveal her name as soon as we're able. No man should be saddled with such a scandalous sinner.

She audibly gasped at the ugly words. Unable to breathe she stood still like the wooden maiden in Bernini's statute of Apollo and Daphne. She tried to swallow her humiliation, but her throat turned drier than a dusty toll road. She clenched her hands into fists to stave off the threatening tears.

"You're writing about Southart, aren't you?" Devan stood and faced her. "I asked him about the scar once, and he told me a magpie attacked him."

She couldn't answer him or shake her head to deny such a statement. But to acknowledge the truth would destroy her and so many others.

"Your secret is safe with me." He took her hands in his and squeezed. "My God, you're terrified. I promise, I'll not say a word."

"I'm ruined." Somehow, she forced the words out. Her voice sounded muffled, buried six feet under in a cave.

"No. You're not. Southart will understand." Devan smiled.

It was one of those compassionate smiles a vicar is known for—the ones she grew to despise after her sister's death. Smiles intended to be sympathetic but, in reality made one furious, since the giver had no clue what the definition of real pain entailed.

Yet she believed Devan truly was concerned for her situation. The genuine warmth in his eyes was designed to soothe and calm.

"That's not what I'm concerned about." She lowered her hands from his and wrapped her arms about her waist.

Devan shook his head. "I don't understand."

"If other pages are published, my entire family will be

destroyed." A sob threatened, but she refused to allow it to escape. It wouldn't help matters. She had to think. Too much was at stake.

Paul entered the room. His face was calm, but the flash of his eyes betrayed his ire with William. He wouldn't handle any teasing from Devan. She could imagine his reaction if she shared the news that *The Midnight Cryer* had revealed one of her diary entries about him.

Paul joined them, but when his gaze captured hers it was apparent she was his only concern. "What's happened?"

Unable to find the words to answer, she gazed at Devon, who smiled in encouragement. With a single small movement, she shook her head. Not now. She couldn't have *that* conversation *now*. She'd hoped she never had to share her writings and the accompanying embarrassment with the Duke of Southart.

Ever.

Yet over the years, Daphne's hopes and her inevitable reality had never proved good bedfellows. Her hand had been forced by the despicable gossip rag *The Midnight Cryer.* For the sake of their friendship, she had to tell Paul. If anyone discovered she'd written about him, his own reputation could be in jeopardy.

"Mr. Farris, would you mind if I have a private word with His Grace?"

Without saying a word, Paul followed Daphne into the sitting room where they had opened their presents together. Their earlier merrymaking was long forgotten. Instead, an icy fear twined around her heart under his steady scrutiny. Silently, she handed him the article and waited for the inevitable.

She didn't have to wait long for her grief to rear its ugly head.

Like a thief, memories of Alice stole into her conscience. When she was unhappy or worried, her thoughts always circled back to Alice. Seeking some distance to control her wayward emotions, Daphne stood in front of the mantle with her back to the blazing fire that failed to keep the cold at bay.

She should be able to manage the pain now. Years had passed since Alice's death, but it simply wasn't enough. Daphne had concluded that even eternity wouldn't promise any peace from the sorrow.

Paul's eyes widened as his eyes scanned the page. He gently shook his head as if denying what he was reading. Finally, the agonizing moment was over, and he placed it on the table before him. She had to keep her feet planted to stop herself from picking it up and hurling it into the fireplace.

"Are you shocked? Revolted?" The anticipation of waiting for his answer made her want to shatter into a million pieces.

"Neither." He arched a brow as only a duke could.

Whether it was a show of haughtiness or arrogance, it was difficult to determine. It made little difference at this point. Whether he was disgusted with her or not, she was repulsed by her own actions.

"I don't know whether to be insulted or flattered. I always considered myself the consummate seducer, but you certainly have surpassed my capabilities with what you've written here." Suddenly, he grinned, and his ice-blue eyes caught the light. "You must teach me some lessons, I see."

He wanted her to laugh, but her grief was too powerful. "It's not a laughing matter, Your Grace."

His grin slowly disappeared. He stared at her in such a manner that she felt as if he could see every lurid and wicked thought she'd ever possessed. The urge to hide grew, but she curled her toes in her slippers, preventing her escape. She forced herself to stare back.

"When did you write this?" His simple question and nonchalance pushed open Pandora's box, spilling all the burdens Daphne had carried for years.

"Several months after Alice died." All she could do was shake her head, hoping to control the surge of grief that flooded her thoughts. The cold gripped her, causing everything within her to still. He had read one of her intimate fantasies, a fiction about the two of them that she'd created out of her vivid imagination. She should be hotter than an inferno with total humiliation. Instead, she stood frozen waiting to crack in two. "It's completely inadequate, but all I can offer you is my sincerest apology."

"Why?" he asked in a calm voice. "Why did you write it?"

She smoothed the nap of her velvet skirt, then forced herself to look at him. "I found it comforting. You were always so kind to me. Then when you and Alex had a falling-out, writing about you and me together like that . . . was a way of lashing out against everyone. You weren't welcomed by my family anymore, and I could say anything I wanted to you in the journal. You were a safe haven from my grief."

"Much like forbidden fruit?" With his gentle gaze, he searched her face for answers—if only she had them.

She shrugged. "You were a fond memory from days long ago. But I've put your reputation into jeopardy. I wouldn't blame you if you went to Martin Richmond—" Suddenly, her mortification at what she'd done burned through her, replacing her earlier cold. Unable to withstand any more, she turned and stared at the fire. She wouldn't shed a tear—she'd done that a thousand times without any resolution to her guilt or its faithful companion, grief. "I'll not ask your forgiveness, as I cannot forgive myself."

Suddenly, strong arms that promised comfort, a safe sanctuary, surrounded her. As desperate as she was, she'd take everything and anything he offered.

"Daphne. I would never be disloyal to you." His deep voice rumbled as if he, too, suffered. Without thought, she turned and buried her head against his chest. His embrace was an escape from the pain.

One tear broke free for the loss of her best friend, her sister. Another tear joined the first as she grieved for her sister's reticence in not sharing all the humiliation and pain she must have suffered.

His arms tightened around her, but it didn't lessen the agony. The wound Daphne battled every day had the power to twist her insides until she felt completely annihilated. How fitting that it reared its ugly head with a vengeance and attacked on this almost perfect Christmas Day.

Not only would she not forgive herself, but she'd also never forgive Alice.

She'd never forgive her one and only sister, the sole person with whom she had shared every secret, every hope, and every fear she'd ever possessed. She'd never forgive Alice for not being there for all the events that made life special. They were supposed to share their Seasons, celebrate their marriages, coo over each other's babies, and write letters to each other in their doddering old age.

Daphne's biggest heartache, the most deceitful and disloyal act that Alice had committed, could never be undone or forgiven.

Never.

Alice had never told her why or said good-bye. Numbness slowly washed away the pain, and she could breathe again. The comfort of his arms was heaven, but she couldn't stay there forever. He deserved the whole truth, no matter how horrible. She owed him that much. "But there's more you need to know."

His lips pressed against her temple offering comfort. "Tell me."

"You mustn't tell a soul, but my sister killed herself." Daphne forced her gaze to his.

"I won't, sweetheart. I never have since the day I first found out."

Chapter Fifteen

Making a solemn pledge, Paul crossed his heart with two fingers. He peered down at Daphne and wiped away the remnants of her tears with his thumbs. Her expression froze in shock. "It hurts, Daphne. I know it does."

"You know?" Her voice trembled. When she stepped out of his reach, he reluctantly let her go. She rubbed her forehead with her hand. "How?"

"Your brother." How to tell her without causing her more pain? "Alex was lost in grief one day and let the secret slip."

She heaved the heaviest sigh he'd ever heard coming from such a small body. "The day he challenged you to a duel?"

He nodded once. "That was one of the blackest days I'd ever experienced. I allowed Pembrooke to believe I was at fault. It was stupid on my part, but at the time, I thought I was helping by taking the blame. Thankfully, he didn't see it to fruition."

With a huff, she blew a loose curl out of her face. "No, it was stupid on Alice's part. She fell in love with a boy who worked at the stable in the village. He'd come to Pemhill looking for extra work." She bit her lip, then locked her gaze with his. "There's no use keeping her secrets hidden. She became pregnant by him."

"Daph, I know," he said.

"I suppose you figured it out when she snuck into your room that night and crawled into your bed." A brilliant blush blossomed in her cheeks. "I was so angry with her over that trick."

"Shush." He took her hand in his. "I was quite foxed that night. When I woke in the early morning hours, she was staring at me. She told me about the baby and how desperate she was." With his finger, he tipped her face to his. "I told her I'd marry her, but we had to tell Alex the truth. She said she couldn't face him or your mother with the news."

"I'm sorry she tried to force you into marriage." She squeezed his hand with hers. "She never shared with me that you actually offered. That was gallant."

"No one has ever called me gallant." He entwined their fingers together, hoping to give her strength—letting her know she wasn't alone to bear the grief by herself. "I could become accustomed to you calling me that."

Finally, she smiled, but her expression turned solemn again. "I find myself so angry with her. All the time. She hurt so many people."

"Shall we continue this sitting down?" he asked. She nodded, and he took her hand and led her to the sofa.

When he took the seat beside Daphne, she looked so forlorn that all he wanted was the power to take all of her grief and claim it for his own. Her normal brightness had dimmed, and he knew in that moment that there was nothing in this world he wouldn't do to ease her pain. "I find that I've an overwhelming need to hold you, Daphne Hall-worth. Will you allow that?"

She nodded. Before he could pick her up, she leaned toward him, making it easy for him to tug her onto his lap.

Once he had his arms around her, she rested her face against his neck. In that quiet moment, the air of her rhythmic breathing against his neck and her gentle weight felt perfect. He realized that his contentment, his sense of place in the world, and his belonging was only attributable to her.

Daphne wrapped her arms around his neck and breathed his scent. In his arms, she felt insulated from all the ugliness of Alice's death.

With his lips pressed against her forehead, he murmured, "Moonbeam, when I feel the sadness ready to descend over losing Robbie, I force myself to dwell on the good things I was fortunate enough to have had with him."

"Like what?" She'd take everything he offered if she could find a way to forgive Alice.

His eyes had deepened into a startling hue of dark blue. "Tell me one thing you remember about her that always made you smile."

She grimaced, then relaxed as fond memories pushed aside the painful ones. "When a mare was foaling, Alice would be the first one in the family to 'introduce' herself. She'd even beat Alex to the barn, and that was his favorite pastime, to wait for the new colt or filly to name." Her lips twitched. "She'd rush from the barn to find me and insist I come and meet the new horse. She'd make an exaggerated formal introduction between the foal and me. It was quite comical."

He soothed his finger over one cheek, and she found the courage to continue, "Alice could find such wonder in the simplest things. She loved Pemhill."

"That's how I remember her. All those times I visited, she was full of mischief and laughter." With his forefinger, Paul pushed an errant curl behind her ear. "Now that you're aware that the estrangement between your brother and me started because of this, you should know the rest of the tale." He grew suddenly serious. "It's doesn't paint me in a very favorable light."

She squeezed his hand encouraging him to share more.

He studied their hands again, then intertwined his fingers with hers. "Mind you this was before your brother married, but I'd told him that his wife-to-be was my lover."

"I know," she said softly. "I hated you for that. I love Claire just like a sister." She released her breath.

"Wretched of me, wasn't it?" He laughed, but there was no humor—only self-loathing. He turned away to study the fire. "I let Alex believe what he wanted about Alice. He was blind with grief, and I thought if he directed all his anger at me, it might help him. But, when he bought my vowels at the Reynolds and forced me to break my engagement to Claire, I was livid and wanted to strike back."

Sweet, kind, and gentle, her sister-in-law had filled a void in Daphne's heart, making Paul's confession painful to hear. Regardless, she'd never rest if she didn't ask the question that begged for an answer even if it tore her world apart. "Why hurt Claire? Did you hate my brother that much?"

"No, I didn't hate Pembrooke, and I didn't mean to hurt Claire. I just wanted her back." When his eyes caught hers, there was a defiance much like a challenge. The muscles in his square jaw jerked, and his angular cheeks deepened in ruddiness.

All those years ago, she'd told him that he was a horrible actor and never to gamble. He proved her right today. This wasn't defiance, but pain. He was protecting himself. "Paul, I'm not going to judge you."

"Perhaps you should. When I was engaged to Claire, for the first and only time in my life my father was proud of me. You see, he wanted Robbie to marry Claire, but when he fell sick, I was the stand-in. When your brother ruined me, my father was livid. Being the vain peacock that I am, I tried to win her back any way I could." His eyes locked with hers.

"Did you love her?" she whispered.

His gaze held hers. "No. I once thought I did, but now I recognize that wasn't love." He took his fingers and trailed them down her cheek until he held her chin between his thumb and forefinger.

"I'm sorry your father was such a horrid man." She leaned in and pressed a light kiss against his lips.

He was momentarily speechless in his surprise. "Thank you, Moonbeam. I'm stunned you're not throwing me out of your house."

"I, above all people, know that grief can make people do the craziest, most illogical things that hurt others." She touched her nose to his. "But you're wrong about you being a vain peacock."

"How so?" He reciprocated the touch of noses.

"You're vain, but I've never seen you in feathers," she teased.

"Someone is feeling better." He chuckled, then leaned close, and his thumb gently traced her lips. "I think it's best if I'm here when your brother arrives."

"I want to have the conversation with Alex alone. Over the last several days, I've decided to find my own residence. I'll explain how far along I am in my plans for the home. He and Claire need to be aware that I'm taking Tait and my lady's maid, Mavis Taylor, with me." She drew back a little and gazed at the fire. "I'll tell them how you saw to my welfare and that we spent time together, including our Christmas breakfast. Hopefully, it'll make it easier to mend your friendship."

When she made the mistake of turning her attention to him, she truly understood the magpie's behavior. He was gloriously handsome today in a dark navy broadcloth coat and a light blue brocade waistcoat. As if he were a shiny coin, she wanted to keep him all to herself.

"I'm not sure that's the wisest course of action," Paul insisted. "If Pembrooke is upset, he can take his anger out on me instead of you."

"No. I appreciate your offer"—she placed her hand over his to reassure him, but the warmth of his skin sent a shiver through her—"but this is important to me."

His gaze, sharp as a falcon's before diving for its prey, flew to where her hand rested. He exhaled deeply before placing his over hers. With a reluctant smile, Paul nodded, but the narrow lines surrounding his eyes exposed his wariness. "Devan and I will take our leave. Just so you know, I told William not to tell Pembrooke about today. I want to stop by tomorrow and explain exactly what happened and why we were here."

His look of worry made her feel even more guilty.

She'd laugh if the irony weren't so heart-wrenching. Paul, who had always courted outrage, wanted to protect her from the scandal, one that he was completely innocent of having any hand in.

It was all her.

She'd have it out with Alex, then the rest of her Christmas holiday required she find Garland. Even if she had to spend the night in the carriage in front of the Reynolds tomorrow, she'd get her diary back.

Like a dropped anchor, her heart sunk.

What if they published another fantasy about Paul?

Or worse, what if they published one of her letters to Alice?

"Devil take it." Halfway home, Paul suddenly knocked on the roof on the carriage, causing it to stop immediately in the middle of a deserted street. All of the fine residents of

London were undoubtedly still at Christmas morning services.

"Such language, from a duke no less. It's a holy day," Devan lectured. "You should have attended the early service with me this morning before visiting Lady Daphne. Perhaps you'd have a cleaner mouth."

"I can't leave her to face Pembrooke alone. I should have insisted I stay," Paul said, completely ignoring his friend's comments. He opened the window to instruct the groomsman to turn around.

"Let her be." The force of Devan's words caused Paul to stop. The vicar only used that tone when he was serious.

"She needs me—" Paul shook his head. "What I meant is she needs us." The words shouldn't have surprised him. From the moment he saw her at the Reynolds, he felt an overwhelming urge to provide for her welfare. Of course, it was only until her brother returned home. Within hours, Pembrooke would arrive to find her safe and sound, ending Paul's obligations to Daphne.

Even he was having a hard time believing that excuse.

But his sense of unease wouldn't abate. In fact, the farther the distance grew from Pembrooke House, the more his disquiet increased. He could have sworn that he saw real trepidation in her glorious gray eyes. Paul could not care less that Lord William made an untimely visit. No, he wanted her to be as happy as when they'd shared their gifts with each other.

She had nothing to fear from Pembrooke. He adored Daphne, always had. When he'd become head of the family, Daphne's only brother always made decisions that kept her best interests at heart. Still, the nag wouldn't leave him be. He needed to be by her side.

The only explanation that made sense was honor. When Pembrooke arrived, Paul would make certain that he understood the situation. It would ease Daphne's burden over the last several days, besides being the honorable and right thing to do.

"Southart, she needs to do this by herself. She wants to do this by herself."

"How do you know so much about her?" Paul growled.

"Because I'm observant, you ducal oaf." Devan narrowed his eyes. "I've watched her with you and you with her. This isn't any of your concern. This is her fight. She chose to stay in London for a reason, and your interference will muddy the waters with her brother. She'll come to you when she's ready."

If he never had to hear "any of your concern" ever again, it would be too soon. "What are you talking about?"

"Save me from fools." Devan tilted his head and studied the roof of the carriage. "It's like watching two moles dance that can't see anything in front of their faces." He exhaled and turned his gaze back to Paul. "Besides, won't your footmen find the boy and the journal today? She'll see you tomorrow when you deliver it."

"Your Grace?" the groomsman called. "Did you want to go somewhere else?"

He did.

He wanted to go to Daphne.

"*Devil take me*," he muttered under his breath. In a louder voice, he called, "No, Carter. Let's continue home."

Merry Christmas, indeed.

As Daphne waited in the salon for her brother, she did the only thing that helped pass the time.

She paced.

Besides having to deal with Alex's questions as to why she stayed in London, she now had to decide what, if anything, she could do to stop *The Midnight Cryer* from acquiring any more of her journal. She still felt the poker-hot flicks of humiliation that Devan had recognized not only that it was her writing but also, more important, that she was writing about Paul. What if someone else recognized him?

Or, God forbid, her?

If her journal wasn't returned to her tomorrow, she might have to find an escort into Seven Dials and try to find it herself. With the publication of her diary page, she was running out of time. She'd call on her solicitor, Mr. Fincham, and ask his advice. He might know of a way to halt the publication of any other of her personal pages.

Frustrated, she let out a sigh. That was highly doubtful, since *The Midnight Cryer* published all sorts of outrageous comments and titillating tidbits of gossip without any harm befalling the paper or its publisher, Mr. Martin Richmond.

She had such a delightful time with Paul until it had been ruined by *The Midnight Cryer*. The house felt empty without his presence. She was in serious danger with him. "Friendship" really didn't even describe them anymore.

Heaven help her, she was thinking nonsense.

Right now, she needed to concentrate on her brother. She rehearsed the points she wanted to make. She continued pacing with deliberate but unhurried movements. If she expelled her nervous energy before Alex's imminent arrival, she'd exhibit more confidence when she told him of her future plans.

All her thoughts scattered like leaves caught in a winter gust when the door crashed open.

Alex stood in the doorway. Mud covered his boots and greatcoat—a clear indication he'd ridden like the wind to reach her. Tait stood behind him.

"Happy Christmas." She surprised herself with her calm demeanor. "You must be cold and famished. Let me get you some tea."

"Not now." Alex's gaze never left hers. "You may leave us, Tait."

As soon as the door clicked shut, Alex examined her from the top of her head to the bottom of her dress hem. Without a word, he swiftly reached her side. She tilted her head and regarded him as she prepared herself for their conversation. Though he'd only been gone a few days, she'd forgotten how tall he was.

Suddenly, she found herself in her brother's embrace. "My God, Daphne, I rushed back here. I couldn't live with myself if anything had happened to you." He released her. "Are you well?"

"Of course I am." She swept one hand in front of her, inviting him to examine her once more. "I'm uninjured, unhurt, and unscathed. To put it concisely, I'm safe and happy. I had a lovely feast this morning. There's plenty left if you'd like Mrs. McBride to prepare you a plate. She's Tait's mother—"

"Daphne, *stop*." Without any regard for the mud, he pulled his greatcoat off and threw it on one of the pink and red chairs closest to him. "I don't want to discuss food."

This was it, the moment his anger would explode like a lead ball from a cannon.

Instead, he continued to stare at her. The silence between them was deafening.

"What would you like to discuss?" she asked while she stood her ground. She'd come too far these past several days to show weakness in front of him. Nor would she, under any circumstances, tell him about the lost journal. "Before we get to me, how was your time at Pemhill?"

"You know damn well what I want to discuss," he growled. "Why didn't you send a note?"

Her heart skipped a beat, but she ignored the warning to proceed cautiously. She'd prepared for this conversation and would not become flustered and apologize. The good girl guise was long gone from her world.

"Shall we sit?" Without waiting for his acquiescence, she took the chair nearest to where she stood. It was her favorite, a high wing-back chair covered in a cheerful rose-colored brocade. "I was angry when I first discovered that you'd left without me."

"Now wait a minute, Daph—"

"Allow me to finish before you answer." She lifted her chin and straightened her shoulders. "But then I realized something. I wasn't your primary responsibility or concern. More important, I discovered that I didn't want to be. I want to be responsible for myself and my own happiness."

Alex shook his head once. Weariness made his face look like he'd taken a direct punch and was trying to get his bearings. He collapsed in the chair opposite her. "You can't imagine the worry I've carried all the way here. I didn't know if you'd be here. You never answered the question. Why didn't you at least send me or Mother a note?"

"What good would that have done? It would have arrived the next day, then everyone's holiday would have been ruined," she said without flinching.

Anxiety etched his face in an expression that told of his true regard for her. Her dear brother had worried about her. Her resolve melted at causing him pain. He knew she was weakening, because he slowly raised an eyebrow.

Guilt raised its hand wanting her undivided attention, but she refused to be swayed. She raised one brow of her own in answer to the challenge. "As soon as you or Claire read the missive, you'd have dropped everything and come for me. I didn't want that."

He leaned toward her and rested his elbows on his knees. "Why didn't you come to Pemhill on your own?"

"There were no drivers or groomsmen who could accompany me," she answered.

"Come now, Daph. You could have borrowed a coach from Langham Hall—"

"I considered it." Abruptly, she stood and began to pace in front of the fireplace. The soft crackling of the fire encouraged her to continue. "But it would have been too humiliating." She stopped her steps and, with a sharp turn, faced him. Anger stirred her thoughts like a witch's brew. "My own family forgot me."

He ran a hand down his face. "I apologize. Claire was beside herself when she discovered you were here. Mother was frantic. When she and Renton stepped into the Pemhill entry, she immediately asked where you were." A smile tugged the corners of his lips. "She missed you, Daph. Just like we all did." He stole to her side and embraced her. "What did you do to occupy your days?"

"I worked on my charity." Moreover, she spent an inordinate amount of time in the company of a charming duke.

"Daph, I thought we'd settled that idea." He leaned back, and his eyes swept her face as if taking inventory again. "What about your work at Emma's bank and Claire's charities?"

"You make my point about me being responsible for my own happiness. Those institutions are their dreams." She smiled. "I need my own. I have to follow my own desires."

"I still don't approve." His voice grew deeper. "It's unseemly for a woman of your stature to have a home for unwed mothers."

"If not me, then who, Alex? Perhaps my stature is perfect, and people will accept it because of my place in society. These women shouldn't be hidden away as soiled goods. They and their children deserve a place where they're safe and wanted."

"This is madness," he huffed.

"If it's madness, then I want to create a Bedlam for them and for me." She wouldn't back down, not now and not ever. "Besides, it's my life."

"It's your life, but you're my little sister."

"Who is twenty-five," she added.

"I don't care if you're ninety-five. You'll always be my little sister."

"No matter how old I am, you'll always see me as such." The graveness on his face told her that the point had been well-taken. It was the perfect segue into introducing the duke. "I met Southart several times over the holiday."

Immediately, that infuriating brow of his shot skyward.

"He's bidding on the same property as me. Once I informed him I was interested, he kindly told me he'd withdraw his bid." Things were proceeding quite nicely, since Alex continued to remain calm.

"Daph, anything Southart's involved in you should walk away from. Let me correct that. You should *run* from. He destroys everything he touches."

"Why would you say that?" Her tone was a tad too defensive for her own tastes.

"I'll explain," he said. "How much was his bid?"

"Three times the asking price."

"And what is yours?"

"What the owner originally asked." She let out a breath.

"There's your proof." Alex shook his head slightly. "Even if Southart's bid isn't accepted, he's muddied the waters for you. The owner will never accept asking price now."

"That's harsh, Alex. I found the duke to be a perfect gentleman." Her trepidation had started to grow stronger. If she didn't tell him about today now, she might lose her courage. "I invited him to breakfast this morning along with Mr. Devan Farris."

His gray eyes, a mirror copy of hers, narrowed. Instantly, the room's temperature dropped. The effect seemed to have frozen her words. Alex leaned close until mere inches separated them. "Daph, how stupid do you think I am? You invited him here to deliberately provoke me for leaving you in London."

"On the contrary, I find you annoyingly intelligent." She refused to blink but exhaled in preparation for battle. If he wanted a war, she would be more than delighted to fire the first shot. "But I do believe you're quick-tempered and have a tendency to jump to the wrong conclusions. I didn't invite him for any nefarious reason. He was kind to me, and I didn't want to spend the day alone. It was perfectly harmless."

"Harmless? I think not. You're entertaining a known rakehell alone while I'm away? That's a scandal in itself." He prowled away from her and poured a fingerful of Claire's family whisky. In one swallow he devoured it, then poured another in a new glass. "Did you ever think of the consequences?"

"What consequences? Now you're overreacting. The duke's friend, Mr. Farris, joined us. He's a vicar. How scandalous could it be? William was here, too," she added.

He held the glass to her, but she shook her head. She needed every wit she possessed to survive this quarrel.

"How long was he in my house?" He'd softened his tone, a warning to proceed carefully.

"William?" She swallowed and tried to find her courage, which had decided to slink from the room.

His stare had grown even more intense, if that was possible.

"The duke was here for only a couple of hours." Her knees knocked together. Somehow, she found her courage again. Instead of retreating, she stood still with her chin tilted in defiance.

"I cannot fathom that he was in my house." The

incredulity in Alex's voice would have been comical if they weren't discussing Paul.

"It's my house, too," she countered.

Silence again descended between them.

"Since when did you become the Marquess of Pembrooke?"

His enunciation made her squirm. Like the time she'd gone swimming at Pemhill and found leeches stuck to every inch of her legs and arms.

"It's my house, and I say who's welcome and who's not." His quiet tone didn't hide the warning in his voice.

"Fine. It's your house," she answered calmly. "I've decided to find my own residence. Though it's Boxing Day tomorrow, I've an appointment with Mr. Fincham."

"My solicitor needs a reminder of who he works for." Alex's retort flew across the room.

She stopped the fidgeting of her hands and fisted them by her sides. She'd come too far to give up her new visibility. "He's worked for the family for years. Not just you. I've instructed him to start a search for a small townhouse. I thought perhaps to lease at the beginning, and if it suits my needs—"

"A proper young woman doesn't live alone." He was getting angrier if the muscles tensing in his square jaw were any indication.

"A spinster does. Besides, I don't answer to you." *Had she really said that?*

"*Daphne*," he growled.

"You're home." The sweet, dulcet voice of her darling sister-in-law, Claire, came from the doorway. She rushed to Daphne and embraced her. "Oh, my word, we were so worried. Thank heavens you're safe."

"Claire, you made excellent time." Alex's demeanor immediately calmed when he saw his wife. A ghost of a smile even teased his lips. Such was the effect of true love. It could calm the most savage beast.

Claire kissed Daphne on the cheek, then went to Alex. She kissed him briefly on the mouth, then took his hand in hers. "Let's all sit and discuss this like civilized people."

"There's nothing to discuss, darling." Alex pulled Claire close to him.

"I agree with Alex," Daphne announced with a smile. "There's no discussion necessary. I'm establishing my own residence."

"Now wait," he said.

"Alex, hear me out. You make decisions all the time that impact my life without any consideration of me. I'll be the first to admit you've done a marvelous job looking out for my welfare. However, the time has come for me to make those decisions. I want to control my future." Whether it was her newfound mettle or Paul's friendship made little difference. She wouldn't capitulate to Alex's wishes. She brushed her gown, straightening the wrinkles. "I'm twenty-five years of age and wealthy in my own right. It's time I live my life the way I want. I look forward to it. Now, if you'll excuse me, I believe I'll go to my room. I'm in the middle of a particularly exciting novel."

"Stop, Daph. We're not finished here." Alex's voice had softened, but there was little doubt it was because of Claire's influence.

"Yes, we are." Daphne walked to the door, then turned. "It's lovely to see you, Claire. Happy Christmas."

"I must tell the whole sordid tale to Mother," Alex warned.

"If you don't tell Mother, I will. I'll start with how I was left alone in London by myself. I'll tell her how the Duke of Southart visited me daily to ensure I was safe while my family celebrated Christmas." Daphne never let her gaze stray from her brother. With each word, her conviction grew. "I'll finish by telling her how I invited him to Christmas breakfast so I wasn't alone." She opened the door but turned back to Alex. "One more thing. Tait no longer works for you. I've hired him as my new butler."

She didn't wait for Alex's reaction but continued to the family quarters. Her decision was steadfast.

Chapter Sixteen

❧

As Paul waited for his groomsmen to arrive with news about Garland and the journal, he considered Devan's argument that Daphne had to stand up for herself. It had merit, yet that didn't diminish the trepidation Paul had experienced. All of this was new to him. In the past several years, he'd spent the majority of his time thinking of only himself and Robbie. Mayhap, the explanation was simple. His responsibility for the duchy had changed his awareness to encompass more concern with the world around him.

The idea didn't soothe any of his restlessness. All morning, he kept thinking of Daphne. More than anything he'd wanted to keep worry from marring her beautiful face. What he wouldn't give to see her smile once more.

A quick knock on the study door broke his reveries. "Enter."

The footman Carter opened the door. "Your Grace, there's a woman asking to see you,"

"Show her in." Half-hoping it was Daphne, Paul suppressed his surprise when he saw the cook from the Reynolds. Elsie Qulin stood outside the door with her hands clasped in front of her without the boy and without the journal. "Come in, Miss Qulin."

Slowly, she made her way inside, then dipped a curtsy. The scarlet hue of her cheeks foretold bad tidings. "Your Grace."

"Did you find the boy or the journal?" he asked.

She shook her head. "When Garland wasn't waiting for me outside my boardinghouse, I took a stroll into Seven Dials. Mind you, I didn't go far as I'm not that foolish. But I found a young boy and asked if he'd seen the lad." She rubbed her forehead with her hand and looked in the direction from where she came. "There's not been a sighting or peep from him, I'm afraid."

Paul reached into his pocket and withdrew another guinea. "Thank you, Miss Qulin. Please keep me informed when you find him. I promise no harm will befall Garland at my hands."

She gingerly accepted the coin with a bow of her head. "I'll have Gilby send a runner as soon as I find Garland. This is the longest he's stayed away."

"Gilby?"

"The Reynolds majordomo." She studied her hands again and sighed. "He wanted me to tell you that you should keep Lady Moonbeam away from the Reynolds. Mr. Richmond has been asking about her."

Paul nodded. Mr. Gilby wouldn't have to ask twice. If Paul had anything to do with it, she'd never get near Martin Richmond or the Reynolds again. "Thank you, Elsie."

"Good day, Your Grace." With a quick curtsy, she took her leave.

Bloody hell.

He rang the bell, and immediately Ives entered. "Your Grace?"

"I'll not wait for Warren or Joseph to return from the butcher's. I'll go to them." He folded his reading spectacles, then laid them on his desk. "We'll take a stroll through Seven Dials if need be."

The butler's white eyebrows shot straight up. "Is it that serious, sir?"

"I'm afraid so." Daphne's reputation was in danger, and he'd allowed it to happen by escorting her to the Reynolds. God, would there ever be an instance where his good intentions didn't turn into shambles?

His coach-and-four made excellent time through the streets of London, since there was little traffic on the roads because of Christmas. Soon, the carriage stopped in front of Hamlin's Butcher Shoppe, the purveyor for the Reynolds and other London gambling establishments.

The coach door opened, and Paul stepped out into the street. Immediately, his groomsmen, Warren Judge and Joseph Campbell, made their way to his side.

"Your Grace," they said in unison.

"Anything?" Paul held his breath, praying for news.

Warren took off his wool cap and shook his head.

Joseph narrowed his eyes and glanced down the street as if still searching. "The boy never appeared. I think he's in hiding."

Warren nodded his agreement. "Your Grace, I searched Seven Dials this morning asking for a chore boy for the day. I got a lot of willing lads, but no one named Garland."

"I'll take one of you and search for the boy myself while the other stays here." Paul slapped his gloves gently across one palm in frustration. "He has to be found."

"Tell him," Joseph said.

Warren dipped his head. "I hope you're not angry, but I took matters into my own hands. While I strolled through Seven Dials, I asked if anyone knew the lad. No one came forward. I even offered a reward if anyone could help me find 'im. I said no harm would come to 'im. Only that the Duke of Southart had a need for a stableboy or two, and Garland had expressed an interest earlier. So far, the boy hasn't come out of hiding."

Paul exhaled. "That's quick thinking. I'm sure you're both cold and tired."

Both men shook their heads.

"We don't mind, sir," Warren said.

"Your wages are doubled this month, then." His men were loyal and deserved a reward for all their efforts.

"Thank you, Your Grace," Joseph said. "I'll send the extra home. My mum will be surprised."

"Aye. That's generous of you, Your Grace," Warren added.

The appreciation in both men's faces told Paul he'd made the right decision. Perhaps being duke was something he could manage after all. "Keep me informed of anything you learn."

Paul took one step into his carriage, then stopped. Down the street, a black lacquered carriage with the Pembrooke seal painted on the side pulled to a stop. With his greatcoat billowing behind him, he made his way to meet it. A woman with a black hat and veil elegantly stepped down. Her smart overcoat emphasized her lean but lush figure.

He exhaled a deep breath. He should have known his Moonbeam would take matters into her own hand.

When he reached her side, she tilted her face to his. The veil was an excellent cover, but he could see the silver of her gray eyes begging for information. He could see the red hue of her plump lips, the ones that enticed him to kiss her senseless. They were the same ones that caused *him* to lose all sensibleness.

"Paul, did Garland—" she asked. The tentativeness in her voice made him want to take her in his arms and never let go.

"Not here. Get in the carriage," he said.

The brusqueness in his voice made her start. Without a quarrel, she climbed back in the carriage, and he followed her in. She sat straight as a ramrod. The defensive gesture tugged at something deep in his chest. He wanted nothing more than to ease her concern, but he had nothing to offer except the truth.

"Do you have the journal?" She lifted the veil from her face, making her whispered voice clear enough to hear the apprehension that tinted every word.

"No. My men haven't seen him, and they searched Seven Dials. They even offered a reward for information. Elsie stopped by my house. She can't find the boy either," he answered. "He didn't meet her where he usually does."

Her hand flew to her stomach as if the breath was knocked out of her.

Instinctively, he reached over and took her hand in his. "I'm sorry, Daphne."

"What if he's hurt or ill?" Her gray eyes impaled him, and he was unable to look away. "Take me to Seven Dials. We must find him. Not just because of the journal, but I'd never forgive myself if he's lying in a gutter somewhere."

"Out of the question. You wouldn't last five minutes in that part of town without being robbed or stabbed."

The downcast look on her face transformed into a mutinous tilt of the chin. For some odd reason, he enjoyed her rebellious streak.

"I'll find a proper escort. Never worry." She settled into the seat and stared at him.

"Daphne." When she didn't move, he closed the distance between them until mere inches separated them. Those strawberry lips taunted him to taste. He slowly took a breath.

"No more excursions." He lowered his voice. "Let me

explain. Martin Richmond is asking about you. He wants
to know who Moonbeam is. If he finds out your true identity, you'll not only face ruin, but your entire family will
be impacted by your behavior."

"If Garland is capable, he will find Elsie," Daphne
protested. "She's all he has. I'll stop by the Reynolds
early in the morning when she leaves work. No one will
recognize me."

"It's too dangerous. You can't go back there. The last
time we ventured into the establishment, we were almost
caught by Richmond, remember?" He certainly recalled
the last time. He'd held her arms as he watched her writhe
and grind against his leg until she climaxed. A sudden on-
slaught of desire heated his blood, but he tamed the beast
as best he could. This woman turned his insides out.

All he could think about was protecting her from those
men. How laughable was that. He'd kissed her senseless
when those same men had been but five feet and one oak
door from discovering her in his arms.

Her defiance melted. "I don't suppose I have a chance
of changing your mind, do I?"

The torment in those beautiful gray eyes looked like a
brewing storm, one that had the power to slash his resolve.
Everything within him stilled, the moment suspended in
time.

He leaned back against the squab in an attempt to maintain his control. What was it about this woman that made
him want to do things so out of character? She couldn't
go back to the Reynolds, not after what Gilby relayed.

"You can't come with me, but I promise I'll find it and
return it to you," he said.

"Of course, it's a tremendous amount of work. Perhaps
I should hire a private investigator. I can't ask you to do
any more." She bit her full, lush bottom lip.

He subdued a groan. "It's best to keep this between us. The less people that know, the better. I promise I'll go to the Reynolds every day. Plus, I have Griffin Witt, another groomsman who grew up in Seven Dials. He's loyal, honest, and hardworking. I'll send him straightaway to see what he can discover. He still has friends who live there."

She looked outside the window as if deciding. Finally, after a moment, she returned her gaze to his. "I suppose that makes the most sense for now."

"If I can't find the journal within the week, I'll hire a private investigator," he said. "I promise."

"Speaking of promises, did you rescind your bid on my building?" she asked.

He blinked slowly. With everything that had happened over the last few days, he'd completely forgotten to send word to his solicitors. "I'm sorry. It slipped my mind."

Her eyes narrowed, and he got the distinct impression that the sudden chill in the carriage had nothing to do with the weather but her demeanor. "Pembrooke said . . ." Her words slipped into silence.

"What did he say?" Paul asked. "I'm anxious to hear how you handled it."

A small grin tugged at her mouth. Immediately, the carriage felt warmer. "He was against my decisions at first, but I have little doubt he'll support me once he gets used to the ideas. Alex is like a fine whisky. He needs to ferment his thoughts for a while, then he'll come around."

"As soon as we're finished here, I'll stop by my solicitors' office." He should have made the call two days ago when he first saw Daphne at Winterford. Instead, he dealt with another gambling debt his father had thoughtfully gifted him on Christmas Eve. Paul had found it on his desk after he arrived home from the furrier where he'd purchased Daphne's gift. "Did you tell him about me?"

He sat motionless except for his hand, which tightened into a fist as he waited for the answer. Whatever this was developing between Daphne and him had the markings of a great triumph or a colossally bad decision on his part. When Daphne's forehead crinkled into nice, neat rows, it didn't bode well for success.

"Yes, I told him." She tilted her head and stared.

"And?"

"Whatever he said is immaterial." She waved a hand, dismissing the subject. "You and I have an agreement. But your lack of action makes me wonder if you're changing your mind about the property."

"No, on my honor." He crossed his heart with one finger. "We have a bargain."

She nodded.

"Daphne." Paul intertwined their fingers and pulled her near. Her gaze pierced his. "I don't know how or when, but I'd like to see you again. Soon."

"Of course." She smiled, but it didn't reach her eyes. "I'd like that, too. I haven't forgotten my promise about Pembrooke."

He almost wished he'd never asked for such a promise from her. It only added more to her worries. But selfishly, it meant she kept him in her thoughts. "If you need me, send word through Tait. If it's urgent, come to the house. My butler is discreet." He brushed his lips against her soft cheek. "Now off with you, Lady Moonbeam."

He knocked once, and immediately the footman opened the door. He sprung from the carriage and, without a look back, proceeded to his own vehicle. For some reason, their parting had felt like a good-bye. The sudden emptiness that rolled through his chest almost made him fall to his knees.

Somehow, he stayed upright until he was seated in his own coach. He thanked heaven for small miracles. Devan must be having some influence on him.

Yet if he'd had taken one more look at her, he would have never left her side.

God in heaven, she deserved so much better than him.

Daphne rushed to the salon once she heard Emma was at Pembrooke House with her precious baby, Lady Laura Lena St. Mauer. It had only been a week since she'd last seen Emma, but during that time Daphne's life had been completely transformed, some for the good and some for much worse. A long talk with her best friend would settle some of the restlessness that had taken over her thoughts.

Once she swept through the door, her heart leapt. Emma looked like a ray of sunshine in a beautiful ivory dress that highlighted her blond hair. She practically glowed as she kissed Laura Lena on her cheek.

"Emma!" Daphne held out her arms for the baby and brushed a kiss across Emma's cheek.

Her friend laughed and handed the baby to Daphne. There were no words exchanged, as Emma knew immediately what she wanted.

Daphne cooed, "How's my glorious girl today?"

"If you're asking after me, I'm fine but tired." Emma settled on the settee in front of the fire. "But if you're referring to Laura Lena, she's in excellent spirits. The holidays agree with her."

Daphne kissed the baby's cheek. Her complexion resembled the color of pink carnations, and she smelled of spring, clean and fresh. Daphne uttered a sigh, then settled next to Emma. "How are you feeling?"

"Much better than when I was expecting Laura." Emma patted her still flat stomach. "Dr. Camden believes that this one will be born around midsummer."

"I'm so thrilled for you and Somerton." While clutching Laura to her chest with one hand, she reached over and laid her hand over her friend's. In that moment, Daphne physically felt the bond between them. Emma was a stalwart confidant, the best type of friend a woman could have. Daphne could share anything with her and there would be no judgments. "It's so good to see you, my lovely friend."

Emma twisted on the settee so she could face Daphne. "Spill."

"What?" Taken aback, Daphne asked, "Spill what?"

"Why didn't you come to Pemhill with us?" Emma lifted one perfectly arched brow. "Don't leave out a single fact."

"It's so humiliating." Daphne gently patted the baby, who fought against falling asleep.

Emma reached over and ran a finger down Laura Lena's cheek. Her mother's touch was magical. The baby shut her eyes almost instantaneously. "I'm your best friend. I'd never judge you."

Daphne drew close to talk without disturbing Laura Lena. "When the time came to leave for Pemhill, everyone had disappeared. Only Tait remained, and I asked him to stay with me. I was certain Alex would return for me, so I waited, and nothing happened."

"Go on," Emma encouraged. "I want it all."

Daphne swallowed the sour embarrassment the best she could, but she could still taste it. "Though I knew Mother and Alex each thought I traveled with the other, I was out of sorts."

"Understandably," Emma agreed.

"To tame my thoughts, I took a walk and settled on my park bench with my journal." She glanced at Emma.

Without any judgment, her friend nodded.

"A boy approached me asking for a coin, and when I gave him one, he stole my reticule with my journal." The words tumbled from Daphne's lips. "My private journal."

Emma gasped. "No."

"Oh yes." Daphne bent and pressed a gentle kiss on Laura's forehead. "I gave chase, but the little fiend slipped into the Reynolds." Daphne caught Emma's acute gaze. "The Duke of Southart happened to be there and escorted me home."

Emma's eyes widened. "Paul?"

Daphne nodded. "He was nothing but kindness."

"Is he gambling again?" asked Emma.

"Paying a debt from long ago." She closed her eyes for a moment. Memories of his gentle teasing and the feel of his lips possessing hers enveloped her in a delicious warmth that no blazing fire could match. "He's helping me find the boy and my journal, but we've had no luck. In return, I'm helping him repair his friendship with Alex."

When she glanced up, Emma's eyes had widened. "You'd never told me, but is *he* the one you were always looking for at those balls and society events we'd attend together?"

She should deny it. Daphne bowed her head and pretended to straighten the baby's blanket. She'd never told a soul why she'd escape from the crowds and find a view high above the ballrooms or a discreet corner at every musicale event.

It was difficult to share such personal secrets, and that left Daphne with one conclusion. If she couldn't be herself with Emma, her best friend, then she'd be hiding again. Today, she wouldn't deny what she wanted in life or what she felt for Paul. This was another step in shedding her self-imposed invisibility. "He's the one."

Emma placed her fingers over Daphne's hand. "You always reminded me of some regal queen surveying her kingdom. You'd find the perfect view and gaze about the room. After all this time, you were waiting for Southart."

Daphne nodded, then looked Emma in the eye. "I

looked for him every night even if he was out of town. But because of my family's regard for him, I didn't dare breathe a word. It's foolish, I know."

"Of course it's not," Emma said.

"I always thought he was special ever since I was a little girl." There was no use denying it. She'd never shared that secret, something precious she held dear. But she needed Emma's help. Too much was at stake. "He's so kind and visited me every day. He's bidding on the same building, but he said he'd rescind his bid."

"Has he yet?"

"No. But I trust him. There's more," Daphne sighed.

Emma tilted her head.

"*The Midnight Cryer* published a page from my journal, one that they bought from the boy who stole my things. It was a secret fantasy I'd written . . . about Paul." Troublesome tears pricked her eyes, but she blinked twice so they wouldn't fall. "They're trying to buy the rest of the journal from the boy and have threatened to publish more. I-I'm terrified. I've written some scathing letters and thoughts about my sister from long ago. It will hurt Alex and Mother terribly."

Emma grabbed her hand and squeezed. "*The Midnight Cryer* has crossed the line here. Somerton uses an informant, Mr. Goodwin, in his shipping business. Not a sneeze escapes London that Mr. Goodwin doesn't know about. Professional and competent, he'll help us find the boy and your journal."

Emma stood with a natural grace and started to pace.

"I appreciate the offer, Em, but Paul is trying to find it for me. The boy has gone into hiding. If he thinks that he's being hunted, he may disappear entirely. I need your help with something else. I promised I'd try to mend the breach between Alex, Somerton, and Paul."

Emma's emerald eyes sparkled when she stopped and faced Daphne. "What can I do?"

"It'll require getting Claire and my mother involved," Daphne announced, then quickly looked at the angel sleeping in her arms. Thankfully, she didn't wake. "I think if we invite Paul to dinner as a thank-you for his considerate treatment of me while I was home alone, it would help start a conversation between the three men. It can't be obvious to anyone. Soon, Paul will be hosting a charity soiree to help establish a hospital in his brother's honor. I thought if the women of the family got behind the effort, then the men might be more inclined to accept Paul and listen to his plans. It means a great deal to him."

"I'd be delighted to help," Emma said with a wily smile.

Suddenly, Laura Lena protested, and Daphne rocked the fussy baby in her arms.

"What harm could befall having a little fun while promoting a good cause?" Emma asked. "You and Paul are destined for one another."

Daphne pressed another kiss against Laura Lena's cheek. If only fate did link Paul's destiny with hers. She couldn't concentrate on dreams now. She had to find that journal before Garland sold more of it to *The Midnight Cryer*.

Chapter Seventeen

Daphne's lady's maid, Mavis Taylor, had returned to Pembrooke House after spending a lovely holiday with her family, and things had settled into the usual routine as Daphne waited for her world to implode. Garland and her journal were still missing.

Today, the runner Tait had hired came with news. Thomas Reynolds was looking for Garland also, which meant the boy would probably be back at the establishment working this evening. Daphne couldn't sit by and let fate dictate her future. There was only one thing she could do—go to the Reynolds tonight. *The Midnight Cryer* had been deceptively quiet, but the morning's edition hinted they were close to acquiring *her* diary. They expected to publish more scandalous entries this weekend. At the end of the article, the gossip rag had thanked its gentle readers for their patience and interest in the *harlot's* shenanigans.

Daphne blew a breath, causing a loose strand of hair to fall across her face. She angrily swiped the offending piece behind her ear. "Gentle readers" was an oxymoron if there ever was one. The entire family knew she enjoyed reading the gossip rag with Emma by her side at the bank. She loved discovering who was pursing whom romantically, and she always read every word to see if she could discover anything about Paul. She'd skip the stories that maligned reputations and ruined innocents.

Now that she was the one they were crucifying, she saw the paper differently. The gossip rags' subscribers were nothing more than vultures who flouted themselves as society's most esteemed members while gleefully devouring and spreading stories, particularly, if they destroyed lives, no matter the cost.

Earlier, she'd sent a missive to Paul asking him to meet her at the Reynolds this evening. Though he was more than generous in his pursuit of Garland, Daphne needed to be part of the hunt. She wouldn't allow Martin Richmond to skewer her family's happiness by publishing another entry without a fight. She had to find the boy, and Elsie was the key. With luck, before she retired this evening Daphne would have her journal in her possession. Her perceptive heart stumbled in its steady rhythm with the thought that she'd have Paul as her escort tonight.

Though he didn't want her near the gambling establishment, the truth was she'd never forgive herself if that gossip rag published one of her entries about Alice and her family suffered. She had little recourse but to visit the Reynolds tonight. She'd never rest if she didn't try once more to find the boy and her journal.

Mavis helped Daphne pick out a heavily beaded silk gown, a color between deep amaranth and purple. An overlay of fine silver netting made the fabric shimmer in the candlelight. Daphne had never worn it, saving the opulent gown for a special occasion. Simple but sensual in movement, the silk whispered with every move she made. A perfect ensemble for a midnight rendezvous with the Duke of Southart.

She straightened her shoulders in defiance. Tonight with her mask and her exquisite gown, she refused to be invisible to anyone anymore.

Including a certain duke with a penchant for moonbeams.

The hired hackney came to a slow halt outside the Reynolds. Mavis tied the mask carefully around Daphne's head, then stole a peek at Tait, who sat across from the lady's maid. Tait's visible exhale was silent, a sign that neither of Daphne's servants was comfortable with the idea of their mistress entering the gambling establishment.

Daphne glanced at the side entrance of the Reynolds. Thankfully, none of the establishment's patrons stood outside receiving the services of the prostitutes tonight.

"My lady, shall I accompany you inside?" The tremble in Mavis's voice sent Daphne's own nerves into flight.

"No, stay here with Tait. We'll only be gone for a short time." She prayed that was true. Fear crept into her veins like the slow movement of ice forming. Though Paul had escorted her inside the Reynolds before, she'd never experienced this type of foreboding.

The carriage door opened, and Paul held out his hand. "Lady Moonbeam, imagine my pleasurable surprise when I received your summons."

When Daphne placed her hand in his, the feeling of comfort she'd been accustomed to in his presence magically appeared, and she released her breath. Such was the power of the Duke of Southart. Her worries fragmented under his touch, and her unruly heart pounded at his roguish smile. "Good evening, Your Grace."

Her squeezed her hand gently, and she responded with the same. He made her feel that anything she wanted was possible. With him by her side, she came to life like a moth dancing in the moonlight.

Paul leaned near as they walked to the side entrance. His familiar scent comforted and whipped her senses into a frenzy at the same time. "I thought we'd decided you should curtail your excursions to this place. This is not wise."

"I couldn't stay away," she answered, keeping her voice low. "Did you see this morning's *Midnight Cryer*? He promises to publish something 'singularly explosive' within days. I have to protect my family."

He pulled her hand to his mouth and rubbed his lips against her gloved knuckles.

A hot ache grew in her throat at his caring gesture. "Please understand."

Within seconds, they were inside the gambling hell. No one guarded the door, and the hallway lacked any signs of life. She released the breath that she hadn't realized she'd been holding. She chided herself for allowing her trepidation to hold her hostage. There was nothing to fear—she was masked and had Paul's escort.

His gaze bored into hers. "I'll never forgive myself if something happens to you. Let us be quick." He took her elbow and escorted her down the abandoned hall.

Suddenly, a boisterous roar from the main gambling room exploded around them. Haunting ripples of laughter followed in its wake.

"If I've inconvenienced you by asking for your escort, I apologize. Perhaps I should have asked Devan, since he also knows about the journal, but I thought he might be offended at visiting such an establishment."

As they continued down the hallway toward the kitchen, Paul grunted. "He's entirely in his element here, but you did the right thing asking me. However, you would have started a bloody war if you'd asked Lord William to help you."

She smiled tentatively. "Indeed. My brother would have been livid if Will had escorted me."

"My lady, you misunderstand. I'm not talking about your brother." Paul's delivery lacked a mocking tone, but his humor was ever present in his tone. "I'm referring to me."

She grinned up at him, and he answered in kind. Suddenly, a door opened, and a large masculine hand grabbed her. Wrenched free of Paul, she found herself pulled into a darkened room with the door slammed shut behind her.

Without any light, blackness surrounded her. Shouting his outrage and pulling on the handle, Paul banged on the other side of the door, causing the wood to crack. Her fear became her ally, rallying her to escape. She turned to open the door as the soft light of a candle flickered to life.

"Lady Moonbeam, here you are *again*."

She stared wordlessly at the club's majordomo. His slight smile and relaxed demeanor immediately calmed her fear.

"What are you doing?" she demanded as her heart slowed its rapid pace.

"What I should have done in the first place. I'm removing you from the premises." He crossed his arms over his barrel chest. "If you ever attempt to enter the Reynolds again, I take no responsibility for any resulting action."

"Please. I'm begging you. I just need to see—"

Without warning, the door cracked like a battering ram was assaulting it.

"Insufferable dukes are the scourge on society. He's going to break the door with his shoulder," the burly majordomo announced as he swooped to open the door.

Paul stood with his feet spread apart. His furious gaze flew to Daphne's, and she nodded all was well. His anger dissolved into his familiar haughtiness. "Gilby, beside the fact that it's bad form to keep me waiting, you should never try to separate me from Moonbeam."

The majordomo shook his head, then pointed at Daphne. "Stay out, understand? There's danger here." He turned his attention to Paul. "You need to leave immediately."

"Please," Daphne said. "I understand Garland is to work this evening. Is Elsie here?"

"No, Lady Moonbeam. The duke has already made his daily visit, and I informed him that she didn't show up today, nor did Garland. It'd be best—"

"You were here?" Her gaze flew to Paul's face.

He nodded once. But his vexation was readily apparent with his clenched jaw.

"Thank you." Her heart thumped in approval as her voice softened. He'd kept his promise. Inside, the small remaining kernel of invisibility that held her captive loosened its hold.

Mr. Gilby nodded. "*Every day.* Now you must leave, Lady Moonlight."

"Moonbeam, not Moonlight."

The voice from the hallway made the hair on the back of her neck straighten in alarm. There was no mistaking the man's identity. She'd heard it in the alley the first time she'd visited the Reynolds.

Martin Richmond, the publisher of *The Midnight Cryer.*

With a smile, he walked toward her until no more than two feet separated them. "Makes me wonder what is so valuable that you'd risk being bodily removed from this fine establishment. Boughs of holly for your Christmas garland? I find I'm pursuing the same things. Perhaps a boy who loves food scraps from the kitchen? Desperation causes mistakes, doesn't it, my dear?" The threat in Richmond's voice was unmistakable. "Your mask does a magnificent job of keeping your face hidden. However, all I have to do is take a couple of steps and I'd be near enough to rip it off you. I'd have my answer as to the diary owner's identity, wouldn't I?"

Suddenly, Paul stood in front of her, and Mr. Gilby drew close to her side.

"I'm certain that I'd mentioned this, Richmond, but perhaps it needs repeating. I don't share. If you touch one marvelous hair on her head, I'll not be responsible for my actions. Understand?" The menace in Paul's voice sounded like a deep guttural growl, the kind that gave warning before an imminent attack.

Richmond laughed and held up his hands in surrender. "No need for that, Your Grace. But there are other ways to find out a person's identity. I find the hunt to solve the puzzle as gratifying as the actual publication of your identity, Lady Moonbeam."

Mr. Gilby took a step in the publisher's direction. "Mr. Richmond, I've been instructed by both Mr. Reynoldses not to allow you to harass the establishment's patrons or guests. Now, the way I see it, I can persuade you two ways. Whether it's by my charming personality or my physical prowess makes little difference to me. But it probably does to you, sir."

Richmond nodded, but the smile on his face didn't reach his black eyes. "I've always been susceptible to charm, my good man." He turned to Paul. "Your Grace, it's always a pleasure. I'm certain I'll see you again. Your duchy must not keep you busy enough. Perhaps I can help."

"I don't need your help," Paul answered.

Richmond stood his ground like a cock sure of his hens. "Come now, a little free publicity would certainly increase your popularity. Imagine the social calls when all of London hears that the newly reformed and *distinguished* Duke of Southart is sneaking—I mean escorting a . . ." Richmond's gaze lazily traveled the length of Daphne's body. "A woman of the night into this fine gambling establishment."

Though Richmond's gaze wasn't lurid, it seemed to

bore straight through her. It took every ounce of strength she possessed not to back away in fear.

Paul leaned close to the publisher and whispered, though they all could hear each word clearly, "I live for these moments, Richmond. It turns my dull life into an orgy of intrigue."

"As you wish." Richmond elegantly bowed to all. "I'll try my hardest. Look for the next edition of *The Midnight Cryer*. You won't be disappointed."

After he left, Paul ran his hand through his blond mane of hair, then held out his arm to Daphne. "Shall we, my lady?"

Still shaken by the confrontation, she grappled with what to say in response to Richmond's vile threats as she took his arm. "I'm sorry."

Paul shook his head. "Let's discuss this later, Lady Moonbeam." He placed his hand over hers and squeezed.

She nodded to the majordomo. "Mr. Gilby, thank you."

"You're most welcome." With his cheeks flushed and smile dimpled, the majordomo ushered them from the room, then pointed toward the side door. "Now, out!"

Silently, Paul escorted her to the hackney where Mavis and Tait waited. Thankfully, the alley was still empty. Instead of assisting her into the carriage, he steered them to the back of the vehicle.

He cradled her neck with one hand and the other encircled her waist. In one motion, he embraced her tightly as if he'd never let her go. Leaning close, he brushed his lips over her earlobe. "Oh God, sweetheart. Enough." The rumble of raw emotion made her heart pound in her throat. "Enough, hear me? Tonight"—he exhaled and his warm breath caressed her skin—"you put yourself in unspeakable danger."

She wrapped her arms around him in return and pressed her lips against his cheek. "I'm sorry, but I'm desperate to

put an end to this. Thank you for coming today and tonight."

"Don't ask me again, Moonbeam. You have to trust
me. The next time, I'll personally bar you from entering."
He kissed her soundly on the lips, then escorted her into
the carriage without another word.

Paul's valet, Brice Tobler, raked his gaze over Paul's jacket.
The fastidious manservant brushed Paul's shoulders once
more before nodding his approval. Paul studied the cravat
in the mirror and made the final adjustment.

Satisfied with his appearance, he dismissed the valet.
Tonight was another hallmark in his endeavor to rebuild
his respectability. A new and unexpected excitement
surged through him. The soiree was only weeks away. Already, the Duke and Duchess of Langham, the Duke and
Duchess of Renton, and the Marquess and Marchioness of
McCalpin had accepted his invitations. Langham had sent
along a note asking if Paul would call on him this week to
discuss the upcoming parliamentary session. The duke
also had invited Lord Kenton so they could discuss committee appointments within the House of Lords.

The request had pleased Paul to no end. His position
within society and the important political acumen necessary to make his mark as the Duke of Southart were
progressing nicely. With the Duke of Langham's support, Paul's wish to develop a legacy honoring Robbie
would soon come to fruition.

When Pembrooke and Claire's acceptance had followed
within hours of Somerton and Emma's acceptance, Paul's
confidence had soared. He wouldn't expect their immediate welcome, but their willingness to attend was a step
in the right direction.

"I'll send word you're preparing to leave for White's.
Anything else, Your Grace?" Brice asked before exiting.

Paul shook his head. Tonight, he planned to socialize at his favorite gentlemen's club. Since there were few of his peers in town, tonight's visit would be informal and a perfect opportunity to renew old acquaintances. The next visit, he hoped to renew even more. His struggle for new respectability would be won battle by battle. "Thank you. You've done a marvelous job in making my foray into society easier this evening. At least I look ducal."

The valet smiled. "You make my job easy, Your Grace."

Paul turned to the mirror and adjusted his sleeves once more.

"Your Grace?" His loyal butler, Ives, entered the room with a paper under his arm. His stance gave Paul the impression the man was hiding it instead of delivering it.

What a nonsensical thought, as Ives had served the family for over thirty-eight years in various positions. It wouldn't be long before the good man would retire. Paul hoped to entice him to stay in the position as long as possible. His history and experience with the duchy were invaluable.

Paul nodded in answer.

Ives shut the door, leaving the two of them in the ducal dressing room. He presented the paper, then swallowed, his prominent Adam's apple bobbing in an odd dance. "You should read this before you leave for the evening."

The Midnight Cryer's familiar type taunted him. Paul simply nodded. The butler's face was devoid of any emotion. A perfect response from a perfect English butler serving a not-so-perfect duke.

Paul straightened his shoulders in defiance. He'd not allow Martin Richmond's spew of stench spoil his evening. "Just lay it on my desk in the study. I'll read it tomorrow."

"Respectfully, Your Grace, you need to read this before you leave for the evening. It's about Lady Moonbeam."

Paul took the offending piece from Ives's outstretched hand. He'd instructed his loyal butler to alert him to anything dealing with Daphne. "That will be all."

He waited until Ives closed the door before he dared to read the headline.

LADY MOONBEAM'S GLOW CAPTURES EVERYONE'S ATTENTION
A CERTAIN "POOR" DUKE IS LEFT IN THE DARK!

Paul's body stiffened while his gut churned as if gutted. In black and white, without relaying any facts that could damage either Paul or Daphne, Richmond taunted them both.

Though he wanted to retch, he continued to read the filth before him.

A new celestial body has been orbiting the Reynolds, a lady by the name of Moonbeam. Her graceful reserve wobbled upon seeing this intrepid reporter. It was apparent to all that my presence broke up a lurid intimate tête-à-tête with another while her duke, who's no stranger to the Reynolds, lost his renowned charm and proceeded to bellow his outrage in the hallway. Meanwhile behind the closed door, Lady Moonbeam used her magic on another. Gentle reader, she's an enchantress ready to devour any man who can't fight against her charms.

What's most fascinating? She's after the same diary we are. Why would she be interested in such a book? The only plausible answer is that it's her scandalous entries!

It's my duty as a journalist to bring you every new detail I can on her wicked adventures. I warn all the great citizens of London. Protect the men of your family from such sorcery.

He swallowed hard, then turned to meet his gaze in the mirror. Deftly, he tugged the expertly tied cravat. His interest in attending White's disappeared faster than snow on a July morning.

His anger blazed at Richmond and, frankly, at himself. He'd caused this—Daphne's dance with ruin. If he hadn't cavalierly escorted her—repeatedly—to the gambling hell himself, she'd be safe. He closed his eyes as the memory of her scent stole around him. More fool he. His groin tightened and every muscle tensed as he recalled holding her close last night. The power of her lavender fragrance reminded him that she'd do what she wanted, and he found that more enchanting than infuriating. He was allowing his fanciful thoughts to control his decisions instead of common sense.

His own actions had caused not only her safety and reputation to be at risk but also his. Instead of trying to be a respectable duke, he'd completely allowed his own interests and desire for her to rule his actions. His time was better spent preparing for the soiree and wooing his peers to support his political and charitable agendas. Always a creature who catered to his baser instincts, he'd allowed his fascination with Daphne Hallworth to consume him.

He pulled the cord for a footman. He'd not go out tonight. Instead, he'd sit by the fire and try to find a way to disentangle her from this web he'd managed to weave around the both of them.

Chapter Eighteen

◠◡

The longcase clock gently chimed the half hour as if announcing the coast was clear for Daphne to escape.

She straightened her cloak while admonishing herself for such thoughts. She wasn't escaping or sneaking anywhere. She had business to attend to, and if that business took her to a friend's house, then so be it. She'd not rest until she saw Paul, especially after today's titillating article in *The Midnight Cryer*.

After she'd arrived home from Lady Ashton's dinner party accompanied by her mother, Alex, and Claire, she made the excuse of a headache—which wasn't far from the truth—and retired to her room. Her mind whirled with the paper's brusque words and innuendo. The threat that they'd soon discover her identity had stunned her so completely that she couldn't think. Once she reached the confines of her room, her brain had functioned again.

What was more, Richmond knew exactly what he was doing. If he could infuriate Paul or her so they reacted to the article, then Richmond had a lead to Daphne's identity.

If the publisher of *The Midnight Cryer* found out she

was Lady Moonbeam, then he'd have the identity of the owner of the journal.

It was a dire threat she'd have to address, and soon. If Paul washed his hands of the whole affair, she wouldn't blame him. His own reputation was now at risk. But she still needed his help if he was willing.

"My lady, Tait has secured a hackney for both of you." Mavis's soft whisper interrupted Daphne's musings.

"Thank you," she answered. They kept their voices low so as not to alert any other servants of her midnight travels.

"Don't worry," her maid reassured her. "I'll stay in your room in case anyone checks on you during the night."

Tait's gentle steps down the entry staircase broke the silence surrounding Daphne and Mavis.

"My lady, are you ready?" he asked.

She nodded, then addressed Mavis. "I'll be back as soon as possible."

"I'll be waiting for you." Mavis handed Daphne the muff that Paul had given her for Christmas. "My lady, this probably isn't my place, but you've been so kind to me." Mavis grabbed her hand and held it tight. "His Grace is a good man with a good heart. He'll continue to help you."

Daphne didn't answer. Instead, she followed Tait down the hallway that led to the servants' entrance where the hackney waited.

Deep inside, her own heart encouraged her to tell Paul the whole truth. She should tell him of her regard for him and for how long. That would mean opening herself to the heartache of his rejection. She reached into her pocket and grasped the heart-shaped rock he'd given her years ago. So many times, it provided the strength she had needed when she didn't think she could endure the sadness. He'd given her comfort when she'd so needed it the most—whether he realized it or not.

Tonight, he would understand how much succor he'd provided in the past.

She'd tell him as much as she dared and only hoped it was enough.

"Your Grace?"

Ives's question broke the silence that had descended in the study. Paul had prepared to retire for the evening, but his chambers offered little solace from the heaviness that weighed on his shoulders, so he'd returned to his desk. He'd finished answering the letters and invitations that had been strewn across the desktop. Afterward, Paul had moved to the sofa that framed the fireplace. He tore his gaze away from his entertainment, the thorough examination of the blazing fire before him, and directed it toward his butler, who stood inside the doorway of his study.

His study. Every day he was becoming more comfortable in his role—his legacy—as the Duke of Southart.

"Lady Daphne is here to see you," the butler said.

"I insisted." She stepped from behind Ives.

Paul nodded. He didn't stand and didn't say a word until Ives left.

"I'm not certain what the proper etiquette requires when a practically undressed man has an impromptu visit from an *unmarried* woman in the middle of the night," he said, deceptively calm.

That should shock her. Freshly bathed, he was naked under his banyan.

A hint of a smile tipped her lips upward. "Ives tried to dissuade me from seeing you, but I told him it was urgent."

He studied her face, which was barely visible under her black wool cloak. A rosy glow colored the tip of her nose. What did it say that Lady Daphne Hallworth had braved the cold to visit?

It said she was desperate to see him to have ventured out in the middle of the night.

It was the only conclusion he could draw, and he'd never had much talent in art.

One fact couldn't be denied—the woman was on the path to ruin.

She pushed the hood of her cloak from her head. The firelight licked her cheeks with an iridescent glow. For a moment, envy surged through every inch of him. Such a nimble light could touch her face, and he couldn't—no, shouldn't.

Lucky fire.

"I know it's late—"

"Or early depending on your perspective," he quipped.

"Clever," Daphne conceded and smiled in earnest.

"How did you manage to travel here so your brother wouldn't know?" He kept his voice even like a slow, meandering stream as he spread his arms in a leisurely manner across the back of the sofa. The movement made his banyan gape at his chest. He shouldn't bait her or make her think he wanted to seduce her.

The problem was *he did want to seduce her.*

"Tait hired a hackney," she answered.

"Ah, the talented and transcendent Tait. Tell me, where is the intrepid fellow and why isn't he by your side? He could play chaperone." His mind warred with his cock. In an attempt to keep the peace and some semblance of his sanity, he didn't invite her to sit. The air between them seemed to shimmer with a restless energy, one ready to explode.

"Ives instructed Tait to leave and said you'd see me home." She swallowed.

"Rather impertinent of the old fellow, don't you think?" He stretched his legs apart, causing the banyan to fall open even more. "You shouldn't be here this late, Moonbeam."

She bit her lip and stared at him.

He wanted to groan at the sight. Her red lips glistened in the firelight.

"I'm going to lock the door. I don't want us interrupted." Gracefully, she turned. The gentle click signaled they were alone together.

Immediately, his cock twitched like a setter ready to point.

Or a pampered lapdog begging for a treat.

Her eyes never left his as she came to his side. His limbs felt heavy as his blood pounded. God, she was beautiful, and he was afraid his best intentions would go awry this evening.

Finally, she stopped several feet away. She dropped her gaze to her clasped hands, then lifted her head. "I had to see you."

"For what purpose?"

"To apologize about the Reynolds." She untied her cloak, revealing a simple ivory gown, nothing like her earlier evening attire.

It was becoming.

But that wasn't where her true beauty resided. Her face would steal men's hearts in a crowded ballroom if she looked at them the way she was studying him now.

He released his breath slowly and discovered that his earlier weariness had completely vanished. "I should be the one with the apologies. Let's not confuse the matter. I should have never escorted you to the Reynolds. A mistake of elephantine proportions."

Her eyes narrowed, and it was the first hint he'd raised her ire. He should be thankful. It would make it easier for her to see his true self if she was angry. His father had taught him that lesson.

"Elephantine? My, you are full of yourself aren't you, *Your Grace*."

For a moment, he heard Devan's mockery in her voice.

"You wouldn't be the first one disappointed in my failings, nor shall you be the last." He leaned his head against the sofa and looked at the ceiling so she couldn't perceive his own disappointment within himself. "If my father were here, he'd gladly point out my natural tendency to spoil anything I touch. And I don't want to spoil you."

At this moment, he couldn't bear the pity that would mar her beautiful face. She was by far the most perceptive person he'd ever met. With one look, she'd see how scarred he was from the countless clashes he'd had with his father.

The bastard wouldn't even leave him be in death. Paul had another debt waiting for him this evening to be paid. This one addressed to "My Misbegotten Mistake."

"He doesn't sound like much of a father." She propped her hands on her perfect hips. "But let me correct your misperception. I would have gone to the Reynolds with or without your assistance. However, I was glad for your company."

The frankness that tinged her mellifluous voice made him want to drag his eyes from the study of the ceiling, but the wounds were too raw. He would reveal the vulnerability that had seeped into every inch of him. Best to tell all of it and destroy what remaining regard she held for him.

"Would you like to know the rest of the truth of why I disparaged Claire to Alex all those years ago?"

For a second, the fire blazed as a log collapsed, then subdued itself.

"Yes." Her voice had grown eerily quiet.

"When your brother stole her away from me, I wanted to destroy him, my best friend, for taking that singular moment in my life when my father was proud of me." The ugliness of his actions nauseated him. "He was the only other person I was close to besides my brother, and I wanted to obliterate him. Now you know what I'm capable of. What a monster, I am. That's why he's leery of me."

Silence reigned through the study. Without looking at Daphne, he could feel the heat of her stare.

"You hurt my sister-in-law and my brother. Their marriage almost didn't survive because of your actions. No, you don't need to remind me of what you did. But I also know you're human. I have no doubt you'll do the right thing." The coolness in her voice disappeared. "Your *father* was the monster. Not you. He should have cherished you." The ferocity in her words took him aback. "Don't let him torment you anymore. He's gone. Look at your own accomplishments. You've survived his ugliness and become a worthy man. Last night you proved how wonderful you are to help me though you'd already visited the Reynolds earlier." The rustle of her dress betrayed her movement. She took a step closer. "The Duke of Langham is supporting you and your idea for the hospital. Everyone thinks it's spectacular. Surely you heard the accolades. I see how incredible you are."

The wall he'd built around his heart to protect him from any hurt she might inflict crumbled like a sand castle in high tide. With what little remaining pride he possessed, he forced himself to drag his gaze to hers.

She nodded. "It's true."

Her eyes spoke a thousand words, and for that moment he actually listened. It was easy to believe she thought him a worthy man, perhaps the most important man in her life. The piercing frankness in her gaze made him light-headed, almost drunk. But for honor's sake, he'd give her a chance to disavow him.

"I haven't done much to remove my bid from Winterford House. I have no excuse, except I forgot once again.

Your brother's assessment of me is correct. I spoil everything I touch."

"I'm confident you'll do the right thing." She pursed her lips. Her heavenly eyes foretold her true regard. They flashed with laughter that resembled lightning from a summer storm. She swallowed, but her mirth still floated around the room, giving it warmth. "Otherwise, I'll haunt every remaining waking hour you possess on this earth."

If that were only true, he'd believe he'd died and gone to his heavenly rewards.

He glanced at her bodice, and his cock tented his banyan in approval. He didn't hide his erection, as he wanted her to see the effect she had on him. For good measure, he widened his legs. He was doubling the ante to force her to see him as he truly was—a complete reprobate. Perhaps she'd think twice before showing up in a man's house in the middle of the night unescorted.

God, he was turning into a prude. He was the one who invited her to come anytime day or night in the first place. "Daphne, you should leave."

"I don't want to." With a lissome movement, she dropped to her knees in front of him—right between his legs. She studied the outline of his erection, then raised her gaze to his. "I don't think you want me to leave either."

He looked into her eyes for any sign of mockery or, worse, any sign of fear. There was confidence and her unique feminine poise. Hotter than any fire, it made him burn.

She made him burn.

More logs collapsed in the fireplace, breaking a well-constructed dam within him. All his doubts were washed away to be replaced with hope for the future. In that moment, he could almost see himself as the man she thought she saw. A man who could carry on his family legacy with pride and accomplish great things. With her belief in him, he could become the man he wanted to be. The man he'd promised he'd become.

All he needed was her.

"Come here," he whispered. He waited for her to reach for him, but Daphne sat back on her heels and studied him.

"I think the world of you. You should know that." She slowly untied his banyan as she continued to study his face. "You asked me last night to trust you. I do, and tonight, I want you to trust me."

His breath hitched. It took every ounce of strength he possessed not to drag her into his arms and kiss those sweet lips as he made love to her.

"What are you doing?" His voice cracked like a schoolboy on the cusp of manhood. In protest, the sofa creaked as his hands tightened on the wooden frame.

Her gaze slid from his eyes to his lips and finally down to his chest. She inhaled deeply and sighed. "You're breathtakingly handsome."

Inch by inch, she regarded him. The prolonged anticipation of her touch was unbearable. "Are you going to kiss me?"

"Eventually." Her husky whisper had lost all traces of her earlier laughter.

Daphne reached with one hand and traced the muscle of his right calf before reversing direction and caressing his ankle. Without hesitation, she placed both hands on the backs of his legs and retraced her movements.

Time stood suspended as he catalogued her every move. Inch by inch, she massaged his skin with her hands like an artist learning every muscle, sinew, and bone. Her gentle movements should have relaxed him but had the opposite effect. They caused a hunger like no other.

She leaned closer and imprisoned him with her familiar fragrance of lavender. He couldn't escape if his life depended on it.

Thank God for small miracles. His blood heated with desire, and his erection lay straight on his stomach, pulsing with need. If he took himself in hand, a mere two strokes would have him coming like an adolescent.

The now familiar virgin witchery she possessed unfurled in her eyes, and he was powerless. She moved her hands over his knees and continued her path of exquisite torment until she reached his thighs. He made the mistake of glancing down. The sight of her hands so close to his cock made him groan with need for her touch. Every nerve of his body was primed to unleash the rabid animal within that wanted her beneath him. His hands twitched to grab her.

He closed his eyes, desperate to gain control. But out of nowhere, the warmth of her hand surrounded his cock and then her sweet mouth took possession. His eyes flew open. When he tried to speak, the words lodged in his throat as the most perfect and intense sensations took over.

She was a virgin all right. She lacked expertise, but she explored him while she touched and teased. She tongued his length where a huge purple vein twined in an aimless fashion. At such superb torment, he pushed his hips forward.

Instead of moving away from him, she took more of him in her mouth. With her tongue, she traced the crown, then slid it over the slit at the top.

Then she did the unthinkable—she moaned. The vibration from her throat against his organ caused every powerful sensation to congregate in his spine.

Without saying a word, he scooped a protesting Daphne into his arms, then had her straddle his legs. The position pressed her mound against his cock. Though it was still an exquisite torture, it was one he could control.

"What are you doing?" The throaty deepness from her velvety voice caused him to grow harder, if that was possible. Everything this woman did affected him.

"I'm going to kiss you." Semen leaked from his tip, crying for her to finish what she'd started.

"Didn't you like it? I thought I was doing it just like the prostitute."

"You are an enchantress. Yes, I liked it. No, I more than liked it." He placed his fingers against the silky skin of her lips, causing his own skin to twitch like a horse before a race. Those very lips had been wrapped around his cock not moments ago. "See what you've done to me. You've stolen my sanity."

He closed his eyes and placed his forehead against hers. If he concentrated on his breathing, he wouldn't come—at least not yet.

She pushed her center against him. Without waiting for him to initiate the kiss, she put her lips against his. Her open-mouth kiss was an invitation, one that Paul readily accepted as he took possession of her mouth. Teaching her, coaxing her into a rhythm they both enjoyed. Her little murmurs and groans encouraged him more.

With one hand he held her close as he used his other hand to push her gown up her legs. He cupped her bottom and pulled her tighter against him. She whimpered her approval. In one move, he flipped them both so that she lay underneath him.

Her gaze captured his. "Are we going to make love?"

If she were any other woman, he'd have already entered her by now. But Daphne deserved the best. Frankly, she deserved the best of him. Making love to her—tonight—was not the best for either of them. He lightly fingered a loose lock of her black silk hair, then brushed the back of his hand gently across one pink cheek. "Sweetheart, is that what you want?"

She blinked slowly. "I don't know. I hadn't thought about it."

"Perhaps we should find another way . . . to enjoy one another."

"I'd like that," she answered.

Slowly, he took her mouth in another kiss as he pushed his cock against her center—skin to skin. The wetness of her arousal caused his heart to pound. Nipping her bottom lip, he continued to move against her. Her breathing increased and she lifted her hips to meet his over and over. She was close to coming. The flush of her cheeks made her gloriously beautiful.

"Paul." She pulled him close as her body tightened against him. The dulcet sound of his name on her lips was more magnificent than the finest Viennese string quartet. He shifted to his side and brought his hand to her hip. A woman's hip had to be the most perfect creation in the history of the world. Daphne's was a masterpiece. He traced the soft skin with the flawless angles, then shifted his hand lower. His fingers strayed to the soft curls that protected her clitoris.

"Let me touch you." He trailed his lips against her temple.

She nodded, then placed her hand over his, directing his touch.

God, she was beautiful and gloriously wet. It excited him that she knew what she wanted. Tonight, he'd help her find the sweetest release she'd ever imagine.

With his fingers, he separated her folds, then found her perfect pearl drenched from her arousal. It was pure splendor in her arms. He caressed her clitoris in gentle circles. In response, she mewled and pushed her center harder into his hand. He continued, and her cries become more urgent, more demanding. Her breathing accelerated, and she undulated her hips. When he felt the first stiffening of her body, he stroked two fingers inside her. Her eyes closed. The pulsing of her orgasm squeezed his fingers. Once again, she'd let herself go in his arms.

Gently, he removed his fingers and caressed her hip once more. The sight drove him to move over her once again as he pushed against her center with his cock, mimicking the act of making love. Each stroke against her soft, wet center sent pleasure careening through him. He was desperate for completion. After fighting his arousal for what seemed like hours, he let it consume him. He roared her name as his climax crashed through him. It possessed him in a way he'd never experienced—the duration lasting longer than he ever remembered. His seed glistened in the candlelight where it marked her abdomen. For some foolish reason, he was proud that she bore the remnants of his release.

He pulled her tight against him as he buried his head in her soft neck, murmuring her name over and over. His heartbeat slowed from its earlier relentless pounding as his body came under his control. He could feel the strong beat of her heart against his. If he died in this position, it would be the equivalent of heaven—he was certain of it.

He placed gentle kisses along her collarbone, then her neck, each one gentler than the last. It was his way of slowing down the tempest they had created in each other's arms. Across her perfect cheek, he pressed his gentlest kiss.

"Sweetheart, I need to get you cleaned up and take you home." He nudged her ear with his nose. He could touch her all night. If he was honest, he wanted to take her to bed, make love to her all night, and then sleep all day beside her.

He stilled at the thought. It had never crossed his mind to take a woman to his bed. His room, his bed, was his sanctuary, a place where no one could invade his space.

But with his Moonbeam, he wanted to whisk her off her feet, walk up the stairs to his chambers, and lock the door.

With her hands on both sides of his head, she gently combed through his hair, the repetitive touch soothing. Yet he could feel his arousal growing again and his desire for her waking from its short rest. He was convinced he'd never tire of her. Never before had he acted like such a schoolboy. He reached for one of her hands, then placed a kiss against her palm. One endearing kiss to help her understand this was special to him also.

Her look of enthrallment mirrored how he felt. She was entranced as much as he was.

"I don't think I care to be cleaned up." The deep huskiness of a well-pleasured woman colored her voice. Her half-lidded eyes delighted him. She was drunk with passion, and he wanted nothing more than to yield to that desire that swirled between them.

He'd always thought her beautiful, but with the gorgeous flush in her cheeks from the remnants of her release along with her strength and regard for him, she could bring him to his knees.

"Why is that?" he murmured.

"Because I'll keep my gown as a valuable trophy." She leaned up and touched her nose to his. "Just like you with your pantaloons that night at the Reynolds."

He buried his head in her soft hair to hide his laughter. The effort futile as his body vibrated with mirth. "You are an incorrigible and wicked woman who's ruining me," he huffed with the right amount of ducal arrogance. "Let it be known, I prefer you that way."

He stood and took his last glance at her half-naked body against the brocade of his sofa. It was now his favorite piece of furniture in the house. While he was alive, he'd see that it was never reupholstered. He held out his hand, and she placed her warm hand in his.

A sign of trust.

"Well, it'd be my greatest honor if you saved your gown as a memento, but your hair is a tangled mess that needs tending." He pulled her to standing. "We need to get you at least presentable for Tait, not to mention Mavis." He took her hands in his and studied her infinite beauty. "How wicked would it be if I asked you to stay with me tonight?"

"Hush." The tender word caressed him. Her smile lit the entire room in a warmth that was fueled by the goodness and pure charisma of Daphne Hallworth.

Without another word, he led her out of his study to a retiring room where she could freshen up. He instructed the footman to prepare the smallest carriage and hot bricks for the short ride to her home in Mayfair. He'd not have her catch a chill.

Within minutes, he was dressed and downstairs waiting for her.

His old emptiness, a near-constant companion, seemed to have deserted him. Instead of melancholy, he had a new purpose, a new cause to consider. She was perfect for him. Her passion matched his, and they got along exceedingly well. There was only one honorable thing to do.

He would offer to marry her. His only obstacle was proving to her family that he was worthy of her. Whatever it took, he'd prove to them and himself that he could be the perfect man and husband for Lady Daphne Hallworth.

After he saw her safely home, he'd retire for the night. He had plans for his Moonbeam. Thoughts of her and their future would keep the old ghosts that haunted him every night at bay.

Daphne woke when the gentle nudge became a shake. She struggled to open her eyes.

"My lady, you must get up," Mavis urged.

Groggy, Daphne pushed herself up to a sitting position

and brushed her hair out of her face. She'd sent Mavis immediately to bed after she'd arrived home. Tired and anxious for sleep, she'd taken off her dress and carefully hidden it in her keepsake chest, then collapsed into bed. She'd forgotten to braid her hair last night, and a mass of tangled strands surrounded her like Medusa's snakes.

"What time is it?" she asked.

"It's after ten o'clock, my lady." After pulling open a drawer, Mavis yanked out a chemise and clean petticoat. She whirled around the room until she stood in front of an armoire. With a pull of the door, she reached inside for stockings and ties. The poor maid resembled a top zigzagging from one side of the room to the other.

The sight made Daphne dizzy. She closed her eyes and, without delay, her thoughts returned to last night. After she and Paul had entered his carriage, he'd placed a hot brick under her feet, then tucked her tightly against him. By then, she couldn't fight her exhaustion, so she'd relaxed in his embrace. Within minutes, they'd arrived at her house. All was quiet in the carriage house. There were no groomsmen or stableboys milling about. A window close to the servants' entrance glowed by candlelight.

Before they exited the carriage, he'd pressed a kiss against her forehead. Silently, he'd escorted her to the door. Before either of them could press the latch, the door opened. With a welcoming smile, Tait stood before them. Paul took his leave after he'd ensured no one, specifically Alex, was awake and waiting for her.

She opened her eyes and sighed with pleasure. It'd been a magical night. They'd shared themselves physically, but there was more. Without saying it explicitly, Paul cared for her. His gentle attentions to her well-being and comfort were proof of his regard. In his eyes, she'd seen—dare she think—deep affection?

How her life had changed. Every new strength she possessed could be attributed to Paul.

"My lady, *pleassse,*" Mavis begged.

"I'm up." Daphne struggled to stand.

"Thank heavens," Mavis muttered. "Your mother is downstairs asking for you. When Simms told me, I rushed up here to get you dressed. Lord and Lady Pembrooke are out all day, and I was going to let you sleep, but this is an emergency—"

"Mavis, it's my mother, not the queen," Daphne assured her. "She'll not mind waiting for me."

Mavis nodded and exhaled a big sigh. The maid ran her hand down her face.

"I'm sorry, Lady Daphne, but your midnight excursions are taking a toll on my nerves."

Instantly, all thoughts of sleep fell away. For the world, she didn't want her actions to have a detrimental effect on her sweet maid. "I'm sorry, Mavis. I never wanted you to suffer because I lost my journal. I promise this will soon be over."

"I'm happy to report that there was nothing in *The Midnight Cryer* this morning." Mavis nodded with a tight smile. "Once that journal is found, we'll all breathe easier."

The vise around Daphne's chest loosened. She had another day to find the journal.

"I want you happy, Lady Daphne." Mavis grew serious. "But I want you to be careful, too."

"I promise." Daphne turned and sat at her dressing table. Mavis's message had been clear, though the words remained unspoken. She was concerned that Daphne would entangle herself in a scandal that would ruin her completely.

Daphne was well aware of the risks, but for the first time in her life, she felt alive. She felt beautiful and admired.

The grief over Alice's death was no longer like a black cloud raining over her every day, coloring every mood. Instead, it had morphed into something different that was hard to define.

Mavis returned to Daphne's side and patted her shoulder in reassurance. Daphne shut her eyes as Mavis's gentle ministrations worked their magic on brushing the tangles out of Daphne's hair.

Daphne would never accept Alice's reasons for taking her own life, but for the first time since Alice's death, she might be able to understand. Her grief would always be there. But she had hope that it was changing into something she could live with—something that would allow her to find her own happiness without feeling guilty.

For this special day, she chose a gown of sky blue with silver netting. Trimmed in navy ribbons, it reminded her of Paul's eyes last night when his desire for her had reached its zenith. When he'd shouted her name, her heart wanted to burst from her chest and reach him.

Her mother wouldn't mind waiting if she took a little more time with her appearance today. In minutes, Daphne entered the breakfast room where her mother was waiting.

Though they'd seen each other yesterday, she missed her mother. Charlotte St. Mauer, the Duchess of Renton, was gorgeous in her late fifties with a lithe figure. Her silver hair and gray eyes complemented her complexion and drew a person's attention to her face. But what made her truly beautiful was her personality. The natural ease about her exuded a kindheartedness and devotion that attracted people to her side.

"What a welcome surprise," Daphne announced as she ran to her mother's side. She dropped a kiss to her cheek, and the sweet fragrance of her mother's familiar scent swept over her. "What do I owe the pleasure of your company?"

"Do I need an excuse to see my beautiful daughter? Have you eaten, sweetheart?" Without answering the question, her mother returned to her chair and lifted the teapot, offering to pour Daphne a cup.

Daphne nodded and took the seat opposite. The room was empty except for the two of them. She helped herself to two tarts and a cold slice of bacon.

Her mother set the cup in front of Daphne and studied her. When Daphne took a bite of the flaky apple tart, fine lines creased her mother's forehead indicating her worry. "Sweetheart, didn't you sleep last night? You're not coming down with a cold, are you?"

Daphne chewed the bite slowly as she squirmed in her chair. Trust her mother to find the weakness in her armor. "No, madam."

Her mother narrowed her eyes. "'No' to the sleep or 'no' to the cold."

The bite of tart stuck in her throat. She took a gulp of tea. The scalding liquid scorched her tongue. She wanted to curse at her slurping instead of a more ladylike sipping. She cleared her throat, and the troublesome piece of tart disappeared.

"I slept well," she offered. "And I have no cold."

"Perhaps later a nice glass of elderberry wine would bring some color back into your cheeks." Her mother leaned closer. "Are those dark circles under your eyes, dearest?"

Daphne took a deep breath in hope of gathering her composure that was slipping out of the room like a guilty thief. "Mother, I assure you, I'm right as rain. In fact, I'm in a marvelously good mood."

But she did tell the truth about her delightful disposition today. She'd practically spent the night in Paul's arms, and it had been pure heaven. She should consider writing her own dictionary. Under the word "heaven", there should be a sketch of him as she found him last night. A glorious archangel welcoming her with open arms.

A deep sigh escaped her. She had to put her thoughts of him aside and discover the reason for her mother's visit and summons this morning. "Tell me why I have the great pleasure to eat with my own mother this morning."

Her mother replaced her teacup on the saucer. She tilted her head and regarded her.

Daphne forced herself to hold her mother's gaze.

"Renton and I had a long conversation about you last night."

"About?" Daphne raised a brow. The movement probably mimicked her brother's trademark expression, which was her intention. She needed a bit of his swagger this morning to stop the conversation from drifting into waters she didn't want to navigate.

Her mother hesitated. "Well, you see . . ."

"Yes?"

A tiny smile tugged at her mother's lips. "After Alex told me Southart had been here with you, and you suggested we invite Southart to dinner, I discussed it with Renton. He and I thought dinner this evening would be perfect as a way of thanking Southart for that whole Christmas business. It was really quite gallant of him to watch over you while you were home alone."

Daphne's anxiety melted. "I think that's a marvelous idea."

Her mother nodded her approval. "Excellent, as I've already sent an invitation to Southart House. Pembrooke, Claire, Somerton, and Emma will attend, also." Her mother's gaze swept over the front of Daphne's gown. "His actions reminded me of how he was when he was a boy and always staying with us at Pemhill. He's really quite dear." Her mother threw her serviette to the table and stood. "Come along, my dear. Let's pick out a gown for you to wear this evening. One that will steal his breath away."

Wary about how to address such a statement, Daphne slowly joined her mother in standing. "Pardon?"

Her mother's smile hinted at a smirk. "Please, darling. I may be old, but I'm not dead. It doesn't take a genius to figure out why a duke would spend so much time with a respectable, intelligent, and utterly beautiful young woman."

Chapter Nineteen

Paul entered the Duke of Renton's London home later that evening, and the butler, a middle-aged man with a proud carriage, soon escorted Paul into a formal pale gold and ivory decorated salon. Bold with an elegant touch, it was the ideal place to meet before dinner. With Daphne and her entire family there, tonight would be the perfect opportunity to talk to the duchess and Alex about his intentions toward Daphne.

It would also provide an excellent chance to tell Daphne that he'd hired the private investigator James Macalester to find Garland and the diary. Time was running out and Martin Richardson was getting bolder in his publication posts. The quicker they got the diary, the better for them both. Paul had even sent Griffin Witt, one of his groomsmen, who grew up in Seven Dials, to visit his old haunts looking for information.

Soft sounds of feminine laughter flooded the room. It reminded him of the sweet jangle of wind chimes or a bubbling brook—such a joyful, happy noise, one he hadn't heard frequently in his life until recently. Paul stood in the salon doorway as the butler prepared to announce his arrival. With a smile, he politely waved the man away.

Feminine laughs, giggles, and gentle snorts came from the direction of two large ivory brocade sofas that faced each other directly in front of the roaring fire.

Whoever they were, they hadn't noticed his presence as the soft laughter continued. Taking matters in hand, he crossed the room and rounded the sofa to a sight that nearly choked him. On the floor, three women rested on their elbows and knees side by side with their bottoms lifted in the air. It was difficult to tell who the other two were, but the one in the middle he'd recognize anywhere.

It was Daphne with her perfect derriere.

He cleared his throat. "Am I interrupting, or do I have the wrong evening for the dinner invitation?"

Three heads popped up like jack-in-the-boxes. Flanking Daphne's sides were Claire Hallworth, the Marchioness of Pembrooke, and Emma St. Mauer, the Countess of Somerton. Daphne was the first to get to her feet.

She gracefully stood with a bundle clenched to her chest. "Good evening, Paul."

Claire and Emma stood back several feet. Both looked guilty as if they'd been caught with their hand in the biscuit jar.

Perhaps it was apprehension with his company. He was a guest, but one their husbands were surely not pleased with. He stood frozen, waiting for a response.

Completely oblivious to Claire's and Emma's discomfort, Daphne walked closer and presented a blanket bundle. "Come meet Lady Laura Lena St. Mauer, Nick and Emma's daughter."

Gingerly, he stepped forward until mere inches separated them. Daphne gently pulled the covering away from the baby's face and smiled.

"Isn't she beautiful?" Daphne crooned.

Speechless, Paul stood there. What was the proper protocol? Ask to hold the baby? Could he touch her? Befuddled and with no clue how to handle the situation, his gaze flew to Daphne.

She must have seen the panic in his face. "Would you like to hold her?"

She held the baby up to him, and he had no recourse but to accept the tiny squirming bundle from her. He looked down at two emerald-green eyes that, in turn, studied him. He had little doubt she could see every hope, aspiration, and hidden secret he possessed. Then she blinked and sighed.

"Good evening, Lady Laura Lena," he whispered as he cradled her close to his chest.

The baby rewarded him with a near-toothless grin, then flailed her hand in the most awkward manner as she tried to grab his hair. Immediately smitten, he studied the little being full of life and deduced she was an expert charmer already at her young age. She'd be giving her father and mother fits long before she made her introduction to society.

He looked to Daphne, who glanced at him and smiled in approval. He grinned in answer like a star pupil who had just received praise from his tutor. Without a doubt, this woman and her smiles could mold him into a man who only wanted to please her. Instead of being baffled at the thought, he relished the challenge. Such was the effect of Daphne Hallworth. Returning his gaze to Laura Lena, he dared to brush the back of his forefinger across her cheek, which was softer than a cloud and more perfect than a rainbow.

"Lady Somerton, there's only one conclusion I can draw." He caught Emma's stare. "You and Somerton have been truly blessed. She's beautiful."

The hint of wariness on Emma's face vanished. "Thank you, Southart."

Those three words broke the invisible barrier surrounding Claire and Emma. They came forward and gathered around him just like Daphne. Giggles broke out again as they marveled at the baby's antics with her hands. The women praised the baby as if she had mastered Newton's law of gravity.

Paul gently returned Laura Lena to Emma. The baby squealed her delight at being back in her mother's arms.

"For a moment there, I thought I might be ambushed," Paul said. All three women turned their attention to him, but their smiles lingered this time.

"What do you mean?" Daphne asked.

Sheepishly, he regarded Claire and Emma. "I made a complete debacle of a betrothal to one of you. The other I offered for and received a resounding rejection. I was concerned that I might have worn out my welcome before I even arrived." He cleared the frog jumping and careening in his throat. "Lady Pembrooke, as time passes, my heartfelt regret grows deeper that I caused you pain when I besmirched your honor and broke our betrothal. You have every right not to believe me, but the only thing I can offer is my sincerest apology. Someday, I hope you'll forgive me. Until then, know I live with my shame every day."

Claire just stared at him. The entire room fell silent. Even the baby quit her wiggling to listen to his apology. He forced himself to continue, though it was painful, but having Daphne by his side made doing the right thing easier.

He turned to Emma. "Lady Somerton, when I asked your father for your hand, I did it out of a sincere wish to help you avoid scandal. As the months have passed, your decision to reject my suit can only be described as sound. If I caused you any discomfort with my impromptu offer,

I apologize. I hope you both accept my apologies for my previous"—he pushed aside the momentary panic that called for him to laugh to hide his embarrassment—"indiscretions."

Claire genuinely laughed, and Emma wrinkled her nose and smiled.

"There's no cause for worry, Paul," Claire announced with a smile. "I've always wanted to thank you for breaking the engagement. I wouldn't be happily married with three beautiful children of my own if you hadn't."

Emma chortled. "And I thank you. If it wasn't for your offer, I always wondered if Somerton's argument to marry him would have been half as convincing."

He chanced a glance at Daphne. Her face had softened with an emotion he could only perceive as love for these two women. She would be a stalwart friend and companion for their entire lifetime. They were lucky to have her as family.

The longcase clock against one wall announced the hour with a succession of low chimes. Waiting for each strike, he'd remember this moment forever suspended in time.

The truth seized all thought and colored every perception he'd ever possessed.

He wanted that emotion from Daphne. He wanted her company every day of his life.

He wanted her love.

With every second that passed, his feelings grew stronger. He loved her.

Dredged from a place beyond all logic and reason, the admission startled him. Never before in his life had he felt such an emotion for a woman. Last night, he'd made the decision to marry Daphne. It was a matter of honor—a way to protect her.

What a fool.

Deep down, he'd wanted her as a wife because he loved her. Overwhelmed, he shook his head slightly and smiled.

The admission made him more determined to make tonight a success when he asked for her hand in marriage and revealed his true feelings.

"If you'll excuse me, I need to put Laura Lena to bed before dinner," Emma said. She gently rocked the baby in her arms and settled her friendly gaze on Paul. "I'm truly delighted you're joining us tonight."

"I should leave, too, and see to Liam, my youngest." Claire rested one hand on Paul's arm. "I want to thank you for all you did for Daphne while we were out of town. You're a true friend."

Emma nodded her agreement, then the two women took their leave. Any concern that things might be awkward with the Hallworth family faded somewhat after Claire and Emma had welcomed him with such warmth and genuine affection. But he still had to face Pembrooke and Somerton.

"Shall we sit?" Daphne waved a hand at one of the sofas before them. "Mother and Renton will be down shortly. I'm not certain where Alex and Somerton are."

Stunning in a seafoam-green silk gown, she exuded confidence. It made her even more attractive. He allowed her to sit first, then moved beside her—close, but not too close, in case someone interrupted them.

"Daphne, I'm not certain where to begin, but I must tell you—"

Before he could utter another word of his declaration, two children peeked into the room. Spying Daphne, they raced to her, then bumbled to a stop. The eagerness on their faces gave them the appearance of little imps.

"Aunt Daph, we want to meet your friend," the little girl announced. Her gray eyes and black hair matched Daphne's coloring.

The other child, a handsome little boy with green eyes and the same black hair, studied Paul as if he were some slimy creature from a Scottish loch, then announced, "Papa says you're here for Aunt Daph."

Daphne's face softened as she regarded the two. She stood and Paul followed. "Let me make the proper introductions. Your Grace, may I introduce Michael Hallworth, the Earl of Truesdale, and his sister, Lady Margaret Hallworth." The affection in Daphne's voice was unmistakable. "Meet Lord and Lady Pembrooke's oldest children."

Paul extended his hand to the little girl, who looked to be about four years old. "A pleasure, Lady Margaret."

Daphne leaned down. "Margaret, you should take his hand in yours and curtsy."

"I don't want to." With a scrunched-up face, she backed away and giggled. "He's not my grace. He's your grace, Aunt Daphne."

"No, dearest. It's how you address a duke," Daphne explained. "He's the Duke of Southart, and proper manners require you address him as 'Your Grace.' Now turn to His Grace and give a proper curtsy like you've practiced."

Lady Margaret shook her head emphatically, causing a riot of black curls to bounce around her face. "I don't want him. You can have him or give him to Truesdale."

"I don't want him," Lord Truesdale declared. "She gave him to you. He's your grace."

Margaret looked at her brother with a seriousness that belied her age. "No, Aunt Daphne said he's yours. Remember when she said 'his grace'? That means he's yours."

Truesdale looked up to Daphne for guidance. "I thought Grace was a girl's name?"

Before Daphne could answer, Margaret propped a hand on her hip. "Silly. Grace is what you say before you eat." With a giggle, she turned her attention to Paul. "I have a cat named Minerva. She had kittens on my *maman*'s best ball gown. I brought one with me this evening. Would you like to meet her?"

Daphne shook her head. "No, dearest. His Grace doesn't want to see—"

"Don't take off your boots around Percival. He'll chew through the toes," Truesdale offered as he pointed to Paul's immaculate black Hoby boots.

Just like her father, Margaret furrowed her brow and nodded. "That's my brother's pug. He's done it twice with our papa's boots."

Holding his laughter, Paul looked at Daphne. "Do Pembrooke or Claire know they talk like this?"

"Yes. They do this all the time, I'm afraid." Grinning, she leaned close to Paul. "They just started deportment lessons with a new governess."

Daphne's happiness made her features more animated. The sight made his smile broaden in answer. "What strange but charming little creatures you live with."

Daphne nodded. "Well, the children adore Percival and Minerva."

"You misunderstand me," Paul whispered in return. "I'm referring to Lord Truesdale and Lady Margaret."

The shock in her eyes melted, and a laugh escaped that caused her gray eyes to sparkle. Another interruption kept her from answering.

"There you are." A nursemaid with a pleasant face entered the room, then dipped a curtsy Paul's way. "Pardon me, my lady, the marquess asked that I inform you that he'll be in shortly." With a smile, she held out her two hands. "Come. I've a special treat for you both. I've some freshly baked biscuits in the nursery."

No sooner than the words were out, Margaret and Truesdale rushed to the nursemaid's side. The trio walked out of the room with both the children talking over each other. The maid seemed to possess the unique talent of keeping track of each child's conversation and responding when necessary.

Still standing, Paul took Daphne's hand. Before Pembrooke arrived, he had to tell her his true feelings. "I have something I must tell you."

"What is it?" Daphne placed her hand over his. "Is something amiss?"

"Are we interrupting?" Before they could sit back down, Pembrooke's unmistakable growl reverberated through the room—more like a warning than a polite question.

"Your brother always did have the worst timing," Paul whispered. He squeezed Daphne's hand before gently letting it go. He turned his attention to Pembrooke and Somerton.

Both men resembled large wolves ready to attack in tandem, and the menacing looks on their faces didn't bode well for a warm welcome. Pembrooke reached them first. With a reluctant sigh, Daphne's brother extended his hand in welcome. The shake was brief and perfunctory. Somerton followed suit with the same courtesy.

Before anyone could utter a word, the Duke and Duchess of Renton entered, followed by Claire and Emma. Pembrooke and Somerton immediately stood guard over their wives but kept a wary eye on Paul.

Depicting an ease he didn't actually possess, Paul greeted everyone. Soon, the entire group entered the dining room en masse. Thankfully, Paul sat next to the duchess at one end of the table. Daphne sat directly across from him. The duke sat at the other end with Alex on his left and Claire on his right. Emma sat to Paul's left next to Alex, and Somerton sat directly across from his wife in between Daphne and Claire.

On the surface, the dinner proceeded with joie de vivre like any other gathering of friends. The duchess, Emma, and Daphne were charming in their attentions to him. When Paul tried to draw Somerton into conversation, it was stilted and awkward. Several times, Alex tried to garner Daphne's attentions, but she ignored him for the most part.

Paul asked Alex about this year's production of barley at Pemhill. Renowned for its excellent yields per acre, Pemhill was a model that other estates tried to mimic with little success. Paul explained he wanted to increase crop production at his ducal estate and would welcome any advice Alex might give.

The marquess grunted some nonresponse about crop rotation.

Daphne's eyes grew wide, but she wisely said nothing. Paul didn't want the affair to grow any more uncomfortable than it already was. Apparent to all, Claire's pointed look pierced her husband's gaze.

Heaven help him, it was going to be a long evening.

Thankfully, the rest of the meal passed without further rancor. Giving Paul confidence—and dare he say hope—that tomorrow he'd be announcing his betrothal to his beautiful Moonbeam to Devan and the staff at Southart Hall.

Before the liveried footmen served dessert, the duke raised a glass of wine in hand. "Here's to renewing friendships. I'd like to offer my sincere thanks to Southart for everything he's done recently for our family and Daphne. When Charlotte first heard that Daphne was alone, she was heartsick. We rushed back to town, not knowing what to expect. Southart, upon our arrival in town, we learned of your generous care and concern for Daphne. Both Charlotte and I can never repay you for your kindness and regard."

Paul chanced a peek at the duchess. Gratitude lined her face. When Paul turned his attention to Daphne, everything within stilled. The flash of her eyes and the smile that tugged at her lips not only enhanced her beauty but also held him spellbound.

The duke cleared his throat. "Please. Will everyone join me in honoring our guest? May the past ties that bind us continue to strengthen in friendship and love."

Soft feminine cries of "Hear, hear" and "huzzahs" sounded around the table.

Everyone lifted their glasses—except Pembrooke and Somerton.

An awkward silence fell across the room like an uninvited guest. Stunned at the obvious rebuke from his two former friends, Paul stared at the table, drawing strength to harden his gut for the blow that was inevitable. As the seconds passed, red-hot heat marched up his neck like a marauding band of Vikings. He'd made a fatal error in his campaign to win her hand. He shouldn't have come tonight. Damage was clearly done, and he needed to exit quickly if he had a chance to salvage his offer for her, especially before tonight turned into a disaster that could never be rectified. If he stayed, words might be spoken that could never be taken back. He could easily see Pembrooke forbidding him from seeing Daphne again. It was too great of a risk.

He took a deep breath, then forced his gaze to Daphne and mouthed the words, *I apologize.*

He stood and faced the Duke of Renton. "I thank you for the kind words and your generous spirit."

No one breathed or moved. The women at the table had paled at the direct cut designed to unnerve him. If there had been any doubt about Somerton's and Alex's regard for him, their quiet disgust was clear to all—especially him.

With as much dignity as he could summon, Paul sat back down at the table. "Perhaps it's best if I leave." He turned to the duchess. "Madam, your generosity on my behalf will be fondly remembered. Always."

The duchess placed her hand over his. "When I invited you to dinner, I expected my family to be civil." She turned her gaze to Pembrooke. "I apologize for the obvious lack of manners possessed by some at *my table*."

Daphne turned in her chair and stared at her brother. "How could you?"

"Daphne, now is not the time," Pembrooke growled.

"I agree. Now is not the time to act like an arrogant arse," Daphne's retort flew down the table.

Pembrooke's expression remained frozen. Claire leaned toward him and whispered something.

"If Mother has invited an estranged friend, one who has been everything loyal and kind to a member of your family, manners dictate that a reconciliation should be forthcoming." The ire in Daphne's voice was obvious.

"If Mother has invited a rogue to dinner, then we all should expect an uproar," Alex murmured.

"Enough, Pembrooke," his mother said.

"If Mother has invited a prig to dinner, then we should expect a sanctimonious spectacle," Daphne answered. "All of us have just witnessed such a performance."

"Don't, sweetheart," her mother soothed.

Daphne's gaze flew to Paul's. "I'll not let him humiliate you anymore."

All Paul could manage was a nod. "I agree with your mother. My presence isn't worth causing a breach with your brother. He's concerned for your welfare."

How could he have foreseen the evening ending any other way? Pembrooke would never accept him as his friend. Stunned, without the ability to move, he let his mortification bleed into every inch of his body. Understanding gnawed at his insides like an incessant worm. He'd never be accepted as a suitable husband for Daphne no matter how noble his intentions or how much he loved her.

His damaged past was too much to overcome.

Further proof of how unworthy he was in the face of people who he'd once considered as dear as family—as dear as Robbie.

Numb, Paul nodded his thanks to Renton and his duchess. He turned to Daphne and simply gazed at her. For as long as he lived, he'd never get his fill of her beauty and, more important, her courageous spirit and kindness.

He didn't care a whit if Pembrooke beat him to a bloody pulp, he'd tell her good-bye. "Thank you for everything, Moonbeam." His whisper was low enough that only she and perhaps the duchess heard the words.

Her eyes suddenly widened, and her pain transformed into glistening tears that caught the candlelight. The sight cut him deeper than a stab wound to the chest. With his heart torn from his chest and his pride left in tattered pieces, Paul left the room with as much grace as he possessed.

Without a second glance, he entered the vestibule and asked a footman to retrieve his greatcoat and beaver hat. The servant nodded and hurried to a room adjacent to the entry.

A small voice called, "Her Grace?"

On the bottom steps of the grand marble staircase, Lady Margaret stood in her nightclothes with a small orange-striped kitten in her hands.

"Good evening, Lady Margaret." He closed the distance between them and crouched on his haunches. "What do you have there?"

"This is Rufina." Margaret studied him. "My brother and I are spending the night at *Grand-maman*'s house tonight. I snuck Rufina over in my coat."

He reached out and scratched the kitten's head. A sound like the rumble of soft thunder burst from the creature.

"Here," Margaret declared. She held the kitten with both hands, letting her small legs dangle. "She's purring. She likes you."

"You suppose?" Paul took the kitten and ran his fingers through the soft fur. The warmth of her body offered comfort, but he didn't deserve it. His actions over the years had come home to roost like a murder of crows. How appropriate that the blackness of their feathers matched his thoughts.

He tried to give the kitten back, but Margaret shook her head. "Her Grace—"

"Sweetheart, it's 'His Grace.'" He smiled at the precious girl's antics and continued to stroke the kitten. He'd steal all the comfort he could find.

Margaret shook her head vehemently, causing another cascade of black curls to swirl about her shoulders. "You're wrong. You're Aunt Daphne's grace. Not Truesdale's." She wrinkled her perfect little nose. "You look like you need a friend, Her Grace."

"I do. Will you be my friend?"

"Of course, silly." With a winsome grin, she declared, "You need a friend to go home with you, Her Grace. Rufina needs you, too. *Maman* says we can't have any more pets. I was going to give her to *Grand-maman*, but I changed my mind. Will you be her friend?"

The earnest question flooded him with a yearning that perhaps could only be answered with the kitten's company. Paul nodded. "That's very generous, Margaret."

"I'll come and see her," she declared.

"I'd like that," he whispered. He bit the inside of his cheek to keep his tight control. "Come and call on Rufina whenever you want."

"I must go back upstairs before I'm caught out of bed."

Margaret leaned close and kissed Rufina's head, then without any hesitation kissed Paul's cheek. Without a look back, she scampered upstairs and disappeared.

With her sharp claws digging into his coat, the kitten crawled up his shoulder and settled next to his neck, her loud purr strangely comforting. Paul stood with the kitten nestled close when the footman returned with his belongings.

At least the night hadn't been a total waste. He'd made two new friends—Lady Margaret and Rufina.

The truth did little to calm the bloody ache in his chest that grew in strength with his every breath. Marriage to him would be nothing but one long humiliation that Daphne would suffer with her family. Such a sacrifice would be too great for both of them. He couldn't let her feel such pain. Thankfully, he hadn't asked her to marry him.

Though he'd lost the one woman he'd ever truly loved, he'd not fail her in securing her stolen journal. It was the only thing he could promise her.

Then, like a bolt of lightning, he understood he was going home with more than Rufina.

His old companion, loneliness, sidled up next to him with the promise to keep him company.

Chapter Twenty

After Paul's departure, silence reigned within the Duke and Duchess of Renton's intimate dining room. The pounding in Daphne's heart lit a fire of anger that refused to die and caused her blood to boil.

"That was beneath you, Pembrooke," she announced, not hiding her rebuke. "Mother and Renton invited Paul into their home to share a meal and friendship. Not only were you rude to him, but to them also. You should be ashamed."

Her mother reached over and squeezed her hand. "Sweetheart, why don't you go home and retire? Renton and I will come over tomorrow to discuss how to make this right with Southart."

Renton caught her mother's gaze and nodded. Empathy and sadness lined his face for his wife's discomfort. "Of course, my love. That's sound advice. Cooler heads will prevail in the morning."

"No, Daphne," Alex warned, his deep baritone laced with resolution. "I'll not be ashamed for trying to protect my sister from ruin or heartbreak. He leaves everything he touches in shambles."

Somerton turned his solemn gaze to hers. "Daphne, your brother is only concerned for your well-being."

"Oh really, Somerton?" she hissed. Though her ingrained manners dictated she not be sarcastic, tonight called for a different type of comportment. "If he's so concerned for my well-being, why would he embarrass my dearest friend and Mother's guest?"

"Not here, Daphne," Alex bit out.

Emma laid her hand on Somerton's arm. "If both of you had seen the way Paul looked at Daphne in the salon before you arrived, you would have seen his true regard. I'd say he cares deeply for her." Emma turned her gaze to Claire. "Wouldn't you agree, Claire?"

Claire patted her mouth with the serviette, the movement an obvious attempt to gather her thoughts. Slowly, she placed the cloth on the table and turned to Alex. "I never like to disagree with you, but I agree with Emma. Daphne and Paul are friends, dear friends, I might add. Your sister is a wonderful judge of character. As such, we shouldn't make judgments about him until we know more. His effort to start a hospital that will benefit those in need is another example that he's taking his ducal responsibility seriously."

Ignoring everyone, Alex took a sip of wine.

Emma straightened in her chair. "Alex, Southart's care for your sister during the Christmas holiday was—"

"Secretive and cowardly," Nick added.

"He didn't come and confess what he'd done," Alex argued.

The thin restraint Daphne had on her anger broke free. Furious, she stood and faced both men. "Neither of you has any idea what you're talking about. He's been nothing but gracious and kind to me. When he first discovered I was alone, he offered one of his carriages and a maid so I could travel to Pemhill. On Christmas morning, he offered

to stay at the house until you arrived and personally ex
plain to you what had happened. I asked him not to."

Not after she'd discovered that *The Midnight Cryer* had
published her fantasy about Paul.

"Proves my point entirely. Any man of honor would
have stayed and seen the situation fully resolved." Alex
stood confronting her.

"It was my duty, not his, to tell you what had happened,"
she countered.

"Daph, he'll break your heart," The gentleness and conviction in Alex's voice cut the distance between them.
"I've seen it countless times."

"Oh, please. What a ludicrous idea," she scoffed. "He'd
never hurt me. He's the only one who puts me first." She
closed her eyes briefly and willed her anger to abate, then
lifted her chin for courage. "Alex?"

Her brother's face had softened, his eyes lined with
pain.

God, she didn't want to hurt her brother or anyone at
the table, but she'd not let him and Somerton continue in
their misperceptions of Paul. She'd not let her brother ma-
lign the man she loved with all her heart.

"Alex, if you don't accept Paul and what he means to
me, you'll leave me no choice. If forced to choose between
him and my family . . ." She paused and held her brother's
gaze. "I'll go with him." She turned her piercing stare to
her stepbrother. "The same goes for you, Somerton.
Whether either of you believes my reasons are sound
makes little difference."

Alex's eyes narrowed. "My God, this isn't friendship
we're discussing. It goes much deeper, doesn't it?"

"Yes, it does." She'd not reveal her regard for Paul in
this fashion. Not when she and Alex were so angry. She
turned and addressed the others. "Mother, thank you for

dinner. It meant the world to me." She nodded her thanks to Renton.

"Daphne, my dear. We'll see you tomorrow," Renton offered.

She forced a smile, then turned to her best friends in the world, Emma and Claire. "Thank you both for your support. You're not only my family, but my greatest strength and truest friends."

Without a glance back, she left the room and soon was in a Pembrooke carriage. Thankfully, Mavis hadn't accompanied her this evening, which made her decision all the easier. She leaned out the carriage and directed the driver to take her to the Duke of Southart's residence.

She'd not rest until she told Paul how sorry she was for her family's behavior. More important, tonight she'd tell him her true feelings.

She loved him and wanted a life with him.

As his wife.

Paul sat at his desk with a roaring fire lighting the room. Flashes of red and gold lit the papers strewn across his desk. A letter from his father's solicitor reminded him of their appointment tomorrow. The old duke's one last rant at Paul's failings would be delivered in the morning.

There was really no need for his father to have extended the effort, as Paul had been reminded ad nauseam about his own deficiencies this evening. He struggled to comprehend how in the world something so rare and pure as his regard for Daphne could have turned into his greatest regret. The humiliation on her face had been a punch to his gut, one he vowed never to be a part of again.

Rufina lay draped around Paul's neck like a pet albatross. How fitting that the tiny purring mass of fur was a

reminder of how devastatingly dire the entire night ha
been.

He shook his head at the sentiment. At least the eve
ning held one bright spot. A small girl with bright gra
eyes had been his own guardian angel tonight, offerin₂
something that few in this world wanted from him—
friendship. Margaret had recognized his sadness immedi
ately, and her gift had already brought him comfort—he
small kitten, Rufina, a keepsake he'd cherish.

He chuckled at Margaret calling him Her Grace. In
deed, he was Daphne's, or at least that black-haired siren
was his—someone he'd treasure for the rest of his days
even if they couldn't share a life together. He raised hi:
gaze from the papers on his desk to the fire. The reality o
his bleak future returned.

The study door opened. Assuming it was a footman at
tending to the fire, Paul shifted his gaze back to the pile
of papers on his desk. Rufina stretched, then snuggled
closer. Paul repositioned the kitten so she wouldn't fall
while giving a few scratches behind the ear.

"What do you have around your neck?" Daphne stood
before him more beautiful than ever. Her tentative smile
had a force that was greater than the moon's pull on the
Earth. "Is that Rufina?"

He fought with every ounce of his strength not to rush
and take her in his arms. Instead, he nodded once. "Margaret gave her to me when I was leaving. If she wants her
back, you should take her."

She shook her head. Her presence resembled a shimmering spirit he had suddenly conjured from his thoughts.
"No. I'm sure Margaret and her mother are thankful you've
taken Rufina as your own. Tomorrow, the kitten was to
make her new residence at one of the Pemhill barns.
You've spared Rufina the long trip and Margaret unnecessary tears."

"That's me, the knight in shining armor," he quipped sarcastically. "At least to a little girl."

"A twenty-five-year-old girl happens to think so, too." Daphne's whisper was as fragile as a moonbeam's dance across the floor on a cloudy night.

"Sweetheart, I'm the antithesis of a knight or a hero." Having forgotten the kitten wrapped around his neck, he leaned back in his chair, only to have the little one clawing at his neck to remain.

Piqued that her sleep was soundly disturbed, Rufina jumped from his shoulder to the desk. Paul scooped the bundle of fur in his hands and set the kitten on the floor. She gave a little stretch, then meandered on the hunt for a cozy chair in the front of the fire where she could curl into a ball.

"What are you doing here?" Paul asked, then added quickly, "Not that I mind." Truthfully, it felt so right to have her with him at home. "But shouldn't you be with your family? What if someone sees you here?"

She stared without uttering a word. The firelight danced with abandon about her ebony-colored tresses. Such a vision reminded him that he'd sell his soul for one more night with her.

"I don't care what others think. I must tell you . . ." She cleared her throat. She studied the floor for a moment, then forced her gaze to his. "I confronted Somerton and Alex about their boorish behavior toward you."

His body stiffened, but he forced himself to relax. He raised his right hand to adjust his left cuff, then dropped it. He was well aware that it was a protective action, but the well-honed movement was as natural for him as breathing—particularly after all the practice he'd had with his father. Deep down, he knew he didn't need to be defensive with her. "Why would you go against your family?"

She chewed on her lips, then with a flutter of her hands,

she wrapped her arms around her waist in a protective gesture.

He stilled at the sight. Momentarily robbed of the ability to think or breathe, he inhaled sharply. He stood slowly, never taking his eyes from hers. Whatever she was about to tell him was excruciating painful for her, and he'd do anything to protect her from any unnecessary heartache or worry—particularly since he'd caused it.

He clenched his fist—the need to take her in his arms turned into a raging hunger, a need he had no right to satisfy. He circled the desk and leaned against it. Like a selfish beast, he craved her and her presence. He wouldn't touch her, but he could feast on the sight of her.

"It wouldn't be honest for either of us if I don't say what I'm feeling." Her quiet determination showed her true strength of character.

The woman who stood before him deserved every happiness life could offer, particularly after all the sorrow she'd experienced. If he had the power, she'd never suffer any further worry or hurt if he had anything to do about it.

She took one hesitant step nearer, keeping her arms wrapped around her waist. "I . . . I meant every word I said to my family because . . ."

The room grew silent with only the fire crackling. "Because why, sweetheart?" he coaxed tenderly.

The lines around her eyes betrayed her torment, but she tilted her chin and looked him straight in the eyes. "Because I love you." She swallowed but never took her gaze from his. "I told them I'd not forsake you."

In two strides, he reached her side and took her into his arms. With his hand around the nape of her neck, he pulled her tight. His heartbeat pounded a staccato rhythm as he rocked her gently in his embrace.

"Believe it or not, that's what I was trying to tell you in the salon. But I couldn't share my feelings with you because of all the interruptions." He tilted her face and concentrated on all her steadfast beauty. "I love you and want to marry you."

Her shyness melted into joy, and the sight intoxicated him more than a bottle of champagne.

Before he could continue, he had to make her understand what marriage to him would cost her. "If you agree to marry me, your brother might not have anything to do with you. He might expect Claire to do the same. I imagine the same would be true of Somerton. I can't ask that of you."

She shook her head vehemently. "No. I don't believe it for one second. Alex wouldn't do that, or allow the others to. I believe his stubbornness is born from his grief over Alice's death. He's trying to protect me, but he's making me miserable." She smiled. "No matter what, Claire loves me, too, and would never cease caring for me. And Emma? She's my best friend. Nothing would keep us apart."

She grasped the lapels of his evening coat and stared at her fingers. "But you see, it makes little difference." Her gaze slowly crept upward until the certitude in her eyes nearly blinded him. "If I can't at least have the chance to build a life with you, the rest of it doesn't matter."

"A break between you and your family might never be repaired. It would be beyond selfish of me to take you from something that is forever yours. Since I don't have a family, in my eyes that is even more important. What I wouldn't do to have a family." He shook his head gently. It was madness to convince her otherwise, but he loved her too much to have her sacrifice her family. "It's too precious, Daphne." He stroked her hair, knowing he shouldn't touch her. It would become harder to convince her not to abandon her family. But he needed to feel her right now.

"Only Alex and Somerton are the ones against it. With time, they'll change their opinion." She gazed at him with conviction and the utter certainty of her decision shone in her eyes. "I'm not saying this out of anger. I meant what I said. I want only you. If you don't want the risk of alienating them for your own reasons, that's your prerogative. But I've made my decision."

The depth of her love became crystal clear, and that simple fact humbled him like none other.

He lowered his mouth to hers, then worshiped her lips—worshiped her. With each kiss, his desire grew until it became overpowering. She was the most precious thing he'd ever held in his arms. With infinite care, he kissed her, trying to bank the fire that roared through his body. She was his, and he wanted her in his bed tonight. He wanted to make love to her until neither of them could remember what days had passed—only that their future lay with each other. His body hummed and his cock throbbed the more he kissed her. On a sigh, she parted her lips, and like a starving man, he took what she offered. The moan that escaped her was a heady sound, one that gave him absolution from all his sins, and he took the freedom she offered. With his tongue, he explored her mouth. Nothing would be rushed tonight. This was a passion built on love—a completely different encounter from anything he'd ever experienced.

With infinite ease, he broke away from her beguiling kisses and kissed the top of her forehead. She was so precious to him, and he wanted her with every inch of his being. He leaned back but kept her locked in his arms. "Lady Daphne Charlotte Hallworth, will you make me the happiest man on this earth and marry me?"

"I thought you'd never ask." She leaned up on her tiptoes and pressed her lips to his. "The answer is yes."

"Then we should seal our betrothal with a kiss," he whispered. Always the consummate lover, he'd never experienced any nervousness around a woman. But tonight, with Daphne and this declaration of love between them, he wanted everything perfect. He wanted to show her how much he loved her. He took her in a kiss, one that caused him to lose himself in her embrace. Lose himself in her goodness.

But he also found his bearings—found his worth—in her love.

With this woman, he could become the duke Robbie and his father always expected him to be.

He kissed a path across her cheek until he nipped at her earlobe. "Moonbeam, would it be presumptuous of me to ask you to my chamber? I have an overwhelming desire to make love to my fiancée."

Her cheeks turned a glorious shade of red, and she nodded. "And I have overriding passion to make love to my fiancé."

Chapter Twenty-One

Paul took Daphne's hand and led her to the door. Still holding her hand, he turned toward her. With his back to the door, Paul swiftly kissed her as he turned the knob. With a blazing smile worthy of a consummate rogue, he tugged her out into the hallway. With her thoughts in shambles from his kisses, she followed.

From nowhere, her mind righted itself and insisted on the appearance of propriety. If the servants saw her enter his chambers, they'd wonder what they were doing, or worse, they'd *know* what she and Paul were doing. What kind of a duchess would they think he'd married? Suddenly, she pulled him to a stop.

His winsome and all too fetching smile eliminated her hesitation. Tonight, all her dreams had come true. No matter what her brother or Somerton thought, Paul was a wonderful man—a kind man. A man who would be the perfect husband and partner for her.

He tilted his head, obviously confused by her behavior.

"The servants," she whispered. "I don't want them to see us like this."

"Like what?" he teased. "You ready to have your wicked way with me while I devour the woman I love?"

An avalanche of feelings rolled through her. Life with Paul would never be dull or tame in the least. They'd be lovers their entire life, she was sure of it. "They'll think you're devouring a woman of low morals."

"I don't really care what they think, Moonbeam," he whispered as he stole another kiss.

"I do." At his touch, she leaned toward him ready to tie their lives and love together. But not like this.

He answered with a single nod of his head. "That's all the reason I need. Come with me."

He took her hand in his and led her to a staircase at the end of the hallway. More opulent than a servants' staircase, the wide granite structure was beautiful, with carved marble busts of gods and goddesses acting as support posts along the way. "What is this?" she asked.

"One of my ancestors thought of this for the ease of his duchess. It leads to the nursery above the ducal chambers, with an exit off the family floor. The idea was that it was a straight path from the kitchen to the family floor to the nursery." He shrugged his shoulders. "I never really appreciated it before, but tonight it's my favorite part of the house."

Within minutes, they were in his chambers without anyone seeing them. The sight of his bedroom made her stop in her tracks—not from nervousness that they'd make love, but from the sheer beauty of the room. Decorated in gold, peacock-green, and red silks and brocades along with a massive ebony bed and accompanying furniture, the room looked like it'd been built for a maharaja.

He pulled her in and locked the door behind them. Without lifting his gaze from hers, he took her to stand in front of a cheval mirror, one that stood just to the side of a large fireplace where a fresh fire poured warmth around them.

"Let me undress you," he whispered.

His gaze captured hers in the mirror—desire burned in his eyes, and the same in her own. He quickly unbuttoned her gown and slid the garment down her arms until it pooled on the floor like a waterfall of seafoam silk. Her stays, chemise, stockings, and slippers soon followed, leaving her completely naked, completely exposed. For some odd reason, though this was a new experience to stand before a man naked, she was confident. How many times had she fantasized about this exact moment? Too many to contemplate. Though her body was bare for his inspection, she welcomed him seeing her thus.

She shivered from the chill, and he slowly rubbed his hands over her shoulders. When he stepped back, she wanted to protest. However, it died on her lips when he shrugged off his coat, waistcoat, then pulled his linen shirt over his head. He balanced on one foot and divested himself of one boot and stocking, then without rushing repeated the move with the other leg.

At her first glimpse of his beautiful body, she practically fell to her knees. Her own body's image in the mirror partially blocked her view, but the swell of muscles that defined his shoulders and upper body was clear. "Magnificent" was too tame a word to describe his physique. A smattering of blond hairs curled around the upper slope of his chest.

He pulled her close. The contact of his hot skin and chest on her back sharply contrasted with the cold air. All the different sensations left her breathless. When he kissed her neck, he gripped her waist and his heat surrounded her. The hardness of his erection pressed against her bottom. When he trailed his tongue to her ear, she was lost.

Convinced she didn't have a bone in her body, she leaned against him for support.

"Look at you," he whispered. His cheek rested against hers as he studied her in the mirror. He placed his large hands on her hips. She inhaled sharply at the sight and touch. This was seduction, and every glorious impression of his hands on her body was a celebration of their love.

One hand drifted up her ribs, inch by inch, memorizing her body. Each ravishing touch caused her breasts to grow heavier, and her nipples tightened into painful peaks, anticipating his claiming caress. Her exquisite torment increased as his other hand crept lower.

"Your skin is softer than silk." He continued the downward drift of his fingers until he stroked and petted her nether curls. She moved her hips in a desperate attempt to meet his touch. He was so close to where she wanted him to ease this overwhelming need.

When he cupped a breast, she groaned her pleasure.

"Moonbeam, you're more beautiful than I ever imagined. I'm not going to devour you just yet. I think I'll savor every inch of you first." He pressed a kiss against her cheek, then pulled away.

She moaned a protest, and in answer, he swung her into his arms. In five eternally long strides, he carefully placed her on the bed. The silk cover beneath her body seemed to ripple around her. Her gaze caught his, and the hunger in his eyes made her believe he truly would devour her. Without turning his attention from her, he unbuttoned the falls of his pantaloons. Bit by bit, they slid down his hips, revealing chiseled oblique muscles much like those of the Roman and Greek statues that littered many of the finest homes in London.

There was no comparison to Paul's body. His riding every day had created a torso that would have been the envy of Achilles. His garment slid to the floor, and her breath hitched at the resulting view of his body.

His legs, covered in fine blond hair, were as muscled as the rest of him. When she focused on his erection, she wanted to touch him. She'd seen his engorged length before and even tasted it. But gazing on it again made her realize that soon they'd join their bodies together.

She held out her hand, and he came to her. He covered her with his warmth and kissed her sweetly before trailing his lips over her sensitive shoulders and chest to her breasts. There he kissed and slowly drew one hard nipple into his mouth. With a gentle sucking, he caused her to gasp as a heady sensation exploded in her body. He cupped her other breast and squeezed with enough tantalizing pressure to prolong her pleasure.

Then he slowly kissed his way down her abdomen. She panted and writhed for more. With a gentle clasp, he took her ankles in his hands, urging her to bend her legs. She blinked and propped herself on her elbows trying to get her bearings. His normally ice-blue eyes blazed with heat.

"What you did to me the other night, I'm going to do to you. It's only fair," he whispered as he pressed a chaste kiss on her folds.

"Like a talion law? Eye for an eye?" Her breathy response floated between them.

With a laugh, he nodded his head. "You wicked, wicked woman. I was thinking more along the lines of a kiss for a kiss." One gorgeous corner of his mouth ticked up in a sly grin. "Perhaps, a lick for a lick?"

He bent and pressed a soft kiss on her thigh, then settled between her hips while he wrapped his arms under her bent legs. With his tongue, he separated her folds and licked from her entrance to the sensitive nub of her clitoris. The texture and curve of his tongue awakened every nerve, causing a pulsating ache in her lower abdomen.

Flooded with desire, she moaned. The sound seemed to encourage him, and he applied more pressure. Each touch, each lick, flicked the flames of her desire higher. She'd experienced releases in his arms before, but this was a new height of arousal, one she'd never dreamed possible.

He now licked with all his attention on her clitoris. She found herself mewling as she repeated his name over and over. He released one of her legs, and she let it fall to the bed along his side.

With his free hand, he caressed her thigh before he entered her with two fingers. God, it wasn't enough. Her body twitched in response, demanding more. His tongue wove a magic spell around her. With her heart racing, she fought for breath and control. He sucked the sensitive pearl, then tongued over her again. He repeated the pattern with each touch of his mouth more urgent. Never pausing, he played her over and over like an instrument, pushing for her release. She ground herself against his mouth trying to climb to where pleasure promised complete control over her body.

"Let go, love," he whispered.

She moaned and twisted beneath him as he continued to feast upon her. Suddenly, she shut her eyes and surrendered to a release that exploded through her like lightning in the night sky. His kisses grew softer and gentler in touch until she had recaptured a tenuous control over her body. With infinite tenderness, he kissed the insides of her thighs, then rose above her.

He was panting, and a thin sheen of sweat covered his body. The hard length of his cock pulsed against her abdomen as he pushed his hips against hers. He growled her name as he took possession of her lips with his. His tongue invaded every part of her mouth ready to conquer and taste every inch of her—no, devour every inch of her.

She tasted herself on his tongue and his lips. The tart, salty taste, a heady aphrodisiac, created another wave of need to course through her. She tilted her hips in invitation. She wanted him inside of her now as the banked flames of passion roared back to life. With his pounding heartbeat next to hers, she met the intensity of his kiss with one of her own.

In response, he broke away and rose above her on his elbows and the devotion in his eyes caused her to gasp. He was desperate for her.

And she for him.

"Daphne," he whispered softly as he swept his lips against her again. He adjusted his length at her entrance, then inched his way inside her. His invasion filled her. The pressure grew until it almost became too much.

He stopped moving and held himself still. The sight of him looming above her with muscles flexed was more beautiful and daunting than she'd ever imagined. Even with all the times she'd created their union in her mind, the physical sight of him stole her breath.

"I want you so badly, every inch of me aches in need. I've been like this since I first saw you at the Reynolds. Are you ready, my love?" he whispered.

His admission made her smile. "I've wanted you for years. Yes, let's not waste another moment."

He kissed her again and, with one move, thrust into her completely. Her body stretched as it fought against their union. In response, she gasped. He swallowed her cry, then cradled her head in his hands as he pressed more deeply into her until he was completely seated within her. Once the shock wore off, she could breathe again.

He placed one palm against her cheek. His troubled eyes roamed over every inch of her. "All right?"

"Yes." Her gaze locked with his. The intimacy of the

moment far outweighed the discomfort she felt. "It's charming that you're worried about me."

"I promise the next time won't hurt," he whispered, then kissed the tender spot below her ear. The soft caress of his breath against her neck caused her to shiver.

"Kiss me," she coaxed.

He took possession of her mouth as well as complete possession of her heart. He pressed his hips against hers, then slowly withdrew from her body. Before he withdrew all the way, he slowed, then entered her again. Her body accepted him more easily this time. In response, she raised her hips to meet his. The only sound that surrounded them was the movement of their bodies, flesh meeting flesh. Their gazes never strayed from each other, and if she wasn't mistaken, his had grown misty with an emotion that made her own suffer the same.

He cradled her close as he began to move with more urgency. He kissed her again, all the while driving into her over and over. His movement once smooth had now turned into something else, a reckless need fighting to be satiated. His kiss turned demanding, and she felt herself climbing toward a release again.

Without a word between them, the explosive pleasure consumed her again. Her body pulsed tight with her orgasm. He roared her name as he poured his seed into her. His eyes were riveted to her face as he collapsed on top of her, his weight calming the turbulent passion that swirled around him.

She took a deep breath. His musky scent filled her, and she released her breath slowly. She wanted to keep his essence in her as long as she possibly could. Carefully, he raised himself on his elbows and stared down at her. His eyes caressed her face and every feature.

"I never roar or growl except with you." He blinked

slowly, and a spark of something she couldn't quiet identify flashed in his blue eyes.

"Have I proved you a liar then?" She lifted her head and playfully bit his full lower lip. Good heavens, she'd never get enough of this man for as long as lived. Thankfully, she was marrying him.

He shook his head once and exhaled. "No. But you've made me discover a great truth about myself. You've proved that I *do* growl, scream, and roar when I make love"—he tapped her nose with his finger and gently laughed—"with you. Enough about me, how are you?" His slight chuckle did little to hide his concern for her.

"You don't have to hide your feelings from me. You do realize that, don't you?" She pressed his lips against his, reassuring him.

He nodded, but the effort did little to ease the lines of worry around his handsome eyes.

"I lack much experience at this. . . ." Her voice trailed to silence.

"You are the most amazing lover," he whispered, then traced her lips with his forefinger.

"Thank you," she said. "I've never felt like this before— so complete and so well loved. I couldn't have imagined anything more perfect."

He bent his head until his forehead rested on hers. For several moments they lay silent, legs to legs and torso to torso. Never had she experienced the incredible intimacy they'd just created.

"I must be crushing you." Without warning, he lifted his body from hers. Without a care for his nudity, he strolled to a small table across the room.

Bereft from the sudden loss, all she could do was watch his elegant stride. The man was magnificent in his carriage. More important, he was wonderfully caring and loyal to her and others.

"When shall we marry? Would within the hour rush you too much?"

"As long as you let me dress," she answered.

"Why? I'll just take it off of you again." He came back to bed with a small basin and toweling. "Whenever you want, love. Just don't make me wait too long." He leaned over and kissed her, then sat on the edge and washed the small streaks of blood and the remains of his release from her thighs. His careful touch soothed her. When he was finished, he made a move to stand, but she halted him with her hand on his thigh.

She struggled to sit up and winced. Muscles tight in places she'd never realized she possessed throbbed in dull pain. His beautiful face grimaced. In answer, she leaned close for a sweep of her lips against his. "I'm fine."

She rinsed the toweling, then with infinite care washed him. A bemused smile lit his face as it became apparent to both that he was becoming aroused again.

Without taking his eyes off her, he took the cloth and threw it in the basin. "Thank you, Moonbeam. You never cease to surprise me with your care. I've never been a gentleman, but after tonight, I shall try my best to become one." He tapped his perfect chin with one finger. "You make me want to be a better person. Though tonight I've delightfully corrupted a perfect innocent. I think I shall start this new endeavor by helping you dress and returning you home."

"Perhaps I don't want you to reform." She ran her hands over his arms. She'd never tire of touching him. "I think you're perfect as you are."

He leaned back and regarded her. "Truly?"

"I love you as you are." The wonderment on his face melted her heart. "When will I see you again?" She couldn't hide the entreaty in her voice, nor did she want to. One day or one night without him by her side represented pure torture.

"My love, as soon as I can call on your mother and brother tomorrow." His words were sweet, but the worry around his eyes was apparent. "I'll tell your brother our plans to marry. It's best if he hears it from me. He'll hate me, but perhaps, if I speak to him, we'll salvage his relationship with you."

"Thank you."

Paul angled his head and kissed her soundly. "In the morning, I have an appointment with my family solicitor, then I'm heading straight to Pembrooke House. Speaking of solicitors, has yours found you a house yet?"

She shook her head, still befuddled from his kiss.

"Excellent. Don't do anything. I may have someplace that will suit your tastes." He waved his hand around the room and smiled seductively. "This place would meet your needs quite nicely." He leaned close and nipped her earlobe. "It even has a duchess suite, but you won't need it," he whispered as he traced the rim of her ear with his tongue.

His touch caused a moan to escape.

"You'll spend most of your time here. I plan on keeping you very busy."

Chapter Twenty-Two

Paul had helped Daphne dress, then they were on their way to her house. His kisses and whispers of endearments filled the ducal carriage and chased the chill away. His coach-and-four slipped through the dark London night making nary a sound. Even the horses were as quiet as a sanctuary the moment a prayer ended as they escorted Paul and her to the mews off the back alley and to the servants' entrance of Pembrooke House. After one last smoldering kiss, Paul lightly stepped from the stopped carriage. He held out his hand and escorted her to the servants' entrance.

"This isn't right, to hide from your brother. I'll ask Tait to wake him so we can discuss what's happened between us." A frown marked his beautiful face. "Perhaps if I catch him unaware, he'll be more likely to accept me."

She placed her hand on his arm, and he stopped immediately. "Wait until the morning. Otherwise, we'll wake Claire, too."

He frowned, then reluctantly nodded his head. "Our love and what we shared tonight isn't something shameful or something that should be hidden. It's honest and pure and full of light." He caressed her cheek with his fore-finger, the loving touch so dear. Playfully, he tapped the end of her nose with his finger. "Just like you."

Paul took advantage with a light kiss, then hugged her close. In seconds, they crossed the short distance to the door. Instead of Tait waiting for her, the kitchen stood empty, with a banked fire acting as sentry.

Daphne reached up on tiptoes and pressed a kiss to Paul's lips. "Until tomorrow."

"Until tomorrow," he answered, then slowly drew away. When she saw the heat in his eyes, her heart pressed against her chest.

He took his leave with a brush of his lips against her hand. Soon, the soft sound of the carriage pulling away reached her through the closed door.

She shivered. After Paul's incendiary kisses in the carriage, it wasn't the cold that garnered such a response.

It was the delightful thought that she'd soon be married to him.

She wove her way up the servants' staircase to the family floor. She opened her bedroom door, then silently shut it behind her. She leaned against the solid wooden panel and closed her eyes, letting all thoughts go except her memory of making love to Paul.

Before tonight, she couldn't have grasped the flood of burning sweetness, passion, and love that united them. For all time, she'd remember how gentle and caring he'd been to her. His love for her was a tender gift, one for which she thanked the heavens and stars above. With him by her side, she'd be forever happy. She took a deep breath and slowly released it. With that breath, all her loneliness subsided.

Tomorrow couldn't come soon enough.

In her room, a brilliant fire snapped, reminding her that in hours the whole household would be up. She pushed away from the door, then stopped after several steps. With the tilt of her head, she studied the fire once more. Why would the fire be so robust this time of the night? It should have burned to embers long before now.

"Should I say good evening or good morning?" The low thrum of her brother's voice broke the quiet. He sat in her favorite chair, an armless creation covered in a mauve-colored velvet.

Her jubilation and merriment scattered like mice spying the cat in the kitchen.

"I suppose the answer depends on whether you've been to bed or not," he said. Alex's gray eyes, a mirror image of hers, swept from the top of her head to the bottom of her feet. "I discovered Tait is incredibly fond of sitting in the kitchen late at night. The first time, I thought it odd. Tonight, I thought it suspicious. At two o'clock this morning, I relieved him of his duty. There was no sense in all of us losing sleep. I told him I'd wait for you."

She didn't look away, nor could she form a word in answer. Instinctively, she patted her hair to reassure herself the loose chignon she'd crafted in Paul's bedroom wasn't falling in a mass of black curls about her shoulders.

"By your appearance, I'd say"—Alex rose slowly and held out his hand in invitation for her to sit in the chair opposite his—"you've already gone to bed. Since your bed is made, I assume you slept elsewhere."

She merely stared at him completely tongue-tied.

"Southart?" His refined voice hinted at his vexation.

What could she say? She loved Paul and wouldn't hide the truth of her feelings for him. Collecting every scrap of composure, she took the seat opposite to Alex.

She interlaced her fingers and rested her hands on her lap. She lifted her eyes to her brother. "Yes, I love him."

Alex squeezed his eyes shut and clenched a fist. Slowly, he leaned back in his chair and regarded her. For a long moment, neither of them said a word. The burning wood crackled in warning.

"There's only one thing to be done. I'll call him out," Alex declared in a whisper.

"No, you won't. To challenge him would destroy me." Daphne gently shook her head. "I've loved him since"—she took a deep breath—"forever, Alex. He's coming to see you tomorrow to discuss our marriage. Whether you withhold my dowry makes little difference."

"He'll break your heart." The deep baritone of her brother's voice shot across the room.

"On the contrary." Daphne sat on the edge of her seat and leaned forward. Now was not the time to confront her brother. She needed to convince him that Paul was honorable and loved her. "Alex, he sees me," she whispered.

Her brother tilted his head and pursed his lips. "Sees you?"

This was so difficult, but he deserved the truth. "For years, I've shrunk into myself until I finally became, for all purposes, invisible." She stole a glance his way. Alex's befuddlement was almost laughable.

"You're a beautiful woman. Think of all the men who've wanted your hand in marriage," he offered. "You are not a wallflower."

Their eyes locked. His gray eyes glowed with an unmistakable pride and bemusement.

"Thank you," she said softly. There was little to be gained by quarreling. Alex truly was a wonderful man who loved her, but she had to make him understand. "There's a huge difference. A wallflower wants to be seen. I, on the other hand, tried to stay hidden. I've never sought attention and have tried to be the perfect sister and the perfect daughter ever since Alice's death." She released a deep sigh. "I can't do it anymore. It empties the soul, Alex."

"Why since Alice's death?" His voice faded to nothing. The fine lines radiating around his eyes betrayed his pain.

"Because we all ached so much from her death. None of us would talk of her. It was if she had disappeared from our lives and memories." She hesitated for only a moment. "I blamed her and myself for her death."

Alex nodded. "I blamed myself, also."

"You did?" Her heart lurched at the obvious anguish on his face. "I thought I was the only one, since I knew what she'd done," she whispered.

"No, darling girl. She left me a note and told me not to blame Paul." He took a deep breath, then slowly released it. "Paul had counseled her, but I thought . . . never mind what I thought. He tried to help, but I mistook his efforts for something else." Alex shook his head slowly. "I always wondered what I could have done. I was head of the family. I should have realized how upset she was."

"I should have known, also. Then I was left with all this guilt." She stared at the flame's reflection against the carpet. "I thought if I was perfect, it might alleviate my culpability at being a failure as a sister." She returned her attention to him. He needed comfort as much as she did. "But I discovered something."

"What, Daph?" he whispered softly.

"I was only hurting myself. I tamped down all my wants and desires, even who I was. I tried to organize my life into a box with a compartment for every emotion. I thought if I could control such things . . ." She let the words fade to nothing as her throat burned in warning that she was about to succumb to tears. "That's why I want to start my home for unwed mothers. I want to help women like Alice. I couldn't help her, but perhaps I can help them. I think Alice would approve."

Alex nodded.

"There's more. Paul sees me. He doesn't let me hide and

helps me when the dark grief rises. He's the first person who honestly sees me, and he loves me with all my faults and mistakes. When I grieve for Alice, he understands and doesn't ignore me. He holds me and comforts me."

He blinked his eyes, not saying a word.

"Alex," Daphne whispered, "a wise man told me perhaps that there wasn't anything we could have done. Maybe Alice wanted something else, and it wasn't here on earth." The fire crackled, encouraging her to continue. "I don't know, but I find it comforting. I've tried putting my grief someplace safe, so I don't have to carry it with me every hour of the day. I'm finding that helpful."

"That's wise counsel. Is that what Paul told you?" he asked.

She nodded. "He's the first person I've been able to share my grief with."

Alex stared with an intensity that made her want to squirm. "Daphne, don't mistake the brief appearance of Paul's humanity for something more permanent. He maligned my wife in the past. I won't let him do the same to you." He ran a hand through his hair.

"He told me everything and is remorseful. He even apologized again to Claire before tonight's—I mean last night's—debacle of a dinner. If she can forgive him, can't you?" Daphne leaned forward and lowered her voice. "You've always been an excellent judge of character. Paul's a good man. You thought so at one time."

Alex gently shook his head.

Daphne placed her hand on her brother's arm. "He was your best friend. Plus, he puts me first in the way that you put Claire first in your life." Her brother opened his mouth to refute her claim, but she held up her hand. "I'm not talking about being left in London. I'm referring to the feeling that you're missing half your soul when your love is absent from your side. The same as if the world tilted in the wrong direction when the person you gave your heart to is elsewhere. Do you understand? Please tell me you do."

He nodded slightly. "Claire is everything to me. I should've been the one you turned to when you needed to talk about Alice. I've failed you."

Her breath caught at the pain etched across his face. "We've both made mistakes, but look at us now. We're finally talking, and I can't help but think Paul's efforts with me have helped us become closer."

"Well, that's a jump in logic, wouldn't you say?" For the first time this evening, a smile tugged at his lips. "I love you, Daphne."

"Prove it, then. Bless our union and welcome him into our family," she whispered. "It means everything to me."

His eyes narrowed, then he sighed in resignation. "You're asking a lot, Daph. But for you and your happiness, I agree to give it due consideration." He stood and took her into his outstretched arms. He drew back and with his fingers tipped her chin so she faced him. "I'm a horrible brother, but I've always wanted you happy."

"You're the best brother." She hugged him as tightly as she could. "I've always loved you, too."

"If I agree to the marriage"—he smiled—"you'll let me punch him at least once?"

If his father's solicitor didn't arrive within the hour, Paul had decided he'd leave for Pembrooke's house. Securing Daphne's hand in marriage was the only thing he could really concentrate on this morning. Since he'd waited for his father's bloody letter for months, it could wait for him until the afternoon.

Standing in front of an ornate mirror that practically covered the entire north wall, Paul straightened his cravat for the second time within five minutes. The noise from the click of two sets of heels on the flagstone hallway announced the solicitor's impending arrival.

Paul let out a disgruntled breath. He'd quickly rid himself of the man, then hurry along his way to see Pembrooke. He smoothed the blue wool morning coat, then turned to the door as his butler and the family solicitor entered.

Morrison Lagan stood a few inches over five feet and had a receding hairline. In his mid-fifties, he'd served the family for over twenty years. He knew secrets about the old duke that would make the devil blush, but thankfully, Lagan had tight lips. One of the well-guarded secrets was that his father kept several mistresses close to various duchy estates. To the best of Paul's recollection, his dear mother never discovered any of the women's existence. If she did, she never acknowledged the duke's sordid proclivities.

His father may have found it acceptable behavior, but Paul found it—frankly—repugnant. For years, he'd observed the Duke of Langham, one of the most respected and admired men in the House of Lords. Langham and his duchess were devoted to each other, and they supported each other's work. The duke helped the duchess with her charitable foundations, and the duchess helped the duke in his political works. Together, they were a strong and powerful presence to emulate. Both were deeply in love with each other after all their years together.

A perfect marriage in Paul's opinion. Like the one he wanted with Daphne. Like a moon emerging from a sea of clouds, his reasons became crystal clear. She loved him and thought him honorable. Just one glance his way with her silver eyes made him want to be the best man he could be for her and their children. The thought of holding a black-haired gray-eyed boy in his arms swept through him with a fierceness like a gale wind. Then, like a calming wind, he imagined a blond-haired blue-eyed girl clasping his hand, enchanting and captivating him just like her obsidian-haired mother.

"Your Grace, Mr. Morrison Lagan is here to see you," announced Ives.

As soon as he finished with Lagan, he could attend to Daphne and start a new, more rewarding chapter of his life. With a smile on his face, Paul turned to his guest.

"Thank you, Ives. You may leave us." Paul returned to his desk.

"Your Grace," Lagan offered as he bowed deeply.

Paul nodded in return. "Please sit."

The solicitor delved into a leather packet and retrieved several items, including a claret-colored missive with a matching seal. Paul's name was written in iron gall ink on the outside of the note.

"Your Grace, your request to rescind the bid on the Winterford House unfortunately is too late. The owner had already accepted it and signed the contract. I'm afraid you own the building now." Lagan pushed a pair of wire-frame spectacles up the bridge of his nose. When he looked at Paul, his eyes appeared twice their normal size, making the man resemble an owl.

Paul ran his hands through his hair, then rested his elbows on the desk. "I appreciate your help. Now I need you to start a search for another property close to that location."

Mr. Lagan widened his eyes. "Your Grace, there's not much available in that area of town."

"Perhaps you could canvas the area and ask other owners if they'd be interested in selling?" He leaned back in his chair. "What else do you have for me?"

The solicitor handed another folded missive to Paul.

He had little doubt it was another gambling debt. He turned it over in his hands. "In his father's bold handwriting, the words "To the spurious scourge of my existence" were written on the outside. "How much is the debt this time?"

"Five pounds, Your Grace."

"Should I expect any more of these delightful gifts?" He didn't hide the disparagement in his voice.

"No, Your Grace." The solicitor cleared his throat and stole a glance at his hand where he tightly held the final paper, the claret-colored missive written on the Barstowe stationery. "The previous Duke of Southart directed that I deliver this only after you had applied for a writ of summons and the Committee of Privileges had ruled you were the legitimate heir to the duchy. Now that you've taken your seat in the House of Lords, this will be the last responsibility I have to your father."

Paul stared at Lagan's outstretched hand. Apparently nervous, the solicitor swallowed, causing his prominent Adam's apple to bob up and down like a buoy in a choppy sea. With a nonchalant ease that belied the instinct to burn the offending missive, Paul took the letter.

"It's best if you read it first. I'll answer any questions you may have." Beads of perspiration dotted the man's forehead. He pulled a clean but wrinkled handkerchief from his waistcoat pocket and blotted his face.

"I take it that I'll not be pleased with my father's last diatribe against me," Paul asked.

The solicitor had the good manners to shake his head.

Paul donned the eyeglasses that he used for correspondence. With a deep breath, he broke the seal and started to read the words his father had crafted.

Southart,
    I can't begin to tell you how sour your title tastes on my lips. I'm certain at my death, my mouth was twisted in disgust. But there's no divine help to change life's course at this point. If you're

*reading this, then your half brother and I are both
dead. A true loss for all. In his stead, you are now
the Duke of Southart. I can only pray there is some
smidge of honor in your debauched body.*

Paul ignored the insult as the words "half brother"
transfixed his mind. Robbie was illegitimate? With his
blood slowing to a crawl, Paul sat frozen. A roaring din of
silence rang in his ears. He forced himself to continue
reading his blackguard father's words.

*You are not my son. But never fear, there's
ducal blood running through your veins. You see,
your mother and the Duke of Renton . . . well,
let's just say that you were the result of their
indiscretion. It shouldn't come as a shock since
you seem to be an expert at creating havoc.
However, you deserve the whole story.*

*My duchess—God rest her soul—was best
friends with Renton's duchess. Since childhood
they remained close. When Renton's wife died in
childbirth, your mother went to console him at his
ancestral estate with my blessing. Apparently, their
grief led them to sleep together. When she told
me of her condition, it didn't take a logician to
determine you weren't mine. I'd been traveling the
Continent on ducal business for over four months.
Though she promised me it happened just once,
you were the result.*

You always did have the devil's luck.

*I tried to find a match for you with some distant
Barstowe cousin, thus ensuring the next duke
would have some familial blood in the next line.
It was the least you could do for the duchy.
Unfortunately, I could only find a spinster, a third*

cousin removed, but the woman was nigh near
forty and, sadly, had the sense God gave a goose.
Thus, I determined the chance of a ducal heir too
remote.

  I didn't want you aware of the situation until
you took your place as the new duke. You, as well
as I, are aware that you can't renounce the title.
You're stuck with me just as I am stuck with you.

  Though you don't have my blood, you are of my
duchess's body. Believe it or not, I loved her.
Because of that love, I tolerated you. In closing,
I do apologize for not being a better father to you.
Under the circumstances, you understand, I'm
certain.

Southart

  One last thought . . . though it's your natural
tendency, try not to damage the duchy too much
during your lifetime.

Paul embraced the silence as long as he could. Finally,
wave after wave of shock pummeled him as he reread the
letter again. Robbie wasn't the half brother—he was.

Paul swallowed the ugly truth.

He was the bloody bastard.

A bastard. A no-name. Since he'd inherited the title,
he'd done his damnedest to make both his brother and
father proud. God, what a wasted effort. For the love of
heaven, his father's insults on the previous gambling debts
should have warned him. "Baseborn son," "Misbegotten
Mistake," "spurious scourge"—it all made sense.

He forced his gaze to Lagan. The poor solicitor shifted
in his seat as if an army of ants crawled over him. With
deliberate effort, Paul removed his eyeglasses and silently

laid them on the table. "Does the Duke of Renton know that I'm his by-blow?"

Lagan stared at the floor. "I'm uncertain, Your Grace."

Paul smirked at the courtesy but didn't say a word. His father needn't have worried. The title left a rancid taste in his mouth also.

Without another word, Paul rose and left the solicitor sitting in the study alone. At that moment, the only thing he cared about was air. He needed fresh air to clear the swirl of putrid miasmas that surrounded him. A footman greeted him in the entry, but Paul couldn't respond. His ability to form a coherent sentence had escaped him.

The footman asked if he wanted his greatcoat, but Paul kept on walking toward the stable at the back of Southart Hall. A groomsman caught sight of him and approached.

"Would you like a horse or carriage prepared, Your Grace?" The fact that Paul had come unannounced didn't seem to faze the man. "You seem to be in a hurry, Your Grace. I'll have your favorite ride saddled immediately."

Within minutes, the man held the bridle of Amor, the white gelding. Paul simply nodded, then mounted the horse. The loyal steed quickly galloped through Mayfair without any encouragement.

The beast must know his every thought. Amor headed to the Duke of Renton's home.

Chapter Twenty-Three

Paul didn't wait to be announced. Instead, he barged into the inner sanctum of the Duke of Renton's study and sitting room. He'd been there once as a young boy with his father. He gritted his teeth and dismissed the disgusting fallacy.

His father was the Duke of Renton.

Surrounded by opulent black, white, and gold appointments, the duke stood on Paul's entrance.

Paul didn't stop until he stood two feet away from the man with silvered-blond hair and blue eyes. They even shared the same build. Paul should have seen the resemblance before. If he had discovered the ugly truth earlier, he'd not have wasted his time in a desperate attempt to capture Southart's attention. He'd always wondered why he didn't resemble Robbie or his father. Nor did he favor any of his past ancestors. Most of them, including Robbie, had sable-colored hair and deep brown eyes.

Now he had his answer, but other questions had reared their ugly heads.

"Did you know?" Paul cursed himself for the transparency of his anger. His normal haughtiness, a trademark reaction that easily transformed into a curtain that hid his true sentiments, had inconveniently deserted him.

The Duke of Renton's easy smile, one that resembled Somerton's, faded on the older man's face. Out of the corner of Paul's eyes, he saw two men approach. With a snarl, Paul turned to greet them or, frankly, attack them. He couldn't have planned a more fitting reunion when he met his father.

Before him stood his half brother, Somerton, with Pembrooke beside him. Paul had kept his anger under control during last evening's dinner for Daphne's sake, but today he'd let it loose with a hurl of insults to match theirs from last night.

"What are you asking?" Somerton growled in return.

"I'm not asking *you* anything but telling. You're my older brother." He let the heavy sarcasm roll from his lips. Though there was no humor in the situation, Paul laughed when he saw Somerton's jaw drop. "Such a response does little for your looks," Paul jeered. "If it's any comfort, I had the same response, but managed to keep my mouth closed."

Paul swept his gaze to Renton. "You owe me an answer. Were you aware that my mother carried your child?"

"No." Eerily reminiscent of Paul's own eyes, the duke's blue ones widened in astonishment. He fell to his seat. "She never told me."

His honest response told Paul everything. He clenched his fist to keep from tearing the room apart. The man had no idea he was his son.

Somerton placed his hand on his father's shoulder in a show of support. Years ago, Somerton had shunned his father. Then after his marriage to Emma, Somerton had allowed his father back into his life. The two of them simply stared, as if he were a creature that had crawled from the bowels of hell.

The description matched his mood perfectly. He trained his gaze first on the man who had sired him, then on his new half brother. Their looks were familiar to him when he was younger, but he never for an instant thought the resemblance meant anything.

More fool he.

"Paul, come sit. Let's discuss this like civilized men." In an uncharacteristic move, Pembrooke placed a hand on Paul's shoulder and squeezed.

Paul wanted to roar at the unfairness of it all. It had been years since his old friend had offered comfort like this. Once again, it was because of the old Duke of Southart's belligerent behavior toward his younger son. Paul had never understood his father's coldness, but how appropriate that today, the one day that held such great happiness for his future, now lay destroyed by his father's actions. Like a mirror demolished into a million pieces, the day he had planned to ask for Daphne's hand and receive her brother's blessing had been ruined by his nemesis.

He stepped away from Alex. There was no comfort here, nor did he deserve it. His maniacal father had taught him to become a selfish bastard, one groomed day in and day out to disappoint others. How fitting. Since he was a bastard. Literally. Today, he'd prove the Duke of Southart's opinion of him was correct all along.

He would have to renege on his promise of marriage to Daphne. His heart twisted with pain, but there was no other course.

For once in his life, Paul would think of someone else first. He'd take the necessary steps to protect Daphne and her future happiness. He'd not ask for her. After everything he'd learned today, he had nothing to offer her. If married to him, Daphne could only look forward to more heartache. She'd suffered enough pain in her life. He'd not add to her misery.

If they had a family, there would be nothing but heartache for all. Their children and their children's children would be mocked and ridiculed. Any heir would be made a laughingstock as he tried to take their seat in the House of Lords. The love of his life would be cut directly. It made little difference Daphne's friendships or the standing of her brother in society. The fact that her mother married his real father added more kindling to the fire of the scandal. Her cause for a home for unwed mothers would be scorned.

"The only thing that needs to be discussed is my behavior toward your sister." Black despair promised no quarter. Why had he taken her innocence last night? Because he was every inch the same rake and blackguard as Southart. Indeed, Paul had learned from the best.

He bit his cheek as he realized there was still a chance Daphne would be tied to his loathsome self. If she was pregnant, he'd ruined her life. "I've decided not to offer for your sister, with what we've learned of the truth of my lineage."

Without a hint of fury, Pembrooke studied him.

The words burned, but Paul continued, "A better husband awaits her. Someone she'd be proud to marry. I can't ask her to ruin herself with me. If circumstances find her carrying my child, I'll do the right thing. I'll marry her, but then I expect you to call me out after the ceremony."

Paul turned to leave, but Pembrooke's hand shot out and stopped his departure. "You bloody bastard, she's in love with you."

"Exactly. That's what I've been trying to tell you," he drawled with a distinct mockery in his voice. "I'm a bloody bastard. If she's forced to marry me, challenge me to the death. Oh, and practice your aim. I don't want to survive. Daphne will have everything she needs for a comfortable life, I promise you."

Without a look back, Paul strode from Renton Hall. He'd made a promise to Daphne, and he'd see it finished.

He would find her diary today and put an end to her distress on that account.

For some reason, the thought offered little comfort. He might stop her worry over the loss of the journal, but she'd suffer from his break with her. He had little doubt she loved him.

If the news leaked about his birth, he'd be ruined. It was his rotten luck that he couldn't renounce the title. Once declared the legitimate heir, he was stuck for life as the Duke of Southart.

But that fact didn't negate the obvious. He wouldn't taint her pureness with the stench of his birth.

He'd rip out his own heart first before he'd allow her to suffer because of the truth of his bastardy.

Which lead to the only truth he could rely on—his entire life was a lie, and he had no idea who he was.

As soon as Paul returned home, Ives greeted him at the door. "Your Grace, Griffin is waiting in the study for you. He found the boy."

With a curt nod, Paul headed down the hallway. The cold pervaded every inch of him, since he'd ridden to the Duke of Renton's home without the accompaniments of a greatcoat, gloves, and hat. He pushed his discomfort away. To consider such trivial matters was a waste of time. When he entered the study, his groomsman stood with his hat in hand.

"Tell me what you found, Griffin." His voice had deepened from the cold, making his words curt. "Was the boy in Seven Dials?"

Without offense, the groomsman, who was slight of build but a master at managing the Southart cattle, simply nodded. "Your Grace, I've visited Seven Dials daily since your instruction with no luck. Then, as if he'd fallen from the sky, Garland returned to the cook's room at the boardinghouse last night. She took him to work this morning."

"Thank you for your hard work," Paul said. "Have my carriage readied immediately. You'll accompany me to the Reynolds."

"Yes, Your Grace." The groomsman nodded, then raced from the room.

For the first time that day, relief trickled through Paul. With any luck, he'd have his Moonbeam's journal as promised. His heart tripped in his chest at the thought. Her diary was the only thing that kept her anchored to him. After he acquired it and returned it to her, there would be no more reason to see her. He fought the war of emotions raging through him. The fulfillment of his promise would be the last thing he'd give her.

He had to remember that she was better off without him.

Within a half hour, Paul strolled through the doors of the Reynolds.

The majordomo looked askance, then lifted one brow with a slight smile. "Good afternoon, Your Grace. I imagine you want your usual private room? I'll tell Elsie you're here."

With a flourish that belied the large man's size, Gilby swept a hand in front of him, beckoning Paul to lead the way. Without another word passing between them, Gilby escorted Paul to the same sitting room as before.

The same room where he'd first sparred with Daphne. A bottle of champagne waited for him just like the first time he was alone with her in the Reynolds. He wiped a hand down his face, hoping to ease his pain or at least brush away the memories until he could retrieve the diary. Only until it was securely in his possession would he allow himself to grieve over all he'd lost today.

"A glass of champagne, Your Grace?" Gilby asked.

Paul shook his head. "No, thank you."

A terse knock sounded on the door, and Gilby answered it. Elsie stood outside holding the ear of a young boy, ensuring the squirming scamp wouldn't escape. Gilby's eyes grew wide. With an unmistakable high temper, the cook marched in dragging the boy behind her.

Paul nodded at Gilby, and the man left.

When they were all alone, Elsie bobbed a quick curtsy while holding tight to the boy's ear. "Tell His Grace what you did." Her fury made her cheeks flaming red.

Paul regarded the young man, who was pleasant of face. "I take it that this is Garland?"

Elsie nodded, then jerked his ear upward. "Show some respect. Bow and introduce yourself."

The boy did as directed, even though the cook's firm hold restricted his movements. Garland winced when Elsie pulled him into a deeper bow. Apparently satisfied with the boy, Elsie let go of his ear. For a moment, Paul had nothing but empathy for the boy as he rubbed his ear. The old Duke of Southart had favored the same corporal punishment when correcting Paul for his misdeeds.

"Where is the reticule that you stole from a young woman several days before Christmastide?" Paul asked. Keeping his voice deep and even, he didn't want to scare the boy into not revealing the journal's whereabouts, but the imp needed to know that what he did was wrong.

The boy pulled the wadded-up reticule out of his pocket and held it out to Paul. The boy's wide eyes and the trembling of his arm confirmed what Paul suspected. The boy was terrified of him. "'Ere you are, my lawd," he whispered.

Elsie made a move to grab the boy's ear again but clenched her fists this time. "He's the Duke of Southart. You address him as 'Your Grace.'"

"Your Grace." Garland's gaze darted to the floor.

Paul took the reticule and checked inside. There was a pencil and several gold guineas jangled on the bottom.

But nothing else.

He returned his gaze to the boy. "Where is the journal?"

Both Elsie and the boy took a deep breath at the same time, then stood still. Every second of silence sounded like a death knell of failure.

"Tell him, Garland, and give him the money." Elsie's voice cracked with emotion. "He has the power to have you arrested for theft and thrown in the gaol or worse."

With his face void of all color, Garland slowly raised his gaze to Paul. "I sold it to 'he fellah who owns '*he Midnigh' Cryer*."

Paul clenched both fists to keep from roaring his rage. Of all the weasels in England the boy could have sold the journal to, Martin Richmond was the worst kind of nightmare. He had to discover how long the reprobate publisher had possessed it. Purposely keeping his voice calm, he asked, "When did you sell it?"

The boy's chin wobbled, and his eyes filled with tears. "I sold 'im some o' the pages righ' b'fore Christmas. 'E bough' 'he res' ov 'he book 'his mawnin'."

Paul exhaled and bit his cheeks to keep from punching a hole through the wall. If only he hadn't taken the time to read the Duke of Southart's bloody letter, he could have saved Daphne from more pain. Not only had he ruined her, but now she would be ridiculed unmercifully by all of London's gossipmongers, too. *God, could this turn any more morose?*

The boy extended his open palm where five sparkling gold guineas lay in a neat row. "Your Grace, 'ere's wha' 'e paid me. Mr. Richmond is in 'he gamin' room. You could buy it back from 'im."

Paul made the mistake of looking at Elsie. With tears

streaming down her face, the girl looked absolutely defeated. Enough lives had been ruined today. These two
had nothing to fear from him. "Give the money to Elsie.
It's the least you can do for the aggravation you've caused
her."

The boy had the good sense to nod his head and handed
the coins to Elsie.

Daphne had wanted to offer employment to this woman.
Giving refuge to Elsie and the boy would be Paul's way of
honoring Daphne and her wonderful spirit. She wouldn't
want the cook or the boy to suffer for the trouble the street
urchin had caused. There was only one thing to do.

"Miss Qulin, you're a fine person for taking responsibility of the boy. You shouldn't be working here. I'd like
to offer you a position as an assistant to my cook. I'll pay
you the same wages as here for the start. We'll see how
you progress."

"Thank you, Your Grace," she gushed. Her sudden joy
disappeared. "I can't take the position, sir. I need to look
after Garland. Even though he's an imp, he needs me."

Paul nodded. The young woman was a good role model
for the boy. "He can come, too, and work in the stables.
Report first thing in the morning." He stared at Garland.
"If you ever steal from me or from anyone again, I'll throw
you out, understand?"

The boy's eyes flashed. "Yes, sir. You won' regre' it,
m'lawd. I mean Your Grace."

Elsie stood behind the boy with her hands on his
shoulders. "Thank you, sir. Your kindness won't go unre-
warded." She shuffled the young man out the door.

Just exactly who would reward him? He had a greater
chance of receiving accolades from the devil than receiving any bounty of a spiritual kind.

Detached, as if watching the events from above, Paul
exited and moved slowly toward the gaming floor ever

closer to the roar of the crowd. At this time of day, most civilized men were at their gentlemen's club or attending their wives during the midafternoon tea. The jackals who littered the floor of the Reynolds weren't civilized. Like wild hyenas, they jostled for positions at the tables, then laughed at nothing but the macabre scene of fortunes being lost.

Thankfully, Paul quickly found Richmond at one of the hazard tables. Wearing a black split-tail coat, matching waistcoat, and black breeches, he resembled one of the ravens that guarded London Tower. His personality matched the raucous birds—quarrelsome and opportunistic. Paul suppressed a surge of hatred and approached the publisher of *The Midnight Cryer.* Paul needed to be his most charming if he wanted to woo Richmond. He angled his way to Richmond's side. Several greetings of "Southart" flitted past him. He ignored them all.

"Room for one more?" he asked as he sidled next to the man.

With a twist of his head, Richmond turned. His look of utter surprise transformed into pleasure, but the crooked, insincere smile ruined the effect. "Your Grace, how delightful to see you at your old hunting grounds. You seem to have regained your taste for the games of chance that you once so favored. Perhaps with your newfound title and wealth, fate will smile more favorably upon your gaming endeavors."

"One can only hope," Paul answered as his stomach roiled in revolt. God, how he despised the man with a passion. But for Daphne he'd go through this hell. "I'm not here to play."

"What a surprise," Richmond drawled. "For a common man such as myself, it's amazing how often the titled seek me out." He threw the dice down the table, and the crowd erupted in a roar. "My luck has been utterly amazing. I've won hundreds of pounds today, and now you're here." The same false smile creased his lips, but his eyes flashed with intelligence. "Let me guess what you want from me. Does it have something to do with the amazing journal I recently acquired?"

"You are as clever as a fox, or at least a raven." Paul returned the same insincere smile. "Indeed. I might have some interest in acquiring it."

The comparison of Richmond to a raven was rather astute, if Paul did say so himself. Richmond resembled the intelligent, cunning bird known for eating the decaying flesh of other animals. The carrion eater before Paul might masquerade as a man, but he also shared another behavior associated with the raven—he liked to collect shiny, bright things that didn't belong to him.

"Name your price, and I'll gladly pay it. You can make a nice, tidy profit, and we'll both be happy." All the unruly noise dissolved into nothing as Paul stared at Richmond, and he returned the favor. They were like two stags ready to fight to the death over a doe, but with one major difference. Paul loved Daphne with every breath while Richmond wanted to destroy her.

Ignoring the calls to take his turn, Richmond fondled the dice in his hand like a lover. "Beg your pardon, *Your Grace,* but why would I want to do that? You're aware of the entries in this journal."

"No, I haven't read them, nor will I," Paul said.

"Really? How interesting." Richmond narrowed his eyes. "To say the writings were earth-shattering and sensational in the content is like saying the Thames is nothing more than a stream running through London." Richmond leaned close enough to whisper, "There's enough material there to publish one entry per day for the next decade. I'll be rich beyond all imagination. Everyone in

London will want to read the titillating and sordid saga of the young aristocratic lady. I must ask, Your Grace, what could *you* possibly offer me that would convince me to part with such a treasure?"

"Ten thousand pounds," Paul countered.

Richmond rolled his eyes. "Tick tock, Southart. The hazard table is calling me. If you don't have anything more valuable than that parsimonious offering, then I shall return to the game."

Everything stilled within Paul except his heart, which beat at a savage frenzy. A tinny sound invaded his ears, and he couldn't respond. Richmond tilted his head, and his gaze pierced Paul.

If he didn't do something, Daphne would become a pariah in society. He was already saddling her with unhappiness once he bowed out of his offer of marriage. If Richmond published her journal and her identity was discovered, she risked society shunning her at every event. All potential marriage prospects would back away from her as if she were infected with a fatal disease. The taint would eventually bleed over to Alex, Claire, and their children.

Like a pebble thrown into a still pond, the scandal would extend outward until it tainted more than the immediate family.

Paul made the only decision that could save Daphne from more ruin. There was one thing he could offer that would entice the man before him to release the diary.

Could he really throw his life away?

The simple answer was yes. He closed his eyes, then smiled. There was no pleasure, only pain, in his decision, but he'd never let Richmond know how he'd gutted Paul's future.

Richmond made a move to return to the table, but Paul

grabbed him by the arm in a vise-like hold to keep him from moving another inch. "I have something much more valuable than a girl's diary," he taunted.

Richmond dropped his gaze to where Paul's hand had gripped him. With a scowl, Richmond heaved a sigh. "Release me, and I'll give you my full attention."

Paul nodded and let go. "In exchange for the diary, I'll give you the story of a lifetime, one that might possibly change the course of history. Political alliances and financial deals will crumble. The story I give you would ruin one of the oldest and most respected families in all of England. Your name would be synonymous with the family's downfall."

"You've piqued my interest, Southart. What's the secret?" asked Richmond.

"The truth of my birth." Paul stood silent as the wheels turned in Richmond's head.

A smile tugged at Richmond's mouth. "We have a deal, Your Grace."

His response reminded Paul of the raven once more, the way the man's eyes sparked in interest. If they find a shinier object than the one in their custody, the birds would readily drop their possession for the gaudier bauble.

The truth of a duke's birth was much more dazzling than a lady's journal.

"Shall we do the exchange now?" Paul offered.

"No," Richmond answered. "My man of affairs took it to my office. Something that valuable shouldn't be treated carelessly. I have business all day tomorrow. Make it the next. I want you to come to my office. It'll be delightful doing business with you, Your Grace."

The condescending look in his eyes made Paul's skin crawl. Once he told everything to Richmond, all ties to his burgeoning honor would be severed. He'd lose his standing in society, and political allies in the House of Lords would forsake him like fleas on a dead dog. As importantly, he'd break his promise to Robbie, all the while descending into the bowels of disreputability, a hauntingly familiar place for him.

But sacrificing his own dreams and reputation for Daphne would allow him to live with his failure and the doubtless demise of the duchy. That was some comfort. He'd protect Daphne with his life. The loss of his reputation was nothing. He'd thrown it away before. Yet there was a deeper, fresher wound that bled and threatened to fester—a breach that would never heal. The gaping hole in his heart would never be repaired. He loved Daphne with every fiber of his being and hated that she'd be hurt by his actions.

But he couldn't see another path to take.

Without a word, Paul turned on one heel and left the establishment. His next course on the path of total annihilation required that he see Daphne, the love of his life, and find a way to make her hate him.

Forever.

Chapter Twenty-Four

Normally, the floral window seat in Daphne's bedroom was her favorite place in the house. She could stare out the window at the garden below and imagine all sorts of fanciful wishes for her life. Sometimes, she'd remember Alice. The painful memories had diminished in potency since Paul had entered her life again. This morning she had wanted to plan her marriage and subsequent move to Southart Hall, but her dreams had dispersed like dandelion seeds in a wind gust.

She tilted her head back until it rested on the recess of the wall next to the window. Paul hadn't come to see Alex as he'd promised. If busy or indisposed, he'd surely have sent her word.

The hair lifted on the back of her neck. Immediately, she sat up. What if he lay ill in bed without anyone but servants to care for him? What if he couldn't call on her? That would explain his absence. But he would have had a footman deliver a note. Something dire must have happened to him. Her chest tightened at the thought.

A brisk knock on the door broke the silence, then Mavis slipped inside. "My lady, His Grace, the Duke of

Southart, is downstairs in the front salon. He's asked to see you." Mavis's gaze perused Daphne from top to bottom, and the maid smiled reassuringly. "I'm certain His Grace will agree with me that you're a vision this afternoon, ma'am."

Daphne reached Mavis's side in two strides. "Thank you." She squeezed her maid's hand in relief. "Silly of me, but I'd wondered if he'd forgotten his promise to call today."

"And why would you think that, Lady Daphne?" Mavis's brows slowly rose a fraction of an inch. "He's here, isn't he?"

"Indeed. That's all that matters." Daphne sat on the edge of the bed to put on her slippers. "Thank you, Mavis."

Within minutes, Daphne swept into the salon. When her gaze found Paul studying the fire, her heartbeat accelerated in excitement. He must not have heard her enter, as he didn't spare a glance her way. She shut the door for privacy.

"Hello, Paul."

He slowly turned. The slump of his shoulders and the tortured dullness in his eyes reflected a man in pain. She rushed to embrace him.

"What's happened?" Before she could touch him, he stepped away.

He clasped his hands behind his back and stared at the floor momentarily. "We should sit." He glanced at the door. "Is your maid coming?"

"No. As we're to be married, there's no need for a chaperone, particularly after the night we shared together," she teased. "Wouldn't you agree?"

Instead of answering with an expected quip, he took a deep breath and extended his hand to a sitting area close to the fire. "I suppose it's best if Mavis isn't here. We'll need privacy."

Daphne bit the inside of her cheek as she chose the sofa thinking they could sit together. He took the red brocade chair next to the sofa.

He rested his elbows on his knees and once again stared at his clasped hands. The longcase clock marked the seconds, and each one grew more ominous the longer he sat silent. Unsmiling, he finally spoke. "I'm at a loss as to where to start."

"Tell me." Her chest tightened, but she pushed aside the dread that thrummed through her veins.

When he shifted his gaze from his hands to hers, the intense pain in his eyes caused her breath to hitch. "I received a letter from the old Duke of Southart this morning."

"Your father?"

"I wouldn't call him that," Paul said brusquely.

"I wouldn't call him that either. But after all these months, why?" She shook her head slightly. Whatever was in it had shaken him to the core.

"Perhaps he thought the day of reckoning could no longer wait. Macabre, isn't it, that he writes to me after death?" Without waiting for her to answer, he continued, "I discovered"—his gaze latched on to hers—"I'm not his son. I'm Renton's bastard."

She sat stock-still as the shock of his words pounded her.

"Earlier, I visited Renton to confront him. When I realized he didn't know, I was, well, rather angry and belligerent." A muscle clenched along his jaw. "A typical day for me."

The cynicism in the remark deserved a rebuke for belittling himself, but she recognized that he was trying to hide his anguish. "Go on," she said.

"Your brother happened to be there, along with Somerton. I'm afraid I said some hateful things to Pembrooke." He glanced at the window as he drummed his fingers on the chair as if anxious to escape. Eventually, he turned back to her. "Daphne, there's no easy way to say this. The truth is I can't marry you."

"Why?" Her thoughts spiraled in confusion.

"I'm a bastard," he said forcefully. "You better than anyone realize the impact of that simple truth on any marriage and offspring from such a marriage. After what you went through with Alice, I'll not let you become fodder for the gossipy *ton* because of my illegitimacy."

"I don't care about that. If I did, I wouldn't be establishing a charity for unwed mothers."

"You should," he said quietly. "My God, look at me, Daphne. I look just like Somerton."

Tears burned, but she blinked them back. He stood and she matched his movement.

"Somerton? Just because of your blond hair and blue eyes?" She forced herself to study him. Their coloring was the same and they both bore a slight resemblance, but that was all. "You and half the men in *Debrett's Peerage* have those same features. Families as old as ours have marriages that have intertwined for centuries. We're all related in some way."

He shook his head in disbelief. "Daphne, I love you too much to—" He tipped his head and stared at the ceiling. "I was going to say ruin you, but I've already accomplished that."

"Oh, my God." Tears welled in her eyes. "You didn't ruin me." One slipped free, and she swiped it away with her hand. "You saved me."

"Saved you? More like destroyed you. Christ, I should have never touched you. But selfish bastard that I am, I took full advantage." He laughed, but it held no humor, only pain.

The desolation painted on his face was perfectly understandable. He'd lost his family and his identity. His actions resembled those of an injured animal that went on the offense to protect itself from further harm. She was desperate to hold him in her arms and soothe his pain.

If they could lock themselves away from the world for a week, she was confident she could help him through this. She took a step forward, and immediately he retreated in the opposite direction.

"Don't, Daphne. This is hard enough to explain. If I touch you, I'll . . ." He walked to the window and gazed outside.

"You'll what?" She didn't move an inch.

"I may never let go." His hoarse voice betrayed his agony. "But I promised myself I'd get through this without touching you."

She faltered in how to respond to his distance as the silence between grew into a chasm that couldn't be breached. Finally, he returned his attention to her, but it was as if she was invisible again. He just stared straight through her.

"If you find yourself with child, we'll find a way to protect both you and the babe. Let me talk to Devan. If worse comes to worst, he'll marry you." The expression on his face was blank—almost lifeless. Her breath hitched at the sight, and she stopped. This man had taught her to believe in herself. He'd taught her how to shed her invisibility. How could he not feel anything?

"Stop it, right now. You can't decide this unilaterally." She let her anger and hurt spill into the room. "None of this makes any difference to me. I don't want you for your ancestry or title. I love you. I want a life with you and *only you*."

"I'm sorry, Daphne." His remorse and anguish were evident from the lines radiating around his eyes. "I wanted a life with you, too. But as a bastard, I'm no one. I have nothing to offer you." He gathered his coat, gloves, and hat. "I'll take my leave." He stood slowly and bowed. "Even a bastard like me possesses a few principles. I made a promise to find your journal. Once I have it, I will send it to you through Devan within the next couple of days. Never worry, its secrecy will be protected from prying eyes." He made a step toward her, then stopped with a clenched fist by his side. The hunger and longing of his expression clear.

"For our sakes, don't do this." Her throat tightened, but she fought to maintain control. "Don't throw us away."

"Moonbeam, that's what I was born to do. I destroy things." Without another word, he quickly exited the room, leaving her with only pain and disappointment for company.

All she wanted to do was disappear and become invisible again. Only then could she grieve for both of them.

If she was hidden no one else would see the carnage that *bloody* letter had wrought on both of them.

Chapter Twenty-Five

Paul rested his elbows on his knees and stared while Devan read the officious letter from the old duke. From the pinched look on his friend's face, the missive had shocked him as much as, if not more than, Paul.

"Your Grace," Devan choked out in obvious discomfort. "This is inconceivable."

Paul studied his hands. His had always been larger and his fingers longer than Robbie's hands. There were so many clues about his bastardy, and he'd never seen them. Paul closed his eyes and let the weight of Southart's revelation settle once again. Once he talked to Richmond, his life, the one he'd valiantly tried to create after the loss of his family, would forever be destroyed. His life with Daphne, the only pure thing he'd ever thought to create, would be shattered. He took a shuddering breath and finally raised his gaze to Devan.

"You simply cannot give Richmond this story." Devan's voice had mellowed into the familiar tone he used when consoling Paul during his grief. "You'll be sentencing yourself to a life of censure from society."

"There's no other avenue. Daphne will not be sacrificed

to that reprobate like a lamb led to slaughter." Paul straightened in his seat. "Besides, don't my previous actions and decisions in life make sense now? I was destined to portray the spurious blackguard, since it's the truth of my birth."

Devan shook his head. "Nonsense. You've changed your life. This"—he waved the letter in the air—"proves nothing about who you are as a man. The only thing it offers is an explanation for why your father was such an arse to you."

"My father is the Duke of Renton," Paul countered.

The door to his study burst open, and Pembrooke and Somerton stormed through the room. If they'd come to battle and conquer everyone in their path, they wouldn't find any opposition from Paul. He didn't even rise at their entrance.

Clearly out of sorts, Ives followed in their wake. "I apologize for the interruption, Your Grace, but they refused to listen that you weren't receiving."

"It's a matter of urgency," Pembrooke stated.

"Thank you, Ives. That'll be all."

As soon as the door closed, Somerton made his way to Paul's side and plopped on the sofa beside him. Pembrooke followed but sat on the sofa next to Devan facing Paul.

Paul leaned back and regarded the two. At one point in time, these two had been his best friends and best allies. "You both probably want to kill me. I only ask that you wait. I have an appointment with Martin Richmond tomorrow morning."

"For what purpose?" Pembrooke asked in a deceptively calm manner.

Paul knew that voice. The marquess probably wanted to thrash him on the spot—the thought was appealing—but he'd not allow it until he had Daphne's journal in Devan's hands. "Richmond has something of value that belongs to someone who means the world to me. In exchange for the truth of my birth, Richmond has agreed to give it to me."

A cold silence descended that froze his three visitors in their seats.

"I want to share something with you. Hopefully, it'll change your mind." After an agonizing eternity, Somerton cleared his throat. "My childhood was a lonely existence, as our father wanted nothing to do with me."

Paul recoiled at the words "our father."

"Ever since I was a little boy, I wanted a brother, someone to cherish as family. I prayed for that every night." Somerton's normally deep voice crackled with emotion. "Now, after all these years, my prayers have been answered. And"—he closed his eyes for a moment betraying his poignant emotion—"our father is a much kinder and gentler man now. He will come to love you as he's done with me. As your brother, I cannot allow you to throw this gift away. You'll be ruined."

Paul bit the inside of his cheek at the bittersweet thought that he had gained a brother in this horrid manner.

"Somerton, you were always a loyal friend, at least until I made it impossible. I should have paid that debt to you sooner." The act still made Paul flinch at his selfishness. "Your friendship and my disregard will always be a regret I'll carry."

Somerton nodded in acknowledgment of Paul's shortcomings. "Your efforts to make things right between us has brought many joys to my life. I'm married to the woman of my dreams, and I've been able to repair the broken relationship I had with our father."

Would he ever be able to consider Renton as his father?

As he gazed at Somerton, he viewed their resemblance to each other. Daphne's words haunted him. It was true that he favored his mother, but his height could only come from Renton. Once he told his tale to Richmond, the reprobate would likely root around like a mole until he discovered the relationship that existed between him and Somerton. The truth of Paul's birth wove a horrid web of destruction for everyone he cherished.

He did care for Somerton and Emma and their children along with Alex and Claire and their family, too. Above all, he loved Daphne. The familiar ache of want twisted his insides. Desires and wants weren't gifts he was entitled to receive. "Somerton, your acceptance of me as your half brother is . . . I truly appreciate your sincerity. However, I think you should reconsider having a relationship with me. When I talk to Martin Richmond, it will impact your family." Paul shifted his gaze to Pembrooke. "And yours."

Against the sofa, the marquess reclined in a pose matching Paul's position. "What is it exactly you want that Richmond has?"

"Something of your sister's that I promised I'd see returned to her." Paul didn't flinch when Alex's eyes narrowed.

"Daphne?"

Paul nodded.

"Tell me." Pembrooke's voice was eerily quiet.

"Something that was stolen from her. Something she values greatly," Paul said.

Taken aback, Alex's face turned white. He leaned forward with his elbows resting on his knees. "Is that why you're willing to ruin your life?"

"I don't believe I'll ruin my life," he drawled. "It was already ruined for me by the previous Duke of Southart."

"Is that why you broke with Daphne?" Pembrooke asked.

"Among other reasons." Paul ran a hand down his face and exhaled. "The church's stand on the laws of consanguinity would forbid marriage between siblings."

Devan put his hand up to stop Paul. "That's only if there's blood shared. For instance, if Somerton had a sister you couldn't marry her, as you'd be half siblings. But there's no blood between you and Pembrooke. More important, no blood shared between you and Daphne."

Paul rose from the sofa to stoke the fire. The domestic act gave him a purpose—at least for the next several minutes. "What difference does it make? It's done."

Somerton scowled. "It makes a hell of a lot of difference. You simply cannot capitulate to *The Midnight Cryer*'s publisher and give him the facts of your birth."

"I'm not giving him anything. I'm exchanging something of value for something invaluable." Protecting his beloved's peace of mind was priceless to him.

But he'd still be leaving Daphne to defend herself against the rumors. He stared at the fire without feeling any warmth. He'd already destroyed her. God, everything he touched he ruined.

"Your rendering of the situation"—Pembrooke rose and stood beside him—"is nonsensical. Such an act would forever make you an outcast in society, not to mention cast doubts on the Southart duchy."

Hot anger exploded in Paul's gut. "I don't give a damn about the duchy!"

"You do, my friend," Pembrooke said. "Whether you carry any Southart blood in your veins is immaterial. You've grown up a Southart, and the future of the great title and estate rests with you. People rely on you for their livelihoods and the livelihoods of their children. In the short amount of time you've been the duke, you've done marvelous things. You've created a charity that all of London is talking about. Your efforts in the House of Lords are nothing but awe-inspiring. The Duke of Langham already sees you as a powerful ally for the important legislation he wants passed. That's not something to throw away."

Devan nodded solemnly. "What Pembrooke says is all true."

Somerton walked to Paul's other side. "If you do this, you'll throw away everything."

"Including my sister. You'll break her heart all over again," Pembrooke added softly. "She loves you. She proved it when she rallied the entire family to accept the invitation to attend your upcoming charity soiree."

Paul's gaze shot to Pembrooke. "She convinced you, Somerton, and the rest to support me?"

Alex nodded. "I was against it, but Claire, Emma, my mother, and the Duchess of Langham informed me they were attending with or without my acquiescence as a way to support you."

"No wonder I love her," Paul murmured to himself. She'd brought Pembrooke and Somerton back into his life. A month ago, he would never have conceived that these men would gather around him in a show of support—in a show of friendship. But for how long? Bitterness stole what little relief he found at that truth. Once he told his tale to Richmond, his old friends could do nothing but distance themselves and their families from his taint.

Every inch of him ached with longing to hold her one last time in his arms. But he didn't deserve such comfort or her. She was pure and he was spoiled to the core like a worm-infested rotten apple. No matter what, for the rest of his life his black heart was hers.

By his father's words and his own actions, he'd lost her. He closed his eyes as the emptiness surged through him threatening to drown him. Once again, his selfishness threatened to take control. His bereavement would have to wait until he'd finished his promise to her.

"I'm sorry, but I see no other way than to speak to Richmond." The steel in Paul's voice meant no one could convince him otherwise.

The wood in the fireplace collapsed signaling his defeat. Sparks flew upward through the chimney trying to escape the devastation that would result from his actions tomorrow.

Devan took a deep breath, then exhaled loudly. "Thankfully, I'm here. Only a vicar could come up with this solution, and I'm happy to be of assistance." He paused dramatically, then rested his gaze on Paul. "When I was at university, I became what one might consider a guardian angel to the boys who couldn't quite, how shall I say, muster the grades to proceed to divinity studies. I saw the injustices and made it my mission to right the wrongs."

Pembrooke exhaled a loud, long-suffering breath. "And the point of this tale?"

Devan ignored the interruption. He stood and approached the fireplace to stand with the three men. "I developed a useful skill to help my fellow students. I learned how to break into the provost's office and change the grades. Thus, I helped my friends in their darkest hours."

"How in God's name does changing grades help Southart?" Somerton queried.

"We'll break into *The Midnight Cryer*'s offices this evening and steal whatever you're looking for," Devan cheerfully offered.

Pembrooke's eyes widened.

Somerton grimaced and slowly shook his head in apparent disbelief.

The walls of the study suddenly closed around Paul. For a moment, he couldn't catch his breath. "No," he whispered.

"The idea has merit," Pembrooke offered.

"It's too dangerous," Paul retorted. "If we're caught your reputations will be shattered, not to mention Richmond would press charges and report about the proceedings every day with a smile on his face."

"We could be in and out within a half hour," Devan announced.

"I'm willing," Somerton said.

"Have you lost your minds?" Paul's voice rose in defiance. "Even if we're not caught, Richmond will know who did it."

"What could he do then?" Alex asked. "Nothing. He'd have no proof and no"—he batted his hand through the air like he was swatting a fly—"whatever it is you're rescuing for Daphne. I'm not going to let you risk this alone if you're doing this on my sister's behalf."

"Southart, this will work. If anything goes wrong, I'll take full responsibility." Devan put his arm around Paul's shoulder. "Trust me, my friend." Devan addressed Pembrooke and Somerton, "Since Lady Daphne is busy elsewhere, might either of you know if there are any extra Cavensham heiresses hiding somewhere in the proverbial family tree? I find I'm in need of one myself."

Pembrooke shook his head, and Somerton chuckled.

All three men, his friends, had come together to help him for Daphne's sake. There was nothing else he could do. He nodded, then the four of them proceeded to plan their evening.

The dinner tray still sat covered on the table in her sitting area. Daphne hadn't asked for it, but Mavis had quietly brought it in after Daphne had sent word that she'd didn't feel well and wouldn't be joining the rest of the family for dinner.

To say she was under the weather didn't accurately

describe her mood. She felt swept away by a wave of epic proportions, the upheaval something she couldn't grasp how to fix. Paul believed his life was worthless because he was a bastard. When she'd explained it didn't make any difference to her, she wasn't at all certain he listened—or if he did that he accepted any of what she was saying.

She pulled the drape in the window seat aside. Night had fallen over London, and the dark gray gloom outside was a perfect companion for her this evening. Earlier Margaret and Truesdale had stopped by for a brief kiss. Though children, they knew she was heartbroken and both gave her an extra hug this evening before saying good night.

She shut her eyes and allowed a lone tear to escape. How could she have been the happiest she'd ever been in her life and now faced the ultimate heartache because of the same man? A man she loved with every ounce of her being. Once again, feelings of invisibility threatened. Desperate to protect herself from the pain, Daphne brought her hand to her chest. The feeble effort provided little relief. Inside, her heart was torn apart, leaving her with the tatters.

A soft knock broke her concentration. Absently, she called out, "Enter."

"Hello, darling." Her mother's sweet voice broke the silence in the room.

Slowly, Daphne turned and faced her mother. She shook her head to keep a shuddering sob from escaping. "He broke our betrothal today."

In an instant, her mother was by her side, and Daphne found herself enfolded in her mother's warm embrace. Normally, her mother's touch comforted, but tonight it did little to tame the disquiet that currently dominated her thoughts.

"Mother, I—" She turned toward the window to stifle another sob that rose in her throat. With several shallow breaths, she managed to tamp down the urge. "Yesterday Paul asked me to marry him and told me he'd talk to Alex. Earlier today he called and said he couldn't marry me." She cleared her throat, then captured her mother's gaze. There was no sense avoiding the pain. "He—he told me he loved me, and I believe he does. But . . ."

What could she say? It was his secret to tell.

"Oh, darling." Her mother's eyes glistened with tears. She patted Daphne's hand in reassurance. "Your Southart received some startling news, and Renton has been devastated by it as well. This won't be easy."

"I don't know what to do. My place is by his side. I want to comfort him." She caught her mother's gaze. "I love him."

"Darling"—her mother took a deep breath—"Southart is angry and said things." Her mother grabbed her hand tighter. "Paul wanted Alex to call him out for . . . ruining you. Your brother was to visit Southart tomorrow after he had some time to think things through."

"Oh, my God." Tears welled in her eyes. One drop slipped free. "He made me feel alive. He gave me my life back."

Her mother slipped a handkerchief into her hand. Daphne accepted it and wiped her face.

"Well, you're not the first woman who slept with her betrothed." Her mother pursed her lips. "I wish you would have waited. What's done is done." She waved a hand in the air. "We'll save that discussion for later. We have more important things to discuss."

When her mother took her into her arms again, her familiar scent of peonies did little to relieve her anguish. She'd lost him. Stabs of grief assaulted her. She had suffered heartache before, but nothing as debilitating as what she was experiencing now.

Her mother's inner strength and beauty were simply remarkable, but her devotion to her family was a force to be reckoned with. Soon, Mavis delivered a tea tray. Daphne's mother dismissed the maid with a smile, then turned to Daphne.

"Let's have a cup of tea, shall we? Cook made your favorite, apple tarts." Holding her hand, her mother led her to her slipper chair, then poured them both a steaming-hot cup of tea.

"I must share something with you." Her mother took a sip of tea, then set her cup down. "I loved your father." She didn't wait for a response. "We were friends, but I never gave him my heart. Of course, we were proud and happy when we had three beautiful children."

Caught off guard at the frankness in her mother's tone, Daphne simply stared before responding, "Why are you sharing such an intimate detail?"

"Because I'm married to a man now who makes me happier than I've ever been in my life. I love Renton with every beat of my heart. When I saw you and your reaction to seeing Paul insulted at the dinner table"—a gentle smile creased her lips—"I recognized how much you loved him."

Daphne shook her head in answer. "He wants nothing to do with me. I'm at a loss at what I should do." She hung her head in defeat. "Mother, he doesn't even want to see me. He informed me that he found something I'd lost." Her hand covered her mouth. Once Paul gave her the journal, he had no more reason to contact her. The journal, which would always remind her of Alice, would now represent the loss of Paul. She let her hand fall to her side in resignation. "But he's not even going to give it to me. He's asking his vicar friend, Mr. Farris, to deliver it to me."

"He's hurting, and because of his pain, you're hurting, also. You've got to fight for your future, fight for your love." Her mother reached forward and patted her knee. "Convince him he's worthy to fulfill the responsibilities of the dukedom. You must convince him that you're destined for each other."

The affection in her mother's gaze brought the hot sting of tears to her eyes. "What if he rejects me?"

"Sweetheart, if he's your true love, then you need to fight with everything you possess to make him understand how rare your love for one another is. Something that great is worth the risk of rejection, don't you think? You'll never know if you don't try." Her mother leaned close and pressed a gentle kiss on Daphne's cheek, then studied her. "My Daphne of years ago, that feisty young girl who took tablecloths for the greater good, was a mighty defender. She'd have fought for this man if she wanted him."

Daphne released a sigh, then stood and walked to the window. A brilliant moon took command of London's night sky, leaving the city painted in a sea of inky blue. Her astute mother spoke the truth. Daphne had allowed her strength and sense of self to wither. Now was not the time to withdraw into the comfort of invisibility again. Everything in the universe had aligned so they could be together. He needed her as much as she needed him. Whatever she had to do, she'd win him back—convince him their love was worth fighting for—no matter the cost.

"You possess a canny, may I say an almost wily, sense of how to slip into Southart Hall. Surely, with all your practice, you can find a way to see him?" Her mother lifted a brow.

The old, invisible Daphne would have been horrified at the gentle reprimand in her mother's voice. The new Daphne relished the advice and embraced it wholeheartedly.

She held her head high. If need be, she'd set up a block-ade in front of every door of Southart Hall. He'd have to emerge sometime.

When he did, she'd be there.

Cold, the kind that seeped into your bones and made you believe your toes and fingers were detached, permeated Paul's unmarked carriage. He sat next to Pembrooke, and Devan and Somerton faced him in the rear-facing seat. With a whispered command and a pull of the reins from the driver, the matched team of horses slowed to a stop in the narrow passage between Martin Richmond's offices and the next building directly across the alley. Without a word, the men descended from the carriage.

A street urchin no more than nine or ten years of age watched the proceedings. Paul nodded at one of his groomsmen, who then approached the lad. As soon as the boy saw the groomsman start in his direction, he ran. Paul exhaled, and a cloud of mist surrounded him.

"Your Grace," another groomsman whispered. "Shall I follow the boy?"

Paul glanced at his companions, then shook his head in answer. He and his companions, all larger than life, were dressed in black greatcoats and beaver hats. The sight probably scared the boy into running to the nearest church for sanctuary. Besides, the quicker Devan broke in, the quicker they could leave.

With Somerton holding a lit lantern over his head, Devan made quick work of the lock. With an echoing click, the door opened, and the four of them entered. Pitch-black except for the illumination their two small lanterns offered, the office itself held little warmth.

"Let's split into two groups," Devan whispered. "What does the journal look like?"

"I'm not certain." Paul reached and touched Devan's arm. "If you find *it*, don't look inside, understand?"

"How will I know if it's the right one if I don't look inside?" he offered with a shrug of his shoulders.

"It's a journal. Probably a leather-bound book." Paul glowered at him. "Don't open it. I promised her."

Pembrooke's gaze jerked to Paul. "For God's sake, what has she written?"

"I'm not privy to that information, but I promised her that it wouldn't be read." Paul stared at Alex. Daphne's words that her brother would be devastated rang in Paul's thoughts. Even with his newfound esprit de corps with Pembrooke and the others, Paul wouldn't allow anyone to read Daphne's writings. Her wishes drove Paul's every action tonight.

With a nod, Pembrooke followed Paul. Somerton and Devan headed toward the opposite end of the building. One of Devan's colorful curses followed the crash of something tipping over and falling to the floor. The brittle sound of glass breaking echoed through the large room.

Paul left his friend's mostly silent yowling for Somerton to manage as he and Pembrooke methodically searched the two rooms closest to the front entrance of *The Midnight Cryer* office. The first offered little in way of hints of the diary's whereabouts. The room contained hundreds upon hundreds of copies of the rag's previous issues. As the piles attested, the paper's talent for finding tidbits of gossip had become its primary focus. Tales of illicit liaisons, curious cuckoldry, and peculiar peccadilloes were rife through its pages and brought in a considerable amount of money. By far, the most popular features were the ones that ruined the ladies of society.

Paul's gut tightened. Daphne would not suffer such a fate.

What a farce.

Hadn't he already ruined her by taking her to bed? Dancing on the edge of ruin was nothing for him, but Daphne didn't deserve the results of his selfishness. He exhaled and pushed the thoughts away. He could mourn later, after he had the journal. Not now.

With quick steps, Paul and Pembrooke headed toward the room closest to the front door. Pembrooke pressed down on the latch and pushed forward, but the door, like a mighty fortress, gave nothing. It was locked.

"Farris," Paul whispered with a low growl. "We're in dire need of your locksmith skills."

The sound of two pairs of footsteps quickly made their way to them. Somerton stood behind with his lantern lifted in the air as Devan knelt and worked on the mechanism. Clicks from the lock and curses from Devan erupted into a quiet cacophony of sounds. Finally, after several long moments, a clack and a snap burst through the night. Devan stood and opened the door. He waved his hand as if inviting them all into the room for a civilized tea.

Before they could enter, a commotion broke outside in the street. A hackney carriage pulled in front of the shop's front entrance with the horses' neighing signaling their displeasure at the abrupt stop.

"Someone is here," Paul hissed. "You need to leave."

After a glance to the shop's entrance, Somerton nodded and gave the lantern to Paul. "Farris and I will have your coachmen wait at the end of the alley. We need to leave immediately upon your arrival. Hurry."

"I'll stay with you," Pembrooke said.

Paul shook his head. "No time to argue. If I'm not out in five minutes, leave without me."

Pembrooke hesitated, then nodded and followed the other two.

None of his friends could afford to be discovered. For

that matter, neither could he. A duke accused of stealing was a rare phenomenon, and Paul didn't want to stir up any more scandal than he already would. He swept into the office and prayed he'd find the journal quickly.

His gaze shot to the large window in the office that faced the street in front of Richmond's business.

"They're in there, Mr. Richmond." The street urchin peered inside. "I saw all four of 'em go in."

Several large men stood behind the boy. The jingling of keys sounded like warning bells.

Paul swept into the office. If there was a merciful God, he'd find the journal before the men discovered him stealing from *The Midnight Cryer*. Richmond would have not only his life story but also another titillating tale of how low the Duke of Southart had sunk. Paul had little doubt the man would bring charges of stealing against him.

As if a beacon guided him, Paul immediately walked to the desk. Notes and inkstands cluttered the entire surface. He swept his gaze across the papers and bent to open a desk door, but in the middle of the desktop a journal lay like a sacrifice on an altar.

The worn claret-colored leather was ordinary, but the sight of a gold-leaf emblem of a diving magpie in the middle of the volume brought a smile to Paul's face. It matched the black one Daphne had given him for Christmas. He picked it up, and immediately an image of his Moonbeam came to the forefront of his thoughts.

The jangle of the keys became louder as the front door opened. Richmond's voice boomed through the interior of the building. "Search the premises. I'll start in my office."

Paul turned with the journal, then stopped. He reached into a small pocket of his waistcoat and retrieved five guineas. With a flick of his wrist, he threw the coins on the desk. As Richmond's heavy steps moved closer, Paul slipped from the room and headed to the back exit.

"There's one of the gents," the boy announced.

One of Richmond's henchmen stumbled over a desk and dropped his lantern. A sudden explosion caused the room to light up like a midday sun had burst on the scene. Paul held his arm up to his eyes to protect his vision. Screams and shouts filled the night.

"Run!" one of Richmond's men called out. "The fire is headed for the ink vat."

Paul watched as the fire gained momentum from the papers strewn in a haphazard manner on the floor. Another sudden explosion rocked the building. The fire had grown three times in size. The level of heat that surrounded him hinted that the building would soon be engulfed in flames. Richmond and his men stood on the other side of the massive fire completely separated from Paul, who held Daphne's diary. The only way they could catch him would be to run out the front door and turn at the corner of the street.

Paul didn't look back but quickly made his way outside. He ran toward the end of the alley only to discover the carriage was gone and the street empty.

Someone yanked the neck of his greatcoat. "Imagine meeting you here, Your Grace."

Paul clenched his fists, then swung around, knocking the blackguard to the ground.

"Whoa, Southart," chuckled Lord William. "I'm just trying to help." In a second, he was on his feet. "Come. We must leave."

Paul nodded, but the effort did little to calm the roar to fight that crashed through him. He chanced a glance back at the building. Through the windows, orange and red flames fought their way outside as others crawled up the interior walls.

William mounted the horse next to him, then gave Paul a hand. With a silent huff of breath, Paul leapt on the horse behind William. The horse shot forward through the alley and rounded the corner into a side street.

Richmond's deep bellow followed them. "Go find them. They left on horseback."

Paul didn't dare turn around to see if they'd been followed. Instead, he asked, "Who sent you?"

"No one." William turned his head sideways and continued, "I was on my way to White's and saw you, Pembrooke, Somerton, and Farris emerge from your house. It looked like a jolly good time, so I followed. I found your carriage and the others running toward it."

"Did they tell you what we were doing?" Paul asked. The sounds of Richmond's men following them had disappeared into the night.

"No." William turned his attention back to the horse. When they approached the main road, he reeled the horse down another side street, then turned his head to address Paul again. "I guess it has something to do with a family member?"

Paul simply stared straight ahead. Under no circumstances would he divulge Daphne's secret to Lord William Cavensham or any other family member.

The exertion of carrying two men together caused the horse to slow to a walk. The easier pace allowed more conversation.

Will turned once more in the saddle and regarded him. "Well, I'll wager it has something to do with Daphne."

Paul fought the urge to snap at the rogue in front of him. Instead, he echoed Daphne's words, "It's none of your concern."

William's deep belly laugh broke the stillness of the night. "That's the exact same look you gave me when I kissed her under the mistletoe."

Paul lifted one brow in haughty indifference.

"Don't misunderstand. I've never had any interest in her

except as family. Since she is part of my family, I don't want her hurt." After meandering through various alleys and passageways, William miraculously led them from a side street to the front of Paul's ducal mansion. "Besides, I can't become entangled in an affair of the heart. I'm off to Northumberland again. I'm managing my great-aunt's estate. It's hard to woo a woman when I'll probably be in the north for at least a month or so."

Paul slipped off the horse with the journal clutched in his hand. "Then why did you kiss her?"

William soothed his black gelding with a pat, then turned his steely gaze to Paul. "You can't deny she is beautiful. Plus, it was Christmas. When else would I get a chance to kiss her?"

Without waiting for an answer, William rode off into the night, leaving Paul with a feeling of accomplishment seasoned with an acute sense of failure. He turned and found the loyal Southart butler waiting for his return. He would never refer to himself as Southart again, since he was nothing more than a bastard—a no-name noble masquerading as an aristocrat.

His sense of failure melted into longing. He wanted it to be Daphne who waited for him instead of Ives. The thought he'd not have her in his life drove him mad. But what could he offer her? He possessed an identity that brought him shame. He couldn't burden her with that. She deserved a man who legitimately bore a worthy title, a well-intentioned man who could love her only as she deserved.

Paul let the pain have free rein over his thoughts and body. Every part of him ached knowing that he couldn't have her as his wife.

As soon as he released the diary to Devan, Paul's last connection to her would be finished.

Chapter Twenty-Six

Rufina gently kneaded Paul's leg. Distracted, he leaned against the winged Bergère chair upholstered in ivory brocade with the Southart seal embroidered in gold thread. A matching chair to the left faced the blazing fireplace that radiated warmth throughout the ground floor library. The fire made little difference as Paul sat frozen.

When he'd arrived home with the journal, it was after midnight. He'd sent Ives to bed, then roamed the halls like a ghost trying to find some contentment so he could rest. Throughout his walks, he'd held Daphne's journal. Eventually, as he always did when he needed comfort, he found himself in Robbie's room.

Paul had sat on his brother's bed for what could have been five minutes or five hours. Time wasn't a concept he appreciated tonight.

He corrected himself—he sat on his *half brother's* bed. The normal peacefulness that usually embraced him when he sat in Robbie's domain had entirely disappeared.

To distract himself, he'd opened a drawer on the table next to Robbie's bed and found a book of children's poems. Paul hadn't seen it in years, but it had been his favorite as a child. Without complaint, Robbie had read them aloud repeatedly until Paul had memorized every one. He gently flipped open the book and a piece of paper, an unfinished letter addressed to him in Robbie's handwriting, fell to the floor. It was almost as if Robbie had reached out to him this evening to offer his own comfort. When Paul had picked up the note, his trepidation had grown acute.

Unable to read it, he sought refuge in the library. He couldn't bear any more pain this evening. Rufina had followed and hadn't left his side since. Lady Margaret had the right of it. He needed a friend, and Rufina was fitting the bill nicely. Even her rough purr offered some solace.

It didn't soothe the hunger that threatened to devour every inch of him. He craved Daphne more than life itself.

Absently, he stroked the soft fur behind the kitten's ears. Rufina stretched, and the slight movement upended Daphne's journal, which rested balanced on his leg. With a soft thud, it landed on the floor open. With his hand grasping the kitten, thus ensuring she wouldn't fall, Paul bent and retrieved the journal.

His eyes betrayed him as he tried to shut the book. The opened page described an event he had a hard time recalling. The date written in a neat feminine hand indicated that Daphne had been ten at the time. Her words caused everything within him to still.

> Today, Paul made my mother cry. He left a wildflower bouquet on the breakfast table. When she asked who they were for, he'd winked at me, then answered they were for her.
>
> He'd remembered it was her birthday when no else did.
>
> Of course, I recalled her special day. I embroi-

dered a new tablecloth for her. I planned to give it to her last Christmas to make up for the cloth I ruined last summer. But it took longer than I thought. I kept missing stitches and having to go back and correct my mistakes. The hem was quite crooked. One spot looked like Athena took a bite out of it, but Mother said it was beautiful.

After breakfast, I took one of Paul's daisies back to my room and pressed it in this journal as a token of the day. I'd never seen my mother cry before.

Proof that Paul Barstowe is a rakehell of the worst kind to make a woman cry—even if they were happy tears.

He skimmed forward and found another entry.

If it hadn't been for Paul, my entire life would have been ruined last night. Mother insisted I attend the local assembly dance as a way to prepare for my upcoming Season. Of course, Alice attended and every man in the room had asked her to dance. I, on the other hand, stood like a tree stump rooted to the side of the room. Not a single man offered to dance with me.

But then Paul appeared. Every woman turned and stared at him as if he were the most succulent cut of venison. Paul and Alex had planned to leave for London today, but Paul convinced Alex to stay.

Paul ignored everyone as he made his way to my side. He asked me to dance, and I swear the whole room grew quiet as we took to the floor. After the set finished, he bowed and took his leave. I could not have cared less if anyone talked to me for the rest of the night. He'd help prove that I wasn't a wallflower.

I'm not exaggerating. When he left, he took part of my heart with him.

In spite of his melancholy, he chuckled out loud. He remembered that night. He'd tried to convince Pembrooke to attend the dance with him, but his friend had declined. Paul had known Daphne had looked forward to the assembly all week. That's all she could talk about. When she'd come down the stairs that night looking resplendent in a simple silver silk frock, she'd been absolutely terrified that no one would dance with her.

He'd decided that he wouldn't attend, but a nag made him change his mind. When he'd entered the Pemhill Community Assembly Hall, he'd found her immediately. Awkward and miserable, she hid in the shadows. As soon as she saw him, a smile lit her face, making her the most beautiful girl in the room.

So many of his happiest memories were tied to her.

Lord Paul Barstowe is by far the noblest man I've ever met. His sacrifices prove he's a man to be admired—and dare I say it?

Yes, I do.

An honorable man who deserves love.

When Alex grieved over Alice's death and became, frankly, unbearable, it was Paul who stood up to him and forced Alex to see how he was hurting all those around him.

When the London gossips were tearing my dearest Emma to pieces because she'd been discovered with Somerton in her bedroom at an inn, Paul came forward and offered for her. Though it broke my heart, his actions that day proved he'd help his friends no matter the cost or sacrifice.

When I was punished for ruining my mother's

best table linen, Paul snuck a basket of tarts to my
room. Every time I see his face, I can't help admir-
ing the scar the magpie inflicted.
  It's his badge of honor.

He closed his eyes as the overwhelming awe crashed into him. She'd thought of him for years. While he'd been busy making a mess of his life, she'd been writing about him—fantasizing about him. A wonderfully kind, not to mention spirited, woman had wanted him for ages. What a fool he'd been not to notice her until this year.

He flipped through the pages again. Any hint of Alice in Daphne's writings Paul purposely ignored. The sexual fantasies about him made him blush. Though Daphne had been an innocent, her imagination was damn near unbelievable. Even he hadn't experienced some of the things she'd described in detail.

If I ever have an opportunity, I hope I have the
courage to tell him that I think I could fall in love
with him easily. Sometimes the heart does what it
wants no matter what common sense says.

His eyes burned at the tender words, but he refused to shed a tear. Such emotions would mean he deserved to be loved by her. As a bastard—even one with a noble title— he had little to offer her. He'd constantly be a thorn in her family's side. Attending family gatherings would amount to torture for them all.

No. He'd not put his Moonbeam through such pain. He'd not make her suffer his embarrassments.

He leaned against his chair once more. The effort did little to relieve the ache in his heart as it shriveled into an empty shell. Rufina raised her head, then settled for a nap.

Tomorrow, he'd have Devan deliver the journal first

thing. Paul would include a note telling her not to seek him out ever again.

If Daphne thought him noble, he couldn't disappoint her.

Sending her away was the noblest act he would ever perform.

"My lady, I'll go with you." Tait stifled a yawn, but the weariness of his eyes betrayed how truly exhausted he was. All the late nights he'd sacrificed on Daphne's behalf had caught up with him.

"No. I think it best if I go in alone." Daphne gathered the fur muff that Paul had given her on Christmas. "Why don't you return home? I'm certain His Grace will see me."

She hoped she wasn't telling a falsehood. But just to be on the safe side, Daphne planned to enter the house through the library doors if they were open. She'd not let Ives or a liveried Southart footman send her packing like an unwanted beggar.

The Pembrooke footman opened the carriage door, and she descended the steps with determination in her every move. She paused at the view of Paul's home. The perfect symmetry of the yellow-brick building always took her breath away. It was breathtaking, just like Paul.

She passed the front door and walked to the left side of the massive Palladian mansion. The Pembrooke footman kept a respectable five steps behind her. Once she was inside the mansion, she'd wave the footman away, then find Paul. Even if she had to wake him from his slumber, she'd find him and discover the truth. One look at his eyes, and she'd know immediately what he felt for her.

A small set of stairs led to a terrace with a large set of French doors. Directly inside was Paul's library. Once Daphne was in the house, it'd be easy to find the private staircase she and Paul had used when they'd escaped to his room and made love. Her chest ached at the memory. His tenderness, devotion, and love that night were gifts she'd never forget. Nor would she allow him to ignore and erase what they were creating—a love rare and true.

She turned the handle of the door, and miraculously it was unlocked. She turned toward Duncan, the footman, and nodded. With a bow of his head, he retreated.

Daphne closed her eyes and summoned every speck of bravery and fearlessness she possessed, then went inside.

A huge welcoming fire roared in the fireplace. Two lovely wingback upholstered chairs flanked the hearth. Her breath caught when she saw Paul relaxing in one. To her complete surprise, he showed no reaction to her breaking into his household. In fact, he didn't spare a glance her way.

As if approaching a wounded animal, she carefully closed the distance between them, then knelt by his side. Gently, she reached out and touched his knee. "Paul?"

Their eyes met, and the tenderness in his expression startled her. This was not the man who had cast her aside earlier.

With infinite care, he reached out with one hand and caressed her cheek. "Have my thoughts magically evoked your image? Are you real?"

She leaned into his hand, then pressed a kiss against his palm. "Do I feel real?"

"Daphne," he whispered.

The vibrancy in his voice made her heart beat in a mad dance. "Marry me," she whispered in return.

Slowly, he shook his head. "It will never work. I'll not see you suffer because of the truth of my birth." His voice faded to a hushed stillness.

"Do you think I give one whit about your past or your birthright?" Gently, Daphne picked up Rufina, then placed the purring kitten in the matching chair. Without hesitating, she took both of his hands in hers and started to kneel at his feet. With nary a word, he pulled her into his lap.

"You should," he whispered as he ran his lips over the top of her head.

"All I care about is the man you've become and our future together." She tilted her head and met his gaze. "You could be a butcher, a baker, or a blacksmith and I wouldn't care. Just as long as we were together."

He exhaled. "I'm a bastard and not worthy of your love."

"Paul, that's such nonsense. I don't care who your father is. Surely you don't believe that I do." She took his cheek in her hand.

The virile, lovely man before her doubted his worth. How could she ever make him realize how special he was? She searched his eyes. The pain and longing reflected in the gorgeous blue depths were acute. The sight made all her defenses rally in support to prevent him from hurting.

She rested her forehead against his for a moment. Once she sensed his guard lowered, she drew back until their gazes met. "My place is by your side. You're the one man in this entire world who's helped me heal. The one man who made me believe in myself." She caressed his cheek once more. "The one man who sees me. I'll not let you go. Nor will you let me go. Our love is too powerful. It's too precious to throw away."

He bit his bottom lip, then reached across the side table next to the chair. A letter and her journal were the only articles present. He picked up the letter. "I went to Robbie's room after I found your journal. These"—he passed the missive to her—"are his last written words. I don't think I can read it and withstand the grief. Undoubtedly, it contains more bad news about my birth."

Daphne opened the letter. After scanning several lines, she knew Paul had to hear from his brother and began to read aloud.

My dearest brother,

By now, you've probably received Father's last letter. He was adamant that you know everything. As we both know, he was a master at leaving out the pertinent details. Allow me to reveal the whole truth of your birth.

Paul, never doubt how greatly you were loved. Our wonderful mother and I would have done anything for you. We'd have given anything to spare you the pain you must be suffering now. But one thing is for certain—you, dear brother, were always the love of Mother's life. It was her way to make up for her past mistake.

The old duke couldn't show much affection, but please hear me out—never question whether he loved you. He just loved you in his own way. As best he could, the duke accepted you and raised you as a Southart because he loved Mother. I can see you now shaking your head. No, it's true. The old man did love her. He told me so on numerous occasions after her passing.

You may wonder why I never said a word about the truth. I thought I'd have more time. I wanted you to make amends with your friends first before I uttered a word. I knew you'd be hurt, most likely devastated. I thought they'd be a source of strength and comfort for you when I'm gone. I'm sorry that I'm not there for you now.

Please remember—it takes a true gentleman to own up to his mistakes, but it takes a real man to be able to forgive.

I hope you can forgive Father, Mother, and me for not sharing this truth with you. Please, learn to love yourself for who you are—an intelligent and

fair man who will bring great success to the
Southart duchy.

Most important, I hope you can forgive yourself.
Become the man you were always destined to
be—not the one you think Southart or I wanted you
to become.

I never said it in life—one of my deepest
regrets—but let me say it now. I love you. Always
remember that.

I know you love me.

I'm proud to call you brother.

With those last words, the room grew silent. Hot tears
fell with abandon as she tried to gauge Paul's reaction. The
love Robbie felt for Paul reverberated around the room.
"There's nothing else," she whispered and took his hand
in hers.

He bent his head and studied their intertwined fingers.

"Marry me." She squeezed his fingers tight. "Let's
make each other happy forever."

He exhaled as if in pain and rubbed a hand over his
face. Gently, he rose and set her carefully away from him.
"I can't." He turned and slowly walked to the door.

If she didn't do something, she'd lose him forever. Without second-guessing her decision, she ran after him and
grabbed his arm.

The lack of his regard seared her resolve, but she fought
it. "Yes, you can."

He stopped and turned to face her.

"I'll never believe you can't. I see it in your eyes. You
want me."

"You're better than me."

She winced slightly at the acute sound of pain in his

voice. He grabbed her as if he'd not let go, then just as quickly set her free.

At his abruptness, she almost fell, but kept her footing.

Both were panting as if they'd run a race against each other—his, the result of anguish; hers, because she'd not let him go.

"No, you're wrong. I'm not better than you. I'm the same as you," she challenged.

"I'm trying to do what is right for us under a very difficult set of circumstances." The deep roughness of his voice reminded her of freshly cut wood. Appropriate since he was determined to cut her from his life and, like a splinter, she refused to let go.

"I'll not let you destroy what we're building together," she answered. "Sometimes doing what's right is the easiest thing to do—easier than you might think."

He stood motionless as if frozen in place.

A spark of hope ignited in her chest. He'd referred to them as "us." Such a small word, yet it held great power.

It meant they were still together—as a couple.

It gave her the courage to move to his side and take his hand in hers. "Plus, I agree with your brother. You are an intelligent and loving man. I've been the recipient of your goodness for years. You deserve happiness. Let me give you that for the rest of our lives."

He stared at their entwined hands, then lifted his gaze to hers. The torture reflected in his eyes made her want to rail at Southart for inflicting doubt in his own self-worth.

"I'm not honorable. I've read parts of your diary, the ones that pertained to me." He lifted his other hand as she started to protest. "I promised, but it fell open when I dropped it." A small smile tugged at his lips. "You were far too generous in your descriptions of me."

"Never. I could wane on ad nauseam about all your wonderful and brilliant qualities." She laughed, but her heartbeat pounded with encouragement—telling her to fight for them. She tugged at his hand.

He gently untangled his fingers from hers and rubbed his hand over his face. The action betrayed his weariness, or perhaps his wavering to send her away. She could only hope that was the reason.

"I broke a promise to you. I read your journal. Not the parts about Alice, but the parts about myself. Proof of my wretchedness. Once a vain peacock, always a vain peacock."

Not willing to let him slip away, she took his hand in hers again. "I'm glad you read it." She searched his eyes for any sign of rebuff and found only tenderness. "It's the essence of me. You know who I am with all my flaws and imperfections. I never want to go back to hiding. Do you still"—her throat tightened, and she squeezed his hand—"love me?"

He searched her eyes. For a moment, she believed he could see what was in her heart. "Always." His voice turned tender, almost a whisper.

"Marry me." Her throat tightened. "You love me. I love you." It was hard to stay coherent with him so near. Really, the only thing she wanted to do was kiss him senseless until he relented. At that moment, she pushed her pride away and used an argument that made no sense, but one she prayed he'd appreciate. "Because I've completely ruined you for any other."

"You think you coming here is a way to save me?" His whisky-dark voice caressed her.

She wanted nothing more than to kiss him, but she'd not allow him to retreat again. "Yes. You're a dissolute rake whom I've come to rescue."

"A rogue rescued by an innocent. Is that it?" he soothed.

"Is that one of your fantasies we acted out in your bed? I didn't see it in the journal."

She boldly met his gaze. "You obviously weren't looking hard enough. It's there." She reached into her reticle and pulled out the heart-shaped rock he'd given her years ago. "You've already given me your heart, and for all these years, I've tenderly cared for it. See?"

She held it in her extended palm.

His eyes widened in astonishment. "I can't believe you still have it in your possession." Carefully, he examined the treasure without picking it up. He shook his head slowly. "I told you to use it as a reminder to harden your heart."

"I won't." She pressed it into his hand. "I safeguarded it for you and will continue to do so along with your love for all of my days."

His hand tightened over hers, then pulled her close. Their lips met. Before she could deepen the kiss, he pulled away.

"You're the most persistent woman I've ever met," he whispered. His blue eyes resembled the warm Mediterranean, and she wanted to swim from one end to the other. "You win. I can't fight it anymore. Without a doubt, I've changed because of you. You're in me."

She snuggled close. "We both win."

"I'm glad you think so." He leaned in and this time gave her a real kiss. Passion seemed to ignite the air around them, but once again he pulled away. "You've made me want to become a better man, one better than my father and even Robbie wanted me to be."

He slipped his hands into her hair and tipped her face to his. Breathless, she waited for his next words.

"I'm not much of a duke, but perhaps with you as my duchess, I'll accomplish some great things. At least I'll be the duke I want to be." He pressed another kiss to her lips, then drew back. "Yes, I'll marry you. I love you."

His promise to her melded into a kiss that she'd remember always. One filled with passion, yearning, friendship, and love.

A perfect kiss.

A perfect kiss that would be repeated throughout a lifetime.

Chapter Twenty-Seven

There was only one word to describe Lady Daphne Hallworth's beauty this evening.

"Enchanting."

All evening, Paul had tamped down the urge to go to her. Every time he tried to see her, one of his guests had demanded his attention, which was fine, as the contributions to help fund the hospital were mounting into an amount that, frankly, was unbelievable. But that didn't keep him from stealing glances toward the mezzanine where Daphne held her own court. Her natural radiance seemed to shimmer around her, and she called to him like some whimsical sprite ready to lead him on some merry, magical adventure.

Paul stopped at the bottom of the steps that led to the mezzanine and planted his feet wide.

It was a bloody feat to keep his emotions in check this evening. All night, he could hardly string two words together to any of his guests. All he wanted was to bask in her warmth and steal kisses in hidden corners and secret passageways.

He breathed deeply, and the gentle wafting of her sweet

scent caused his nostrils to flare. Would her effect on him ever cease?

God, he hoped not. The entire evening had been his crowning achievement, all because of his darling Moonbeam. Immediately after arriving, the Duchess of Langham and Claire had shown great interest in his plans for Robbie's hospital. Their perceptive inquiries and support for the cause shouldn't have surprised him, yet it did. Claire, an heiress in her own right, had promised a generous contribution, one that the duchess had matched. Emma had also pledged support.

Pembrooke and Somerton had milled around the group, not taking part in any of the conversation. Both feigned boredom, but it became obvious to everyone they were keenly listening to the discussion. Paul had done his best to acknowledge both men with a simple nod. As Devan had alluded to earlier, it said a great deal that both men had bothered to appear.

Before he reached the top stair, a thought stole his breath and stopped his ascent. He'd be married to this marvelous woman in the morning.

As he closed the distance between them, her smile grew to a brightness that made a thousand lit candles pale in comparison. He answered her smile with one of his own. With every ounce of self-discipline he possessed, he fought the urge to race to her side and fall on his knees like a fool before her.

But why fight it? He was a fool for her. Lucky him.

He shook his head in a desperate attempt to quell his confusion. This had to be some type of moonbeam magic, one that he never could resist.

When he reached her side, she dipped into a deep curtsy, the movement elegant and seductive. "Your Grace, I'm delighted to see you." Her honeyed voice was the sweetest sound he'd heard all evening.

"Lady Moonbeam, look at what you've accomplished this evening." He pointed at the floor below, where his guests mingled. "With the funds pledged tonight, Robbie's hospital will be built in half the time. It can be operational in a year. Your brother and Somerton promised to match their wives' contributions."

"You did this, Paul." The love in her eyes stole his breath.

"Let's say we did this together." He raised her gloved hands to his lips and pressed his mouth against her knuckles. "Let's kidnap Devan and find a room. We'll have him marry us immediately, then I don't have to spend another lonely night without you in my bed."

She squeezed his hand with hers. "I can't wait until tomorrow either. I'll not sleep a wink tonight."

"I always regretted that I never sought you out at these affairs in the past. I'd just gaze upon you from afar." He continued to hold her hand close to his lips, knowing the crowd slowly started gawking at them. "Truthfully, I was a smidge hesitant to talk to you. I don't think I could've withstood your rebuff."

"That was a mistake. I'd have talked to you." The huskiness in her voice made his heart beat faster.

"Why did you always find refuge in those perches of yours?" He turned her hand and pressed a kiss against her wrist.

"Are you calling me a bird?" she teased.

"A bird of paradise," he answered.

"Need I remind you that is a flower." A deep blush colored her cheeks.

"Your beauty causes me to say the most absurd things, love. Now tell me, why did you stay away from the crowds?"

She bit her lip, and the sight caused him to groan. How horrible would it be to sweep her away right this instant and kiss her until the morning when they married?

"I was looking for someone." Her gaze never faltered as she answered.

He couldn't keep from touching her. If she was a flower, then he was a bee starving for her sweet nectar. "Who?"

"You. It was always you." Her whispered words held the strength to level him.

He found himself lost in her shimmering silver eyes. For now and always he'd think fondly of the Reynolds Gambling Establishment where he'd found his glorious Moonbeam who led him out of the darkness and into the light. "Do you have any idea how much I love you?"

She lowered her lashes and smiled. "As much as I love you."

He drew her near. "I'm going to give you your wedding present now."

"Here?" The confusion on her face was simply adorable.

He leaned down and pressed his lips against hers. "I never had much patience when gifts are to be opened." Still holding her hand, he addressed the crowd below them. "Ladies and gentlemen, I have an announcement." He pulled the deed from his waistcoat pocket.

The murmurs in the crowd grew to a low roar, then quieted like children anxious for a treat from their nursery-maids.

"Tonight is not only a celebration for the hospital that will be built to honor my late brother, but it's also to honor another new charity, Aubrey's Place. My wife-to-be is starting a home for unwed mothers."

The crowd grew silent. Daphne's hand tightened in his.

"This is the deed to the Winterford property, the location Lady Daphne has chosen for Aubrey's Place. In addition, I'm pledging twenty-five thousand pounds. The Marquess of Pembrooke and the Earl of Somerton have matched my pledges. Please join me tonight in support of this worthy cause."

The Duchess of Langham and the Duchess of Renton nodded their approval. The smiles on their faces made his throat tighten. Pembrooke, Somerton, Langham, and Renton lifted their glasses in a silent toast. With a tilt of his head he acknowledged their support. That was his new family, and because of the woman beside him, he was accepted.

"Paul, what have you done? I thought you were going to use that building for the hospital." He'd done the right thing if the trembling in her voice was any indication.

"No. I had my solicitors purchase the property surrounding Aubrey's Place. Our charities will be next to one another. Mrs. McBride has agreed to be the house manager." He raised her hand to his lips again. "Are you happy?"

"I'm stunned and ecstatic. But why?" she asked in bewilderment.

"I promised I'd make this right between us. I don't want there to be any confusion about my motives—selfish as they are."

Her adorable brow crinkled into neat lines. "What are they?"

"I want us to be lovers for the rest of our lives."

"Always." The tears in her eyes took his breath away. "How will I ever thank you?"

"By loving me and staying by my side forever."

THE MIDNIGHT CRYER RETURNS
WITH A VENGEANCE

Gentle readers, never fear—a fire may have destroyed our office, but the press will not be silenced. Not when there are tales to tell.

Would it surprise any of you, my dear readers, to discover that a certain reformed duke was seen purchasing a fur muff on Christmas Eve? What makes this piece so unusual is that His Grace paid twice the asking price for this gift . . . AND . . . purchased the most exquisite moonstone pin as an accompaniment for his lady love. Indeed, the nuptials are set in the very near future. Once this intrepid reporter discovers the secret wedding plans, I will divulge all!

MOONSTONE, MOONGLOW, MOONLIGHT . . . MOONBEAM?

I must ask your opinion, intelligent readers, coincidence? I think not.

Well, whatever the truth, this paper wishes the betrothed couple a happy life.

As for the story we'd promised you regarding the truth of the "reformed" duke's birth, it seems there is no story at all. This intrepid reporter scoured the city for retired servants of Southart House who could shed light on the scandal. One such person, the old housekeeper, Lucy Porter from Leyton, was only too happy to share what she knew. Seems the duke was born in a parsley bed. The servant chuckled, then changed her story by saying that his birth occurred under a gooseberry bush. Immediately, this reporter knew he'd had the wool pulled over his eyes.

What a disappointment. Alas, gentle readers, as is the case with a few of our stories, the truth is exceedingly boring.

Now we're on the hunt for a new story— hopefully one that promises lots of lurid details. We've heard that the second son of a powerful duke (rhythms with "Havensham") had his heart broken when, as a young lad, he'd thought he'd fallen in love at first sight. His wounds so deep that he's sworn off all women.

Now, my faithful readers, whoever brings me his story will be the recipient of a five-thousand-pound fortune.

Good luck and Godspeed, my gentle friends. However you celebrate the holidays, may they shine like a pot of gold and overflow with riches.

> Trustworthy and respectfully yours,
> **THE MIDNIGHT CRYER**

Epilogue

◡◠

Christmas Eve—one year later
Southart House
London

No jumping on people. Nor shall you eat from someone else's plate. It took the duchess over an hour to calm Cook down after she'd spent all morning dicing the candied dates and cherries, then you found you in the middle of it all. I am too busy with the hospital plans to continue with these lectures. I'm considering hiring someone to give you deportment lessons. Don't look away when I'm reprimanding you, darling. It's unbecoming. Now, where was I?"

For a moment, the hallway was silent.

"Ah, I remember. No climbing the garlands ever again. Ives tendered his resignation over that fiasco. Because of my excellent persuasion skills, along with our under-butler Tait, I convinced Ives to withdraw it."

The gentle admonishment in her husband's voice drew Daphne away from her errand to hide their nieces' and nephews' presents in the rose salon. Slowly, she entered their bedroom. In actuality, it was her bedroom, but every night Paul slept with her. His bedroom was drafty, or so he said.

She didn't care as long as they were together.

"That little incident of unwrapping Lady Margaret's

present was absolutely uncivilized. You know better," Paul scolded. "Now hold still so I can adjust your ribbon."

"Paul? What on earth?" Her husband stood in front of the middle window seat tying the most elaborate bow she'd ever seen—on his cat, Rufina. The feline was not amused if the rapid flickering of her tail was any indication.

"Hello, Moonbeam," he drawled. "You're just in time. Tell me if you think this is too tight." He pushed two fingers under the ribbon measuring the fit.

Daphne leaned over his arm for a peek. "It looks perfect. But why so formal? It's just family."

"Rufina is dressed for our Christmas Eve festivities." Paul lifted an eyebrow. "Renton and your mother won't be here until later. However, I invited Pembrooke and his family along with Somerton and his family over early. Lady Margaret suggested it."

Daphne tried hard to hide her smile but failed miserably. Ever since she and Paul had married, Lady Margaret came over regularly for tea with Paul and Rufina. The majority of the time her father, Pembrooke, attended, too. Throughout the halls of Southart House, laughs and giggles bounced against the walls when those three were together.

The little girl had wrapped Paul around her finger as neatly as the bow on Rufina's neck. Just like she'd done with her own father.

It was really very sweet and dear. Alex and her loving husband had put their differences aside and were now as close as brothers once again.

"Margaret and Truesdale want to sing Christmas carols this evening. Out of the goodness of my black heart, I invited the Duke and Duchess of Langham, the Marquess and Marchioness of McCalpin, along with that infernally irritating Lord William." He leaned close as if divulging a secret. "Truth be told, I like the irreverent fellow. I'm glad Devan is traveling to Northumberland with William after the New Year. Devan will have some friends in the area when he takes his new position."

Her husband's heart was anything but black. Pure gold was more like it. After they'd married, all of Daphne's family, including the Duke and Duchess of Langham, had embraced Paul into their welcoming folds. Paul and his father, the Duke of Renton, had become close because of Paul's half brother, Somerton, who had helped ease the troubled waters between the two men.

Paul gifted Rufina a scratch under her chin, and the cat carefully curled into a neat ball on the window seat almost as if mindful of her bow. Paul stretched out his hand, and Daphne wrapped hers around his.

"Do you realize, love, at this time last year I had no family at all?" He brought her hand to his lips and held it there while his gaze settled on hers. "After I learned Renton was my father, I thought my life was ruined, but you, my dear darling one, gave everything back to me."

"Proof that Christmas miracles are real. Now hold me." Daphne moved into his outstretched arms. When they closed around her, she sighed with contentment. "You have more family than you know what to do with."

His hand caressed the back of her neck as he rubbed his lips against the top of her head. "Hmm, can one ever have enough?"

Staying in his strong embrace, she leaned back and studied his handsome face. "I suppose not."

"I've gained a father, two brothers, and two sisters-in-law, and all sorts of nieces and nephews. Don't get me started on our relationships with the Duke and Duchess of Langham's family." His hand gently cradled her cheek. "Didn't Shakespeare say, 'What a tangled web we weave'?"

"Walter Scott wrote it in his poem *Marmion*," Daphne murmured while pressing a kiss against his palm.

"I stand corrected by my beautiful wife who is also my stepsister."

"Don't say that. It's indecent and ribald," she scolded.

"You mean 'wife'?"

The innocent expression on his face made her laugh. "You, my dear duke, are incorrigible."

"Such a terrible thing to say about your husband when I have your Christmas present." He picked up a black box and gave it to her. "Open it."

The smile on his face was breathtaking.

Slowly, Daphne opened the lid. "Oh, Paul," she gasped. Inside, her heart-shaped rock was set in a gold pendant surrounded by rubies. "It's beautiful."

He rocked back on his heels and smiled. "The jeweler thought I'd lost my mind when I told him I wanted to give a rock to my duchess for Christmas."

"Will you help me put it on?" She turned, and he quickly placed it around her neck and secured the clasp.

His lips trailed up the side of her neck. "You have the softest skin, Daph. Let me tell you a little secret." He kissed the sensitive skin below her right ear. "You are the most beguiling, beautiful woman a man could ever fall in love with. Thankfully, you chose me."

"I did choose you, didn't I? I'm the one who asked you to marry me." Daphne turned to face him and kissed his cheek.

"And without a proper courtship, I might add. You ruined me." He brushed his lips across hers. "I liked being ruined. Will you ruin me again tonight after our guests leave?"

"It'd be my pleasure, Your Grace," Daphne whispered. "Now I have a little secret to tell you."

"Intrigue from my darling wife? Do tell."

Daphne stood on tiptoes and nibbled on his earlobe before she whispered in his ear, "Your Christmas present will be late this year."

"How late?" he asked in a similar whisper before kissing her soundly.

She broke the kiss. "Six months."

"What is it?" He kissed the indentation at the hollow of her throat. "You have the most glorious neck. I should write an ode—"

"A baby."

Slowly, he raised his head. "A baby?"

Her throat tightened. Tears came so easy these days. "Mm-hmm."

His beautiful blue eyes glistened while he bit his lip and slowly shook his head as if trying to contain his emotions. "What have you done, you wicked, wicked woman?" He held her at arm's length and slowly examined her from head to toe.

"Well, whatever I've done, I didn't do it alone." She smiled.

"I'll tell you what you've done," he whispered as he once again drew her into his arms. With the softest touch of his thumb, he wiped away a rebel tear from her cheek. "You've made me the happiest man in the world." Gently, he pressed his lips against hers. "How are you feeling?"

"Fine. Dr. Camden made a call this afternoon while you were out with Alex and Somerton. He confirmed my suspicions."

He kissed her again. "I don't think we should wait until this evening. I think you should ruin me right now."

She buried her head against his chest. "What about our guests?"

"Sweetheart, what good is it being a duke and a duchess if we can't be fashionably late to our own party?" He swept her up into his arms and carried her to bed, where he proceeded to let her ruin him.

Twice.